Wonder Cruise

One woman's romantic adventure of a lifetime

Ursula Bloom

DEDICATION

There was a Commander
and also a Cadet, here's to
them. God bless them …

PART ONE

CHAPTER I

I

The extraordinary happenings began to occur in Ann Clements' life that particular morning in mid-April. It was very warm for the time of year, muggy some people might have called it, but Ann would have described it as being just nice. There was the strangely sweet earth smell in Onslow Square, and a thin veil of green about the grey trees. The birds were singing, too, with a new note, and the men and women in the London streets were selling gay bunches of tulips and gold daffodils, so that everyone knew that it was spring-time. 'How wonderful it would be in the Mediterranean!' thought Ann, which was queer – perhaps the first of the extraordinary happenings, for Ann wasn't the sort of person who thinks about the Mediterranean.

Ann was thirty-five. What was worse, she looked thirty-five. She had, in point of fact, never been young. She had soft brown hair with little gold threads in it at times, but generally it was knotted back so closely into a firm bun that the gold did not get a chance to show. She had been blessed with a good skin, but she had never done anything to help that skin. It struggled manfully with soft pink roses in the cheeks; it could not do more. Ann's eyes were grey, and she had soft dark lashes. Her mouth, innocent of lip-salve, was too pale. She was just the ordinary woman you see in any London street, going to business, or coming back from business, and who you know, by her very look, lives an entirely nice life at home.

Ann had lived a sheltered but somewhat unfortunate life.

For twenty years she had dwelt in a country rectory where nothing that was in any way nasty ever happened. This had, though she did not know it, been a tremendous disadvantage.

Her mother had died when she was eleven, and from that day there had ensued a life of earnestness, of zeal, and of praiseworthy though somewhat narrow attempt.

Ann's only brother Cuthbert was ten years her senior, and he had gone into the Church as soon as ever he could. He was now comfortably settled in a suburban parish, just outside London. He had an evangelical outlook, and a robust figure and florid countenance. Cuthbert had married a plump and exceedingly worthy wife called Eleanor Higgins, whose family had been chapel but who had turned C. of E. in order to marry Cuthbert. They had one daughter, Gloria, whose birth could only be looked upon as a miracle, seeing that Cuthbert was for ever declaring that marriage had no physical side; she was now nearly eighteen.

Ann was her godmother.

Ann had lived all through infancy, adolescence, and early blooming in the country rectory, where nothing ever happened. The red house on the hill was graciously flanked by laurels and yews, which gave it a depressing effect in winter, and a certain sombreness in summer, which Ann's father thought extremely right and proper.

Ann could only remember the grinding monotony of the twenty years spent there. The little interests which were so essentially mundane. The hens, who never laid when required to do so by the prohibitive prices of the egg market. The Easter offering, which never came up to expectations. The baptisms and churchings, and the weddings, often of no connection with the baptisms and churchings, and the funerals one after the other. The children smiled upon when born in wedlock, and scowled upon when born out of it. 'It all seems to be very wrong,' Ann had been wont to remark, and her father had replied, 'Yes, you see it *is* wrong, all very wrong, and that is why one can but frown.' Which was not quite what Ann had meant.

Sometimes on a Sunday, when for the third time in the rigorous day she tramped back from the church, which was inconveniently marooned in a muddy field – the original village having been destroyed by fire by some Elizabethan practical joker – she would say to herself: 'If I live to be seventy, I shall be doing this, I suppose. Tramping to church, playing the harmonium, tramping back.'

Only fate took a hand. Fate had isolated Ann for twenty years, so that when her father died and she left the village she had, by very reason of her surroundings, grown into a placid, well-meaning young person, who lived a well-ordered but terribly monotonous life. This had not been her choice, but had been her unfortunate necessity.

Her father's stipend had been so small that saving had been out of the question. They had no private means, and Ann had found herself in the rather difficult position of being left practically penniless. On the proceeds of the sale of furniture she had come to London to undertake a secretarial course, and had lived for six months with Cuthbert until she would be qualified to earn for herself.

Living with Cuthbert had been far from amusing, in fact nowadays Ann could not imagine how she had put up with it. It had been even worse than living at home. Cuthbert was arbitrary and dictatorial, and Eleanor was afraid of him. Cuthbert had a horrid time-table to which his house and his parish ran. Woe betide the stranger who inadvertently fell foul of this time-table. He was both punctilious and exacting, and he expected everybody else to order their lives as he ordered his own. He had no patience with novelty or disorder. He classed every individuality as a heretic. Even Gloria, who was only two at the time, seemed to realize that she could not do as she would with her father, and never howled for her own way with him. Eleanor had of course given up trying and was a mere shadow of her former self.

The time spent in the manse at Balham was disconcerting, and, despite the fact that Cuthbert emphasized that in common gratitude the least she could do was to go on living with them as a paying guest after she had qualified and was earning, Ann went off to rooms the moment that she could.

'Such gross and heartless ingratitude,' said Cuthbert scathingly.

Ann worked in an office in Henrietta Street, that street of publishers which lies so close to the great flower-market of Covent Garden. She had been very grateful when the appointment had been offered to her, but that was a long while ago now.

And during the ensuing years she had grown a little sick of doing the same thing at the same time in the same way. When she had first come to London she had thought: 'Now this is going to be very different from Wadfield.' But London wasn't so very different from

Wadfield, at least not the London that Ann knew. The same deadly monotony had encompassed her again, and she had arrived at the conclusion that it encompasses all life; in particular all spinster life.

And Ann would never marry now. She was thirty-five, and, as I said before, she looked thirty-five.

She had rooms in South Kensington, just off Sussex Place, and they were 'nice' rooms, both cheap and convenient, but again they were dull! Ann inhabited a big bed-sitter, and the bed could be converted into a sofa by day, which she had thought at first to be most ingenious. But it made neither a satisfactory bed nor a convincing sofa in reality. The carpet was tired and worn, the one easy chair had adapted itself to Ann's frame, so that she could see the vague outline of herself for ever sitting in it. For over fourteen years now Ann had spent the complete twelve months in Onslow Gardens at Mrs. Puddock's, save for the one fortnight when she took her annual holiday and went to Worthing with Cuthbert and his family.

Even that was extremely dull.

They always stayed at the same place in Worthing too, at a Mrs. Simpkins' on the Parade, which was equally drab. Mrs. Simpkins was only another Mrs. Puddock, and Worthing was only another Onslow Gardens when you came to analyse it.

Mrs. Puddock was a pale-eyed woman with a large flabby bust, and large flabby hips. She had taken Ann as a favour, for she generally only took in 'gents', as they gave less trouble and were not so finicky. It did not do to be finicky over the Puddock *ménage.* Her arrangements did not bear too close an investigation. There had not been a draught through the house for years, and there was the faintly frowsty smell of stewing tea and of washing up, and of dust that had accrued. The thin hall led to thin stairs, all hung with an impossible paper on the walls, and where the paper was not, there were rather grim pictures of famous generals meeting at different Boer War relievings, and of Queen Victoria in *négligée* having just learnt that she was Queen Victoria. There was one picture of Princess Mary's wedding. Patriotic history ceased there as far as Mrs. Puddock was concerned.

On the first floor was Ann's room, and outside the window the plane tree in its green-gold brightness. The plane tree meant much to her, for it was her one link with the country. The room caught the sunshine, which in its turn caught the dust, and disclosed much of Mrs. Puddock's haphazardness. There was plenty of accommodation and space, and a gas fire fitted with a useful ring.

In the beginning, Cuthbert had approved the rooms, because there was a lithograph picture of the Bishop of London hanging over the fireplace. He felt that Mrs. Puddock must be a good woman if she had a picture of the Bishop of London hanging there. He little knew that this had been obtained in the same way as the other more patriotic engravings, in a job lot at an auction sale. For Mrs. Puddock was not at all a good woman at heart. She was mean and grasping, and Mr. Puddock had had no qualms about departing and leaving her to fend for herself as best she could.

He had walked out on her one evening when the may was in bud.

'I'm just going round to the "Toy and Hoop" for a quick one,' said Mr. Puddock (familiarly referred to by his wife as Mr. P.), and she had never set eyes on him again.

Mr. P. had gone off into the blue; he had in all fairness divided his savings, leaving her half, and where he and the other half had decamped to nobody knew. Certain it is that the 'Toy and Hoop' had never seen him, not even for the 'quick one'.

Ann, finishing her breakfast – brought up to her on a japanned tray – would get ready for her office, and then she would walk through Church Street to Chelsea Town Hall, where she could catch her number eleven 'bus. On fine mornings she would usually get out at the Ministry of Health, and she would walk briskly up Whitehall, and across Trafalgar Square, and up to the Strand. But to-day she went all the way to Charing Cross.

The sunshine was very gay indeed, and the houses looked bright and impertinent in the light, and round the column where the great little Admiral stood, the fountains glittered.

In one of the basins a flower-seller was moistening her flowers. Deep red and full pink tulips, golden daffies in armfuls.

'It's a shame to go into that dull old office where nothing ever happens,' thought Ann …

II

The office was always exactly the same. You said good-morning to the man in the enquiry office downstairs – Brockman was his name. You mounted the stairs, carefully carpeted in hair cord until you reached the second flight where clients never ventured, and where opulence had descended to mere linoleum. It was quite patchy in parts.

On the first floor was Mr. Robert's office, with Mr. John's alongside, and the outer room where the three secretaries sat. You went upstairs to the second floor, and hung up your things in the derelict little cloakroom, with the tap above the cracked wash-basin that invariably leaked – drip, drip, drip! And the tired towel behind the door which nobody used, for you kept your own in a drawer of your desk and brought it up with you when you wanted to wash.

You powdered before the mirror which gave such a distorted reflection and which was set over the marble mantelshelf. For once the building had been a private house, and it had never been properly converted from its late-Victorian grandeur. A thin wood partition railed this corner off, that was all.

By the litter along the marble shelf you could tell which of the other secretaries had arrived. Miss Thomas, if it were a little – a very little – Nilde powder in Rachel. But if Miss Gelding had preceded you, there would be rouge fluttering about, and a liberal supply of *Quelques Fleurs*, and perhaps a dash of thick red paste where a lipstick had rested.

Ann, who only mixed rather aloofly with her fellows, knew them in this way. Nilde, reserved, discreetly applied. Rouge, *Quelques Fleurs*, lipstick in a smother.

Then you went downstairs and, sitting before your desk, drew the lid off your typewriter and cleaned it – a hateful job! You were all ready to take down Mr. Robert's letters when he came in. Little Gelding was Mr. John's secretary. He was younger than Mr. Robert, flighty and bright, and Ann had always been truly grateful that she had been employed by the elder brother, who was dignified and prim (inclined to be irritable at times, it is true), but, as Cuthbert had said, 'always a gentleman'.

Mr. Robert was fifty. What was more, he was a sedate fifty. He was punctilious and pernickety as to his correspondence.

'Oh, I could never put up with him,' little Gelding would say; 'now Mr. John ...' and she would roll her eyes round in appreciation.

For Mr. John was not punctilious and pernickety, and he was not fifty – not by long chalks!

Having taken down Mr. Robert's letters and brought

them out, and typed them and taken them in again to be signed, the morning would have gone. It would be lunch-time. So ran the day.

You took down your hat and coat and your umbrella – the umbrella was considered to be an insurance against bad weather, a ruse which did not always work. You went out to lunch at the nice little restaurant round the corner run by two ladies, and on affluent days you had soup and entrée and a sweet; on days when you were not quite so affluent, Thursdays and Fridays for instance, you had just a poached egg on toast, or chips, and a cup of coffee.

Just sometimes you went there with Miss Thomas, never with little Gelding.

Little Gelding was mysterious about lunch. There was always some 'boy' in the background of little Gelding's picture. She would prink and perk before the mirror with the distorted vision, and she would give her scarf an extra tie, or tilt her hat a little more, and giggle excitedly. Little Gelding found life delicious, such a joke, and always something more amusing round the next corner. *Billets Doux*. Assignations. Flirtations. Flippancies. Parties and Palais de Danse. She believed secretly that both Ann and Miss Thomas were jealous of her, but then they were old. Poor old things, she would say to herself. Never mind! They had had their fun, or perhaps they had not had their fun. Much more likely not, little Gelding told herself.

Ann and Miss Thomas lunched with each other twice a month. At the beginning of the month, Ann paid. Towards the end it was Miss Thomas's turn to return the compliment. They had entered into this arrangement when they had started their work together in the office, and now, though Ann was quite sick of the whole system, she could not think of a good but polite excuse to terminate the agreement.

Miss Thomas was inclined to be a little trying, for she was interested in charitable associations, and had always got subscription lists, and raffle tickets that she wanted to dispose of. The subscription lists were all very well, only Ann had not the money to subscribe to them, but she was not at all sure about the system of raffles. Once she had won a yellow silk cushion with a one-and-sixpenny ticket. She had been very pleased about the cushion, for it had all happened at Christmas-time, and, although she did not want it herself, she had been worried to death about a suitable present for Eleanor; the appearance of the cushion had solved the difficulty. She had taken it along to Balham in its tissue wrappings, and there in a fit of truthfulness she had confessed to her sister-in-law how she had come by it.

Cuthbert had been very shocked.

He disapproved of raffles, in the same way as he disapproved of theatres and dancing-places and playing cards and strong drink. He was intensely angry about it.

For her own part Ann could not see anything very sinful in a one-and-sixpenny raffle, but all her life she had been taught that Cuthbert knew better than she did, so she was quite willing to abide by his all-superior judgement. All the same she did not feel that she could explain to Miss Thomas that she was unable to buy any more raffle tickets because Cuthbert said that raffles were wicked. Ann was not brave enough for that.

She gave some halting explanation and she salved her own conscience by saying that, although she would give the money to the charity, she would not accept the actual ticket. She would just pay the price.

'Then,' said Miss Thomas, 'I will keep the tickets and just hand you over the prize if you win anything.'

Under that arrangement they continued. Ann had not got the heart to refuse to contribute to Miss Thomas's raffles over which she always waxed so eloquent, but at the same time she always scuffled over it, because of that guilty conscience that assailed her on the subject.

She could not help it, but she suffered from the Cuthbert Complex, and, although she herself knew that raffles were not sinful, because he had said that they were she could not hope to escape from the recurring obsession.

So nowadays the twice-monthly lunch out with Miss Thomas had ceased to be the thing of joy which it had once appeared.

Afterwards, at two o'clock to be precise, you returned to the office, you typed out contracts, or you took down more letters, or you filled in the petty cash and the account books, all dreadfully dull jobs and sickeningly monotonous.

She wondered sometimes what other occupations were like, really thrilling ones, like working in a flower shop or a beauty parlour, or being a mannequin; then she would banish all those dreams, remembering that they were very unsuitable to a plain woman of thirty-five with life and youth lying behind her.

At four you made the tea. Every third day it came to your turn to supply the biscuits – shortcakes if you did not want to be extravagant, Bourbons if you did. Sometimes you took in a cup to Mr. Robert – little Gelding always did Mr. John's, she knew how many lumps of sugar he had, and the milk to the very drop; she prided herself on these details.

At five-thirty the day ended.

Mr. John would come out of the office first, grabbing at hat and stick and attaché case, and rushing across the outer office. 'Good night, Miss Clements. Good afternoon, Miss Thomas. Gelding …' Through the door and down the stairs and out into the street, obviously glad that work was finished.

Mr. Robert next, more sombre and slow, always

decorous. 'Good afternoon,' gravely, with a calculated coolness. 'You can leave those contracts until to-morrow, Miss Clements. Has the Clarke one gone out?' and then, 'Good afternoon,' again, and out into the street.

After that the ramming on of typewriter tops, the crashing down and fixing of tin lids. Papers pushed into drawers, things put away tidily in readiness for the morrow, all the little details, and finally the last chatter in the cloakroom and the burst out into the street. Lovely fresh coolness of it in spring and summer; sparkle and chill in winter. You welcomed it.

That was life at the office.

It went on and on as it had gone on and on for years, as it would go on and on, Ann felt, long after she was dead. It was a phase that she had been sucked into by the giant machinery of life. An intricate pattern of living, and always dismally the same. You could not escape it. Change was not. Things happened to time, to order, in much the same manner ...

'If only something different would come!' she thought.

III

The evenings were alike too.

She spent them sitting tiredly in Mrs. Puddock's bed-sitter, or in walking round Onslow Square. She very seldom went out and about. She had never sought entertainments, for her family had always insisted that anything in the nature of such amusement was wicked. Ann was a creature of old shibboleths and warnings; she was the child of inhibition. She had allotted her week into separate little duties, and although she hated the monotony of them, and they irked, she still stuck to them meticulously. She did not see how else she could manage. After all, things had to be done, and if you stuck to your schedule they got done, and if you did not they were left undone. She had got to be exact. The pattern of living had got Ann, wholly and entirely. It was inescapable.

Monday night she washed out her stockings and her hankies, and her *crêpe-de-Chine* collars and cuffs which she always wore on her office frock. There were lots of little things to be washed, and she went through them all on a Monday evening.

On Tuesday she ironed them surreptitiously with her electric iron. Mrs. Puddock did not approve of electric irons, and she had very definite laws concerning them. Ann had tried to argue, but she had been defeated. She had instead taken (very wrongly, she knew) to the secret application of the iron. She always worked at it in fear and trembling lest Mrs. Puddock should catch her, though usually after supper the good lady was rather past investigation of any nature and was verging on the comatose. But Ann, hurrying through the ironing and putting the iron on the window-sill to cool – she was always terrified that one day it would fall down and kill a passer-by – was in a state of panic. She hated putting the iron on the window, but knew of no other way to cool it, and the young man at the shop had been most emphatic about the use of cold water in such a circumstance. Ann was secretly afraid of her iron, and it caused her a good deal of consternation, what with the voltage trouble, and the cooling-down process, and the terror of fusing and of Mrs. Puddock's immediate discovery of all that had been going on.

Wednesday night she mended.

Ann loved sewing, and it took her the whole evening to make those neat little darns and patches on which she prided herself.

Thursday was given over to manicure, for she was

particular about her hands. Alternate Thursdays she washed her hair, and sometimes if time permitted she cleaned her face with cream, which she felt would have met with Cuthbert's strong disapproval had he only known of it. But Cuthbert did not know. She had never dared to admit the simple truth that she was the possessor of one of those sensitive skins to which the wholly virtuous soap-and-water is merely irritating.

Friday nights she wrote her letters, keeping them in a little bundle in her desk, neatly bound round with an elastic band, until they could be attended to. It was never a large mail, but she prided herself on her faithful correspondence with old servants and vague cousins. Ann was dutiful in the extreme to all who she felt had a call upon her time and attention.

Saturdays were supposed to be free days, yet for all that they seemed to get themselves filled up, cluttered by little duties of no real consequence, yet requiring attention.

Sunday was the day when she went down to Balham and lunched with Cuthbert and Eleanor and her goddaughter. They ate cold lunch because it was the Lord's day, and it would have been wicked to ask the maid to cook a meal, which certainly was some manner of work. They ate cold mutton alternately with cold beef. They ate roast potatoes in winter because they could be pushed inside the oven to cook themselves and therefore could not be considered to be any manner of work. In the summer time it was just a salad. Afterwards there was served stewed fruit and custard.

Ann loathed cold mutton nearly as much as she loathed cold beef. She had no stomach left for roast potatoes, which she had had thrust upon her every Sunday of her life, and she hated chilly stewed fruit and that insipid pool of custard in a glass dish. Those horrible shrivelled prunes, or the pink strings of rhubarb!

Stewed apple in a sickly pale green mess!

Eleanor had no imagination.

They talked Cuthbert, and Cuthbert's sermon. Sometimes Ann wondered how she stood it. If they didn't talk Cuthbert they talked Gloria – who was pert and precocious – which was almost worse. She could do no wrong in her parents' eyes, this *enfant terrible* of a flapper.

During the afternoon Cuthbert took the Sunday School, save on the third Sunday in the month, when it became a children's service and was held actually in the church instead of in the parish hall. Whilst he worked thus, Eleanor slept on the drawing-room sofa. Ann only wished that she could claim the joys of oblivion, but she was expected to play with Gloria all through her childhood, and now, when Gloria was eighteen, they were supposed to have what Eleanor described as 'a nice talk together'.

Tea at five provided a meat dish for Cuthbert, who needed sustenance, as he had Evensong ahead of him. But Ann always left before Evensong. She always supped at Mrs. Puddock's and afterwards in the summer she would sit by the open window in the half light, and listen to the people returning across Onslow Square, their day of gladness over.

She would hear young lovers, with slow steps, soft whispers and the faint sound of kisses in the darkness. She would listen wonderingly. Ann, who was thirty-five, who had never had a lover, who would never have a lover now. Something precious that she had missed in life. Something tender and delicious which had passed her by. For the pattern had absorbed her; the mechanical adjustment of living which had caught her into its toils and which drove her round and round with dynamo-like force. Throb, throb, throb! It beat on and on, remorselessly, and now she could never hope to escape from it.

In the winter she sat on a hassock before the gas fire, which roasted you in front and left you to freeze at the back. She hugged her knees and thought of Christmas, and of trees hung with tinsel and toys, and of little children laughing as they danced round them. They were the dream children of a rather sweet imagination.

For there were dreams still left even to a spinster of thirty-five, who had never had very much from life, but who had been spun on and on in the weary monotonous pattern of just living. But I believe that some of those dreams were bitter-sweet.

CHAPTER 2

I

But this particular morning it was mid-April.

Ann decided that she would walk down Church Street and on into the King's Road, and that she would catch the number eleven 'bus outside the Westminster Bank there. Sometimes they would stop for you, and sometimes they wouldn't, but more often than not they would.

The first green was on the trees, and in the gardens there were crocuses and daffodils, and a tree not as yet green was pale pink with blossom. It was one of those mornings which you felt would be full of lovely happenings, and somehow, as she crossed the Fulham Road, the idea of the Mediterranean occurred to her. It was absurd that the idea of the Mediterranean should occur to anybody in the Fulham Road, but it did. It may have been the sight of the policeman on point duty, or the old curiosity shop opposite with its bundles of dusty old books, and its quaint china ornaments, or more likely

– much more likely – the flower shop on the corner. In the flower shop there were bunches of cream freesias, and great white arums and dark red roses.

Ann thought, 'And I've never been further than Worthing. And what is more, I am never likely to go further than Worthing,' and again she dreamt of the blue of that almost tideless sea, and the smell of Africa, hot and sandy and aromatic, and the flowers of Southern Spain, heliotropes and verbenas under the oleanders.

And all this in the Fulham Road!

She went down Church Street, and she saw all the lovely houses in Mulberry Walk, and wished that she were rich enough to live there. She saw the more stately houses of Mallord Street which thrilled her. There was always the chance of seeing the real Christopher Robin in Mallord Street, and she came round the corner by the bank with a jerk.

What was the good of thinking of the Mediterranean when it was April in England? What was the good when your salary was three pounds ten shillings a week, and ten shillings went on insurance against the future? For old age threatened her as it threatened every other lone woman who was not provided for. Cuthbert had been very helpful over the insurance policy, and it ensured three pounds a week when she was sixty, or in preference two thousand pounds down. Cuthbert had said that it was Ann's duty to take the two thousand down, and to leave it all to Gloria. After all Gloria would want prospects as much as anybody else. So Ann was saving diligently for Gloria's future, and very dull work she found it.

She timidly hailed the approaching eleven 'bus.

She was always a little timid, for she disliked it so much if they would not stop, but went on unheeding. She felt so silly left with her umbrella up, pointing into space. The 'bus stopped, and she climbed gratefully into it.

It was one of those spring days when the conductor was facetious. He was chatty. As he clipped the tickets he whistled.

'Looks like a bit of decent weather, miss,' he volunteered.

Ann said yes.

She had no wish to be offhand, but she knew that Cuthbert did not approve of her speaking to conductors.

At Sloane Square a running gentleman caught the 'bus only by a fraction.

'Nah then, nah then,' said the conductor as he helped him inside, 'do you want to bust yerself up?'

In confusion Ann saw that the running gentleman was Mr. Robert. She felt very embarrassed, for one's employers present a knotty problem out of hours. She did not want to appear pushing or over familiar, and she certainly did not want to seem icy and reserved. She only hoped that he would not get off at Charing Cross and embarrass her further by walking to the office with her.

As they bowled up Whitehall she turned the problem over in her mind, and decided that the thing to do was to let him get off first, that was if he were getting off at all.

Mr. Robert did get off at Charing Cross. He did not hurry himself about it, but allowed three fat girls and a flower woman with an armful of tulips to get off first. The result was that at the last moment, just before the 'bus was starting again, Ann had to spring up and rush for the step.

'Nah then, nah then,' said the facetious conductor again, clanging his bell, 'why can't you get along while we was a-stoppin', instead of 'angin' about until we was a-startin'? What's the idee?'

All confusion, a much embarrassed Ann jumped to the pavement, and practically into a little knot of people who were busy staring at the 'own unaided efforts' of a pavement artist as vouched for on a flag which he had inscribed with coloured chalks.

Ann went along up the Strand.

It was a warm and perfect morning, and it would have been delicious in the country. She thought of the buttercups, and the close dark buds of lilac against the new vivid green. Again she thought of the Mediterranean, and her mind was recalled to it by the sight of a poster outside Charing Cross station. The Riviera. A ruined temple, draped in bougainvillea, a cypress in the background. A poster that made Ann think.

Ahead was Mr. Robert walking in leisurely fashion, stopping to light a cigarette in a doorway – for there was a light wind blowing – or to study a spring display of shirtings. Ann turned up a side street to avoid him. He was very early this morning; she did not know when he had been so early. It was certainly most inconvenient of him to have been travelling on the same 'bus as herself.

In the side street the sun was brilliant; a newsboy was screaming out the latest sweepstake news, and he rushed past her, nearly knocking her down. Ann would have loved to dawdle, to linger out here in the yellowness and the pleasant warmth, and never to go inside the office at all. The office always struck her as being gloomy and dark, although in reality the secretaries' room was almost due south. It was the surrounding leads and chimney-pots which seemed to close it in.

A nurse fluttered into St. Peter's Hospital; a Covent Garden porter, whistling a cheery tune, shouldered a basket of oranges. Again she thought of the Mediterranean. Funny, but she could not get it out of her mind this morning. Orange trees and lemons growing alongside one another. The clinging perfume of stocks; warmth, blueness, an atmosphere that was different. Queer how she could not help thinking of it.

She turned in at the office door.

II

Brockman was fussing in the enquiry office; he did not notice her as she passed, for his back was to her as he opened the small attaché case which he always carried with him. He brought his own lunch, his wife packing it, for by that means it only cost him half what it would otherwise have done, and he could be sure of getting reliable food. Brockman was particular about food, seeing that it represented his sole remaining interest in life.

He did not drink or smoke, and twenty-eight years of marriage with Mrs. Brockman had stemmed his ardour in the lists of love. But, as he told his associates, he might be getting on in years and one thing and another, but thank God he had still got a good stomach left.

The good stomach stood him in good stead.

Ann went through the swing doors, and started up the stairs. Instantly she was aware of a strange atmosphere hanging about the place. At the first sound of her foot on the hair cord leading to the first floor, Miss Thomas and little Gelding had darted out of the room above. They were clinging to the banisters and gesticulating.

'Hurry, hurry,' they called.

Ann thought that there must have been an accident, or a fire, or something unusual. She hurried as well as she was able and arrived breathlessly on the top stair.

'You can't think what's happened,' said Miss Thomas. But little Gelding, always over enthusiastic, screamed: 'You've won three hundred pounds! Just think of it! You've won three hundred pounds!'

Ann Clements looked at Miss Thomas red and rumpled, and she looked at little Gelding, clinging to the banisters and springing up and down like some excited child, and she said quite sharply, 'Don't be silly.'

It was very silly indeed. They did not seem in the least

surprised at the iciness of her tone, and their enthusiasm was not damped. They came towards her, talking so fast, and laughing so much, that Ann simply did not understand what was happening.

'It was one of those tickets,' Miss Thomas was saying. 'I didn't explain, because you wouldn't let me. You said you did not want to know anything about it, so I just did not worry you, but that is what it was.'

'What what was?' gasped Ann not too lucidly.

'Isn't it luck?' gasped little Gelding, and she was springing up and down on her toes. 'What shall you do with it, I wonder, what shall you do?'

Ann shook herself free. 'Look here,' she said with a firmness surprising in so gentle a creature, 'don't be idiotic. I don't know what has happened or what on earth you are talking about – do try to explain things if you can.'

Miss Thomas produced from her handbag a letter. It was typewritten, and it bore an impressively good heading. After the first few phrases Ann saw the words blurring. She heard a peculiar thumping going on and became suddenly aware of her own heart beating within her. She felt herself going quiet, as though paralysed. For the letter explained that the ticket numbered – never mind what – had drawn a horse, and that the ticket had been booked in the names of Thomas and Clements, and that even if the horse did not start the ticket was worth six hundred pounds.

'But,' said Ann helplessly, 'I never bought a ticket for a sweepstake in my life.'

'No, but I did.'

'I wouldn't have bought one. It would have been altogether wrong,' said Ann definitely.

'Oh, isn't it marvellous? Too marvellous?' chanted little Gelding, going on and on with her refrain like some sort of chorus.

Ann began to get quite cross.

Miss Thomas was trying to explain. In among the raffle tickets there had been this one, and of course she hadn't been able to show it to Ann seeing that Ann was so funny about things and never wanted to know what she was buying. She just had not bothered, never supposing that either of them would ever hear another word about it, and now this enormous piece of luck had happened. Three hundred pounds each. Three hundred pounds, and the chance of quite a lot more, flinging wide the gateway to all manner of possibilities. Lovely clothes, cities of enchantment, exotic holidays. Private means, why, with some building societies you could get five per cent, tax free, and then you would have fifteen pounds a year.

'Oh, do shut up,' said Ann crossly.

'Well, if that isn't the limit! Really it is, dear, and if I had not troubled to tell you, you would never have known that you had won anything at all, seeing that you did not know you had even bought a ticket for it. And that would have been six hundred pounds to me, and at five per cent, tax free that would be thirty pounds a year, over ten shillings a week. Why, thirty pounds a year would keep the wolf from the door, wouldn't it?'

And then into this bewildering world which had become altogether too complicated for her comprehension there walked Mr. Robert. He had stopped to look in Stanley Gibbons' *en route.* He had a very fine collection of stamps which interested him very much indeed. Last night he had received a telephone message from Stanley Gibbons' that amongst a collection that they had just purchased there was a certain stamp that he had been wanting for some time. This it was that had brought him out so early in the morning, and now he came in with the precious stamp in his pocket feeling as though the whole world were his.

He had actually pranced up Southampton Street. The whole world was epitomized in one stamp, which for a long time he had been aching to possess, and of which he had almost given up hope.

He walked into the office and up the stairs, and into the pandemonium of the secretaries' room.

'What's all this?' he demanded.

Miss Thomas and little Gelding blurted it out together. Ann, flushed and confused, stood aside. He had never noticed before how pretty she was. She had a delicate colouring, and when she blushed her eyes seemed to turn unbelievably blue.

He looked at her again.

'When you are ready,' he said, 'come in and tell me all about it.'

III

Ann, beginning to believe the most extraordinary news of this extraordinary morning, went into the cloakroom to take off her hat and leave it there with her coat.

Along the mantelshelf was the drift of Nilde, and the rouge and the Houbigant that were the hallmark of little Gelding. There was a torn envelope addressed to Miss Thomas, obviously the envelope that had contained the good tidings of great joy.

Thrust aside was a circular addressed to Ann.

The circular was the second of the extraordinary happenings. She opened it quite mechanically, and the coloured paper fluttered out and down to the floor at her feet. It had been sent by a steamship company. Why it should have been addressed to her she had no idea, nor how they had got hold of this address. She saw a big white ship against a deep blue sky. Turning over the page a phrase caught her eye. 'A cruise to the dream cities of Europe. Naples. Venice. The Mediterranean.'

She caught a glimpse of a gondola in St. Mark's basin. Vesuvius dark and glowering across a bay, and Naples gleaming white and wreathed in wistaria and rambler roses.

She saw an impossibility suddenly become possible; it was a dream city within grasp. For a moment she felt quite faint, and, not knowing that she still held the circular in her hand, she went downstairs and in to see Mr. Robert.

And now she was convinced that the whole thing was some absurd practical joke, or some mistake that would be bound to be discovered soon and put straight. The amazing piece of luck which always happens to other people and never to yourself had suddenly happened to her. It was the miracle of miracles, and most miraculous of all because it was her own.

Suddenly, as she crossed the threshold into Mr. Robert's room, an acute horror gripped her. She remembered that (if it were true, and she still had doubts about it) Cuthbert would have to be told, and that most undoubtedly he would be disgusted over the whole thing. A sweepstake! Surely a sweepstake was, if possible, a great deal worse than a raffle, and both were inventions of the devil, and milestones to be passed along the road to Hell.

She felt herself going quite white at the awful thought of Cuthbert's wrath when she told him what had happened. That was if it had happened; she was not sure about that.

It seemed that this morning, bright with April sunshine, Mr. Robert's office looked a great deal gayer and more convivial than usual. It might be that the knowledge of the miracle had helped her to change her outlook, or that it really was different.

She closed the door behind her, and approached the chair where she always sat to take down his letters. Mr.

Robert was surveying her quite affably. In truth he was feeling affable. The stamp had proved to be an extremely good specimen. It would fill that gap in his collection which had worried him for so long. He was very well pleased with himself for getting it. He was also interested in the surprising piece of good fortune which had happened to Ann. He had never noticed her closely before. Funny, that, for his brother John always noticed his secretaries a great deal too closely.

But to Mr. Robert these girls were just secretaries, so much machinery; he classified them as being good or bad, poor or indifferent. Ann was good. You could rely on her to put the right letters into the right envelopes, and to spell carefully and correctly, and not to be too reckless over her punctuation. Secretaries were amazingly erratic over punctuation, and sometimes their spelling made you weep. But Ann had proved herself to be a very excellent machine. She did not plead temperament or headaches. She never asked for an extension of her holidays. She kept her desk neat and tidy, and did her work conscientiously.

Young men who were clients did not leave their sticks behind them to provide excuses for a return, as they usually did with secretaries of John's choosing. On the other hand she was not disturbingly hideous, but of quite pleasant appearance. In fact now that he came to look more closely she was of a little more than pleasant appearance, if only she had had her hair cut short and would wear better clothes. Ann, it seemed, filled all the qualifications necessary for a secretary, and until to-day he had never looked twice at her face.

'Ah well,' said he, 'I must congratulate you on being a very lucky young woman. A very lucky young woman indeed.'

Ann did not know what to say, so she just nodded. Mr. Robert surveyed her across his desk littered with papers, but he seemed to be far more interested in her than in the papers. He went on gaily enough.

'I wonder what you will do with your windfall?' he asked; and then his eye fell on the gay circular that the enterprising steamship company had sent. 'Oh, I see,' said he, 'and very wise too. I congratulate you on your choice.'

Ann, glancing down in the direction of his eyes, saw the circular, and started. It was all very irregular to have brought it in here with her, and she did not know what he would think, but really she had been so flustered.

She said, 'Oh no, no. This is just a coincidence. I'd love to go of course, but I couldn't. I mean I've never done anything like that in my life.'

'I see' – he nodded gravely; 'and may I ask why you could not do that? A really good holiday would be the making of you. You have got the chance now, why don't you take it? The least you will win is three hundred pounds, and it may be a great deal more.'

'Oh, well, I …' began Ann, and then she said, 'You see, I shall probably have to return the money – that is if I have really won it; my brother, who has a living in Balham, thinks such things are very wrong. I doubt if he would let me keep it.'

Mr. Robert surveyed her calmly. 'But that is all nonsense,' he said, 'they would not take it back; besides, where would be the sense? Don't you do anything ridiculous like that.'

'But I feel that Cuthbert …'

Mr. Robert felt himself getting quite cross with her. How could any woman of that age allow some bossy little parson to treat her like that? 'To invest three hundred pounds would be foolish,' he said; 'you take a hundred and spend it on happiness. Give yourself a holiday.'

'But,' said Ann, 'my holiday is in September, and I

am going with Cuthbert and Eleanor to Worthing'; she ended lamely, 'we always do!'

She did not know why she was talking like this, and so familiarly, to Mr. Robert. Probably it was all part of the miracle, the extraordinary things that had started happening and were going on happening.

'If you like,' said Mr. Robert, 'you can take a holiday now, a month, but on one condition.'

She stared at him aghast. 'Yes?' she said.

'On the condition that you go on a cruise. Anywhere you like, but *not* Worthing.'

Ann thought that the world had suddenly gone mad. She thought that something had happened to change everybody and everything. She was not to know of the precious stamp which had got Mr. Robert up so early, and had managed to put him into such a good mood. She was not to know that only this very morning he had heard from a secretary whom he had employed and liked in his way, years ago, and who had asked if he could possibly give her a spare-time job. She was married – Mr. Robert had disliked her husband intensely – and she had got wrong with him, and had had difficulties one way and another. Mr. Robert had wanted to help her; he had a big heart and was of a charitable disposition, only he had not quite seen his way to giving her a hand. All the three secretaries in the office were efficient and worthy. He did not want to get rid of any of them. He could not afford to employ more, especially in these hard times.

Now he saw the way.

He saw how to help Ann too, and he was thoroughly interested in Ann, who was behaving, he thought, like a silly little ass frightened to death by a pompous brother who thought he could do what he liked with her. Worthing indeed!

'Now, look here,' said Mr. Robert, 'you go straight

down to that office in your dinner-hour and book a cabin for that cruise. I'll lend you the deposit money until you receive your cheque.'

'Oh, I –'

'You want to go? I mean those are the places that you want to see?'

'I – I've hardly looked.' She glanced down at the paper in her hand as she spoke, and she saw the names, the magical names, of dream places. Each one conjured up a picture in her mind. Gibraltar, a hulk of rock against a sky, a little town straggling at the foot of a great hill, raggle-taggle music, the warmth and languor of Southern Spain. Naples, a city actually on the hill-side. See Naples and die … Vesuvius across a bay inconceivably blue, Pompeii within a stone's throw. Malta, little square stone houses, the grey outline of warships in the Grand Harbour. Sand and glare. Venice. She felt almost sick with the apprehension of the beauty of Venice.

'Oh yes, yes,' she said suddenly, 'of course they are marvellous. The very places I'd choose.'

'Then choose it, my dear young lady. Take the chance while you have got it. Book that cabin in the lunch-hour.'

She glanced again reluctantly at the circular, and her eyes caught the one sentence 'Anchor in St. Mark's basin'. She became tensely still. Into the stillness she heard his voice penetrating.

'And now, what about the morning's mail?'

She came to with a start.

IV

The more she thought of it, the more the idea fascinated her, and at the same time frightened her. She conjured up pictures of the places, and pictures of her own fright. She thought about everything that she had ever heard and a great deal that she had wholly imagined. Miss Thomas asked her what she was going to do with her money, for Miss Thomas felt that she had a right to participate in it a little, seeing that she had been the one who had actually bought the ticket.

Perhaps wholly for effect, Ann said, 'I thought of going on this cruise,' and tossed the circular across to the others.

They pored over it.

'Oh my,' said little Gelding, 'it'd be fine. You'd meet some beautiful boys too I'd be bound, and perhaps sheiks! It'd be like a film, wouldn't it?'

Miss Thomas, who felt that if any cruise were contemplated she ought to be asked to share it, since the whole thing had happened through her, was a little huffed.

'I've never been interested in foreign parts,' she said, 'they always strike me as being fast. They are not meant for people like us at all.'

Queerly enough, the fact of Miss Thomas saying that in that particular tone was the match to tinder. It piqued Ann. It infuriated her.

'I'm sick of England,' said Ann, which was not strictly true. 'I am sick of office life, of living in diggings, and what's more I don't know that I am not sick of being respectable.'

Until this actual moment she had not realized that she *was* sick of diggings, and of doing the same thing in the same way day after day. She had not realized that Mrs. Puddock's rooms were awful, and that Monday washing, Tuesday ironing, Wednesday mending, and Thursday hair-wash were much like a pair of handcuffs set like shackles on her wrists.

'Oo-er,' said little Gelding, 'I think that's fine. That is just what I would do.' But in her heart she thought, 'Poor old dear, over thirty and all that. She'll have a sticky time wherever she goes.'

Her own bright life made a vivid comparison. The glitter and accompaniment of Palais de Danse and theatres, of meals at glamorous restaurants. She did not know that she envied the poor old sticks their three hundred pounds apiece, for all their being so mighty quiet about it, and never even offering her a share in the ticket. Mean of them! Oh, rottenly mean, but she did not grudge it to them all the same. The cats!

All the morning Ann, busy over her typewriter, played with the idea of the cruise. She niched it in the corner of her mind, taking it out as it were, and looking at it. She told herself that she supposed she had really truly made up her mind to go. What a heavenly time it would be! She thought of the ship rising and falling a little, of wearing comfortable gym shoes on the decks, of sitting in a deck chair. She thought of everybody being very friendly and pleasant, she had always heard of them being like that on the sea.

All she had ever heard came back to her, every picture she had ever seen was recalled, until she really did not know where the cruise was going; she had got into a wild jumble of camels in deserts, of snows in Russia, of glaciers and volcanoes, and Heaven only knows what.

When lunch-time came round she had put a living wall between herself and Worthing. The picture had grown too big for her, and now it was something that she could not hope to destroy.

Mr. Robert called her into his office and handed her the notes. 'There,' said he, 'you take my advice and book a cabin.'

'Oh, I don't know. I ought to consult Cuthbert first.'

As if she didn't know what Cuthbert would say!

'Opportunity,' he warned her, 'never comes twice; don't you be a little goose. The things we regret are the things we haven't done, not the things we have.'

True, dismally true! She *did* regret all those wasted yet worthy years. She regretted the rectory at home, the respectability of Mrs. Puddock's rooms, the lunch at Balham on a Sunday. She had sought for just this opportunity and had never been able to find it. Surely the chance would never come again; he was right there. She went out into the office wondering. Miss Thomas was putting on her hat. It was an old felt thing that she had bought at Lewis's sale very cheaply because it was faded. It looked much more faded now in the spring sunshine.

'I was thinking,' said Miss Thomas, 'that we might have a bit of lunch together, seeing as how it is a sort of a celebration.'

Lunch with Miss Thomas was more than Ann could stand. She would talk five per cents, and Building Societies and what the three hundred pounds would bring in a year.

She said, 'I'm just going down to book my passage first.'

'Oo-er,' said little Gelding.

V

For the look of the thing she had to go down Cockspur Street way. She would invent some excuse later; she could say that the cruise was already full, anything – there would be time enough to think of that during her meal.

She entered the street in the bright sunshine. It seemed quiet as though caught in a hush, just as though the cars ran more smoothly, and the 'buses put on silencers when they passed down it.

She thought that it was very nice, a great deal nicer than the noisy Strand, or Henrietta Street always so full of vegetable carts, and their quarrelsome drivers. She liked this far better. In this mood she came to the frontal of the enterprising steamship company.

In one big window was a model of a great ship. She stopped to look at it, and the wonder of it held her. To the side was a little panorama of what would be seen on the cruise. You looked through little windows, and you caught glimpses. The glimpses were entirely breathtaking. She thought of Worthing and the esplanade which she had once thought to be so grand and imposing. Why, it wasn't grand at all, it was just dingy – or worse!

She passed into the big portal to peep through the wide door at another picture of Pompeii. It held her attention. Ruins. A rutted road. A cypress which stood like an old lady wrapped in a dark shawl, hooded and still. Ann stood there watching it and her thoughts flew along the route, for with all this fascinating loveliness before her she could not control them. If only it were possible for her to go, but of course it wasn't. It would be ridiculous, for after all she was thirty-five, and she had never been out of England in her life. Little Gelding had said that there might be sheiks, and, although Ann held no exaggerated ideas of her charms, well, you did hear of such things happening! After all, whatever Mr. Robert said, and even if she had won three hundred pounds in this illicit manner, she could not go gadding about Europe on it.

As she stood there, a large American gentleman, supported by an even larger American wife, came blustering round the corner. He had not expected anyone to be standing just inside, and when he saw Ann it was too late to stay himself. He and his fat wife actually swept her inside the door of the steamship office before them.

She had got inside.

The gentleman who was all American did not attempt

to apologize. Ann was standing in the office alone, on a carpet that was like moss into which her feet sank. There was a square table in the middle and on it forms waiting to be filled up. A beautiful young man with hair that shone like an advertisement for brilliantine came forward.

'And what can I do for you?' he asked.

There was nothing that he could do for her, but somehow Ann could not say so. She could not possibly say, 'I have been pushed in here by accident, and now I am going out again.' She felt herself going red, and she glanced down at the paper which she still carried for the address. The young man glanced down too.

'Oh, of course,' he said, 'the Mediterranean cruise.'

Then things started happening.

If Ann had been brave it would have been easy enough, but she wasn't brave. She had not got the moral courage to tell him that she wanted nothing of the sort. Around her were people booking passages to the other side of the world, people who wanted to go to China, and to Australia; it seemed such a silly little thing only to want to go for an insignificant cruise lasting a modest three weeks.

She saw a plan of the ship, and the young man, who was still of the opinion that she had come into the office in good faith and that she really wanted to go on the cruise, indicated the cabin which he considered would be the most suitable. The bath was so close. The dining-saloon was so handy. He dwelt on the advantages of swimming-bath and library, of music-room and cinema.

Suddenly the fever of travel seized hold of Ann like some dreadful disease which drags you remorselessly into its clutches. She recalled Mr. Robert's suggestion that life does not offer you its opportunities twice. In case she might miss anything she handed over the wad of notes before she had time to change her mind.

'I'll have that cabin,' she said.

She had forgotten Cuthbert; she had forgotten Mrs. Puddock; she had forgotten the rules and regulations by which she had lived for five-and-thirty years. Her only anxiety was that someone would snatch the chance from her before she could grab it.

And now she was filling in an impressive-looking form her name, her age, her parentage. The helpful young man was giving her details as to how to obtain a passport; he was murmuring something about labels being sent to her, special trains, embarkation forms. She turned to leave the office like a woman in a daze, and she did not know what or whom she had to thank for all this. The sweepstake, or the circular, or Mr. Robert, or the large and impetuous American gentleman who had swept her willy nilly into the offices of the most obliging steamship company.

But she had done it now.

Ann felt that a new spirit had settled down upon her, the new gay spirit of adventure. She had reserved a cabin for herself on a wonder cruise. For the second time in the day she found herself outside Charing Cross, and she knew that she had had no lunch.

She could look at the poster of Naples and say with satisfaction, 'I'm going there. I'm going there almost at once,' and it gave her a delicious feeling of complete satisfaction.

She thought that she would buy herself a packet of sandwiches and take them back to the office to eat; that way you saved money. Not that money mattered so vitally at the moment. Not that anything mattered.

She went back to the office a quarter of an hour too soon, and she sat down in the deserted secretaries' room, and she started to eat the sandwiches, spreading her hankie in her lap, for it would never do if she got her good fawn frock soiled, and fawn did show marks so quickly. In between bites of somewhat tough ham sandwiches she let herself indulge in day-dreaming. They were the most remarkable dreams of a most remarkable day. Every little while a vision would float before her, a broken Colonnade, a little fountain at play in an orange grove, the white glare of Malta. And when the distracting visions came, Ann would stop eating, and would just sit staring owlishly into space.

That was how Miss Thomas found her. Miss Thomas was disgruntled. After all she had bought the ticket, and Ann did not seem to be any too pleased with her. The offer of lunch had been refused, and Ann, entirely obsessed with the idea of this idiotic cruise, had gone off to book a passage. She had not even suggested that, as the money had been won by their united efforts, her company might have been desirable on the journey. And now Miss Thomas had a vague idea that in spite of her protestations she would have liked to go. Her father had been an archaeologist, and he had been interested in old stones. Miss Thomas felt the sudden pangs of archaeology. She came in exceedingly annoyed with Ann, and she was a great deal more annoyed when she beheld her sitting before her desk, eating her sandwiches over a distinctly crumby pocket handkerchief.

'Well, my word,' said Miss Thomas hotly (she had got to vent it on somebody), 'you're too grand to come out with me, and this is what you do. I'm sure I don't know what has come over you.'

'I'm very sorry, but by the time I'd finished at the steamship offices I hadn't time to get lunch anywhere, so I just bought some sandwiches and brought them along.'

Miss Thomas sniffed. 'So you did get your ticket?'

'Oh yes.'

'My goodness!' Miss Thomas began pulling off her gloves. 'If that doesn't beat the band! You really do surprise me.'

'I've always wanted to travel, and now I've got my chance.'

'But alone? Nice women don't travel by themselves,' and Miss Thomas looked down her long nose.

'I'm thirty-five; surely at that age it is all right? It is nineteen thirty-two, not eighteen thirty-two.'

Ann was getting irritated, though she hoped that she was not showing it. She knew quite well that Miss Thomas wanted to come with her; she also knew that she wanted to go alone. She wanted to cut herself adrift. To go out in a great white ship which reminded her of a beautiful white bird with spread wings. She wanted to see things for herself, all those precious things that were so beautiful that they made you feel like crying! She had a vague idea that they were going to affect her that way.

'You'll need clothes,' Miss Thomas was saying, 'and the tips will be awful, and you won't understand the people you mix with because they won't be our sort of people. You will be sorry that you ever went.'

'Then I'll *be* sorry,' said Ann obstinately.

Somehow all the keen opposition was making her feel obstinate. She finished the last sandwich and, taking up her hankie by the corners, she shook the crumbs into the waste-paper basket. 'That's that,' she said.

Miss Thomas eyed her coldly. 'You aren't angry?' she asked. 'After all, if it hadn't been for me you would never have won the three hundred pounds at all. Only you do seem to be so funny about it, batchy I'd call it; I am sure I can't understand you.'

'I haven't meant to be funny,' Ann apologized in all humility; 'it was very good of you to do it for me, because of course alone I should never have gone in for it. I'm very grateful.'

'I shall invest my money,' said Miss Thomas; 'it will be something for my old age. You'd far better have done that yourself; still, I suppose it is no good talking to you,

you seem to have taken leave of your senses.'

They heard little Gelding coming up the stairs, two at a time, singing to herself as she came. For she had had a most successful lunch with a new boy friend and he had given her real salmon mayonnaise – not that nasty tinned stuff – and chicken and a meringue. Although little Gelding was supposed to be dieting, for there was a certain fullness just above the waist-line, over the ribs, she had however succumbed to the meringue. It had been a most *recherché* lunch, and he had suggested dancing together one night at the Café de Paris too. All so select. Little Gelding was thrilled to the core.

'Well, I've got it,' said Ann, very flushed.

'Got what?' And then little Gelding remembered: 'Oh yes, your passage. Good egg! I'd give something for your chance, reely I would.'

They heard Mr. John coming up the stairs, and little Gelding fled rapidly to the cloakroom. She always lived in fear and terror that her face might be in need of 'doing-up'. She was over-elaborate with powder-puff and rouge-pad, and to have Mr. John see her not titivated for the occasion would have been too awful.

The office settled down for its afternoon ritual.

Typewriters broke the silence with their chatter. There was the sound of paper crackling as it slipped into the carriage. The Mediterranean seemed to be far away, and no longer did the world dance to fantastic music. It was the monotonous, everyday office world, with the chirruping of typewriters and the constant use of rubber – for never had Ann made so many mistakes. She just could not settle to it. Round the corner, across the chimney-pots and the leads, was the enchanted world, and she could not forget it.

It was little Gelding's turn to get the tea. Because it was a celebration, it was Bourbon biscuits and a whole quarter of a pound of *petits fours* from the little grocer's round the corner. And because little Gelding was extremely hard up, she borrowed perforce from Ann to pay for the biscuits.

'I'll be flush again on Friday night,' she explained, 'but I laddered my new stockings yesterday, and that did me. I'll be better off next week.'

So really the celebration tea came out of Ann's pocket, although it wasn't her turn. When she took the last letters into Mr. Robert to sign, he said, 'Well, did you do as I said?'

'Yes, I booked the passage.'

He nodded approval. 'You won't regret it; you are a wise young woman.'

But Ann, as she passed down the stairs into drab London, was not at all sure that she was not beginning to regret it already.

CHAPTER 3

I

Mrs. Puddock entered into the affair of the ticket in the sweep with an enthusiasm which quite surprised Ann. Ann mentioned it when she got back, and instantly Mrs. Puddock launched herself into innumerable 'Well, to be sures', and 'Fancy that nows'. It appeared that Mr. P. had very often had a bit on a good thing. Not that it generally turned out to be such a good thing as he thought. He had been a great man for sweepstakes, though as far as she knew he had never won a prize in his life. Mrs. Puddock's chief regret at the moment was that she had not had a ticket herself. She should have done, of course, but she just hadn't. Then, seeing that someone she knew had won, it had, so to speak, brought it home to her. Next year, she told herself, she wasn't going to act so silly, that she wasn't.

'I knew there was a bit of luck coming to the house,' she informed Ann, 'because this evening there was two black cats a-fighting in the area. That's always a good sign,' and she went downstairs.

She cooked an extra dish for Ann's supper, a nice bit of macaroni cheese, for after she had had her poached egg on baked beans, and her bit of cold bar tart. Mrs. Puddock prided herself on her bar tart. It had been the first thing that had attracted Mr. P. to her, he having a rare sweet tooth. 'Not the first tart as has attracted me!' he had been wont to say. Such a one for his jokes! And some of them none too nice!

It was Wednesday and it should have been the mending night, but somehow Ann could not mend. The sweepstake and the circular, and the ultimate booking of a passage, had been too much for her. She eyed the basket of stockings – those last elephant-grey ones had worn disgracefully – and, although she knew that she ought to be busy with her needle, she couldn't. All the broken colonnades and the tremble of red roses and the still shapes of cypresses seemed to come between her and her work.

She would need clothes, different clothes, to go on that cruise. She would get a new jumper, one of those light crocheted ones; her big coat would do, perhaps a new semi-evening frock …

Then suddenly she remembered that the news would have to be broken to Cuthbert. She would have to tell him on Sunday, and it was not an enviable task. He would somewhat naturally be disgusted at the way in which the money had been won, and probably equally disgusted at the way in which she intended spending it. Anything in the nature of a cruise was quite outside his comprehension.

She would have to tell Cuthbert, and she had no idea how she was going to do it. Usually under difficulties she would enlist the sympathies of Eleanor, but she did not feel that under these circumstances Eleanor would be sympathetic. She would take Cuthbert's part. For anyway a very considerable portion of the money had been wasted – they would probably use the word 'frittered' – on travelling to a part of the world where people had no morals at all. Cuthbert had the usual outlook of an Englishman, with the beautiful belief that though the Almighty had made the British Isles, with the possible exception of Ireland, which was Popish and Sinn Fein, the devil had undoubtedly made every other part of the world. And that was that!

It would not be easy to tell Cuthbert, and Ann was dreading Sunday. She went to bed very frightened, and through her dreams she wandered in an Italian orange grove, and listened to the alluring music, but every now and then the devil would peep out at her. The devil was in his accustomed uniform of horns and a tail and nothing much beside. And then it would not be the devil at all, but just Cuthbert with his neat little jam-pot collar, and his silly little saucer hat. It was most confusing.

II

Between the extraordinary happenings of that most extraordinary day and the Sunday, the cheque was sent from the sweepstake offices and cashed, for their horse was scratched. The balance due on the ticket was delivered to the offices of the steamship company, and the amount lent by Mr. Robert was returned to him. The remainder was locked into the office safe, for Ann had a terror of a banking account, and Mr. Robert said she could leave it there if she wished.

'I'll be your banker,' he said brightly.

Instead of feeling wicked and damned for ever, Ann found herself feeling amazingly thrilled and all the better for the venture. She would not let herself think of Sunday.

On Friday she put up office tea, éclairs and cream

buns, and Miss Thomas forgave her her previous sins, and over the friendly kettle they all became fast friends again. Little Gelding borrowed a whole five shillings – another pair of stockings had done it on her, she explained; and it seemed to Ann that there was very little chance of seeing the fourpence for Bourbon biscuits the other day or the five shillings to-day back again.

Still Ann tried not to think of Sunday.

On the Saturday afternoon she and Miss Thomas, feeling too rich for words, attended a matinée of *White Horse Inn,* sitting in the upper circle, and feeling just like duchesses. And *White Horse Inn* whetted Ann's whistle for further travel. Why was she going to a stupid place like Italy, when there were lovely places like the Austrian Tyrol? Of course she oughtn't to have rushed off like that and booked herself a passage for the very first cruise that had attracted her attention. She ought to have waited a little while. There were so many places to choose from.

Only she knew that if she *had* waited, she would never have gone at all. She would have provided herself with a hundred and one satisfactory reasons for not going; she would have thought of what Cuthbert would say, she would have told herself that she ought to save the money, and eventually she would have saved the money. Undoubtedly she would have saved it.

On the Sunday morning she simply had to think of Cuthbert. Within an hour or two she would be faltering out the truth to him, and hearing his opinion. It was a horrible thought. Ann put on her clean underclothes, which, in deference to the precepts of her youth, she faithfully aired by placing them under her pillow all Saturday night. She put on her best dress, the navy-blue one with the little spotted vest which Cuthbert and Eleanor thought looked so nice and ladylike. At South Kensington tube Station she bought some pink tulips to take to Eleanor. The very fact that she bought the tulips showed that she was disturbed and not in her proper senses, for Cuthbert had very definite ideas about shopping on a Sunday. In the first place he considered that it was breaking the commandment which bade you to keep the Sabbath day holy; also it was aiding and abetting other people not to keep the Sabbath day holy.

The kind-heartedness which had prompted the gift would never be taken into consideration by Cuthbert, who had an unfortunate aptitude for looking on the worst side of any situation. In the train bound for Charing Cross, where of necessity one changed on to the Balham and Tooting route, Ann suddenly remembered Cuthbert's rooted objection to people who shopped on a Sunday, and she realized that, instead of assisting her cause, she would be very seriously damaging it.

She tried to leave the pink tulips behind her at Charing Cross station, getting up hurriedly and rushing for the door as fast as she could go. A well-intentioned but misguided young Cockney grabbed the tulips and pursued her.

'Here, miss, yer flaws!' said he.

Redly Ann accepted them and thanked him with a heart that was overfilled with embarrassment and fury. She must rid herself of the hateful things.

Just as the Balham train came in she crammed the tulips into one of the wire baskets which desired you to place your rubbish in its depths. Two women watched her and said loudly, 'Oh my! Look at her! Such beautiful flowers too.' They gazed at her as, hot and confused, she leapt on to the train.

She had not cooled by the time she got to Clapham. Naturally she was worried. Usually she felt that there were too many Claphams on the tube, but to-day there could not be enough. She wanted time to think. She did not want to get to Balham with the painful necessity of explaining the somewhat complicated matters to Cuthbert. The train got to Balham too soon, and she got out and walked as slowly as she could up the road. She thought to-day that it looked very Balham-ish. Far more Balham-ish than ever before, and all because she was thinking of the cruise, and the cruise was going to be so wonderful.

The first green lay on the trees of Tooting Bec Common. The first dim reflection lay smudgily on the stillness of the pond. The youth of the year with its beauty attracted her, and suddenly she felt that, whatever anybody else might say, she knew she had done the right thing. Mr. Robert had known what he was talking about, and she was glad that she had taken hold of the opportunity while she had the chance. Whatever Cuthbert might say she was not going back on it now. However he tried to dissuade her, she was determined to go through with the project. In any case the company would refuse to return the passage money, so anyway it was spent now, and she meant to have something for it.

She turned in at the gate full of determination.

It was a neat wooden gate, with 'The Manse' in beaten copper upon it. Inside was a square of green, with a round flowerbed in the middle, and triangular flower-beds at each corner. Up one side ran a neat asphalt path. Cuthbert had had the path asphalted because it saved weeding, and although he had conscientiously allotted this task to his wife and daughter – 'A labour of love,' he airily termed it – in time their constant complaints had become irksome. There were laurels at the side of the path, which led straight to the house and was neatly tiled.

Behind the porch stood the house itself, and it was essentially the right setting for Cuthbert, just the right background. There was the bow window of the seldom used drawing-room which jutted out of the ground floor, and up above it the corresponding window of Cuthbert's bedroom, the windows firmly closed and discreetly draped in Nottingham lace. At the back of the house there was the dining-room, and the spare room above it, with Gloria's and the maid's rooms at the side.

Ann opened the front door a little timidly; they always left it on the latch about the time that they knew she would be there. From inside there came the familiar smell of furniture-polish and of soap, and Ann, stepping on the aptly named slip-mat, proceeded to slip violently. Eleanor was enthusiastic about cleanliness. She rather overdid it. One of these days Ann firmly believed that Cuthbert would break his neck entering his own house.

There was a square hall, with a hat-stand on the right, where Cuthbert's saucer hat (token of his being within) hung, and on the left what the house agent had been pleased to term 'the usual_offices'. Cuthbert had been very pleased over that, for the old house which they had had before this had been ill equipped, and he was always telling people about the excellent arrangements in this new house of his.

He now came out, drying his hands on a small towel and smelling very pungently of disinfectant soap. Eleanor did not believe in scented soaps; disinfectants appealed to her imagination, perfumes she considered to be a little fast. Cuthbert was a small man, a round little man, with a small cherubic face and a bricky red colour. He wore a rather old-fashioned clerical coat, on which there were traces of previous meals, for Cuthbert had always been careless about eating. He wore steel-rimmed glasses, and his hair was rapidly retreating from his forehead, leaving a smooth and polished band of whiteness, in rather unpleasant contrast to the brick-red of the rest of his face. He was wiping his small fat hands carefully as he came out.

'Oh, hello,' said he, with the rather dreadful

cheerfulness that he sometimes adopted to Ann, 'and how is Ducky to-day?' If there was one thing that Ann disliked, it was being called Ducky. When she had been born, Cuthbert, a large flaxen child believed by his mother to be what is known as a beautiful boy, had looked at his young red sister and had called her an ugly duckling. This remark had been considered to be clever. Still, although the years rolled by, whenever he assumed one of his playful moods he addressed Ann as Ducky! She loathed it. She loathed it insistently, and more especially at this moment. She had prayed that Cuthbert would not be playful. She had prayed desperately hard about it. Always when he was in this mood he was particularly deadly, and she had got to break her news to him. Cuthbert had a paralysing effect upon Ann.

She said, 'Oh, hello,' and waited breathlessly.

Eleanor came out of the dining-room. 'That you, Ann? It's your auntie, Gloria.'

Eleanor hadn't worn well. She wore tweeds and she had not got a complexion suitable for tweeds. As a matter of fact her face was not unlike a good heather mixture itself. She had little eyes, dark and beady, whereas Cuthbert's were pale blue. She was getting a stomach. Behind her came Gloria, who was pale, for she outgrew her strength. She was sandy and had freckles. A weedy-looking girl, Ann thought. A striking-looking girl her parents thought. Having inherited her father's unfortunate astigmatism, she wore glasses, and this gave her the appearance of poking forward. They were not an attractive-looking family though their worthiness was most apparent.

Ann kissed them: Cuthbert who was warm and moist, Eleanor who was hot but dry, Gloria who was cold and flabby.

'Such a lovely day,' said Cuthbert; 'twenty-five communicants at the eight o'clock, and such a lot at eleven. You counted them, Eleanor?'

'I'm afraid …' she faltered.

'You certainly should have counted them. It was most irregular. There must have been over thirty.'

'Oh, certainly over thirty,' from the flustered Eleanor; and then, 'lunch is quite ready, I think. Run up and take off your things, Ann, or Gloria will run up with them for you. Take Auntie's coat and hat, dear.'

Ann handed them over, and while Gloria tramped upstairs with them the other three went into the dining-room. Lunch was set, with a highly polished brass bowl of ferns in the middle and the cruet alongside. The cold leg of lamb lifted itself mutely from the dish.

'You *ought* to have counted,' Cuthbert was saying. He was still concerned with the number of communicants.

Ann said: 'The garden is looking very nice. The daffies are coming on beautifully. You have got a lot more out than you had last week.'

'It was the warm Wednesday,' Eleanor told her; 'there was such a lot of sunshine.'

'There must have been over thirty,' remarked Cuthbert, though he was not talking of the sunshine.

'Any news?' asked Ann as they sat round the table. 'Has anything happened?'

Cuthbert, as he carved the lamb, which bore sorry marks of his previous maltreatment, gave her the news in a nutshell. 'We had the Mothers' Meeting on Tuesday, and it was most successful. On Wednesday Eleanor and I went round and collected in several of the envelopes of self-denial, which were out for Lent. The results were hardly up to our expectations; they were distinctly disappointing.'

'I'm sorry.'

'On Friday we started our mission services, and I think I may say that the first was a great success, oh, a very great success. Now, what have *you* been doing?'

Now was the moment. She knew that it was the very moment in which she had got to speak. All the way here she had been telling herself to be brave and go straight at it. And now here she was at it. Only she couldn't. Not with Cuthbert looking at her like that. Not with Eleanor and Gloria in patient attitudes of meek attention. Ann funked it.

She said, 'Oh, nothing much,' knowing perfectly well that it had been the week of her life, that it had epitomized the one week when everything had happened, just everything.

'Mr. Robert is well?' asked Eleanor. She had a great respect for Mr. Robert, whom she had never met, but whom she looked upon as being some lesser relation of the Deity Himself.

'Oh yes, he is all right.' She thought to herself: 'This is awful,' and then consoled herself that she would tell them after lunch. It would be easier then; they would be full fed, and Cuthbert would have got over Eleanor having failed to count the communicants. It had been very remiss of her.

With very little appetite Ann settled down to her lunch. At the end of it …

III

They talked of all manner of things, and all the while it kept recurring to Ann what nonsense it all was. All the little events had been quite eventless, the matters quite matterless. None of them had been of the least importance. Cuthbert was mercifully so full of himself and his own absurd little doings, that he did not notice that Ann had gone quiet. Eleanor rambled on, then she remarked on Ann's silence when she refused a second helping of rhubarb.

'Not feeling well, Ducky?' she inquired.

Ducky! As if that helped to make you feel well! 'Oh, I'm all right,' she said.

She saw the pock-marked cheese coming out. Soon she would be obliged to tell them. Soon. She felt quite sick about it. Unfortunately the conversation took on a turn of its own. Cuthbert full of cold lamb and pink rhubarb remarked on the happenings of the week.

'I never open a newspaper but what I realize that as a nation we grow more and more degenerate,' he said. 'Now there is this appalling sweepstake business.'

Could anything be less propitious? she asked herself. She put up a foolish defence, fully realizing its futility. 'I think the hospitals benefit.'

Cuthbert looked at her over the top of his glasses. 'Hospitals benefit indeed!' said he. 'Nobody benefits by money sinfully obtained. Nobody ever will,' and he looked at her as much as to say: 'deny it if you can!'

After that of course the only thing left was to mention it quietly and casually as best you could even though your heart sank. 'Well, I won something though I never knew that I had a ticket in it.' Never had her voice seemed so loud! She felt the atmosphere grow tense. She heard Eleanor's sharp intake of breath, and Gloria's sniff (she suffered from a chronic catarrh). She felt Cuthbert galvanize all his senses.

'You – you won in a sweepstake?' he demanded.

She started telling them, and it was the more dreadful because they waited to let her tell them all. It sounded too silly. She had not realized that it was a ticket in a sweepstake at all; she had thought that it was something to do with a raffle, and anyway she had not expected to win anything out of it. Then she had heard the great news, she had received the cheque, she was the richer by three hundred pounds.

'Of course,' said Cuthbert sententiously when she had finished, 'you will return it?'

'Certainly not,' she replied, 'why, I have spent some of it already.'

The worst was yet to come!

'Spent it?' he repeated, 'spent it? Why, it might have been invested in a trust fund.'

'A trust fund?'

'Certainly. You have responsibilities, you know. There is your goddaughter.'

Ann did not see why she should be made to hand over any of the money to Gloria. That was the sort of idea that would present itself to Cuthbert! He had more to say.

'Of course,' he went on, 'I think it was disgraceful of you buying a ticket in such a thing, even though you were not fully aware that it was a sweepstake. Ill-gotten gains never did bring happiness with them.'

'That's why I shall not put them into a trust fund for Gloria,' declared Ann. Usually Cuthbert paralysed her with fright so that she dare not answer back, but to-day she felt different. The knowledge of the ticket for the cruise gave her a certain assurance. Cuthbert was not used to argument; while he was recovering from the shock of it Eleanor said, 'Tst, tst,' between her teeth, and, 'I don't think you ought to speak to Cuthbert like that, Ducky, really I don't.'

He recovered himself. 'I am pained,' he said. 'I am surprised. I cannot tell you what a shock this has been to me. To think that a sister of mine has stooped to gambling!'

'I didn't gamble.'

'You won three hundred pounds for five shillings. A pure gamble,' he said, and an icy tone had come into his voice. 'And now let us hear what you have done with the money.'

They waited with a rather dreadful patience to hear what she had to say next.

'I – I have kept most of it,' she began, 'then the rest I am spending on a holiday.'

Cuthbert brightened considerably. Undoubtedly she was contemplating taking them all to Worthing to a good hotel. That was not so bad. Most of his Easter offering went on his holiday. It was never very large, for Cuthbert was not popular in his parish. If he could save the Easter offering he would be able to have the spare bedroom papered and painted, and some new bookshelves put into his study. Of recent years he had not found the Worthing lodgings too comfortable, though habit drove them back there every June. It would be far preferable to be in one of the hotels. Nothing with a palm lounge or a ballroom or a licence of course.

'Undoubtedly,' he said, 'that is an excellent idea. Then we shall all participate.'

Eleanor looked relieved, even Gloria smiled wanly. Ann felt her heart sinking. 'I,' she began again, 'I am not going to Worthing. Mr. Robert suggested that I should go on a cruise, and I have booked a passage. I start Thursday week for the Mediterranean.'

Whilst she had been speaking a change had come over the three faces before her. She knew that Cuthbert was conjuring up visions of what the Mediterranean meant. For him the ruined temples still held ghosts of Vestal Virgins – misguided young women with strange motives. Naples was a Papist stronghold. They used incense. They burnt candles. They did not recognize the same God however much they might stipulate that they did. Liners were full of vice. They had intoxicating liquor out of bond, whatever that might mean, and they danced all night.

He said, 'It would be an abominable thing for you to do. To go off like that into foreign parts without a chaperon, I have never heard of such a thing.'

Ann had expected to be entirely crushed by Cuthbert;

deep down in her heart there was the secret terror that she might be tempted to give up the project because of his interference, but now it had an entirely different effect upon her. She felt rebellion stirring within her. She was amazed at her own courage.

'I am thirty-five,' she told him, 'chaperons are out of date. I've always wanted to see the Mediterranean and now I am going to see it.' She added in a fit of daring, 'So there!'

The effect was extraordinary.

First of all Cuthbert was longing to tell Ann exactly what he felt about it all, but he was sadly handicapped. He remembered that she had come into a certain sum of money. It was not a very large sum it is true, but Cuthbert had an extremely material outlook, he was also a dutiful father, and he would not stand in Gloria's way for a single moment. He was torn between his fury at the impossible attitude adopted by his sister, and his paternal duty. Obviously Ann's success had gone to her head. She did not know what she was doing. In a crazy moment he thought of fortune-hunters whom she might meet abroad. In this mood anything might happen. He composed himself for argument.

IV

Nobody ate any cheese. Nobody ate anything else. Cuthbert, controlled and cool, argued along every line of illogical reasoning. He argued with a tendency to fierceness which he did his best to check. Eleanor resorted to tears soon after the argument began; she knew that crying made her nose red, but she couldn't help that. Gloria, who did not quite gather what it was all about, looked from one to the other and sniffed. Her sniffings had the effect of infuriating Ann to distraction. The black marble clock which had been presented to

Cuthbert by grateful parishioners when they heard he was leaving his previous parish to come to Balham, tinkled out the hour. It was getting late. The urgencies of the Sunday School must break up any argument. Cuthbert realized it. He rose.

'We will continue this at tea-time,' he said.

Ann, seeing her chance, took it. 'I can't stop to tea.'

'What? But you have always stayed to tea.'

'I know, only I can't to-day.' What she really meant was that she daren't to-day. She did not know how she had been brave enough to suggest it, but now, as she had suggested it, she was going to stick to it. She was not going back on it, for if she did stay to tea, life would be intolerable.

'You can't go,' said Eleanor, and she clung to her arm, 'oh, Ducky, you *can't* go. We must talk about it.'

As if they hadn't been talking a great deal too much in the last half hour! As if …! The maid came in with a large tin tray to clear away the unlovely debris of the meal. They went into the hall.

'I'll run up and fetch my things,' she said. She must go now, right away. She could not stay another five minutes. What with Cuthbert being pained, and Eleanor's tears, and Gloria's sniffings, it was unbearable. She actually ran upstairs.

When she came down again they were grouped together, and they eyed her reproachfully.

She was sure that in her absence they had been discussing it in whispers.

'I will walk down the road with you,' announced Cuthbert coldly.

She felt like a child about to be whipped.

***

V

'It's no good my not saying that I am surprised over all this,' he said. 'I do not understand you. Frankly, Ann, I do not understand you at all. You are behaving with no consideration for others at all.'

'I'm sorry.'

'There is our reputation to be considered. As the Rector of this parish, people will doubtless be very surprised that my sister should behave like this. A certain stigma will attach itself to us through you. We shall suffer. Oh yes, we shall all suffer.'

'I am afraid it is my own life.'

'Certainly. Haven't you always lived your own life?'

'Well, no, I don't think I have.'

As if you could argue with a woman whose logic ran along those lines! Cuthbert tried hard not to lose his patience as he strutted along by her side. 'And now to go tearing off home, not to stay to tea ...'

'I've got so many things to arrange.'

'You should have stayed to tea.'

'Well, I haven't stayed to tea.' She also was beginning to lose her temper.

It was queer that she had never lost it with Cuthbert before. She hadn't dared. She now felt she might do anything. Cuthbert gave her only one look, but it was singularly expressive.

At the corner of the road they parted company. He went to the Sunday School, she went to her 'bus. She did not know what she would do for the rest of the afternoon. Mrs. Puddock's house would be empty, for that worthy woman did not expect Ann back to tea. In fact there would be no tea for her. It was a fine afternoon, and, tempted by the sunshine, she went back to Kensington and walked into the gardens there.

It was green and lovely, and quite serene. She knew

now that everything was settled. She was really going to the Mediterranean. Cuthbert by his very perversity had settled it for her. She sat down on a green bench under a chestnut thick with its sticky brown buds. She let her thoughts wander through the adventure of the next month. She dwelt lovingly on the beauty; she had known so little real beauty that this in itself would be wonderful. In the grass opposite, the first daffodils were flowering.

She saw them swaying in the wind, like little bells, she noticed them appreciatively because they were so essentially English. Most of the English flowers were pale, whereas the semi-tropical flowers of the Mediterranean would be richer and fuller. She tried to imagine them, but they were beyond her powers of conception.

A man came and sat down by her side. He was, she supposed, nearly forty, with amiable grey eyes and soft darkish hair thinning at the temples. He did not look rich, yet his clothes were not shabby; she knew that he was not poor. He sat there smoking a cigarette and looking at the daffodils in the wind, then he said, noticing that she was gazing at them too, 'They look very pretty don't they?'

Before she thought she replied. 'Lovely. I've been watching them some time.'

'England is rather beautiful at this time of the year. I don't know of any country that can hold a candle to it.'

'I've never been abroad,' she admitted. 'I'm going on a cruise on Thursday week. I want to see the Mediterranean. I've never seen anywhere,' she added regretfully.

Then suddenly she realized that this man had quite deliberately picked her up. Never in her life had she spoken to a strange man before. She felt hot with shame, yet really she could not be ashamed, for his manner was eminently respectable. There was nothing of the touring Romeo about him, nothing at which she could take offence.

He smiled. 'You'll love the Mediterranean. Where are you going?'

Although she knew that Cuthbert would not approve, she was so anxious to tell someone that she could not restrain herself. 'Gibraltar and Naples. Malta and Venice. Ragusa, some of those little islands ...' Her geography was vague, therefore she hurried over it. 'You know them?' she asked.

'Yes. Gib. is amusing. It is an excellent place for a start. It has an attractive atmosphere and you will love it.'

'The flowers?'

'Lilies and roses, heliotropes and freesias. You are fond of flowers?'

'Very,' and somehow – she did not know why – she was reminded of the prim daffodils in Cuthbert's garden, and the clipped laurels. Cuthbert only grew ordinary flowers, those that everybody else grew; the unconventional had always struck Cuthbert as being 'nasty'. He eschewed anything that was 'nasty'. He believed an orchid to be as lascivious as an aspidistra was pure. He thought in those terms.

She sat on talking in the pleasant afternoon, and it was quite hot in the sun, one of those pleasant April days when the cold wind dies down, and in the comfortable warmth you can almost imagine that summer has come. He told her quite naturally that his name was Oliver Banks, that he had independent means and that he was a nomad by nature. He lived in a flat near Victoria Station when he lived anywhere at all, and she told him that she lived in South Kensington, and that she worked in an office in Henrietta Street.

All the time she felt that she ought to be ashamed of

herself, for never had such a thing happened before. And it was entirely wrong. Properly brought-up young women of thirty-five did not speak to strange men, even though the first remarks were quite commonplace and ordinary. She realized that she had been very foolish and she got up in confusion.

'I must be going back now,' she said and hurried from him in embarrassment.

She did not dare to look back.

CHAPTER 4

I

The following morning brought a letter from Cuthbert. He had broken his steadfast and sacred rule never to write letters on the Sabbath day, in case it should jeopardize his chances of immortal life. For an extremely good man Cuthbert lived in an abiding fear of missing salvation. He had a suspicion that fate might not play fairly with him, he suspected injustice and he risked very few chances. But he felt that this was such an important occasion. Was there not three hundred pounds at stake? He must do something about it. Something to bring Ann to a sense of responsibility and the excess of foolishness which seemed to have possessed her.

So he settled down and he wrote several pages on his best notepaper. On opening the envelope, Ann was aware of the honour done her by the best notepaper! It was not usually wasted on relations, but was reserved for such people as patrons and bishops. The letter was voluminous. It said everything that could be said, and a great deal that couldn't. Cuthbert was pained; worse than that, he was grieved and shocked. He could not think how Ann could ever have been so cruel and thoughtless. The whole family had been left shattered by the news. It was bad enough that she had won the money in such an undesirable manner; though that was of course a matter for her own conscience. But to contemplate this insane sojourn abroad; to go off entirely alone to these fast places, where only the dissolute collected; that was more than they could bear. All this had happened in one week. Surely matters had not gone so far that the project could not be cancelled? It *must* be cancelled. He knew of a most excellent investment, where her money would be perfectly safe, and although the interest it would yield would not be very large, it would be there. He dwelt upon the joy of knowing that every quarter day would bring in your regular thirty shillings. He agreed that it might not sound very much, but it was always comforting to know that it was there. And in case of need or illness – you never knew when a long and serious illness might not swoop down upon you – it would be a godsend.

He suggested that he should come to see Ann one evening during the week. They could discuss it together. Ann knew that she did not want to see Cuthbert. She read his letter through laboriously, and she folded it up. Her reply was terse.

She was now terrified that Cuthbert should persuade her in some magic manner to give up the whole scheme. She was afraid that it might be possible to cancel it, and that the steamship company might be persuaded to return her the money. That would be terrible. The wistaria would be out in Naples. That thought haunted her more than all others. Wistaria in heliotrope clusters. She would not miss it for the world.

And, spurred on by Cuthbert's pain and grief and

general shock, she went into the West End one dinner hour and bought herself some clothes. They were serviceable garments of course, because all Ann's attire was serviceable. She could only think in tailor-mades and woollen jumpers. Her shoes were severe, and she hated the extravagance of silk stockings.

The saleswoman listened to Ann's nervous enquiries. She listened to the ports to be visited on the cruise, and all the while she thought what a waste it would be. Fancy somebody like Ann going, when there were lots of girls only too anxious, who would have such a marvellous time. She advised a lace dinner frock that would not crush in packing, and a good tweed costume, and brown shoes.

'And a scarf?' suggested the saleswoman, and held up a prettily fluttering affair of many colours. Blue and green and mauve.

'Oh no,' said Ann, 'I couldn't,' then she thought how pretty it was. 'Perhaps I could make it into a work bag,' she said.

She had it sent round. The saleswoman packed the box with no interest, She did not care if the holiday was unsuccessful.

Ann did not look the sort of person who ought to be having such a holiday. And anyway if she intended sticking to tweeds and semi-evening frocks, she'd have a rotten time.

'It does seem a shame,' said the saleswoman to Miss Phyllis, who was second in command, 'if I'd got that chance I'd pick up someone and come back married.'

Miss Phyllis, who was manicuring her nails, looked up casually. 'Oh, well, I daresay she needs that chance more than you do, dear,' she said, 'did you see her face?'

***

II

Cuthbert was as good as his word, and he called round to protest. Mercifully he came in on one of those evenings when Mrs. Puddock was indulging in a tantrum. Her tantrums were as difficult as they were inexplicable. For no reason at all she would suddenly become huffy. It was very obvious that she had taken offence at something. Mrs. Puddock would be insolently haughty. All her conversational tides would be of a sudden stemmed. No longer would she indulge in that gay chattiness which was so much part of her. She would bring in the meals, and bang the door as much as to say: 'So there you are!' and she would flounce out again.

These tantrums would last either for a few hours or a couple of days. It all depended. Ann was sometimes at her wits' end to account for the strange behaviour of Mrs. Puddock, though of recent years she had been forced to the lamentable conclusion that the condition of the cellar was largely responsible for these various moods.

Mrs. Puddock did not suffer from the artistic temperament, nor did she have nerves, though she always informed the neighbours that that was her malady. Mrs. Puddock tippled, and when she overdid it she drank sourly. She was ready to pick an imaginary quarrel with anyone, even if they happened to be so entirely harmless and innocent of blame as poor Ann.

Ann herself suffered from a periodically guilty conscience (most guilty of all on Tuesday nights), and she had previously connected Mrs. Puddock's huffiness with the electric iron.

Perhaps it had been discovered. It was really a very mean form of cheating, she told herself, and she should not stoop to it, but necessity, the stern necessity of three pounds ten a week, drove hard. Necessity allied with bad example, for both Miss Thomas and little Gelding admitted to similar sinning.

When Cuthbert arrived in Onslow Gardens, Mrs. Puddock was in one of her very worst moods. She wasn't having no truck with no one, she said. She had only seen Cuthbert twice before, and she did not recognize him again. On the whole she did not hold with parsons, seeing that you did hear such things, and read such things too in the Sunday newspapers. Being a parson only made it worse. So she conveniently forgot that Cuthbert was Ann's brother, and she declared that Miss Clements was not at home. After all, she argued, if Miss Clements was going to start having gentleman visitors, brothers or no brothers, where would it end? Winning a prize in a sweepstake, and then going off gallivanting to foreign parts, well, what would happen next?

'No, she ain't at home,' said Mrs. Puddock. She did not speak so badly usually, but she felt like it to-night. She was going to put a stop to gents coming visiting once and for all.

'Then I'll come in and wait,' said Cuthbert.

'Not in my 'ouse,' said Mrs. Puddock.

'But I'm Mr. Clements, Miss Clements' brother. We have met before.'

'Ho yus,' said Mrs. Puddock and she shut the door firmly. She wasn't going to have any truck like that. That she wasn't.

At the moment she was feeling a fierce enmity towards Ann, but she had all unwittingly done her the best possible turn that she could. For, had Cuthbert gained access, had he pleaded his cause, playing on Ann's sentimental feelings as only Cuthbert knew how, why anything might have happened.

But then all life is suspended on the slim thread of chance. If Eve had not fancied fruit, well, where might we not have been now?

III

The steamship company supplied Ann with a passport, and a most attractive-looking and varied bundle of labels. They intrigued her tremendously and she felt the thrill of voyaging coming rapidly closer.

It all sounded most important.

She took her time packing her nineteen-and-sixpenny trunk (she was always grateful to Mr. John Barker for that), and to have hurried it would have spoilt the whole thing. She took all her woollies. She would need them, she believed, for since this amazing series of coincidences she had read every newspaper article on the Mediterranean that came her way. Unfortunately they contradicted themselves badly.

She read disturbing warnings about sandflies and mosquitoes, and they frightened her. She tried to put them out of her mind, and furnished herself with an antidote for midge bites provided by a thoughtful and solicitous chemist.

The articles had suggested thin silk frocks, but Ann decided that was futile. No, she told herself, her woollies were quite useful, and it was senseless waste getting other things. She never felt the heat very much, and it could be quite hot at Worthing, especially in a heat wave. People made a lot of fuss about the heat, she thought, and anyway if it was a little trying she must put up with it. After all, it would not be for long.

The trunk went off two days before sailing, in accordance with the printed directions on the back of the form, as supplied by the obliging steamship company. The actual hour itself was fast approaching.

The day before she was to go she asked both Miss Thomas and Miss Gelding out to lunch, and she ordered it to be an extra special.

She could afford this now. Cold salmon, roast

chicken, and a fruit salad. A bottle of wine. This she felt
was not entirely right, in fact it was, according to
Cuthbert, most definitely wrong. But in deference to the
fact that it had been Miss Thomas who had originally
bought the ticket, she felt that even though sinful she
must stand by it. And as she had started sinning, a little
more or less did not make much difference.

Little Gelding did not accept. She had a new boy
friend. He was a professional dancer, she said, and
taught the terpsichorean art at a school in Regent Street.
He wore lovely suits, and silk shirts, and smeared his
hair down with the most beautiful smelling hair cream.
He had It. He had personality. He might look a little
Nancy, but he wasn't really. No, truly he wasn't. You
should just feel how he kissed you! Little Gelding had
high hopes that this time it would be the real thing. It
was always the real thing on her side, but the young men
did not feel quite the same way about it. They had their
own ideas, and more often than not those ideas were not
marriage. But, touched by having been asked, little
Gelding, always generous, bought Ann a very ornate
sponge-bag in silk, all fitted up with soap and flannel
and sponge.

'Just as a remembrance,' she said amiably.

It was really most touching. Most good of little
Gelding, and Ann only wished that, on the strength of it,
she had not borrowed seven and sixpence from her; as
Miss Gelding put it, 'to help her round a stiff corner'.

Ann and Miss Thomas lunched together and grew
intimate over the cold salmon and hot chicken. Miss
Thomas had invested two hundred pounds of her money
in an insurance scheme, by which she would benefit
enormously in those years of the mid fifties, when, as the
prospectus tactfully put it, she would need a little extra
comfort. Already the money had made a difference to
her. She grew warmer and more confiding, aided by sips

from the glass of wine at her elbow. At the corner of the road there lived a commercial traveller. For years Miss Thomas had thought that he cared for her, only thought, mind you, for she had had no cause to do anything more. It was the way he looked – oh, you know! He was poor, because he was only paid on commission and it was difficult to sell these days. Marriage on his vague pay would have been impossible. But Miss Thomas wasn't proud, and she did not see that it mattered which side the money was as long as it was there. And, since the sweepstake, he had been very friendly indeed. First he had congratulated her, then he had remarked upon his interest in her and her future, he always had been interested, he had informed her. They had grown quite matey, Miss Thomas assured Ann, over the hedge, discussing his roses overburdened with greenfly, spray them as he would. And after that, Miss Thomas said, Why, anything might happen, mightn't it? You could not have more auspicious circumstances. Congratulations. Interest. Greenfly. Well, there you were. And Ann, not quite seeing where you were, said, 'Oh yes, of course.'

They walked back from the restaurant arm in arm. Ann could not believe that to-morrow she would be at Tilbury; that she would not be in England at all later, but would have set out on the great adventure.

It was too marvellous.

They walked along contentedly, then Miss Thomas said, 'I have got a little souvenir for you too, only a bottle of eau de Cologne, but it's a very ladylike perfume, and it's nice if you are feeling sick.'

'How lovely of you!' said Ann. Really, they were all too good, very much too good. Last of all Mr. Robert, she was almost afraid that he might have bought a gift for her, but he hadn't.

'Good luck,' he said, 'and a pleasant voyage.'

She was passing down Henrietta Street for the last

time for a month. She was going out into the world. And now she felt a twinge of regret as the door of the office shut fast behind her, and Brockman locked it. It was as though she were shutting out an epoch.

She walked down Bedford Street and along the Strand. It would never seem so beautiful, she felt. Trafalgar Square at the end and the evening light on the still pools of water. The stone grown dark with smoke and grime, and through the Admiralty Arch a glimpse of trees growing green.

She took the 'bus home, and somehow it seemed that there was a queer peace about South Kensington. It was a new peace, something that she had never discovered there before. She wondered if it were always like this on the eve of a journey.

She turned into the house and went up the stairs. The room still bore traces of her packing, it was all turmoil and confusion, and Mrs. Puddock (mercifully not in one of her moods) was hovering on the stairs.

'I made you a buck rarebit. I thought it'd be a treat, and you going to these nasty foreign parts.'

Ann did not like to tell her that everything on the liner would be English, people had always told her how wonderfully they fed you on board ship, and she was rather looking forward to that part of it. It would be nice not to have to consider price, would be lovely to have chicken every day, and no Thursday and Fridays when it had to be a glass of milk and a bun if you were really 'stony'.

On the supper tray there was a last appeal from Cuthbert. He had been most persistent in his appeals to her, and had apparently not yet given up hope of persuading her to abandon the adventure. His last appeal was more truly Cuthbert than any of the others had been. In it he had let himself go. He could not understand her. He had tried, but either he was very stupid which he did not think was possible, or she was behaving in very odd fashion. Undoubtedly that was what he believed. He was, to put it frankly, quite disgusted.

The whole family were disgusted, and in particular it was extremely hard on poor little Gloria. Ann seemed to have forgotten that poor little Gloria was her godchild, and as such she had a right to participate in anything that was Ann's. It was all typical.

Even now, Ann felt that in spite of Cuthbert's rooted antipathy to gadding about, if she offered to take poor little Gloria with her, the suggestion would not meet with disapproval. She hated to think that her brother was a hypocrite, but she had been forced to that conclusion.

She went to bed early, and as she curled up between the familiar blankets, and listened to the noises which she knew by heart, she dreamed daydreams. The old noises, the clipping together of the tree branches in Onslow Gardens, and the traffic passing.

She thought, 'What will have happened to me before I sleep here again?' It was an old game that she had played with herself ever since she was a child. Anything might have happened. Certainly she would bring back with her memories, fragrant memories of the most beautiful places in Europe. She prayed that there might be no regrets.

The next morning Ann Clements started on the wonder cruise.

PART TWO

CHAPTER 1

I

The *Allando* lay at anchor in the middle of the stream at Tilbury. She looked very much larger than Ann had expected, and she was confused by the crowd all anxious to get on board. 'Passports this way.' 'This way for the tender.' 'Postcards of the ship.' 'Telegrams. Telegrams.'

She had never expected that there would be so many people or so much bustle, and she proffered her passport to an official timidly enough. The photograph inside was very bad. She was almost afraid that he might not recognize her from it, and that even now she might be turned back within the very sight of the ship itself. But apparently he did recognize her. He slapped the passport together with a bang, and pushed it across to her in company with an embarkation ticket.

Ann, fumbling with a bag, a cabin ticket, a passport and now an embarkation ticket, became more embarrassed than ever. It was very bewildering, not a bit like going to Worthing. There were telegraph boys proffering forms – as if she had anyone to telegraph to! – boys with postcards of the ship, others with magazines, some selling fruit. One little lad was so persistent that she bought a postcard, borrowed his pencil to address it with, and sent it to Cuthbert.

He would probably take it as an insult.

Ahead under a big archway, she saw the tender drawn up alongside. The hour had come. She approached it a little nervously, not quite so sure that she was enjoying herself now. She was still clinging to the embarkation ticket, and the passport and the more important-looking itinerary with the cabin number on it. She stepped into the tender, and viewed the *Allando* herself anchored in mid-stream.

There seemed to be a great many people about, and what was so disturbing was that they did not appear to be her sort of people. Some old ladies with a strange hand luggage, many baskets and bags, and umbrellas and parasols. Young men who in London she would have supposed were cultivating art. Very modern girls, all lipsticks and berets and fixed stares. One thing she had thought was that she would meet 'nice' people, gentlefolk, that cultivated and refined class to which she herself belonged. But these people were different, they were extremely mixed.

Cruising had come within the purse of everybody, and everybody had taken to cruising in an amazing manner. Perhaps, she told herself, they were not so different as rather surprising. She hoped it was only that their appearances were against them.

The tender, filling up, sounded a siren, and slowly began to chug her way out to mid-stream. As the *Allando* came nearer she grew very much larger. Within Ann's heart there came the first faint yearning to turn and to run back home. At this particular moment she would have given a good deal for the solemn mounting of the stairs to Mrs. Puddock's bed-sitter. She would have given a lot for the office, and the mantelshelf littered with little Gelding's make-up. She felt sick with fright.

If it had not been for Cuthbert, she would have returned then and there and have sacrificed the money. What was money compared to acute misery, anyway? But he would have been so delighted and so cocky about it, and she could not have borne that. He had predicted failure and disappointment, and very well satisfied he would have been that failure and disappointment had come about. He was like that.

She filed up the gangway and in at the door at the side of the ship. A steward – she thought he was an officer – looked at her ticket.

'This way, madam.'

Then she knew that he was not an officer, and she followed him timidly. She would never find her way alone, never, never. She was sure of that. She tried to etch into her mind some manner of the way they were travelling. She tried to remember the blue lights marking ladies, and the red lights marking gentlemen. She felt that it was a vulgar method, but what else could she do? Nothing else broke the monotony of cabins, cabins, and still more cabins!

This one,' said the steward.

It was all beautiful, small of course, with a port flung wide, and a little brass bedstead standing under it. She had never thought of a ship having a bedstead, nor had Cuthbert, because he had been most emphatic about the immorality of a single woman sleeping in a bunk! The trunk stood there in readiness, the cord removed and rolled into a bundle, and laid carefully on the top. There was an efficiency about it all that left her gasping.

In the wash-bowl there was a bouquet of flowers, she could see the deep red glow of carnations through the tissue paper wrapping. She felt herself turning red. Never before had such a thing happened to her, and while she was amazed at the sheer wonder of it, she felt a sharp pang of recollection that they could not possibly be for her. They must have been delivered here in error. They were quite obviously somebody else's.

She went outside to look at the number of the cabin. Yes, it was cabin 241, just as it had said on the ticket, just as was written on the flowers. There had not been a mistake. Gingerly she approached the bunch and lifted them, and instantly there came the delicious perfume of cloves and carnations. A little card dropped to the floor, and she picked it up. On it was written:

Bon Voyage, from all at the office.

It made the tears come.

She stood there blinking at the full crimson heads, and marvelling at the exquisite smell of them.

Then it was that the stewardess arrived, very efficient, very starched, very important.

She consulted the passenger list that she carried. 'Miss Clements? Yes, that's right! Now in the morning do you like an apple or a cup of tea?'

Ann, who had never had either before, said rather vaguely, 'Oh, an apple, I think.'

The stewardess (her name was Brown according to the instructions printed and put up in the cabin) realized that Ann was new to travel, for she said, 'You had better see the chief steward and arrange about your seat in the dining-saloon. There will be lifeboat drill at five o'clock, you'll hear the bell go and you will find the instructions on the card.'

All of which left Ann cold with horror.

The joy of the carnations faded in a sick fear of the chief steward, and the dreadful significance of a station at lifeboat drill. She had all the shy person's horror of making herself conspicuous, and had already sighted a horrible photograph of a gentleman, involved in all the intricacies of becoming equipped with a life-saving apparatus. And furthermore, investigation produced a complicated arrangement of cork and strings – she would never be able to put it on, she was sure, and even if she did get into it she would never get out again, and she would loathe to be inspected in it. She felt lonely, rather terribly lonely, as she sank down on the bed. Of course she ought never to have attempted the trip really, twenty years in a country rectory and fifteen years in a London office, plus South Kensington and Balham, were not conducive to making friends.

Then she remembered the chief steward, and the necessity for booking a place in the saloon and finding a table, and also for locating the nearest place of retirement to the saloon, where, if needs be, she could be comfortably and privately sick. The thought of sickness had not come to her until now, but suddenly she was not quite so happy about it.

She went out to find the dining-saloon, which with difficulty was located. It was magnificent, a great deal finer than the Lyons' where she was wont to go on special occasions. She was also much disturbed at having to approach so obviously important a person as the chief steward. He was, however, in command of a plan of the room, and he showed her a table close to the door (very useful in emergencies) and she marked it down in her own mind so that she might recognize it when dinner time came.

'I think you will be happy there,' he said, 'and you sit where you like for the first lunch.'

As lunch was being served she thought that she might as well have it now. Anyway she would never dare to enter the saloon again. She sat down and ordered a meal.

It was the loveliest meal that she had ever had, save that it was entirely spoilt by the memory of stations at lifeboat drill, which must inevitably follow later. Which were starboard and port side anyway? And how could you locate your lifeboat when as far as she could see each was identical with the last? She objected to going about dressed up, and more especially when you were dressed up like that.

She did full justice to the meal, and afterwards she followed an ornate staircase – it was queer having staircases – into the lounge above. The lounge had marble pillars and bowls of pink tulips in it. There were magazines and newspapers lying about, and the chairs were the most comfortable she had ever sat in. It was like a magnificent hotel, not like a ship at all. And in this it disappointed her. She had wanted a ship; she had wanted the wind-blown wildness of it, a prow cutting its way through the waves, masts, rigging in a dark lace against the sky. In a way she had wanted it to be uncomfortable, because she had associated discomfort with the sea, and this she felt was far too much like a Park Lane hotel.

She watched the people with trepidation. She was afraid of them. She longed desperately to speak to them, yet she was frightened to death that they would speak to her.

As she sat there she realized that she was part and parcel of this scheme; she, who had never been used to anything save the rather solid discomfort of the rectory at home, and the bedsitter complexities of Mrs. Puddock's establishment in South Kensington. She had started on this strange adventure, and it was worth while.

She glanced out of the porthole and she saw suddenly that the grey outline of Tilbury was moving. They had already weighed the anchor, or whatever the correct term might be. They were passing down the river on the first stage of the wonder cruise towards the wide ocean which lay beyond.

She felt inside her the delirious sensation of joy that she had not experienced since she was a child, and the feverish excitement of some anticipated pleasure suddenly fulfilled in its promise. Now she had really started! Nothing could make them put back again, nothing in the world; not even Cuthbert or Eleanor or Gloria, nor the sudden illness of both Miss Thomas and little Gelding, and the urgent need of Mr. Robert.

Nothing whatsoever.

She had disconnected herself from England. She had cut it off from her. There wasn't anything that represented normal routine left. No postman at eight. No morning newspaper. No convenient telegraph forms. No milkman in the morning. No putting out the cat at night!

She gave a cry of pleasure.

A man sitting a little away from her turned at the sound and looked at her curiously.

'Well, upon my soul!' said he.

It was Oliver Banks.

II

Although he was practically a stranger to her, and they had certainly met under peculiar – Cuthbert would have called them promiscuous – circumstances, she found that she was overjoyed to see him. She was quite surprised at herself.

'Fancy you being here!' she exclaimed.

'I wanted a cruise, and quite frankly you put the idea into my head.'

Later she thought, 'Heavens, he followed me! How awful! But at the time she was so enchanted by the sight of a friendly face that she never thought anything of the sort.

'It's nice to see you,' she said.

'How are you liking it? Is it what you expected?'

'It's much more magnificent. It is so gorgeous that it rather frightens me. I – I hadn't thought of it being like this. I am afraid I shall be awfully out of it.'

She was remembering the tweeds and the two-and-eleven-penny plimsolls that she had bought on Eleanor's advice as being just the things for wearing on deck. So far nobody was wearing plimsolls. Most of them had those white shoes with brown strappings which she had thought to be fast and conspicuous. The plimsolls would be far more conspicuous, she felt. It is odd how one's standards change.

'I don't believe I have brought the right clothes,' she commented.

'Nobody ever does the first time. It is the easiest thing in the world to shop in Marseilles! You just nip ashore, and get some more, that's all.'

Ann couldn't see herself nipping ashore and doing anything of the sort. In the first place her French was limited, very much limited. Dr. Ahn's First French Course had never been completed. She had stuck at page sixty-seven. The *le mien, la mienne* page.

'There's another thing,' she said, glad to confide her difficulties in someone, 'there is this lifeboat drill. I don't know how I put the thing on.'

'I'll help.'

She voiced the thought that had lurked like a ghost in the back of her mind for a while. 'I suppose I'm bound to turn up? I can't dodge it?'

'People frequently do. It isn't wise. Nor is it very fair on the Commander in case of an accident. But people *do* hide.'

'I suppose they'll look for me in my cabin?'

'Obviously. You could say you were sick.'

She thought very hurriedly of the only other place where she could hide, under the pretence of sickness, and she felt herself reddening.

'I think I'd better turn up,' she said.

'You won't find it so dreadful really. Everybody is

very friendly, and they all take it in good part. It is rather fun.'

Ann, who by reason of an isolated and introspective life was not a good 'mixer', wasn't so sure about the fun part of the business.

'I shall feel better when it is over,' she admitted.

All the same when eventually the bells went clanging through the ship, and she proceeded to her cabin for her life-saving apparatus, she did not fancy it at all. She was assailed with sheer panic. The bell went on insistently. She picked up the bundle by the strings, and went out into the alleyway. Nobody was there. Had there been other people, she could at least have seen what they looked like; as it was she felt more dismally afraid than before.

She did not know what to do. If she stayed here, with the awful apparatus dangling from her hand, she felt sure that she would be discovered by some steward or official, who would hustle her along to what she now depicted to herself as a veritable shambles. She could not face it. She did not know what to do.

Then she saw opposite, like an oasis in her desert of doubt, the most blue light above a doorway. This at least offered sanctuary. She dithered for a moment, then the sound of a bell and of footsteps sent her hurrying inside.

She waited. Footsteps shuffled up and down the alley. She heard voices calling. The bell again, harsh and insistent, sending her heart down into her boots. And all the while the wretched contraption in her hand, the infernal life-saving apparatus that she simply could not get rid of.

'I think I'd rather drown,' Ann told herself.

Silence at last, only the heavy sighing of the ship, the rising and falling, the heaving and the swaying. She did not know what to do. Was it over? Had anybody missed her? Had the Captain sent down for her, and had her absence been discovered? She felt quite unable to think.

Cautiously she came out, and looked up and down. She went back to the cabin, and tried to fold up the apparatus to look as though she had never touched it. Whilst she did so, she heard running footsteps, and peeping round the corner saw a young man, still wearing his apparatus and looking strangely distorted, like pictures she had seen of Chinese punishments in a book her father had had.

Seeing her he called, 'Lifeboat drill,' and ran on.

It wasn't over. It hadn't begun apparently. In her dilemma she went back and dragged up the hateful apparatus again. Just as she had thought it was all done with. Just as she had been happy about it again. Now this! She heard more running footsteps, and now determined that nothing short of death itself should entice her into this contraption, worse than any Chinese punishment, she dived into her precious sanctuary She did not know how long she waited this time. The ship had taken on its normal noises; it had become again like every other ship in the world. She emerged. A stewardess with a hot-water can surveyed her with reproach.

'Oh, the lifeboat drill is postponed,' she said, 'the Commander has decided to have it to-morrow. Nobody hardly turned up to-night.'

And after a whole hour of hiding! After this dodging like a truant child! Ann Clements re-entered her cabin and plonked the apparatus down with a bang. Regardless of what Cuthbert would have said she gave vent to her feelings. The new atmosphere had got her. The wonder cruise was beginning to work its miracle.

'Damn,' said Ann Clements with emphasis, 'damn.'

***

III

After that things went on in a daze. There was dinner.
She entered the saloon nervously, for she had suddenly
become quite sick with fright. If she could have escaped
this meal she would have done so, only she had to eat.
She was far too afraid of the stewardess whose name
was Brown, to ask her to bring food to her cabin. She
had a sick longing for the homeliness of Mrs. Puddock's,
for the baked beans and the poached egg set on a tin tray
perched perilously on your knee over the fire in winter,
or on the table pulled under the window in summer.

She tried to tell herself that everybody was feeling
strange and therefore it was as bad for them, as it was for
her. Everybody whom she met seemed to be beset with
too bold a swagger, or too nervous a tread. Nobody was
at their ease.

She entered the saloon at a run, owing to the lurch of
the ship, and she cannoned into an old gentleman who
did not appear too pleased. He was obviously North
country (there seemed to be a tremendous amount of
North country people on board), for he shook himself
free and he said 'Naow then.' It frightened Ann a good
deal.

Already other passengers were at her table. A large
middle-aged woman with the fast-looking daughter. Ann
had noticed them earlier in the day on deck, and she had
decided that she did not like them; they were not 'her
sort'. The fast-looking daughter was apparently called
Ethel; she had too red lips in a too white face, and she
wore a skimpy black chiffon frock with a knot of white
violets on the shoulder. Ethel looked discontented, she
looked as though she were prepared to grumble. In truth
she and her mother had come here on a man-hunt. Ethel
was getting on. Men were scarce. They had thought of
cruising as an original idea, and they had hopes of

picking up a count. Titles were four a penny on the Continent, they had been told. Ann recognized a difference, subtle but certain, between her own lace dinner frock, as recommended by the shop assistant as being 'so useful for all occasions', and Ethel's. As she sat down she glanced across at the other two inquiringly. Did they speak or not? She recalled the one time when she had stayed in a boarding-house in Worthing, and there it had been etiquette for everyone to speak. Apparently it was etiquette here.

'Good evening,' said Mrs. Duncan, the large middle-aged lady.

'Good evening,' said Ethel indifferently.

'Good evening,' said Ann.

That was that.

Everybody waited for somebody else to say something intelligent and so set the ball rolling. At last Mrs. Duncan thought of something original.

'It's a large ship,' said Mrs. Duncan.

'Yes, isn't it?' said Ann.

'Larger than I expected,' said Ethel.

'Oh much,' said Ann.

It was really rather dreadful. It was the desperate and hopeless attempt of people feeling their way in conversation. Three people who had got to be friends whether they liked one another or not. Ann would so much rather that people did not talk at all than talk like that. There were four other empty chairs, those on either side of her. She did hope nice people would sit in them, her sort of people; that would make all the difference in the world.

The next arrival was a ship's officer, young and dark, who took the seat on Ann's right. He wore the red stripes of a doctor, though that conveyed nothing to Ann, who presumed that some wore one colour, some wore another, just by way of a change. He said 'Good evening' and sat down. Ann thought that he looked what she called 'nice', and certainly Ethel brightened considerably. She darted him one of her looks. But the doctor did not brighten. He had been on these damned cruises ever since he had started; there had not been enough money left from the fiasco his father had made of business, for the son to buy a practice, so he had come straight to sea, and had been going backwards and forwards ever since. Once he had been ambitious and keen on surgery, but now – he was thirty-four – all that seemed to have been left far behind.

Nothing ever happened here, nobody ever got ill, not decently ill with something that was interesting. Once there had been an appendix, but they had been close to shore, and he had had to let it go into hospital. His only touch with that surgical life which had once so inflamed his ambition was the *B.M.J.* and the *Lancet*, delivered to different ports to await the arrival of the ship. He was sick to death of it. He saw no way out, for he had to continue like this to live. Fergus Simmonds was a soul in chains, and the chains were there for eternity. He knew that.

Every cruise provided him with uninteresting table companions, and the painful necessity – urged by the Company – of making yourself pleasant to your fellow travellers. They liked having an officer about, especially the women. His uniform gave them an emotional rapture. Fergus hated it. Voyagers were of few varieties. Fast and amorous like the red-lipped girl opposite (the passenger list had told him that her name was Ethel Duncan), or dull and stupid like the old trout on his left. The passenger list had told him that her name was Ann Clements. She wasn't really old in years, he supposed, but she had got into the way of appearing old. She thought oldly; she wore frumpish clothes, and she had the old personality.

Fergus had seen too many of them not to recognize

them when he found them sitting at his table, glancing at him with that admiring yet inquiring manner; Ethel wondering if he epitomized her romance, Ann wondering if she would ever dare talk to him. 'Same old people, same old cruise, same old everything,' he thought desperately.

Monsieur Paul Vallé came next. He was twenty-four and he spoke extremely bad English, but thought that he spoke it very well. He sat the other side of Ann, and before the meal started she realized to her horror that he was a distinctly French eater! He spiked her with his elbows as he ate; he was very noisy; he masticated freely and thoroughly. He was little and rotund, with small dark eyes peering at the red-lipped Ethel through goggle glasses. She intrigued him – he called her Mees – if he had been the girl sort probably he would have had an *affaire du coeur* with Mees. But he wasn't the girl sort. He was the food sort. He had come for the menu, and he wasn't going to allow Mees to distract him from that menu.

So far Ann was disappointed in her fellows. She had believed that at sea everything took on a new glitter and a new glamour. She had not anticipated dull people, people who had come for the food, people who were frankly bored before they had started. Old people in stacks, Lancashire and Manchester people in hordes.

Old gentlemen in tweeds and bowler hats, young gentlemen in flannels and panamas, and this although they were as yet only off Dover.

The last couple to make up the party were the final straw. Mr. and Mrs. Spinks. Mr. Spinks had pioneered a particularly successful brand of cheap jam, and he had done so well by it that now he was in his own parlance 'quite a gentleman'. He had emanated from the board schools, and Mrs. Spinks had at one period in her life been a cashier in a Brixton butcher's shop. She believed that it was her proximity to the meat that had made her full-blooded and florid. She was also massive, for she had run to over much flesh on the good food that nowadays they could afford. They had come to do the things that everybody does, without being hampered by the difficulties of foreign lingo and foreign exchange. Last year they had done Juan les Pins, or Juan les Pins had done them. Juan les Pins had recognized them for what they were and had deliberately misunderstood their execrable French, and had fleeced them badly. Being a self-made man, Mr. Spinks was extremely mean, though he wished to give the impression of being lavish with his riches. He was a little man with such untrimmed and bushy eyebrows that he gave the impression of an inquiring shrimp. A little round man in a black velvet jacket, and carrying a large cigar. It was an expensive cigar, and he wished everybody else to know that it was an expensive cigar, and what was more he'd have them understand that he could afford it.

His wife, half a head the taller, full busted, and buttoned into a lace frock, was emblazoned with diamonds, and tactlessly wore a very full-blown rose over her heart, where she was unfortunately a great deal too full-blown herself.

'Well, here we are,' said Mrs. Spinks, settling herself into her chair, and she remarked affably, 'Good evening, everybody.'

'Good evening, all,' said Mr. Spinks.

Fergus groaned. This was going to be a worse trip than ever. It was positively vicious.

Disappointedly, and yet she hardly knew what she had expected, Ann looked about her. She felt that she had nothing in common with any of these people. There was no neutral ground upon which they could possibly meet. She ought not to have come. She was too old to mix with others, too shy, too self-conscious. She wondered how she could live through the entire cruise with people of this kind, and if perhaps it was not a just retribution for having won the money as she had done, and having spent it entirely on herself.

A little while ago she had been congratulating herself that now they could not put back. Nothing would put them into port again until they got to Gibraltar. Now she could only deplore the fact. She could have wept for herself as she sat there spiked by the noisy Frenchman on her left, and trying to converse with people whom quite frankly she did not like.

Although the ship was bound for sunshine and blueness, for the joys of the Mediterranean, and for the grandeur of Naples and the glamour of Venice, she felt herself entirely alienated from them all.

Instead of going up into the lounge to partake of coffee, she shrank down into her cabin and crept into bed. She was cold. Her first night at sea, Ann wept tears of bitter chagrin.

IV

Daze. Haziness. Queer jumble of thoughts all tangled, and of events equally involved. She was seasick. She wasn't very seasick, yet enough to keep to her cabin, feeling giddy and wretched, and apprehensive that surely this was the hand of God in wrathful adjudication on her unfortunate head. She lay there in a cabin, the porthole of which had of necessity to be closed, owing to the ferocity of the seas through which the *Allando* was ploughing. They were quite unexpected. From adjacent cabins there came sounds of other sufferers in even deeper agonies. Ann felt giddy, confused, and her head ached. She was also in that unfortunate position which warned her that though she was not actually sick, it would take very little to make her so.

She lay there and time ceased to be. There was only the eternal rising and falling. Only the sounds of stewards hurrying to and fro, and the stewardesses' starched gowns rustling, and the desperate brightness of the gramophone at the end of the alley, which played jazz music incessantly to two dreadfully hearty young men obviously undisturbed by the weather conditions.

All the meals took on a sameness, and none were appetizing. She did not know how long it lasted. Sleepy periods. Periods of acute misery. Darknesses. Lightnesses. Gloomily lying on her heart Cuthbert's grim warning, 'Well, didn't I tell you not to go?'

Then a new morning. A sea grown amazingly calm, the sunshine stronger and warmer than any she had known at this time of year. Finistère passed. The porthole was flung wide and the warmth and the new light came in in a golden wash. She felt restored; pale, a little green and decidedly thinner, but herself again. Ann staggered on to the deck.

It was an eternity since last she had stepped upon it, she felt, and now it was a new ship stirring with ship life, moving rapidly into the warmth and the blueness. 'It is quite horrible,' thought Ann, 'to remember that I'll have to come back this way and go through all this misery again,' and she tried to console herself that that was over three weeks ahead. A lot may happen in three weeks – even Judgement Day.

It is absurd to fret over the coming back on the going out. In the sunshine she found strength returning to legs that had been inclined to wobble. She found colour being fanned back to her cheeks. Fergus passing said, 'Hello, been sick? We've missed you from the table.'

She inquired how the others had fared and learnt that the Spinkses had been unable to leave their cabins, and that the Frenchman should *not* have left his cabin, but had done so injudiciously and had fled back to it, but unfortunately not in time. The result had been calamitous. The Duncans, mother and daughter, had held firmly on to their seats, and though at times pale green and having obvious difficulty in seeing the food set before them, and a reactionary dislike of poached eggs, pork and pastry, they had however managed to stick it out. Fergus remarked that the very sight of the 'fiddles' had been enough to send the unwary back to bed. Ann, who had no idea what the 'fiddles' were, smiled as though amused. Probably they had music in the saloon.

When Fergus had passed on, the old lady sitting in the deck chair alongside made herself acquainted. She mumbled very much. 'You must excuse me, my dear,' she said, 'but I had an accident the very first day out. Mo' unfor'nate.'

'Oh, what happened?' asked Ann.

The old lady, who had to unburden her soul to someone, launched into the story. She and her husband had come for the food. They liked good food, and it was better at sea than anywhere else, particularly on this line. It had been rough the first night, and after dinner she had felt rather seedy. They had gone for a walk along the deck. 'I feel sick, George,' she told her husband; George felt the same. Being both equipped with what is more gracefully described as an 'artificial denture', George suggested that they should take them out in case of accidents. Very unfortunately the accident happened first in the lady's case. Dinner and the artificial denture had gone over the side together. Now she could eat nothing but slops until she got home. They had come for the food, and this was what had happened! Bread and milk would have been possible at home, and bread and milk was all she was going to get here.

Ann did not know whether to be disgusted or whether to laugh. Cuthbert had artificial dentures, but he did not mention them. He thought they were rather indecent, like

Eleanor's underthings. You had to have them, but you never alluded to them.

When she could, she got up and she walked away.

The deck steward brought round beef tea. It seemed to her to be very funny having it at this time, and she had supposed that the smell of it would make her sick again. Instead she suddenly found that she was very hungry. She sipped it gratefully. She could survey her fellow passengers with a new interest. After all had they not all suffered together? Most of them were bright young people, rather terrifying in their brightness and their youth. Blazers were out. White shoes strapped with brown, berets, dark glasses, field glasses, blue jumpers with brass buttons, American sailors' caps. They were all the equipment of cruising. There was a new tone about it all.

She saw Oliver Banks.

'Well, and how did lifeboat drill go off?' he asked.

'I didn't go. I never got as far. I was sick!'

He laughed. 'We get into Gib. at ten o'clock to-morrow. What about coming ashore?'

The thought of getting to Gib. was worth all the misery and the chilliness, and the sense of desolation which had descended upon her in the throes of seasickness. It was worth the panic of hiding from the intricacies of lifeboat drill, and of the shambles below decks when the ship pitched and tossed. This evening she would have a talk with the bath steward – it seemed all wrong having a man arrange your bath for you – and she would have a proper bath this time. Before she had been too frightened. Bathing had been so complicated, it was most confusing. The big bath greenly full, and the funny little nursery tub set in a wooden tray before you. One for the face and one for the body, she had thought, in the extensive way that they did things on board. That evening the steward disillusioned her. He explained that one was salt water, and one wasn't. You could not soap with salt water. Ann, testing it for herself, came to the conclusion that this was true. She went down to dinner feeling like someone rejuvenated.

V

The saloon was full, though considerably paler than it had been on the first night. Mr. and Mrs. Spinks were still absent, but the noisy eater was noticeably present. Monsieur Vallé was making up for previous losses in the food line. Mrs. Duncan, decidedly limp, and Ethel, much as before, seeing that her makeup was applied like a paste, and her lipstick like an enamel.

The room was hot, for already they could feel the warmth of Southern Spain. Ann's hair behaved as it did in heat waves in England. It stuck to her head, and she had to keep pushing it back. 'Long hair,' she thought as she surveyed the neatly cropped heads of her fellows, 'is not all a blessing. I wish I'd had it cut off ages ago, only Cuthbert was so violently opposed.'

She ventured a few remarks. 'She's not a bad old trout,' thought Fergus, and gave her a closer observation. He wasn't sure that she was an 'old trout' after all; it was just the clothes that she wore, and the way she put them on, and the lack of make-up.

'You can't think,' said Ann, 'how I am looking forward to to-morrow. I've never been out of England before, and it is going to be wonderful.'

Before Fergus could reply, Ethel leaned forward and said languidly, 'But it's only Gib.! Nobody could get up a thrill over Gib.'

He felt that he ought to say something to help Ann. 'I've been to Gib. a good many times,' he commented, 'and I always think that it is a place with a personality. It always thrills me.'

Ann gave him a glance which said gratefully, 'Thank you so much. I felt it would be.'

He thought, 'She is really rather nice.' …

VI

Early next morning Ann felt the ship slowing down. She moved no longer with the same urgency, rising and straining, her beams complaining, her decks groaning a little. Looking out of the porthole as she dressed, Ann saw the land on the far side. It was bluer than any hills in England, and it rose in acute peaks. She was looking for the first time on Africa, which until now had been only associated with the hymn,

Where Afric's sunny fountains
Roll down their golden sand.

No sunny fountains, no golden sand … just blueness, unending blueness …

She dressed quickly, for now she was fired with the keen desire to see what lay on the land, and she hurried on deck. Land lay on either side, and ahead of them she saw the gloomy hulk of that rock which is Gibraltar. She saw the light of early morning, rose and amber on the hyacinth points of the fountainless, sandless Afric, and on the opposite side the little white city of Tarifa, curled like a necklace of pearls into the dip of dark hills.

A few people were clustered together under the bridge, viewing the approaching land with approval, but for the main part the ship was occupied with bath and breakfast.

'I don't think much of it,' said an old lady peevishly; 'travel is not what I thought. Not so gay. Why, it might be anywhere.'

'There are places round Sheffield that could knock it into a cocked hat,' said an obvious North-countryman.

'Oh, you come from the provinces?' suggested someone with the superiority of Bayswater.

'No, I don't. I come from Manchester, and Manchester's a fine city.'

Ann burned with indignation, for how could you compare Sheffield or Manchester with Africa? She went down to her food, hurrying through it, depressed by the sight of travellers who had lost their enthusiasms and who intended to remain comfortably below until the anchor dropped. She would not have missed this precious moment. The hot sun rising and piercing through the mist which lay like a grey blanket over the top of the rock. Golden shafts of light piercing down into the sea beneath, like so many golden spears. There was just a little wind, probably of their own making, and it fanned her face. She felt the flush of exhilaration; this was so far from home, something new, something so different. And here there was no Cuthbert.

A thousand miles stretched between her and convention, and all the difficulties and throes. A thousand miles between her and a powder-speckled mantelshelf, an office where typewriters jangled and jarred, a bed-sitter where Mrs. Puddock indulged in her moods. She was approaching a new land, and she would go ashore. She wanted to be alone. She would probably cry at the sheer beauty of the dream come true. She felt that she would enjoy that cry enormously, and that she would not be able to indulge it so comfortably if someone were with her. She had that beautiful feeling that you get when you are in the middle of a very sad but fascinating book, which you are convinced will reduce you to pleasurable tears.

There she stood in the bows, staring at the approaching land.

'It'll be a good hour before we drop anchor,' said a man beside her; 'it's a goodish way off yet.'

He was looking through glasses, which his wife had bought for the opera (not that they ever went to the opera, but they were useful from the upper circle at a musical comedy). 'Would you like a peep?' he asked.

Ann peeped. In her excitement she had forgotten that he was a complete stranger. They talked animatedly.

But were they really strangers? They had all seemed to be very formidable strangers when first she had come on board, and she had been frightened to death of them. But now they were no longer like that. They were fellow voyagers. There was a difference. Whereas at first she had felt that it would be fast and forward to speak to any one of them, she now believed that it was uncivil not to speak. With a smile for each, she found herself a new being. 'Something is happening to me,' she said, 'something is changing me. It just shows what travel will do.'

She went down to her cabin to get her hat. How her hair had blown about her face! Again she wished that it was close-cropped like her fellows. She ought to have had it cut. She wished she had been brave about it; it made you look years younger. Suddenly she wanted to look years younger. She wanted that blessed youth which slips away so quickly. Fine sand running through your fingers, something you cannot hope to keep.

'If I'm brave enough I'll get my hair cut one of these days,' she told herself. Courage. That was what you wanted. Courage carried you far. She rushed back on deck. They did not seem to have progressed an inch. Ann had yet to learn that it takes a ship a long time to make harbour.

VII

At last they had steamed up the bay to their anchorage. The officials had come on board, the tenders were coming out from the Commercial Mole. Ann, bewildered, half drunk with the thrill of it, leaned on the taffrail and watched. There were little fruit boats rowed by dark-skinned lads; she looked at the glow of oranges and of green grapes, and figs darkly bruised one against the other.

'For all the world like Berwick Street market,' said a clever young man.

She turned on him angrily. 'It's not a bit like Berwick Street market. How could it be?'

'Only my little joke.'

'A silly little joke,' she commented. She wasn't going to listen to people joking about the lovely new land. It was the land of new promise to her.

And now she was in the first tender, sitting against the side, and watching people swarming down the gangway. They were moving away from the big comfortable sides of the great liner. The people around her were mostly familiar by sight, although she did not believe that she would ever know their names. Names were difficult on a cruise; people were just people. You did not label them. Ann had discovered from her stewardess that Gibraltar was not a dangerous place. British money was in circulation, and it was quite English – she would be safe there.

Unfortunately, before Ann had gone a hundred yards from the Commercial Mole she had discovered that it was not so English as she had supposed, and that she was doubtful about the safety of it.

In the little street she was met by an array of odd-looking, rickety little carriages.

'*Carozzi?*' called a darkly smiling driver.

There were remarkable horses, and cadaverous coachmen all armed with enormous whips. They called to her, they hailed her as a long-lost friend.

'Hey, Mees. Rosia Bay. Europa Point. I take you.'

She tried to pass them by without deigning a reply, but a more persistent jehu stirred her tenderly with a long whip.

'I take you. Rosia Bay. Europa Point. See-a the sights.'

She said, 'No, thank you,' and hurried onwards, her cheeks flushed a little. They had reminded her of the four-wheelers you saw outside Worthing station years ago when they had first gone there. A dingy array.

She came to the Water Port gate, and here, rounding the corner, she found herself face to face with a Moor. She had not expected this in the so-English Gibraltar. A Moor, who walked in stately fashion, his eyes seeking those of no woman; his long clean robes sweeping the ground. He walked so proudly, with that grim majesty of mien which is wholly Moorish, and she saw behind him the kaleidoscopic glimpse of the markets and the women selling flowers. It wasn't at all English. It was 'India's coral strand' and 'Afric's sunny fountains' and 'spicy breezes' all rolled into one.

Ann never knew how she braved the dangers of Main Street on that bright morning. Women with dark handkerchiefs tied over their heads sat on the kerbs or on the cathedral steps. They were selling baskets of flowers, freesias, roses and lilies. Their scent came to her as she walked. There were donkeys with laden panniers. Little foreign shops from which came the aromatic scent of sandalwood and cedar and incense all in one. From the windows there fluttered Persian rugs and Spanish shawls, embroideries, laces, and leatherwork in one mingling collection. The Indians standing at their shop doors each seemed to recognize her as an old friend.

'Good morning, Madam.'

'This way, Mees.'

'Step inside. Have a look round. No need to buy.'

One after the other, and she with quickening tread and

heightening colour tried not to listen. It was disturbing, the insistence of the tradespeople desirous to do business, and not a bit English; she could not think what on earth the stewardess had been talking about.

It was hot too. She ought not to have worn a tweed coat and skirt, and her hair was heavy on her neck. She told herself if, later in the cruise, it was going to be hotter than this, she really would have it cut off, and not care what Cuthbert said about it. It would be too late to say much then anyway! She took off her coat and carried it. It was far hotter than Worthing even in a heat wave. Sticky hot! 'A lemonade,' she thought, 'would be lovely, but where dare I get one?' She decided that she daren't.

She came out of the South Port gate into a strange peace. And she knew now that she was standing in the new land, the land that had been the torch with which to fire her imagination. The burial ground of the heroes of Trafalgar lay on her left; she saw the trees as they bent together in green communion. In the grass, among the tangle of verdure, crimson geraniums ran riot; a pepper tree blew its fragile branches, and a little monkey climbed out of the boughs and clambered higher for safety. She said before she could stay herself, 'Oh!' for it was an amazing sight. She had never before seen a monkey save on a hurdy-gurdy, or at the Zoo, where she had taken Gloria when she was younger.

She went on ahead into the Alameda, and for a little while she walked and actually wept for the beauty of it all. She smelt the exquisite smell of flowers blend together in a divine essence. She walked in the grateful shadow of the trees clustering side by side. She rose higher and saw the brilliant blue of the bay, all the bluer for being seen through the dark tracery of branches bent together. Already *carozzis* were galloping past, packed with people from the ship, dashing for Rosia Bay (where there is nothing to see) or for Europa Point (which is practically the same place and where there is still less to see). Those dreadful people who would probably compare lovely, lazy Gibraltar with Northern England.

She climbed higher still.

She reached a road and she saw another woman on that road. She was old and withered, wrinkled like some summer apple stored over long into the spring. She was an old Spaniard in a tired black frock, which hung limply like a shroud over her half-dead body, which was veritably all bones. A small black shawl hooded her head, and she clutched the ends together with brown hands horribly reminiscent of bird claws. Ann had sat down on the low wall to pant. She really would have to do something about these tweeds, and her long hair, and her woolly underclothes. This was unbearable!

There was no one else in the white road, deep with dust, with cacti lifting fleshly arms on either side, and some burning red with flowers. Ann wondered if some horrible situation was about to develop. She would have gone back into the Alameda, save that she had all the Englishwoman's reserve; she did not want to do anything at all *outré*. Habit had made Ann dreadfully afraid of the *outré*. She stepped down from the wall and walked forward determined to take no notice. The woman, approaching, adopted a fawning attitude, and held out her hand.

'*Malo* piccaninny,' she whined.

Ann tried to steel her heart.

'*Malo, malo* piccaninny.'

It wasn't any use. She tried not to meet the old eyes of the woman who had nearly finished with life; eyes sunk back into two pits on either side of her beak-like nose. She was like a vulture, a vulture living on flesh. Somehow Ann felt that if she did not do something about it, she would be consumed by this old woman; drawn up and out of herself, and there would be no staying it.

She fumbled in her bag and felt inside the purse for some coppers. For a moment there burnt a light like a savage flame in the eyes of the woman who had nearly finished with life. It was the flame of a burning and besetting greed. A little shamedly Ann held out her hand with the money jingling together.

'Here you are,' she said.

'*Grazzi, Señora, grazzi*'; then she broke into a mumbled English. 'All happiness, *Señora*, make much of life while you are still young. Look at me!'

She indicated the gaunt face with the folds of the shawl about it, emphasizing the holes and the hollows. The gums in which only a few yellowed teeth remained. The shrivelled skin, the colour of a decaying apple. The wisps of greyed hair. Her gesture was dramatic.

'Look at me!'

Suddenly Ann felt in vigorous contrast her own firm flesh, her brownish fair hair, her even teeth. She turned sickly and she hurried away, the little pebbles and the hot dust of the road flying under her feet. She heard the old woman laughing bitterly. A poor old woman, who had nothing left, not even that outer appearance, the husk.

In the shelter of the Alameda, Ann felt her knees shaking. She sat down on a rock seat, and whether it was the beauty of the place or the shock she did not know, but suddenly she was glad that the incident had happened. She had grown so used to being old; well, of an age! She had never been actually young, but always like this; reliable, friendly, romanceless, eventless. She supposed she had always envied those glamorous young people who had had youth, the joy of that time, and she had grown to believe that most certainly now, when she was past thirty, she had not any right to that precious heritage. She wasn't young. She was almost middle-aged; soon she would be like the old hag on the upper road. Not exactly, of course, because climate and poverty had withered that old woman more entirely, but disfiguring old age would eventually descend on Ann. She took a little glass out of her bag and glanced at the reflection. The lovely languid heat of the Alameda received her. She saw the reflection of a mild-eyed placid woman, with a low brow and thick folds of hair drawn back into a bun on the nape of her neck. She thought, 'I've got to get that shingled; I'd look years younger, and it is hot, and it makes my head ache.' It did not matter how distasteful it might be to Cuthbert, she told herself; he was remote and matterless, and the picture of the old hag and her warning was distinct and close.

The recklessness of the mood did not pass.

It accompanied Ann, a somewhat new Ann, up the Main Street again. Even here she might have demurred (save that she was so dreadfully hot), but outside the English hairdressing saloon a man was standing who was obviously really English. She inquired the price, and after that there was no escape. Doubts dissolved themselves into nothingness and she found herself sitting in a chair, with her long thick hair in a smother on the floor. Well, she had done it now!

It seemed that the years fell off her with her hair, and she was almost afraid of the youthful reflection in the glass. The barber clipped and chattered. He told her stories of the Barbary apes who come down from the Rock and have strange carryings-on in people's houses. One lady had in fact woken at dawn to find a great and hairy ape there, lying in bed beside her. Children, after watching the apes playing in the gardens, were wont to ask embarrassing questions, usually at the most awkward moments. Ann was extremely worried as to what he would tell her next. The truth of the matter was that the barber was glad of someone to talk to, after 'Rock

Scorps' and the old *clientele* of English inhabitants, and he was making the most of it.

Finally Ann left.

Ann, who had taken a great step forward, and who was now a little afraid of it. Also her hat felt queerly large; she felt that on the slightest excuse it would spin round, or go rolling off and up the road. She dreaded passing through the narrower part of the Main Street, but it had to be negotiated. She clutched at her hat. It was indeed a passage perilous, and she asked herself why she had ever had it cut off. An ingratiating Indian gentleman in a tightly waisted suit approached her warily.

'You want a nice shawl?' he suggested.

Ann, who wanted nothing so much as to get back to her cabin with the hat still on her head, said, 'No, thank you.'

He laid a coffee-coloured and detaining hand upon her arm.

'I make a good bargain. I like you,' he said. 'Come inside and have a look round.'

Ann entirely misinterpreted his intentions. Contact was new to her, and entirely alien to her nature. She felt a flood of horror, she felt a rather dreadful quivering inside her. She wrenched herself free and fled. The familiarity of the detaining hand had horrified her. In her progress up the street she had discovered the futility of argument with these people; frigidity was no more helpful. She quickened her steps and went hurriedly onwards.

Ann in her frantic hurry was nearly run over by a galloping *carozzi*, full of people from the cruise who had been beguiled into paying a large sum of money to 'see-a the bull-fight, bull-ring, and brigands', and were now being conveyed towards La Linea, which, although they did not know it, was entirely peaceful, but where they would be convinced that they had seen ten shillings' worth of fun. The Gibraltarian had had some previous acquaintance with the credulity of 'cruisites'.

Crossing the barrack square and not looking where she was going, Ann found herself in the centre of a squad of soldiers. It was very difficult. When she was actually outside the market, the hat did blow off, rolling along giddily, and rescued by a street urchin. The short ends of her hair blew up over her head, and she felt that she looked like a caricature. It dismayed her.

The little boy came up with the hat. 'Penny,' he said brazenly.

Years of Sunday-school teaching came to Ann's head. 'You shouldn't ask for money,' she said impressively as she searched in her purse.

He said again more definitely, 'Penny.'

In her fluster she gave him sixpence. Anything to get back the hat and to perch it on her head. She thought she would never get to the ship. Now she did not care how she looked. Why should she?

VIII

The *Allando* had weighed her anchor, and in her cabin Ann sat staring gloomily at the bulkhead. Why had she ever had her hair cut? What madness had tempted her to make such an utter fool of herself? It was so desperately final, something she could not possibly undo. Now it frightened her. The ship was cool. No longer was she wrapped in that terrible sticky heat, and it did not reveal itself as an additional excuse. The hairdresser's glass had been flattering; now she was sure that she looked a fright, and could do nothing to change it. She told herself that she could not possibly go down to the dining-saloon like this, even the stewards would laugh at her. They had all seen her with long hair and must notice the difference.

Facing Cuthbert and Eleanor and Gloria would be nothing like so bad as facing the dining-saloon full of criticizing people. For a moment she wished that she had never attempted this silly cruise at all. Then pictures precipitated themselves into her mental vision. The Alameda, rich in colouring, filled by the tender and languid heat, the old woman like something already half dead, and the crimson glory of geraniums, the cacti with the whiteness of the lilies. They stood out in contrast to the drabness of her own life at home. Mrs. Puddock's and the allotted nights for ironing and for washing. The problem of the disallowed electric iron, and the difficulties of cooling it off. The office with little Gelding and her flirtation with bad Mr. John which had to be winked at. It was all like some hideous machinery; you fed it at one end with the raw material, and it champed and champed, and then delivered you the finished object at the far end. She knew that there was no chance for you once the machinery of life caught you in its ceaseless grind. You came out at the other end – dead. There was no escape.

Only by the aid of a miracle had she got away from it all, and she would have to go back. The very need for money would drive her back remorselessly, there was no getting away from that. This was a phase, a fleeting, flashing holiday phase, that had for a moment changed all her being. It could not last. It was like a dream, and there would be the awakening. Unfortunately the shingled head was not like a dream, that was the real thing, and wake with it she must. That was what disturbed her.

She looked so strangely young. She felt so naked about the back of the neck. She wasn't herself at all. She would have to go down to dinner, and quite probably someone would remark on her hair, and then she would cry. She felt most unhappy about it. Slowly, very slowly indeed, she began to change.

CHAPTER 2

I

Ann did not believe that she would ever go down to the saloon. She stood before the mirror, combing the refractory hair this side and the other, arranging it in ways in which it would not arrange, and distracted by the ways in which it would arrange. She was full of doubts and dilemmas. Finally she gave it up in despair, and crept out into the alleyway like a child ashamed of itself.

One of the ship's officers met her. She had seen him before; he was, she believed, the second officer, dark, with deep-set eyes and long lashes.

'Hello,' said he, 'just joined?' and then, recognizing her, 'Sorry, for the moment I didn't see who it was.'

She crimsoned and went on. She would not for the world have told him that no man had ever spoken to her like that before. Just for the moment romance had glittered on her horizon. She felt a new thrill and was instantly ashamed of it. Ashamed that she had had her hair cut; ashamed that she had aroused that interest in some man, and much more ashamed that she liked it.

Mrs. Duncan and Ethel were already at the table. They were usually quick on their meals. They had been shopping and were occupied with the bargains they had bought.

The Spinkses arrived, large and pompous.

'Good evening, everybody,' from Mrs., and, 'Well, and how did you find Gibraltar?' from Mr.

They were not so full of their bargains as of the immense sums of money they had paid for things. That was the besetting sin of the Spinkses. They wanted everybody to know that they *had* money to spend. You might have thought that Juan les Pins would have taught them the folly of it, but they had forgotten Juan les Pins now, and were starting all over again in the ship. They had been ashore and they had paid a fortune for a shawl, but after all what did a few pounds matter either way? They had bought perfume in a black glass bottle, like a goblet.

'Five pounds for a bottle of perfume,' said Mr. Spinks; 'just think of it!' He pursed his lips violently. When he pursed his lips the enormous moustache jerked like Harry Tate's. It gave him a queerer, more prawnish appearance than ever.

So far no one had noticed Ann's head. They were much too full of their own doings. Ann was of no interest to them. The Frenchman had bought green figs, baskets of them; he had a passion for them as he had for most foods. He ate heartily and masticated with a frightful noise.

'I'm dancing on B deck,' said Ethel to all whom it might concern.

'And there was a bedspread,' went on Mrs. Spinks, who was not in the least interested in the dancing on B deck, 'made by the nuns at Seville, he said, but I had my suspicions. I thought it was too cheap. Only fifteen pounds. You can't expect much for that, can you?'

Evidently other people could! Ann most certainly expected a great deal for fifteen pounds. It was far more than she would have spent on any bedspread, or any bed either for the matter of that, and she wanted to tell Mrs. Spinks so, only she daren't.

Fergus Simmonds was late. He was furious. It was queer, but during the whole of his term of service he had never been mistaken for a doctor, very seldom for an officer. Now, to-night, a woman had leapt out upon him in a state of undress, and, snatching at his arm, had demanded, 'Steward! Bring a cloth quickly, I've upset a bowl of water all over my cabin.' Coldly he had replied, 'Madam, I am not a steward,' but she had not withered. She had only said that he looked like one, and that he ought not to go about looking like one and not being one; it was most misleading. He had not recovered from this fracas, when he found himself swallowed up in the Spinkses' bragging.

He felt that he would like to hit somebody.

He hated these cruises. The mail run was bad enough, when the first fortnight you loved everybody, and the next you loved them not quite so much, and the last launched you into a definite hate. But this …! This …! People who had never been in a ship before; who had, he felt, no right to be in one now, and who he hoped, for the sake of all shipping companies and all respectable passengers, would never be in a ship again. People who mistook officers for stewards, and probably the other way about for all he knew. One old bounder who had worn a bowler hat on deck, and the fates (which are never discriminating) had not seen fit to blow it overboard.

He chose fish – starting at fish made the meal go quicker!

Then he saw Ann sitting there, and for the first time he became aware of her finely shaped head, and of a new girlishness about her. Why, he had thought her old.

'What have you been doing to yourself?' he asked.

There was the faint tremor of tears in her voice. 'I've had my hair cut short. Isn't it awful?'

'No, it makes you look a different person. I like it. It's a good thing you had it done. I believe in women making the best of themselves.'

Ethel Duncan, listening with lowered eyes, looked up furtively, and for the first time she realized that there was a difference in Ann. She leant forward. She was annoyed with Ann for attracting Fergus's attention, Ann who was old and ordinary and dreadfully old-fashioned and dull.

'Fancy *you* having your hair cut!' she said, and there was something aggressive about her.

'I think it is a great improvement' – from Fergus.

And then the Spinkses: 'Forty-three pounds he was asking, not much I thought, but what was the good of a carved bidet to me?'

Only Monsieur Vallé did not interfere. He had paid four thousand francs for this tour, and he meant to have four thousand francs' worth of food out of it. What was the good of spending all that money if you did not get something back for it, and how could you get something back if you chattered hard all through the meal-times? Social amenities did not appeal to him. He was not attracted by beautiful views, nor by the idea of travel, but, like the lady who had unfortunately lost her artificial dentures on the first night at sea, he had heard that the food on this particular line was excellent, and that was what he had come for. He put his heart into the engrossing business of eating. There was the noisome accompaniment of mastication and gulping.

***

II

Dinner was over.

Coffee had been served by the stewards in the lounge. The gentle Mediterranean heat had tempted Ann out on to B deck, where she walked to and fro. The ship was settling down to life at sea now. Faces were becoming familiar. The sick were no longer afflicted. The people who had saved up for this one marvellous holiday of their lives and who had been at first a little over-awed by the luxury and the efficiency of the ship, were beginning to feel at home.

One daring old gentleman had actually breathed to the steward that he preferred tea to coffee after his meals – he always had it at home. The steward had conveyed with a single look that he certainly would not have it here.

In another day or two they would warm completely. The strangeness would wear away. They would be one enormous family of friendly people at home in this wonderful floating hotel. And then the hates would start. Not being able to stick that woman in brown. Not standing Mrs. So-and-So. And all the rest of the fierce savage hates that emerge at sea.

As Ann walked up and down she saw a young man in a blazer that only a suburban tennis club could have devised, and capped by a beret, his arms fondly entwined about the slender body of a girl whom four days previously he had never even met. It was sea-fever. The beginning of a romance at sea; it was the strangely subtle atmosphere of a great liner urging forward, bent on pleasure; it was the wonder cruise.

There was a quiet sea, palely blue, with little lines like smears of milk across its translucent face. On the horizon, land, dim as clouds, the undulating coast-line, and rising out of a mackerel sky a moon which seemed to Ann's imagination to be far larger and of a more golden hue than that old friendly moon she had so often seen rising over Onslow Gardens, shedding beams that were dimmed by the lights in Sussex Place.

The ship sighed and whispered as she steamed along. The throb of her engines was so distant and indistinct as to be merely remotely audible. From either side came the sound of water, crushed into a heavy tide, split into two great waves by the giant bows of the S.S. *Allando*.

As Ann stood there she heard someone come up from behind, and felt him standing there. It was Oliver Banks.

'Looking at the moon?'

'Yes. Lovely, isn't she?'

'She grows a great deal lovelier further along.'

'How can she? It is the same moon really,' she smiled a little, 'it's the Pimlico and Putney moon at heart.'

'No, not quite the same. Nothing is the same at sea. Haven't you realized the danger of the atmosphere? The subtle, indescribable danger of a ship?'

Ann did not understand. She only associated danger with shipwrecks and with lifebelts, with fire drill and alarm. He saw instantly that she did not follow his meaning. 'No, not that. I was thinking of the false glamour, the new gaiety of flirtation that this place gives us.'

She thought of the old woman in the Alameda. 'Make much of life while you are still young, look at me …' And now she had almost forgotten the hair cut short. Perhaps that also had been glamour and the atmosphere.

'It gets us all in time,' he said, 'wonder cruise, sea-fever. What do we get out of it? Just something to remember.'

She turned and faced him. 'Why are you talking like this to-night? Has anything happened?'

'I got a letter at Gib. It worried me.' There came a silence, and she felt that it was an inquiring silence, so after a moment she said:

'Would it help you to tell me? Sometimes it does help a little to tell a stranger.'

'You aren't a stranger. You seem to me to be like a friend. Years ago I married, it was one of the impulses of my boyhood. In Bermuda. There was this atmosphere there. The lilies and the palms, lime cocktails. It goes to youth's head, inflames his senses, and I believed that I was in love. Later, but too late, I found that I wasn't.'

Ann was profoundly shocked, but curiosity lit her imagination. Somehow she felt that he ought to have told her that he was a married man. A respectable married man ought not to have spoken to a strange woman in Kensington Gardens. Then perhaps he wasn't respectably married! He went on.

'We separated almost at once. No good doing anything else. If we had gone on trying to make the best of a bad job we might have had children. They complicate life dreadfully.'

She did not know what to say. It was a difficult conversation for one only used to the extremely 'nice' remarks of Cuthbert and Eleanor and Mr. Robert, and the perhaps quite not so nice remarks of Mrs. Puddock. Cuthbert had always kept up the difficult pose of believing that God, and God only, was responsible for birth, which in the face of the definite establishment of Gloria with Cuthbert as her father was more than a little absurd. Mr. Robert would never have mentioned such things; he would have considered them crude. Mrs. Puddock only referred to them when she mentioned the agonies of a lady friend in labour. Mrs. Puddock liked agonies. She would have believed it indecent to connect consummation with conception, but quite decent to discuss the more ghastly details of first and second stages, of instruments and stitches.

To Ann it was startling to hear a man discuss quite

casually the facts of birth and beginnings. In her confusion she could not think of any way of stopping him.

'We split. I paid up. It was the only decent thing that I could do to acknowledge my responsibilities. Lilia has not had anything to complain of there! Now I'm a bit staggered. She is thirty-seven, and after having been married, or rather separated, all these years she wants a divorce.'

'How *dreadful*,' said Ann.

A young couple sharing the same deck chair just behind them, imagining the conversation to be engrossing, grew louder in their caresses. 'I'm mad about you, plumb crazy,' said the young man. 'Oh, go along,' said the girl …

'Let's move our pitch,' suggested Oliver. They went further down the taffrail. 'It isn't really dreadful. Ordinary, I suppose, only Lilia seemed to be getting on. I never thought she would want an affair of her own. She went on a pleasure cruise on a luxury liner, the American ones are pretty snappy I can tell you, and she has met someone. She wants me to give her her freedom.'

'But divorce! It is so wicked,' said Ann. It was Cuthbert's teaching. Those whom God hath joined together. Naturally it was like breaking a promise, the sort of thing no gentleman ever did. There were indiscretions in divorce, frightful scenes, you could not think of them.

'I don't know about it being wicked,' said Oliver, 'it is more likely our system of marriage that is wicked. So absurd tying people up, looped together in chains like prisoners. That's wicked if you like it.'

Ann was vaguely uneasy, yet the loveliness of the surroundings drew her along with them. She felt that no decent man should talk like this, and yet in her heart she was sure that he *was* decent. Perhaps he was a little drunk. Spirits being out of bond and all that. It did go to people's heads. She felt it was a mistake having spirits on board at all. She glanced at him nervously. No, he did not look drunk; he wasn't flushed. His face was palely cut against the background of sea and sky, and the tender, gleaming loveliness of moonrise. He was certainly not drunk.

'I think,' said Ann sententiously, 'that it is your duty to go to your wife and talk to her about it.'

'You think divorce wrong? You've been taught to think it wrong. Isn't this a case when we should think for ourselves?'

For a moment she wondered if he were making improper overtures to her, and then banished the thought, angry with herself for allowing it to cross her mind. Perhaps for the first time in her life she was aware that people had different ways of thinking, quite nice people too. Cuthbert, and the dogma which was Cuthbert, insisted on dividing people into two herds, the people who abominated divorce, and the adulteresses who revelled in it. Sheep and goats, nicely labelled. For the first time there merged on the horizon of Ann's thought a third herd, a herd that dare think for itself and which refused to be labelled. Instantly she knew that she had never dared to think for herself, but had allowed her father and Cuthbert to mould her views and set their own opinions in her mind, like little flags pinned to a map to denote the route. She had never formed a single opinion of her own, and it dismayed her.

Because she could see sense in what Oliver Banks was saying, she could see sanity in a sea of insanity. It might be that marriage was wrong in its definite need of divorce. It might be that her whole method of thought had been wrong, and that she herself had been nothing but a mirror, reflecting the unlovely images of her father and of Cuthbert. And they were unlovely too!

She had hated the disloyalty which allowed her to realize it, and yet she could not choke it down. She said, 'I wish you would not talk like this. I don't suppose I have ever proved anything for myself. I've been a sort of a chameleon.'

'Life is full of chameleons.'

'That doesn't make them any more original.'

From B deck came the sound of the ship's band, diligently assisted by the young man who helped in the post office. From the side came whispered caressings in deck chairs.

'I'm plumb crazy about you.'

'Get along, do.'

'You know what I feel. You know what I want?'

'I know what you aren't going to get.'

Other voices, girls in conversation together.

'Oh, my dear, I'm having a simply *marvellous* time. A most *marvellous* time. Two boys tried to kiss me to-night. *Two boys.* Won't the tennis club at home seem awful after this? The office hops too, they'll be agony! Oh, it's *marvellous*.'

Oliver said to Ann, 'Shall we dance?'

III

Ann had no time to refuse, for Oliver accepted it as the natural thing. She had never danced since her youth. Then her mother, less narrow than her father, and decidedly obstinate, had insisted on escorting the child into the local town on a bicycle, to Miss White's dancing class. She remembered bicycling through the snow, her slippers in a neat little bag that her mother had embroidered, dangling from the handle-bars. And once on the way Ann had broken a suspender, and had been terrified in the cloak-room when she had tried to pin it up with a safety pin. It had snapped again in the reel steps – abominable steps they were too – and now Ann could only connect dancing with a broken suspender, and the reel steps, and the instructions 'Behind and out, behind and hop,' of Miss White standing up before her little flock.

Ann had danced nothing but the old-fashioned waltz, and the schottische and the reel steps and the positions! Yet for all that she had a sense of rhythm. Music was a pulse within her, a pulse that set her moving. It was more than just a tune; it was a pattern of sound in space. Something that the wind and the rain and all Nature had. She was dismayed to think how much she wanted to dance, and how against all nice standards it was.

'I … I haven't danced these new dances at all,' she said in a little frightened voice.

'Oh, they're easy, you'll just drop into them.' He put an arm about her, and drew her to the deck.

After that Ann did not know what happened; she did not care much. Forgotten the shingling and the dancing, and the sin of it all. It was an adorable sensation. The lovely, rather tragic tune of 'Auf Wiedersehen', the appeal of it, the ship rolling just slightly so that every little while one's feet slipped away. Gay lanterns. A laughing, merry crowd. The urge for movement. It was all intangible. She knew nothing of dancing, only some vague intuition taught her to allow her body to follow his, pliant and yielding.

'Splendid,' he said approvingly.

A new entity stirred in Ann, a new knowledge, a new world which opened up before her, a world dominated by music, by movement as an expression of that music. She would have liked to go on for ever, but she could not.

The tune died down. The feet were silenced. The deck chairs on either side were filled again, and the ship pressed through the separate tides on either side.

'Well, I have to write some letters,' said Oliver.

'And I must go to bed.'

She was thinking, 'When I get to Marseilles I'll get an evening frock. I'll get something worthy of it. I'm sick of semi affairs, and of good serviceable lace that doesn't crush in packing.' The stir of life was within her.

Before she went down to her cabin she crept on to D deck. She knew it would be deserted. She passed the barber's shop, shrouded and veiled for the night; she went along the alleyway where a steward was whistling brightly as he cleaned the shoes. Beyond was the after end of D deck. It was very still.

She stood against the taffrail, leaning her head to a wooden stanchion which supported her. Something had happened to her; something that was unreal. The old woman in the Alameda had awakened some realization of the curfew to youth already tolling within her. Youth that had not yet gone so far as to be entirely out of her reach. She could still touch it with her finger tips. Then to have had her hair shingled; left behind in Gibraltar, that very hair that she had cared for and brushed so repeatedly, now blown into somebody's dustbin in a Spanish courtyard. Men talking to her, highly improperly Cuthbert would have said, and she was still uneasy as to whether Cuthbert was not right.

She had realized that there were other ways of thinking, less definite and more tolerant ways, and that they were the lines along which she had always wanted to think.

She stood there very still indeed.

An old lady who had come on this cruise to please a daughter who had 'got on' in life, and had 'got ideas' that were above their position, came on to D deck.

'Looking at the sea, my dear?' she asked kindly.

'I was.'

'Funny, that is one of the things I can't do. Never could. Not even off the end of the pier. It always turned me up. Liver, you know.'

'I see,' said Ann gravely.

It was a very grave matter.

CHAPTER 3

I

When the ship was passing the Balearic Isles, Ann was indulging in daydreams as to the frocks she would buy at Marseilles. Her things were much too hot, they were unbearable, and they were also far too serviceable. She must have been mad to suppose that she could have stuck out three whole weeks of tweeds in the Mediterranean. Why, she would have melted! Now, in the hot sunshine, with the blue water being swept away from the ship's side, and the almost bewildering blue above, the only garment of them all that looked to be even wearable was the scarf; blue, pink and mauve in a maze of colour.

And she had nothing suitable to wear the scarf with.

She'd buy a white frock, much older women were wearing white, and some of the clothes on board were queer enough. She did not need to worry on the side of peculiarity.

At Marseilles, she promised herself, she would go

shopping. It would take some courage in a strange country, and she was convinced that her French would not meet the strain. Miss Brown, the stewardess, informed her that everybody spoke English, but then Miss Brown had said that Gibraltar was so English, whereas now Ann knew it wasn't. It wasn't English at all. Miss Brown gave lucid details when she brought in the apple in the morning. You took a taxi at the docks, and drove to Fifinelle; the stewardess said that was where most of the ladies shopped. Ann promised herself a silk frock, which she could wear with her scarf, and a linen frock, and a small hat – something more suitable for the newly-shingled head, and for deck wear. At the moment nothing fitted her. Her hair blew about, it was most trying. She must have some strapped shoes, she told herself, everyone had those. It was queer that in England she had thought they looked the height of fastness, yet here she was contemplating buying a pair for herself. She thought it must be the sun. In the brightness of this sunshine, which had lost all the thinness and the paleness of England, things looked so different, colours were not the same.

It was just as the moonlight made the nights different. Each night since they had left Gibraltar, she had danced in the enchantment of the moon. She had experienced great difficulty in writing a laborious letter to Cuthbert, because she had not dared to tell him the truth. The truth which was, '*I am finding my real self at last. I thought I was growing old, I thought youth had been left behind, and instead new things are developing within me.*' So she sent Cuthbert different postcards which she had bought in Gibraltar – views of the Neutral Territory, which he would not understand; Europa Point; Rosia Bay; Mediterranean Steps. She sent postcards which she had bought in the barber's shop, of the Lounge, and B deck, and the boat deck, and the games deck of S.S.

Allando. She sent postcards of S.S. *Allando* in profile so to speak, with her three funnels against a deep blue sky.

Ethel had commented on those funnels at table.

'The last ship we travelled in had nice red ones with white rings,' she had said. 'I think I liked those better.'

Fergus had groaned inwardly.

It was a little trying when people chose their cruises by the colour of the funnels, with entire disregard for the efficiency of the line.

On a postcard one was not supposed to say much, nothing that mattered anyway, and that was something. So Ann posted numerous cards in the letter-box of C deck marked, 'To be cleared at Marseilles,' and she felt that she had done her duty.

II

Marseilles is a city of tumult.

It is more essentially docks than other dockyards, it is a riot of cobbled streets, and over it all broods the golden Madonna who keeps guard over the goings and comings of the sailors. Fergus told Ann all about the golden Madonna the night before the ship drew alongside the mole, but somehow Ann had not thought that Marseilles would be like this. It was breathlessly hot, with the town rising in tier upon tier of houses, and the mountains rising behind. She had not supposed that it would be so noisy, or so bustling, or so entirely commercial.

'Just like Leeds,' said a nice old lady who had been born in Leeds and swore by it, 'only I bet the shops aren't half so good. They are honest in Leeds, and I wouldna say so much for these here Frenchies.'

That was not the sort of shopping that Ann intended to do, also she was in no mood for golden Madonnas, for now she was thinking of frocks and still more frocks.

The heat had increased considerably, and she had

discarded the woolly vest that her mother had always insisted on. ('You've got a weak chest, dear, promise me you'll always wear wool next to your skin,' her mother had begged, and Ann had promised.) But now wool was unbearable. It had to go. She really did not care how indecent it might be; indecency and comfort, she felt, were even better than this extreme discomfort of a frightful decency.

The new blood flowed in her veins and filled her like a warm fire. For to the woman over thirty who hears for the first time the call of youth, it is an urgent call. She knows that the years are piling up against her, but she has still a handful of precious months. To Ann they were weeks, three weeks, for assuredly youth would end at Tilbury when the wonder cruise terminated.

After that – she dare not think of it; a drabness, a dullness, a sinking back into the greyness of Mrs. Puddock's bed-sitter, into the office routine. She did not care now if she spent every penny on this cruise, or at least a great many of her pennies, she would have the memory, and she must get cool!

The purser obligingly changed her money into francs. In francs it looked a great deal more. She took up the little wad of notes, and she thought that surely she would not need a whole two thousand of them. She counted them out on the desk, and tried to get their arrangement into her head, then boldly, like a condemned man about to walk the plank, she marched down the gangway. Halfway down she was overtaken by Miss Bright. Miss Bright was a little lady well past middle age, who was in the habit of introducing herself as 'Bright by name and Bright by nature'. She had spoken to Ann several times, nothing more than 'Good morning' it is true, but she now buttonholed her.

She was wearing a strange costume about her small tubby person, a navy blue skirt and a blue print blouse of a style one would never have expected her to be able to buy in modern times. About the bosom of the blouse were pinned all manner of pendant belongings. Miss Bright's gold watch, which had belonged to her mother, who had conveniently provided her daughter with the same initials. The watch dangled, its dial to the print blouse; its C.F.B., scrolled and so ornamented as to be undecipherable, blazoned to the outside world; it hung from a gold chain which ended in a golden bow artfully designed to conceal a pin. Beside the watch was a gun-metal disc with a button in the middle, and from this disc hung Miss Bright's pince-nez. You pressed the button, and out flew yards of gun-metal chain. You pressed it again and the chain miraculously recalled itself, winding up inside the disc and drawing the pince-nez taut, despite the fact that quite often the button had been pressed accidentally, and the glasses had been perched on Miss Bright's nose. On her head was a panama hat. Some of her family had lived abroad and this was a relic of that time; she had brought it at the instigation of her sister Emily, who had been quite sure that it would come in useful. It had come in useful. At Gibraltar it had blown off into the sea, and one of the sailors, endeavouring to reach it with his boat-hook, had overbalanced and had fallen in. Unfortunately the wetting had not irretrievably damaged it. Miss Bright insisted that nothing spoilt a real panama, and to prove her words was wearing it to-day. Perhaps it was a little more salt-stained, a little more shapeless, but it remained now spiked by the serviceable hat-pin to Miss Bright's grey bun of hair.

'Excuse me,' beamed Miss Bright, 'but if you are going ashore, might I come with you? Just up to the town, you know? Just up to the town?'

Ann did not want her but she could not think of any good excuse by which to avoid her. It is rather difficult when you are accosted on the gangway. There seems to be nothing left to say. So they went down together, with the master-at-arms standing at the bottom in his beautiful and spotless white drill, and with his knowing, roving eye from under his cap. He had once driven a 'bus, and very hot work he had found it. This was much easier, though hot enough at times in the Mediterranean, and with some of the young ladies you got on these cruises … Funny, but you got so many of that sort of young lady!

'We sail at eight, Madam,' he warned them.

Miss Bright sniggered. Fancy his thinking they would be away until then, all that time!

'I was only going to have a look at the place,' she told Ann as they climbed into a taxi.

'I'm going to buy some clothes. Fifinelle is the shop.'

'How interesting! French frocks! I do envy you.'

Now it was obvious that she intended coming too. At heart Ann was not sorry, for her courage was beginning to fail her a little. Marseilles was not like Gibraltar, where she believed she might have managed. The difference was apparent by the way the taxi started over the cobbles, flinging the occupants each into the other's arms. Small boys ran by the side, screaming demands in atrocious French, and equally abominable English. They offered themselves as guides; they clamoured for pence.

'Oh dear, isn't it cosmopolitan?' purred the delighted Miss Bright. 'I'm quite glad I've got you with me. You make me feel so safe. My mother always said girls should go about together.'

Now Miss Bright's need for caution must have ceased many years ago. She seemed however to believe that her virginity was in grave danger of attack, and she was taking every care. Ann did not know whether to laugh or to cry over her.

Marseilles was not what she had expected. It was noisy, it seemed dangerous, cars rushing this way and that, chattering milk wagons. Little *tabacs* where people argued and fought; the whole city seemed to be confused and angry.

'I am glad you are with me,' she said to Miss Bright, 'I hate driving about a strange place alone, and I have quite dreaded going into this shop alone, but cooler clothes I simply must have. The stewardess assures me that they all speak English.'

'I'll come too.'

The taxi was driven as only French taxis can be driven. They spun round corners on one wheel, they missed other vehicles by the merest fraction of an inch. They climbed hills, zooming up them like an inebriated aeroplane; they boomed over crossings at grotesque speeds. Eventually they pulled up with a most disconcerting rattle outside the shop. The jerk of stopping was so unexpected, that both Ann and Miss Bright were again flung forward, and collided violently with the vase of dusty paper carnations with which the taxi was adorned. For the first time Ann noticed the advertisements for the prevention of *mal de mar*, and other strange but useful pharmaceutical accessories which hung about the cab. A little disgruntled they alighted.

'I wait, *oui*?' enquired the taxi driver.

Ann was torn between the need for economy which had distressed her all her life until now, and the horror that no other means of locomotion might be available, and then she would be marooned. For never, never would they be able to find their way back alone. Marseilles was a positive labyrinth of streets and turnings, a wilderness of docks, all much alike, more streets, lots of hills, and then the commercial centre of the shops. She had noticed green gardens with trees under which amazing French nurses flirted with more amazing French *poilus* and *matelots*. Open air cafés –

she knew what Cuthbert would think of them – and secretly she would have liked to partake of refreshment in them.

'You may wait,' she said impressively.

'Oh dear now, isn't that extravagant?' said Miss Bright. They went inside together.

III

When the stewardess had suggested Fifinelle's, she had mentioned it primarily because they spoke English there, and secondly because all the young ladies shopped at Fifinelle's. It was essentially a young ladies' shop.

Ann saw it as very modern, rather a daring place, with its black glass portico, and the revolving door of cut steel. It glittered in the light; it twinkled wickedly and invitingly. Only two windows were to be seen, and they were disappointingly small. In one a single under-garment was displayed. It was an *entoutcas*, it announced, scanty in the extreme, perfectly cut. A chemise which ended in adorable knickers. Peach *crêpe-de-Chine*, with here or there an embroidered violet. It was, Ann, considered, a most immodest garment; she would have been quite frightened to have worn it. Why, in such an affair anything – or everything – might happen. It was obvious that this was the type of underwear destined for ladies of easy virtue. She did hope their frocks were not like that.

In the other window a jaunty-looking doll, dressed in an over-French fashion, perched above the notice *Fifinelle, modes et chapeaux*. It gave no hint as to what else there might be within. If Ann had been alone she would certainly have turned back, but she was not alone, she had Miss Bright to consider, and the impression that would be made on Miss Bright's mind. Boldly, she opened the door and marched inside.

A delicate perfume assailed her; a satin-clad young woman; unbelievably *svelte*, seemed to swim towards her. Ann began with the Englishwoman's inevitable formula abroad.

'Do you speak English?'

'But of course,' said the lovely young woman who was entirely curveless.

Ann explained hesitantly what she wanted, and all the while she clutched her franc notes in her hand. She had the vague idea that they might be stolen from her. She suspected Fifinelle. She suspected everything that was French. She wanted some cooler frocks for the cruise, her things were all wrong, she knew, and she wanted to buy some others.

The young woman called Madame, and Madame settled down to the business as only a Frenchwoman who is also an artist can. She disposed of Ann and Miss Bright (whom she insisted on alluding to as *Maman*) in spindly gilt chairs, and she waved before them young girls in the frocks that she considered would be suitable. Ann thought she had never seen anything so unsuitable. The girls looked lovely enough. They looked just as Ann had always wanted to look, young and glamorous and alluring.

'This,' said Madame, 'is *gentille*,' and lo, she waved to the dais a girl in a slim white frock with a tiny madonna-blue cape.

'But too young for me ...'

'*Jamais*,' said Madame gallantly.

Madame was inclined to stoutness but she had severely buttoned that stoutness in. She had an extremely French bust, poised at the angle only Frenchwomen can poise their bosoms. Above it was Madame's face framed in her henna-ed hair, and her ears in which hung elaborate pearls as big as little billiard balls.

'You try heem,' said Madame.

Now Ann had not meant to 'try heem'. She was however beguiled into a fitting-room and persuaded. She found herself looking quite unlike herself, for Madame banished the woolly underclothes. She waved aside the corset upon which Ann had pinned her faith for all those years since she had been promoted from a Liberty bodice.

'*Ridicule*,' said Madame.

She found herself sheathed in satin. Over it there slid cami-knickers which she could only describe as being fast. A petticoat that was all allure. And last of all the frock. It might be Madame's way of disposing it about her, a twist here, a tweak there, but the material no longer looked too young, or the cut too slim.

'I could never put it on like that,' said Ann plaintively.

'*Vous fautes* – I teach you,' said Madame, and her bright little eyes shone and the pearl knobs quivered in the rouged lobes of her ears. Madame was the perfect saleswoman. Her mission in life was to sell frocks, and she saw to it that she sold them. She had a positive genius for showing you yourself as you wished to look; just as you had always wanted to be. Every dress that Ann put on, she felt that she must buy. She could not resist it. To a woman who has been suppressed for thirty-five years, there is a desperate allure about the blossoming. She grew reckless, and undoubtedly Miss Bright egged her on. Miss Bright sitting there on her little gilt chair, with the gold watch and the pince-nez quivering and gibbering together on her bosom. She kept saying, 'Well, really now,' and 'Just look at that,' and 'That one is a dream.'

The inevitable happened.

Ann had not enough money.

'I shall have to go back to the ship for more,' she explained.

Madame shrugged her shoulders. To her a few francs more or less did not matter. She thought only in thousand franc notes. Her *modes* were very reasonable, absurdly so when they were so chic – *ridicule*, she explained. Perhaps Ann could leave a small deposit, hey?

Ann left a thousand francs and thought that it was a very large deposit.

'It is usual, and *commode*,' said Madame, 'it secure the garments too.'

Ann thought that it ought to.

She and Miss Bright bundled outside and into the taxi. An array of vivid boxes splashed with audacious French flowers was dashed in beside them. The rest, waiting under seal of the deposit, were put on one side in the shop.

'The ship. *Bateau*,' said Ann, becoming quite violent in her French according to Dr. Ahn.

The taxi-man had expected that. *Mesdames* who shopped at Fifinelle's usually ran out of money. Inevitably they rushed back to the ship, and kept a car waiting for their return, and they never complained how fast you drove either. *Mais non!* Their minds were entirely centred on *les chemises*, *les robes*, *les pantalons!* They were picturing how superb, *comme gentilles*, they would look in their new finery.

He drove recklessly, skidding deftly along the streets, while Ann and Miss Bright clutched at each other and prayed that their end might not be yet, though it looked very much like it. Then, righting himself, he proceeded to spin perilously down towards the docks.

'This is life,' said Miss Bright, 'this is really living. Oh, my dear, isn't it all fun?'

But Ann was remembering the old hag in the Alameda – 'Youth goes. Look at me!' She was thinking as the taxi-man had supposed that she would be thinking, in terms of peach *crêpe-de-Chine*, and lavender georgette. Perhaps she had been a little fool! Well, she had enjoyed it. She only regretted that she had not bought the other frock, the one that Madame had described as being *tout á fait chemise*! Perhaps she had squandered her money, but she had bought happiness with it, and that is what counts. She had bought a certain yet subtle thrill of joy which centred within herself.

That was something.

IV

Ann actually ran into the purser's office to get more money. She had thrown caution to the winds. Outside Miss Bright sat prinking in the taxi as though it were a private car. The scum of Marseilles tried to divert her attention. Lean, cadaverous-looking gentlemen offered their services as guides. Little boys attempted to sell her all manner of useless commodities, from postcards of a very dubious nature, to local guide-books and beadwork.

'Go away, my little boy,' said Miss Bright, for she still smiled in that gay manner of hers, which the little boys who understood no language (save that of the stick) took to be encouraging. Eventually she found the taxicab becoming too conspicuous. She began to wonder when Ann would return. She began to have grave doubts as to what might have happened to her.

Ann had cannoned into Oliver Banks, who also had returned for more money. It is the eternal quest of all cruising passengers, this hurried and humiliating sojourn to the purser's office, this demand for more of the wherewithal to spend.

'Oh, you've been done down too,' Oliver commented. 'Frocks?'

'I've been a tremendous *bust*,' she admitted, 'I've never done such a thing in my life before.'

'Well, go on. Have some more. It will do you good.'

Ann decided in her heart that after all she would have the little frock that Madame said was *tout á fait chemise.* She had not meant to melt, but why shouldn't she? You might as well be hanged for a sheep as a lamb. Mrs. Puddock was always saying so. ('And by the bye, I *must* send Mrs. Puddock a picture postcard,' she thought).

'A frock,' said Oliver, 'is a tonic. Go a good bust, and you will feel a new woman.'

So Ann returned to the taxi and she saw all the rag-tag of Marseilles gathered round, and Miss Bright sitting there very erect and very perky, and saying, 'Go away, little boy,' to little boys who did not mean to go away. Ann got into the taxi beside her new friend, and they started off again.

En route they met the Spinkses being driven along in a gigantic car which they had commandeered, looking most hot and uncomfortable in the sun. Mrs. Spinks habitually sat upright with her amply upholstered bosom before her; she felt the heat badly, and was both crimson and damp. They were not enjoying themselves, and all the better-forgotten memories of the miserable holiday at Juan les Pins had come back to them. For Mr. Spinks had gone into a café to get something for them both, and had had an 'umptarara' with a girl there! She had been bad, downright bad through and through, Mrs. Spinks could see that at a glance. Brazen too, for she had winked at him, and it had enraged his wife. She had recalled the horrible affair when they had occupied separate rooms at Juan les Pins. In France all the best couples had separate rooms, it seemed to be the proper thing to do. Mr. Spinks, fussy and fidgety, had been convinced that his bed was damp. To make certain he had put his watch into it, and had found the glass (as he had expected) misted. He had called the *femme de chambre*, and there unfortunately his French had failed him. He had tapped the glass, and had indicated the bed. She had understood. *Mais oui*, she understood *parfaitement*. '*Un moment*,' she had said, and only one moment had she been. She had totally misunderstood his need. She had reappeared in the scantiest chemise, she was well used to the exigencies of English gentlemen with fat and old wives.

Mr. Spinks had forgotten himself so far as to scream. His wife had come rushing out. She too had misunderstood everything. Never to this day would she believe that he had not staged the whole affair. Never to this moment would she understand that he was no good at languages. The language of the eye was the same with every nation that ever was, and Mr. Spinks was good at that, too good at it. And here he was, starting it all over again with another little girl in a café. No wonder she was sitting bolt upright in the car, and keeping a watchful eye on him. She was taking him to Grasse. It sounded pure, lovely scenery, hill-sides and mountains, pastoral and simple. No more French hussies for Mrs. Spinks. And she'd take good care there were no more French hussies for Mr. Spinks either. That she would.

Ann saw that they were miserable. She saw it as her taxi hustled past them. For the second time that day she drew up with a clatter outside Fifinelle's, and rushed inside.

'You wait here,' she told Miss Bright, 'I shan't be a moment; it is only to have the boxes sent out.'

She couldn't have Miss Bright witness her weakness about the frock that was *tout á fait chemise.* With the pressing need of a woman who already sees forty coming out of the shadows ahead and twenty lost in the mist of the twilight behind, she was daring. She did not care. This was her entire spring and summer wound into the one St. Martin's summer which comes at the end of the year and is too brief, too lovely to be believable. She intended living every moment of it, getting the most out of it, giving the most to it. Time enough to regret when she returned to Mrs. Puddock's and the office, and the humdrum monotony of the mechanical pattern of living. Time enough for all that then.

She went flying into the shop.

Madame had other customers, and as she believed that she had finished with Ann she did not come readily to her assistance. Ann had bought all that could be reasonably expected of her, therefore Madame did not trouble herself too much. A young assistant appeared.

'*Mais oui*,' she lifted the boxes – '*l'addition* …' she read out the amount.

'And the frock, the other little frock,' breathed Ann hurriedly, 'I'll take that too.'

Madame, who had strangely furtive ears for overhearing what she wanted to hear, turned quickly. '*Aussi le petit chapeau*,' murmured Madame.

It seemed that there was a *petit chapeau*, a mere *morceau*, but it went with the frock that was *tout á fait chemise*. It was the very thing for cruising, tiny, provocative, and very sweet.

Ann had told herself that the frock really must be the very last thing of all, but when the assistant fitted the *petit chapeau* over her head, she knew that she had to have it.

'Oh, very well,' she said.

She counted out the notes. There seemed to be dozens of them. Little fluttering notes, and now Ann was in a hurry to leave the shop where she had spent so much. She was in a hurry to leave before she spent more, for the tide of wild and reckless extravagance had overtaken her, and in it her wiser and better self was drowned.

The boxes were crammed into the taxi, where Miss Bright still sat in all her dangling jewellery. She was sitting there saying softly to herself, 'Broom, broom, broom.'

As they drove down the hill, Ann said, 'Why are you saying "broom, broom, broom"?'

Miss Bright laughed. 'Oh, it's just a little way of mine. My mother always said it gave a pleasing expression to the face, moulds the lips, you know. I used to laugh and to say that I was one of those girls who always said "brush, brush, brush". Not at all the same, you know, not at all the same.'

'Oh,' said Ann.

In a few years' time she would be as old as this, and perhaps as silly as this. She might wear her mother's brooch, and pince-nez. She might be saying 'broom, broom, broom', or 'brush, brush, brush', to herself. It was rather an awful thought.

And now she wanted to open the magic boxes with the gay flowers on the lids. She wanted to strew the bed in her cabin with the contents, to glory in the kind of materials in which she had never gloried before, but had always been forced to admire on somebody else.

'We seem to get on well together,' said Miss Bright, 'what about doing some of the churches this afternoon? They're Roman of course, and not quite nice, but we'd be safe, the two of us?'

'I'm going to have a quiet rest.'

'I don't believe in quiet rests in foreign parts, except of course the siesta, but that's India.' Miss Bright was not always reliably informed, but liked to give the impression that she knew a lot. 'And although Marseilles is hot it isn't quite India.'

'Not quite,' Ann agreed.

She thought she would never get rid of Miss Bright, but eventually she had greater trouble in getting rid of the taxi. The taxi-man considered that he had been grossly underpaid, whereas truly Ann had in ignorance overpaid him. The mere fact that she obviously did not understand the value of the franc, and that she was a lady travelling alone – he did not count Miss Bright as being of any consequence whatever – encouraged him to demand more.

'*Ma'm'selle* not understand,' he said, 'the extra for wait?'

Ann began fumbling with further notes. The sight of the fumbling put fresh hope into the taxi-man's soul. Really these English were so very easy, they hated being considered mean, they hated people to presume that they did not understand the difference between francs and sous.

Doubtfully Ann inquired as to what more she owed.

'What *Ma'm'selle* will,' said the obliging driver, and he doffed his cap and held it over his heart, standing in a pretty attitude of respectful attention.

Ann had no idea what she wanted to pay. She thought she had given him enough, and she was covered with confusion. 'There must be some set sum,' she protested. There had always been an accepted fare at Worthing.

'It is what *Ma'm'selle* wish,' and again he bowed with all the perfidious courtesy of the Frenchman.

At that moment the master-at-arms noticed the scene. He moved forward ponderously, his advance much like that of one of the 'buses he had driven in his days along the Number Nineteen route.

''Ere, what's all this 'ere?' he demanded.

Instantly the courtesy of the driver faded into thin air. He knew masters-at-arms of old. They had no scruples as to the justice of so much and no more. They did not care who thought them mean or ungenerous or ungallant.

'Now then, come off it,' said the master-at-arms. 'Money for waiting, why that's on your meter. You 'op it, me lad.'

The driver professed a complete ignorance of the English language. He waved his hands in deprecation.

'And don't you start doin' of that there at me,' said

the master-at-arms, 'I don't like it,' and he turned to Ann. 'You pop inboard, Miss,' said he, 'and I'll settle this 'ere.'

Gratefully Ann popped.

V

Ann had all the precious clothes laid out on the bed, cyclamen georgette, tissue in golden folds, a green floral threaded through with little quick rivers of fire, the frock that was *tout á fait chemise*!

She would never dare put them on, and yet they were so lovely. Even supposing she never wore them, she would have got her money's worth out of them, she told herself. Just looking at them was enough.

But the heat of Marseilles, coming down in its exhausting high noon, and the realization that she was tired to death, overcame her. She laid aside her serviceable costume, which she had once thought so smart. She drew on the white frock with the cape that was the colour of a madonna's cloak. She put on the appropriate underthings, and discarded the old corsets that had steeled her through life.

'All nice women wear them,' her mother had said, when as a child she had protested against promotion from the Liberty bodice to the drab courtil corset 'for maids' wear'.

She wasn't going to be a nice woman any longer. Sheer satin clasped her close. She was surprised that she was so slender, that she did not bulge. The freedom was delightful.

She tied the narrow sash of the frock about her waist. She had never before experienced the exquisite joy of drawing a string together like that, soft in the fingers, crushing into a tie. She put it on and fluffed out her hair, drawing it forward over the low smooth brow. She looked a new person.

She had lunch like that, a rather desolate lunch, for no one was about, even Fergus had gone ashore.

Later she went down to tea. The band was playing in the café when she slipped in for her cup. A few couples were dancing languorously. Stewards were standing about awkwardly, for fire stations had been warned for five o'clock, and they were expecting the bell to go at any moment.

Ann sat down at the nearest table and she asked for China tea. It was funny but China tea gave her a thrill. It seemed so remote from Balham and Onslow Gardens and the office. It intrigued her. At first she had not liked it, the stewardess had brought her some in error when she was ill, and the name had fascinated her. It sounded like cocaine, or something frightfully wicked. Yet the taste had reminded her of her childhood when she had sat in one of the church pews, and for want of something better to do had sucked her kid gloves. Yet it was a taste that grew on one. She did not believe that she would find it easy to go back to the strong black Indian tea that she had been used to. And it would never do for the office to think that she was giving herself airs and graces; what was more, Mrs. Puddock wouldn't hold with it, and as to Cuthbert, he would make scathing allusions to the new-fangled ways she had got in foreign places. But now she could enjoy its fragrance unmolested. She sipped it contentedly enough. An officer came up to her. He was the assistant purser, and he believed in making the most of his opportunities. He saw a brownish fair head, and the delicate curve of her neck. Ann had a dear little curve, rather childish, most attractive. He saw the flutter of a blue cape, and a white frock cut as only a Frenchwoman can cut clothes.

He said, 'Will you dance?'

'I – I'm awfully stupid at it.'

'Never mind, I'll teach you.' He thought, 'Where did she get that quite divine blue? It matches her eyes.' And he slipped his arm round her. The assistant purser could dance. He had joined the merchant service because he believed that it would give him facilities for exhibiting his terpsichorean powers. He had stipulated for a line where he would be permitted to exhibit this skill, and had finally emerged from Pangbourne here. Now he wasn't so sure that he was so well pleased with himself, or the line, or the terpsichorean arts. Such amazingly old women danced, and when they were on the mail run, all the women seemed to be old. Dear old trouts with long earrings and coy frocks, and the I-will-be-a-girl expression. So far he had been disappointed in pleasure cruising also. He was no better than a gigolo. A gigolo of the line, he told himself. Because he danced so well, and was so junior, the purser had a little habit of allotting aged-partners to him.

'You must dance with old Lady So-and-so; she is a special friend of the directors,' or 'You must give that fat old lady a turn, she hasn't had much of a time.' And, as to Mr. Collins himself, he seldom had much of a time! There was usually only one good-looker a trip, that was the average; and if the Commander could be persuaded to keep off it, there was the first officer, and the second officer – he was the Spanish type, and that always has a mean advantage – and the third officer who had a 'way wid him'. You could not defy competition of that sort.

So the A. P. had formed a convenient habit of drifting into tea dances, when the others were busy, and when the purser was enjoying a prolonged siesta, which, as he was getting old and somewhat stout, ran far into the afternoon, and was only broken by cocktail time. The A. P. having thus arranged things to a nicety, quite often contrived (as he expressed it) to pick a daisy during tea. Ann could not dance, but she had rhythm. He knew that the moment he put an arm round her. He gave her a few hints which she received gratefully. He admired her frock, and finally he told her that she was the best looker in the ship, which left her entirely bewildered.

The A. P. was in the habit of telling every girl that she was the best looker in the ship, but Ann was not to know that. She danced as only a woman can dance when she suddenly finds all the elusive fantasies of youth no longer elusive and no longer fantasies. Suddenly life seemed new and different. She supposed she was old enough to be the A. P.'s mother, he could not be twenty, well – almost his mother! All the same that did not lessen the delight of the dance, of the atmosphere, of the new knowledge of fantasy come true, of the elusive overtaken and become reality.

She said with the ingenuous enthusiasm of a girl, 'This is the loveliest cruise in the world.'

VI

Night in Marseilles.

Late night, just before sailing, a night of sapphire and of emeralds. High up on the hill twinkled the little lights, like so many stars in a new heaven. And above them all the golden Madonna who guards the goings and the comings of the sailors. The sea was an unbelievable blue, and Ann, watching it, leaning on the taffrail with Oliver by her side, knew that it was carrying her away. The water was clear, and very still; in it lay further stars, drowned.

'I never want to leave Marseilles,' she said, 'it is a city of romance.'

'But you are going to Naples. If ever there was a city of romance, it is Naples.'

She shook her head. She was the new Ann clasped in satin, with a pink chiffon frock frothing about her in little cascades and frills. 'In Marseilles I grew young,' she said.

'Had you never been young before?'

'No, never.'

He nodded. 'I know. There are too many women who live life and never know youth. You're lucky.'

'I'm terribly lucky,' she said.

She was enjoying it to the full, this new precious youth. Now she did not care if he were married, or divorced, or what it might be. What did anything matter? Well, of course it didn't.

'I had a cable from Lilia,' he said. 'Funny that she has found her romance on a pleasure cruise that is ended, and she wires to me on a pleasure cruise that is starting.'

Ann clung to the taffrail. Sapphire water, sapphire hills, and above it all a great deep sky in the same sapphire. It was just as though the whole world had become a brilliant and beautiful jewel, and she was wearing it on her heart. Her world. Her jewel. She said, 'To-night everything looks unreal and very beautiful.'

'Yet in our hearts we know that it is real and not very beautiful. Marseilles is one of the most sordid cities in the Mediterranean.'

'Yet to-night she looks lovely.'

Then the A. P. came up and asked her to dance. Later, much later, when she went to her cabin and unclipped the pink chiffon frock from about her, and slipped out of the satin corselet which was so graceful and which gave such a new feeling of liberty, a horrid thought assailed her. Pink chiffon frock. Fifinelle. She did a rapid mental sum. There had been some four thousand francs owing, and she had left one thousand on deposit. She had rushed back to the purser's office, and in her hurry, and harassed by the somewhat irksome companionship of Miss Bright, she had paid the entire four thousand francs. She had forgotten all about the thousand on deposit, with the lamentable result that she had grossly overpaid Madame. And Madame, her little red tongue in her cheek, had said never a word. Why should she trouble to remind someone of a little error of that type? argued Madame. Why indeed?

Ann, the new determined Ann, told herself that she would cable in the morning. She did not suppose that she stood a ghost of a chance of getting the thousand francs back, but she would try. She would at least tell Madame what she thought of her, and that would be some small comfort.

As she undressed, stepping carefully out of peach-coloured cami-knickers of the type that Cuthbert would have attributed to Jezebel, she thought unrepeatable things of Madame. There was an immense comfort even in being able to think them.

CHAPTER 4

I

In between the ports, the ship settled down into its normal routine. Its breakfast and beef tea; its lunch and tea dance; its savouries and supper routine.

Ann was beginning to fit into the scheme of things, she was beginning to think of the ship as home and to enjoy it. She knew nearly everybody at least by sight, and most of them to speak to, though it seemed to be impossible to discover what their names might be. But what did names matter really?

Miss Bright had after the affair at Marseilles attached herself to Ann, who did not reciprocate the feeling of extreme and rather overpowering friendship. She made excuses, unfortunately feeble excuses, and she tried to dodge Miss Bright round the decks. But large as the liner was, and many as were her decks, it seemed very difficult to lose anybody you wanted to lose; just as it was also very difficult to find anybody you wanted to find.

Ann went to the purser and he helped her to devise a Marconi to Fifinelle. He was strongly biased against traders in foreign ports. In the Mediterranean, he said with more than a little truth, they were a very dirty lot. The Marconi was handed in, and despatched.

Through a sea unbelievably still, the *Allando* urged forward. She steamed with hardly a sound, seldom a movement, only an occasional tremble of her engines, beating within her.

'It's very seldom that we get both the Bay and the Gulf of Lyons bad,' Miss Brown told Ann when she brought her her morning apple, 'it's one or the other, but not often both. Best to get it over in the Bay and have done with it.'

Under the fine warm weather the ship prospered. Fans became busy. The roses that the chief steward had brought aboard at Marseilles stood about in bowls, rising and falling a little with the ship. It was summer on board. A summer born miraculously soon of the dead English winter.

Ann had rolled her tweeds into a bundle and had forsaken them. They were useless anyway in this heat. Now she could not think how she had ever tolerated them for a moment. Badly-made, and with ill-fitting cut. What had induced her? Soft silk, piquant little coats, sheer stockings, strapped shoes. It was a new Ann. It was a woman enjoying the St. Martin's summer of her life.

Long and lazy mornings with the beef tea arriving as an agreeable break, and the thrill of the tote. Ann had resisted the attractions of the tote, knowing full well how Cuthbert would have thought about it, but unfortunately Oliver exploited a shilling for her one day. She found herself surging forward in the little crowd which awaited the arrival of the officer from the bridge soon after noon, in such breathless anticipation. She experienced all that fever of excitement, she glowed. The number was the one on which Ann's shilling had been placed.

It seemed to be all wrong that Ann, who was very well aware of the sinfulness of such forms of amusement, and who was dragged into it by other people, first Miss Thomas and now Oliver Banks, should habitually win. She overcame the first intention of giving it to charity, which had seemed to her to be the only way to condone the offence. She put a whole five shillings on the tote the next day, not a single one of which brought her in a farthing. 'And that serves me right,' she told herself.

The swimming bath was in constant demand, a pale green pool aft, deliciously clear and refreshing. Until now it had been more or less avoided by the passengers, save those more daring males who had taken their morning dip in Spartan fashion from the beginning. Now young women besieged it. Young women with fat legs, young women with thin legs, young women in home-knitted bathing dresses, and in bought bathing dresses, some a great deal too revealing, and others not half revealing enough. Fergus, who was a stickler for the swimming pool, and attended it vigorously every day of his life, seethed in wrath. There were the young women determined to grow brown, who covered themselves in oil, 'guaranteed to give that sun-bronze tone which is so distinguished'; they then went into the water. 'Now it is nothing but an oil bath,' he protested, 'always having to be changed, always coming out like a blinking sardine!' He hated it.

Above was the deck reserved for sunbathing, and here people in various attitudes of undress sprawled and disported themselves. Many an illusion of the previous night in a Paris frock of superb cut was shattered by the simple bathing dress on a figure that could not cope with its revealing lines.

Ann thought at first that it was most indecent, but the heat becoming fiercer as the sun beat down on the decks, she made up her mind that at Naples she herself would buy a bathing dress, a modest one of course, and she also would enjoy the coolness of the pale green swimming pool. Supposing she could go brown? Supposing she could return to the office and show arms and neck sun-bronzed according to the directions on the bottle? She had half a mind to try. The spirit of competition entered into it.

'You'll come to Pompeii with me?' said Oliver as they danced that night.

Pompeii! It was true then. She was standing on the threshold of the dream world of Naples; of ruined Pompeii; of the blue bay with Vesuvius across it. She was glad. She was tremendously, supremely glad that she had not saved the money, but had come here. Mr. Robert had been quite right in his advice. She had bought happiness, she had bought youth. The old hag in the Alameda had warned her: 'Make much of life while you are still young, look at me!' This was making much of life; paying in coin but gaining in kind.

'I'd love it,' she said.

II

As Ann went down to her cabin, Miss Bright buttonholed her. Miss Bright was standing on D deck aft, near the little door where at stipulated intervals Fergus held his surgery. In her young days Miss Bright had been 'sort of engaged to a doctor, nothing settled, you know, but an understanding'. She believed that this period of her life had given her a strange insight into the medical profession. She was surprised when doctors did not reciprocate her interest in them.

'I wanted to see you,' she said to Ann. 'I wanted to

ask; if you would let me come to Pompeii with you in the morning. I would be willing to share expenses.'

Now on the Marseilles trip, although Miss Bright had volunteered to share expenses, no actual money had been forthcoming. At the moment of settling up, she had been entirely preoccupied with something else. She had not been very helpful in the purchasing of the frocks, and her French had been execrable. Ann started telling her about Oliver, but she would not listen. She was full of other theories.

'I hear,' she said, 'that the Pompeians have the most peculiar signs in the streets, really odd. And some of the frescoes cannot be shown to decent women. Personally I am broad-minded. Little things like that do not upset me. I look on them in the spirit of art, which is the way they should be looked at, I feel. I thought, you see, that if we were together we could enjoy everything to the full.' By which it was very obvious that she meant the strange street signs, and the frescoes that could not be shown to decent women.

'Well, I'm very sorry, but I've fixed up to go ashore with Mr. Banks.'

'Oh' – Miss Bright registered extreme disapproval – 'now isn't that too bad? Perhaps he would not mind if I joined you?'

Ann thought that probably Oliver would mind very considerably. She was trying to think out some suitable and wholly polite excuse, when three girls came down the companion laughing together and talking.

'He wanted me to meet him on the boat deck,' one of them was saying, 'and what's more I'm going to. I believe in having my little bit of fun.'

'Oh, but you don't know what he said to me this evening. I tell you I was absolutely shocked, and it takes a lot to shock me.'

'Well, I may be shocked too after to-night, and I hope

I am. I don't believe in being too good …'

They passed along together, laughing, with their arms intertwined, going down to E deck.

'Well now,' said Miss Bright, 'I do not approve of how these modern young people behave, really I don't. It is most odd.'

It was easy enough for Miss Bright who would never see fifty again, but Ann was in the unfortunate position of not being of Miss Bright's generation, and not of the post-war gay girls who believed in their little bit of fun, and wanted to be shocked. For a long time she had believed herself to be of that older generation. Was she not born in Victoria's reign? But now she had abandoned herself to the joy of the wonder cruise.

If she had come here five years later it would have been too late. But, thank heaven, it wasn't too late. She ran her fingers over her hair where it was clipped close to her neck.

'I'm afraid I couldn't very well ask Mr. Banks,' she said.

'I don't mind asking him,' declared Miss Bright.

'I don't think we could. I mean he would not understand. I'd rather you didn't.' And Ann felt herself reddening as she turned away.

'Oh well, if that's the way the land lies …' said Miss Bright in snorting indignation, and she blundered up the companion. She was going to have a look round the boat deck. Other people seemed to find it very interesting and she did not see why she should not investigate.

'Oh dear, now I've offended her,' thought Ann, 'and she is old and has no fun, and it is rotten of me.' She went for a little stroll round D deck. She went softly, watching the pale gold ribbon of moonlight reaching right across the water, which was so still as to be almost rippleless. She heard two people talking and recognized the blasé high-pitched voice of Ethel.

'I call this cruise bloody, perfectly bloody.'

With a start Ann realized that she was not of this generation. She never could be. She wasn't even of this cruise. It was just a cinema, a film flickered before her eyes, bright people, people she did not really know, like a patchwork quilt thrown across her. Patches of silk. Gay colours. Dull colours. People.

She would wake up and find herself at home, with a good white honeycomb counterpane, and life would be all the deadlier for this. Perhaps she had made a mistake in coming. Perhaps…

III

They were alongside the mole when she went on deck the next morning. The town of Naples rose in little white terraces with the palm trees standing erect, and the heliotrope veil of wistaria laid finely like a lace on balustrade and portico. The houses came right down to the mole, alongside which the ship was tied, and where all the touts and rascals you could possibly imagine were collected. The taxicabs drawn up rank upon rank, were all driven by men who looked as though they could easily have filled the roles of the robbers in the Babes in the Wood. Lean horses, almost dropping in their shabby harness, pulled crazy carriages, and were only beaten for their pains. Opposite, blue, serene, and entirely oblivious to the pain and suffering that might go on in this day of surpassing beauty and woeful brutality, stood Vesuvius.

When first Ann saw Vesuvius, she felt that here indeed was a dream come true. Only the merest filament of smoke curled about the summit. There was little outward sign of it being anything but a mountain, standing as it had always stood, and not the shell, the husk which concealed the fire devil who had wrought such vengeance. But, as she watched, her mind going back to the days when she had pored over the tragedy of Glaucus and blind Nydia, she saw the faint wisps of smoke trembling upwards until they became cloud and part of the heaven, instead of part of the hell that was volcano.

It fascinated her.

'Well,' said the cheery voice of Mr. Spinks alongside her as he watched, 'I don't think much of it. No more than a little hill, I think, and as to the fire coming out of the top of it, a fat lot of nonsense that is!'

'I suppose it depends on when you happen to see it? At night any fire would show. It wouldn't in this bright sun.'

But Mr. Spinks had expected something like his kitchen stove at home, with the damper out. He was disgruntled. 'I once saw a really good chimney on fire,' he said, 'and it was a lot better.' He went down to breakfast with the air of a man who considers that he has been grossly cheated.

Ann stood there a little while, stood and marvelled at the loveliness about her. She marvelled also at the woman who was keen on knitting a jumper, and sat there without taking her eyes from her work, but murmuring repeatedly to herself, 'Knit two, purl one.' Fancy knitting a jumper in Naples! In the very shadow of Vesuvius occupying yourself with purls and plains. For to Ann it was all a wonderful city. A wonderful city of terrible people.

She hardly dared to look at the crowds on the mole; at the skeletons of horses, sweating and panting in their last efforts to appease the wrath of those tyrants who drove them. She also descended to her breakfast, for they were to make an early start.

The dining-saloon was in a state of uproar, for everyone was anxious to be off on the day's excursion. On E deck was situated what was known as the excursion office, where Mr. Thomas Cook made adequate arrangements for this, that and the rest of it. A fleet of large charabancs classed ambiguously as 'private open cars' was lined up alongside the ship at Mr. Thomas Cook's instigation. They were to undertake the tour which was in the little illustrated brochure of the line described as 'Exclusive tour to the ruined Pompeii, under the very shadow of Vesuvius. (Glimpses of the island of Capri to be seen). The cars run alongside the vineyards. Time occupied – all day. Lunch included at the famous hotel at Pompeii. £2 9s. 6d.' Miss Bright had considered the excursion to be too dear, even though it might include lunch. She had had previous experience of the continental lunch on a spring cruise she had once undertaken to the Riviera.

She had gone on 'an excursion to the little town of Grasse, giving unrivalled views of the Alpes Maritimes. N.B. – Corsica can be seen en route on a fine day'. (N.B. – Corsica had *not* been seen though it was a very fine day.) The lunch at Grasse had been what Miss Bright had called sketchy, much like the continental breakfast only more *recherché*. Half a boiled egg on a couple of runner beans, the inevitable veal, cheese and fruit. Miss Bright was wondering if she could inveigle the chief steward to make her up a parcel of good ham sandwiches, and picnic amongst the ruins. The chief steward however had had other ideas. He had left a little notice on the tables the night before, instructing people who were desiring picnic baskets to put in their orders before the morning. It was too late now to do anything about it.

Ann realized when she saw Miss Bright groping about the tables, and bewailing the expensive tour and the need for a picnic basket and the obstinacy of the chief steward all in one and the same breath, that unless she was quick about it, she would be saddled with Miss Bright. She made an early escape. She met Oliver Banks on the gangway, the longest she had ever seen, and they went over the side together.

IV

Ann had never supposed that there could be anything so wonderful as Pompeii. And, although she hated herself for the thought, again she surmised that it would have been much more wonderful if it had not been for the hordes of sightseeing tourists prowling about. It was not a ruin as she had been led to expect; it was a town in ruins.

'I did not know that it was so big,' she faltered, half afraid to enter it.

It was, it seemed, a town suddenly cut short in its prime. It had been. It had ceased to be so suddenly that it still was. That was the most strange part about it. These people were not dead. It did not seem possible when so much that was real and vivid and entirely of their era was still in existence, that they had long since died. The ruts of chariots, and here and there the impression of feet; the imprint of a finger against a porch; a column worn away because some long-dead sentry had leaned against it in fatigue.

Beyond, the blue of Vesuvius, towering over it, calm and implacable, Vesuvius which had done this thing.

It was more than a little overwhelming. Again, hundreds of years later, Pompeii flourished in its ruined beauty. Grass grew in the dead streets. A cypress curled close like a deep blue cocoon, a wistaria struggled up and tumbled about an old stone loggia in a cloud of heliotrope loveliness. Nature had forgotten that this hideous tragedy had ever been, and already the little houses growing out from the suburbs of Naples were coming dangerously close.

'But supposing it happened again?' she said in wonder.

'It wouldn't happen without warning. There is a laboratory right up on Vesuvius, you know, where men live and spend their lives, they would send word if anything were likely to occur.'

'But before, it did not give warning then?'

'They probably did not understand.'

'The witch knew in the Last Days,' she said, and in fancy began to plan where it had taken place. Nydia and Glaucus, the bold beauty of the arena. And now, all over Pompeii radiant in the bright Neapolitan sunshine, the excursion poured. It is always rather a frightful thing when you meet your fellow countrymen abroad, but it is a far more frightful thing when they are on an excursion and *en masse*. And still more frightful when the city they are visiting is the ageless, deathless, yet entirely deathly city of Pompeii.

'I should think,' meditated Oliver as he surveyed the approach of stout ladies and perspiring gentlemen, 'that the combined tonnage of our ship is pretty gross. The majority of them seem to be fat.'

They approached. They were very earnest about their sight-seeing. They were armed with guide-books, and escorted by a courier gentleman who bore the name of the indefatigable Mr. Thomas Cook round his hat.

'Supposing,' said Oliver, 'that we had lunch first, while they pour over the place? Then, when they have done with it, we can come back. At the moment it is not fit for a decent person.'

Ann was loth to leave the ruins, yet she had to admit that the excursionist party were doing their best to spoil it. They turned and went out of the ruined city, and came to the hotel built alongside, where all the tourists go.

'Now,' she said, 'before we start, I want you to understand that this is all on the fifty-fifty basis. I have not come to Pompeii to sponge on you.'

'Rot! Look at the fun I get out of your companionship.'

Ann cherished no illusions about her companionship, and she coloured as she said, 'That's nice of you, but it makes it most embarrassing for me. It wasn't at all my idea to let you pay, and I am not coming inside to have lunch with you unless you let me contribute my share.'

'You can't possibly go anywhere else for lunch. This is the only place there is, and it would take you much too long to go back to Naples.'

She realized the futility of the threat which she had suggested, and was more than a little dismayed, because she was not used to people paying for her. In her world, the Miss Thomas and Miss Gelding world, the price of a lunch meant all the difference between bankruptcy and affluence in the weekly pay envelope. You just could not treat other people. And now he was being silly, because she had the money to pay, and she wanted to do so.

She said, 'You don't realize how uncomfortable it makes me. I don't know what to do about it.'

'Then that's simple. Do nothing.'

She thought when she got back she would buy him some cigarettes, and send them to his cabin. They would probably be the wrong sort, Virginian when they should have been Turkish or Egyptian, for at any rate she knew nothing about smoking, but they would show that she meant her word.

'If I get you some cigarettes, I wonder if they will be the wrong sort?' she mused.

'If you do I shall be most offended.'

'It is all very difficult.'

'Not at all. Let it be. It is quite usual for a man to pay for a woman, I can assure you,' and he laughed as he gave her a little push into the hotel.

***

V

There was the scent of tuber roses, and of lilies and wistaria all blending together. It was far more beautiful than anything that she had ever imagined, far lovelier than any picture she had seen, even the one inside the portal of the steamship company in Cockspur Street.

Cockspur Street!

How terribly far away that seemed – and was!

This was vivid and real; the cypresses were not like old ladies with dark blue cloaks drawn round them; they were alive. The light wind blew them and ruffled them, so that they broke into little blue feathers which the sun kissed to gold.

The picture in Cockspur Street had not been able to convey the exquisite sunny scent of it all; the hot earthy smell of the field, and the acrid smell of ruins. She glanced at the grass which lay on the other side of the dusty road, and behind them in the city of dead yesterday.

The lunch was not so sketchy as Miss Bright had thought it might be. Thin soup, fish, cold chicken (the inevitable *poulet* of the Mediterranean), fruit in a wire basket. There were deep dark grapes nestling against vivid oranges; there were inferior peaches and luscious peaches. Oliver insisted on Chianti.

'It will make me talk,' she urged, torn between the wild desire to drink it, to shock Cuthbert, and to cry shame on all her upbringing, and the knowledge that it would be dreadfully wrong.

'Does that matter? I want you to talk. You interest me. Tell me why have you never married?'

It might be the Chianti, it might be Pompeii which rushes to the head, but she answered the truth. 'Nobody axed me, sir,' she said.

'Well, that's candid enough! Tell me about yourself.

You've lived in the country?'

'In Gloucestershire until I was over twenty; six months in Balham, the rest in South Kensington.'

He nodded. 'A good mixture. Did Balham leave much of an impression?'

'The worst of the lot. My brother is a rector there.' She stopped dead. The loyalty to Cuthbert sealed her lips, and her colour came and went so that she turned her face from him.

'I had an uncle once who was a doctor in Tooting. He got run in for illegal operations, and had to go to Nigeria and start a practice of a strange nature there. It is odd how in these respectable suburbs people's morals go to pieces. Haven't you noticed it? You might expect that sort of thing in Mayfair, but not in self-righteous Tooting.'

She knew that she ought to be angry that Oliver should dare to mention such a thing as an illegal operation to her. Yet somehow the queer change that had come over her ever since this cruise was encroaching. She wasn't angry. She was interested.

'You are lucky that no man ever asked you,' he said, 'that's to come. Some new experience in life. Lucky fellow.'

Something to come! But of course she would never marry now. She felt a glow and a tingle, for is not proposal and refusal or acceptance the great adventure to every woman? When she believes romance to be behind her, then she becomes old. Women who have believed this have been old at twenty. Women who have found it still before them, have become miraculously young again at forty. Romance is the rejuvenating hand of time upon a woman's high noon. It sets back the hours. It is without any doubt her daylight saving bill.

Ann could actually feel time slipping from her, discarded like those dreadful tweed clothes she had brought with her; it was ridiculous!

'I shall never marry,' she said, 'this is what you might call my swan song! I won three hundred pounds in a sweepstake, and I am spending it like this. My brother is furious. He said I ought to have invested it and left it to his daughter. She's my godchild. I suppose I ought really.'

'I don't see why. Buying happiness! It is worth all the capital in the world. I wish I'd done it, but I met Lilia and there we were.'

'Don't you think you could go back to Lilia?'

'God knows. She doesn't want me. There's the other chap too.'

'But Lilia is your wife.'

'That doesn't give me the right to make her miserably unhappy, does it?'

'No, but it insists that you should not give her up. You ought to make her see the folly of her ways, and come back to you.'

He laughed as he lit a cigarette. 'The six months in Balham has stuck, hasn't it? I am afraid I find your high morality quite immoral. It's just that we look at these things in different ways, that is all. Good God! Look at this.'

For the excursion, hot and breathless, was arriving.

They were red in the face. Daring old gentlemen had unbuttoned their coats and flung them wide, showing vast expanses of chest and stomach. Retired gentlemen who had obviously lived in the East at some remote time of their lives, had come in Shantung suits which gave them a feeling of superiority over their flannel-suited fellows. There were straw hats, and panamas, even felt hats and tweed caps … and one bowler. There were old ladies in Edwardian attire, in pre-war hats, in print blouses, and one trimmed with jet. There were young girls who had come for a fling and meant to get it; young men who had come for romance and had got it. Blazers and berets, little round crochet hats and large flopping hats, parasols and pince-nez, lunch baskets bought *en route,* sandwich parcels packed by the steward, everybody seemed to have something to carry. And in the midst of all this the tall and miserable-looking courier as supplied by Mr. Thomas Cook, who must have wished himself anywhere else in the world than where he was at the moment. And this in spite of it being one of the loveliest spots on earth.

The excursion was bearing down on the hotel, the more opulent hopefully contemplating lunch, those with food hoping to cover the fact by ordering a bottle of something to drink, and eating under cover of the bottle!

'This is where we get out,' said Oliver, and he signalled to the waiter. The waiter was a morbid-looking fellow. He eyed the approaching people with interest.

He said appreciatively, 'Mr. Thomas Cook.'

He had an eye for tips.

VI

Ann was very tired. The Neapolitan sun was hot; it had beaten down upon her fiercely enough and she had not realized how weary it could make you feel.

'Tired?' he asked.

'I am rather.'

'We'll go straight back to the ship.'

It seemed a pity, for she knew that she would only be here once in her life, here with the broken colonnades and the crumbling balustrades, in the dead city which still continued to live. There was something remarkable to her in the fact that it still lived, and as the car went along – she thought far too quickly – she wondered whether it was thought or spirit or ghost which trod those dead streets. She wished that she could have gone on walking about it, while the excursion ate heartily at the famous hotel where the lunch was provided and included in the itinerary, but she couldn't.

Her head ached terribly.

She was glad to get back to the deserted ship, glad to curl up on her little bed, with the fan playing on her, and to sleep. She slept late.

Ann had made the mistake which seems to be inevitable to the Englishman who has never left England before. She believed in sunburn and tan as being both beneficial and healthy. Always returning from Worthing she had waited with a thrill for Miss Thomas or little Gelding to say, 'My, but how brown you are!' That was the hallmark of a successful holiday. It meant that the fortnight had done her good. She had the purely British theory that the sun could do no wrong, instead of the superior knowledge of the Mediterranean, which believed in the sun as a god of vengeance who can kill at will.

Although the little hat that she had bought at Fifinelle's with such pride most successfully shaded her eyes and gave her the idea that it was protective, it left the nape of her neck naked to the rays. Ann was suffering from a touch of the sun. She was sick. In her head there beat a pulse like that of a dynamo, and she could do nothing but lie there and suffer the ministrations of Miss Brown, well used to such catastrophes.

'Having given her so much trouble, her tip will come to something *awful*,' Ann thought wretchedly. 'I'll never know what to give her, and I'll be frightened to death …'

Still it wasn't much use bothering about that now.

Existing on grapes and ice water for the rest of the day, Ann rose extremely weakly the next morning, long after the second day's excursion, as organized by the persevering Mr. Thomas Cook, had started on its way. They were doing the Blue Grotto, and the island of Capri – including, so the itinerary set out, a car ride along one of the most exquisite pieces of coast road in Europe, and a delightful boat trip. The idea of a delightful boat trip set Ann dithering; she had, of course, no idea that part of that trip had to be spent lying flat at the bottom of the boat, so as to escape being decapitated when going through the entrance to the grotto. Several of the more obese had trouble with this.

The Blue Grotto itself sounded attractive enough, but she had not wanted to see it in company with the people on the excursion. There were far too many people in the ship, she thought, far too many of the sort who had come only to get their money's worth. In their earnest endeavour to miss nothing they managed to see only the obvious. Ann, struggling wanly on deck as suggested by Miss Brown ('Only now do keep in the shade or you'll find it all comes back again'), collided with Mrs. Spinks.

She was the last person whom Ann wanted to meet, but she could not escape. Mrs. Spinks had not gone to the Blue Grotto, nor had Mr. Spinks. He had heard some home truths about the delightful boat trip, and the difficulties to be suffered by the obese, sprawling at the bottom of a boat to circumvent the entrance. He had had other ideas.

'You heard what happened to us last night?' said Mrs. Spinks. 'And a nice thing it was too.'

'I was in bed, with the sun.'

Mrs. Spinks buttonholed her, and they sat down on one of the lounge sofas, side by side. There was no escape. It seemed that in the evening several of the older ladies of the party had been anxious to see something of the night life of Naples. Their husbands could not help them, they knew nothing about it. Having heard that it was a particularly disgraceful city, the elderly ladies' respectable whistles had been whetted. One of the cadaverous-looking guides who frequented the mole had accosted some lady, and had told her that he could show her a most extraordinary cabaret where the most peculiar dances in Europe were to be witnessed. 'Nevaire see anyzing like-a,' he had said.

He wanted a considerable sum to act as their escort, because, as he informed them, the Fascisti had to be squared and it was a very dangerous business. Mrs. Spinks had been consulted, and, being only too anxious to show that she had money and to spare, she had offered to put up half. What was half to her? The result of all this argument and bargaining had been that at ten o'clock, five indiscreet ladies, in the fascinating pursuit of something which they considered would not be 'quite nice', had departed over the side.

There the dark-haired, dark-eyed guide had joined them. He had been wearing a cloak, which had stirred the ladies considerably. A cloak was dangerous-looking, it was romantic. Brigands wore cloaks. They had all been squeezed into a taxicab, which had proceeded at breakneck speed over the cobbles of Naples, jolting them into one another's arms. The guide had been very agreeable over it, very amusing, laughing all the time, and to the ladies in search of the disgraceful, it had really seemed that their adventure had already started.

The car, climbing the hill, arrived after a devious route left them entirely bewildered, outside a somewhat seedy-looking café, which had obviously been forewarned of their arrival. A long conversation took place between the guide and the manager, before admittance could be obtained. Once inside, they were escorted to two small tables set on a sanded floor, the whole place being very ill-lit, and a great many soiled paper roses and shell flowers being entwined about the roof. Just at first it had seemed dull enough. Girls had danced, but so wholly respectably and in so many clothes, that the ladies had protested to the guide. He had charged them abominably for a very third-rate affair. The guide had shrugged his shoulders. All of a sudden he had become surprisingly ignorant of English. He held up hands in protest. But anyway after that things had started to happen. And such things! Oh, my dear, I thought I should have died!

The ladies' protests had certainly enlivened the proceedings. Suddenly the lights had fused. In the scuffle that proceeded, one lady found herself deprived of her bag, but as she said afterwards, she was so glad to escape with her life that she did not care. A wild scream reverberated through the café, oaths, a mysterious knocking. Then they had been aware of the guide clawing at them, '*Signore*, queek, this way. The Fascisti.' They had no idea what it might all be about, but it had epitomized their way of getting their money's worth. They had been only too glad to follow him down a queer little passage and out of the darkness into what was very obviously the café's back yard.

One of the ladies had had a heart attack in the subsequent ride back. Mr. Spinks was very angry with his wife for having embarked on the expedition at all. Anything might have happened, he said. Unfortunately when you came to analyse the whole thing, nothing of what they had expected had happened, and the guide had got away with a fat sum of money and somebody's bag to boot, though it had all been very exciting at the time.

Ann found it rather dull. People's adventures are seldom so thrilling to others as they are to themselves. Ann would have hated to have been in a low Neapolitan café, while women screamed and fainted, and the Fascisti pummelled at the door. There was too much of Cuthbert in her for that, but she had to listen to Mrs. Spinks's narrative at length and to agree that it had been amazing.

And as she listened, her mind wandered away, and she remembered sitting on the veranda of the Pompeian hotel, and she was not at all sure that she had not had a wonderful time there with Oliver. Afterwards it is so easy to look back and to see the singular beauty of moments. At the time it is not so simple, you are too close to them, they do not stand out against the background of everyday drabness. She had been happy, radiantly happy.

'Did you see Pompeii?' asked Mrs. Spinks.

'Yes.'

'So did I, and I can't say that I thought much of it. All in such a mess, I thought. So bitty. I felt sorry for the people who had gone on that wretched excursion. I would not go to such places if I could not afford the best. Do it in comfort, I say or not at all.'

'Quite.'

'Ah, there's the beef tea.' Mrs. Spinks watched the tray coming up in the lift with approval, though her figure cried shame to the very thought of beef tea. 'That's one of the little luxuries I always treat myself to. I must have my drop of beef tea.'

And she moved off.

VII

They danced that night, with the lights of Naples astern, and beyond the bows Vesuvius, now and again throwing up a red glow, a marvellous sight against the darkness of the night sky.

Ann could not dance because her head still throbbed a little, and Miss Brown had warned her about it.

'I think you'll do what I tell you,' said Miss Brown, 'though some of them – Lord, bless your heart – it all goes in one ear and out the other. That's the worst of these cruises. Some of all sorts. Now the mail run's different. There you sort of get to know your people. This is all chop and change.'

So Ann drew a deck-chair to the taffrail and sat there with the sound of the band in the distance.

'Looking at our little volcano?' enquired Miss Bright cheerfully as she pattered by. She was wearing plimsolls. The cobbles had lamed her, for she had that afternoon done a prowl of the docks, until so beset by gentlemen who wished to sell her goods of a doubtful variety, that she had had to lay about her with an umbrella. The language of the umbrella as wielded by an irate female is the esperanto of the dago. Miss Bright had returned victorious, left severely alone, but quite lame from the cobbles; hence the plimsolls.

'Nobody is likely to ask me to dance,' she said.

The ship was already full of its romances. Most of the young people had made friends. From where Ann sat she could see them grouped in couples.

'So amusing to watch them,' said Miss Bright, 'sea fever, that's what that is … *I must go down to the sea again*,' and she hummed to herself.

The A. P. had struck lucky. His eye had been attracted by a peroxide blonde, whom he had first sighted at Marseilles. The peroxide blonde was no sailor. She took to her bunk whenever the ship took to sea, and the A. P. had unfortunately not made enough progress when in harbour to take to her bunk too. He had hopes anon, having had some experience of the young girl who saves up and goes the whole hog on a cruise in other things beside money. He had a remote idea that there was some wholehogging to be done here, and he wasn't going to be left out of it. Not likely.

The A. P. brightening considerably, pursued the lady with avidity in port, because undoubtedly when at sea she would be missing. He was suggesting the boat deck, and he got such a view going up. The A. P. had been in the merchant service so short a while that he was still full of enthusiasms, still keenly interested in what came his way. And the purser himself never went on the boat deck! He had informed the A. P. of that only this morning, when behind the wrought iron bars of their office he had been occupied in converting passengers' money into lire. And that was an advantage about the boat deck, thought the A. P. as he trundled up the companion with the lady of his affections just ahead.

Ann watched him a little reproachfully. What a thing it was to be in the teens. What a joy to be a peroxide blonde. She was wondering whether, if she had had her life to live again, she would not have chosen fastness, and yellow-gold hair, and powder and lipstick galore. You had more fun that way. And when you got on you didn't regret the things you had done, but the things you hadn't. Queer, that.

Three girls were giggling together. She could not help overhearing their conversation. She listened languidly, feeling a little guilty, but they were so close, and anyway her presence did not seem to worry them much. It was quite obvious that they were in the passenger list as that part of the cruise that started from twenty-five pounds.

They were three shop girls, she supposed, who, rather like herself, had never been farther than Margate before.

'And oh, my dear,' said the longest and leanest, 'how was I to know that he wasn't an officer? He looked like one. He had on one of those funny little short jackets, and a cap with a peak, and all, and then when he tried to kiss me I made sure that he *must* be an officer.'

'And wasn't he?'

'My dear, he's a steward. Isn't it awful?'

'I dunno,' said the third, 'a steward is better than no one. He does wear a uniform, and what with the shortage of men and all that …'

But the longest and leanest was highly indignant.

'All the same he ought to have been an officer. I can't get over that, and it is so awkward meeting him again.'

'You must have encouraged him. Stewards don't try to kiss passengers.'

'Oh, I encouraged him all right. You see I thought that he *was* an officer. It isn't my fault that he isn't.'

The band struck up again, sparkling happy music of Congress Dances, and they drifted away. Flotsam and jetsam of a wonder cruise. Happenings. Events. Romances. Illusions. Disillusion. All crammed together into one bewildering whole.

Ann sitting there heard a voice behind her.

'What are you thinking of?' asked Fergus.

'I was thinking how funny a ship is. Listening to people talking.'

'Some of all sorts.'

'Yes, all sorts. My stewardess tells me the mail run isn't like this?'

'We don't get such a mixed crowd of course. This is all one class and it produces that. There we have the people we like and dislike, more for themselves than for what they are. Now we take dislikes just because people look dreadful and do dreadful things. Mean of us perhaps; still, human.'

He leant against the taffrail, and she noted the long slender lines of his body, the little short coat that fitted closely about the waist, and left the smooth line of his hip defined against the sea. Ann for her part interested Fergus. She was the most interesting woman he had met this cruise. In his own mind he could not 'place' her. She was different from the others. She seemed to be growing younger every moment, both physically and mentally. She was so rapid in this youthful development that she took him by surprise. Soon he believed that the real and rather lovely Ann would blossom out, and she would be worth noticing.

He said, 'Why did you come this trip?'

She told him about the sweepstake.

'And you are still in a whirl about it?'

'Of course.'

'You are coming out of it quickly too. You are shaping, finding your real self at last.'

'And then there will be the going back.'

He said slowly, 'You'll never go back. That isn't in you. Nobody can go back in life, you know, that isn't possible. You will go on.'

When she undressed that night, she stood a little while peeping out of the round port to where Vesuvius stood lowering against the night sky. She thought, 'He says I am never going back. I'm going on and on.' And then she remembered what Oliver had said only yesterday … 'You are lucky that no man ever asked you. That's something to come. Lucky fellow!' Life was dropping amazing possibilities into her lap.

CHAPTER 5

I

Before the S.S. *Allando* cast off from the mole at Naples, a letter from Cuthbert was delivered on board. The letter was reproachful. He had received only postcards, and he felt that he had been grossly neglected.

Cuthbert had never been geographically interested in places, much less in places that he was never likely to see for himself, and Ann had, in a fit of aberration, sent him a picture of the Spanish Cathedral at Gibraltar. It had been a match to the fuse of popery, for ever latent in his mind. He felt it necessary to rebuke Ann. It was all very well, but although she might be having a very good time, they were having nothing of the sort in Balham. It had rained dismally ever since Ann had left, and the seeds that had been put in in anticipation of a delightful summer, had been washed away, which was a wicked waste of money.

Cuthbert was hard up. He was furious because his sister was not hard up. It wasn't fair, he argued. There was never a time in his career when Cuthbert was not hard up, but he felt that it was worse now than before, because of Ann going and squandering that vast sum of money. He ought to rub it in. He did not suppose that there would be any holiday for them this year, not even such a simple holiday as Worthing. A pity! A hard-working man like himself needed his annual holiday. It meant that the winter would be additionally hard on him, and he wasn't as young as he had been. Cuthbert's letter was full of righteous self-pity, and it covered a good deal of ground. He had got as far as next winter, and his financial status next year, and he had deplored the unfortunate affair of the Spanish Cathedral.

Ann sat down in the lounge and reviewed Cuthbert's letter, and thought how much angrier he would have been had he known that she had had her hair cut short, and had bought new clothes – thousands of francs' worth, and a thousand francs extra because she had forgotten the deposit – she had bought what he would have called fast clothes, that could be of no possible use to her when she returned to her drab life in the office and in South Kensington.

And she had changed so much that she had actually gloried in the extravagance, that was the most extraordinary part of it.

She sat down at a little side table in the lounge and she wrote to Cuthbert. She had an idea that he might consider the letter rude. There had been quite enough of this 'you are wasting your money' business. Whose money was it to waste anyway? She had had her fill of fraternal interference, and there was going to be a terrible row when she got home, she knew, but a lot lay between her and that time. Malta, Venice, Ragusa. Why, the cruise was not half through yet.

Whilst she was writing her letter, Oliver Banks came across the lounge. He was holding a Marconi in his hand, and there was something a little odd about the way he looked; his mouth was caught and puckered, his eyes were dazed as though even when seeing her still he did not recognize her. He came straight to the other side of the writing desk, and sat there opposite her, with the pile of stationery all marked S.S. *Allando* between them, and the curtain of the porthole flapping a little in the light breeze, for they were running before the wind.

'What do you say to that?' he asked, and he laid the Marconi along the top of the papers so that she could read it. It had been sent from California, and it stated with brutal candour that Lilia had been killed in a car accident in Los Angeles.

For a moment Ann did not know what to say, then the words came in a flood. 'I'm most awfully sorry, and coming like this just when you are on a cruise, enjoying yourself. What can I say? What will you do?'

But he was obviously thinking of Lilia and what she had meant to him.

'It would have been so much easier if I had loved her, only I didn't. I can't be sorry. Not really sorry.'

'But you *must* be sorry! You mean the grief is so great that you do not realize it?'

'No, I don't mean that at all. I mean what I say, and I am not going to be a hypocrite about it. I can't express what I don't feel, I'm not made that way. Lilia and I separated years ago, we were disappointed in each other. I should not have expected her to have been upset if I had been killed.'

'But she *was* your wife?'

'I know, only having split we were like strangers. You cannot live on a memory, that is the cruel part of life. I feel so wrong because I cannot feel sorrier. You see, it just doesn't mean anything to me at all.'

Ann stared at him in amazement. 'But it must do. You were married to her.'

He shook his head. 'Long long ago I had a romance and it faded. When a flower dies in your coat you forget its loveliness in its withering. It is like that with women.'

She did not understand him in the least. She had never known any man at all intimately save her father and Cuthbert, and she had been afraid of both of them. It is difficult to ally romance with one's father, almost impossible. Somehow she did not believe that he had ever loved and wooed and had children. Cuthbert had made a very prim marriage which left you wondering if and how consummation had taken place; still, there was Gloria as proof of that, or of Eleanor's infidelity, which was more unlikely still. It was hard that now she could not understand Oliver in the least when she wanted most to help him.

'I suppose,' she said, 'my world is so different that it makes it impossible for me to understand you, only I cannot think how it is that you are not despairing.'

He lifted his head and looked into her eyes. 'If you were now told that your mother was dead, would you be despairing?'

'I couldn't be, could I? She has been gone so long.'

'That is my predicament. Lilia has been gone so long. It is very hard that she should die in this way, very hard indeed, though I don't know that a car smash isn't the best way of passing out, provided you are killed immediately. Lilia as she used to be is nothing but a ghost, and whether she is alive or dead it makes no difference to the carryings on of that ghost.'

She sat there chewing the end of the pen. She wished that she could think of something to say, something sympathetic and sweet which would comfort him. But she realized that perhaps he was not in need of actual comfort, and that was the most amazing thing of all.

He got up uneasily.

'I'll have to cable back,' he said.

II

Ann sat on dully.

She ought to be able to think of something to say to Oliver or in her letter to Cuthbert, but she couldn't. Her mind was a blank. It seemed like blotting paper, events smudged in, and that was all. It wasn't any use for anything else at all.

Then the disposal of the savouries in their silver dishes diverted her attention. Green lettuce, prawns in pink curls, white and yellow egg against the gleaming silver of sardines. Caviare. The caviare gave her an idea. Oliver loved it.

She approached the steward cautiously, for she had always had an idea that he was a sort of officer, though what sort she really did not know. She enquired if some caviare could be sent down to someone's cabin? The steward looked at her in the manner that conveyed that he had not realized before that she was 'that sort of young lady'. He said coldly that doubtless it could be arranged. Ann interpreted his glance, turned crimson, and stammered out the number of the cabin. As it happened she had only come to know that by accident, because he had made a fuss about the first cabin allotted to him, and it had been changed.

The steward said it should be fixed, and his fingers closed over the half-crown timidly proffered. It seemed to her a dreadful lot of money for a very little job, but seeing the way that he had looked, she had not dared to offer less. Even now she was quite sure that he looked upon her as being promiscuous. Caviare in a gentleman's cabin *did* sound a little odd, when you came to think about it. No one would ever believe that she had done it out of pure goodness of heart, out of an overwhelming sympathy for a fellow-being in distress, though when she considered it, she was not sure that he *was* in distress. And all her upbringing told her that was the worst part of it, and all her recent experience of human nature told her that, under the circumstances, it was quite understandable.

She got up to go across the lounge, for the steward was getting a small silver dish out of the locker, and was filling it with strips of toast decorated with caviare. He poised them on a couple of forks with the air of a professional juggler. Every little while he glanced at Ann coldly and critically. Even the half-crown had not silenced him. He still looked things.

As she moved to the companion, he pursued her. He held the small silver dish at arm's length as though it contained a bad smell.

'Will that be sufficient, Madam?'

Caviare cuddled among shredded lettuce of a delicate pale green shade.

'It will do very nicely indeed,' she said and hurried away, redder than ever.

She went down to the deck beneath and pretended to interest herself in the barber's shop window. It was not in the least interesting. Inside a large and flamboyant Jewess was being begged to 'choose something for herself' by a little fat man who had obviously had a success with her.

'Anything you like, dearie,' begged the little fat man, and he pointed to a stand of morocco handbags.

But the Jewish lady was interested in bags of a different nature. The barber had some lovely sets of Chinese embroidered underwear. The lady examined them carefully; she even held them up to the light, to study the cut, which was most embarrassing for the little man and even for Ann outside. How could the woman do it? she asked herself. But the woman could. You can do a lot when you are used to being trotted down to the barber's shop every few minutes by different satisfied clients. She had morocco bags in abundance; she did not want any more. Now lingerie was a different matter; she fingered it lovingly. She was not going to be hurried for anybody.

The little fat man had been what she called 'fussy'; one of the persistent sort, and she considered she had earned any little souvenir that he liked to give her.

Ann could bear it no longer. She went along the alley slowly. What should she do? Perhaps she could have a bath. The bath steward disillusioned her on that score. All the baths were booked.

In the café the A. P. had had the ping-pong table erected and was busily engaged in trying to do what he called 'wipe the floor with the third officer'. But the third officer was a dark horse. He had, it transpired, once beaten Borotra at ping-pong! It wasn't Borotra's game, of course, but still it was a bit of a feat. The A. P. was enduring such a slamming that he was seething with indignation. He liked to win games. He was years younger than the third officer, and he had more 'puff'. He was furious at having met his Waterloo.

Ann went on to D deck, where there was the last glimpse of Vesuvius, unrelenting against the sky. As she watched, it threw up a crimson glow, the same deep glow as the sunset. She thought of the dead city lying under it, the dead city where they had walked and had talked and had been so completely happy just about the same time as poor Lilia had been killed.

A dead city, and Lilia was dead too.

'Life seems to be all wrong,' she told herself.

III

She did not see Oliver at dinner. Mrs. Duncan and Ethel were gaily exaggerating about what had happened at Naples. They had been ashore to a very grand hotel to dance, and everybody had been quite mad about Ethel. Oh, quite mad!

'Of course with that fair hair of hers,' said her mother, 'she does attract the Latin races so much.'

According to her mother it was very difficult to find the man whom Ethel did not attract. Everyone loved her. Everyone! Why, she had once met a Russian Grand Duke who had put the second shot into Rasputin, and he –

'Oh, shut up,' from Ethel, who in spite of a certain show of modesty was vastly pleased at stories of that sort.

In this hotel however things had gone with too much of a swing, for while mother was purring her satisfaction over a cup of tea in the corner, and Ethel was dancing with an Italian gentleman ('I'm sure that he was a duke or something, dear, he had that kind of manner'), another had come in. He had challenged the first to a duel. It was all on account of a *signorina*, they protested, and they had rather persuaded Mrs. Duncan that the girl was Ethel. There had been such a scene, with dark eyes flashing, and white teeth gnashing, and Ethel and her mother enjoying it to the full.

But the sequel had not been quite so pleasant. They had kept this to themselves, only telling it to their own advantage. The first gentleman had not been a duke at all, he had been the professional dancer who danced at tea dances. He had had an affair which had been more than indiscreet, with a chambermaid in the hotel. She had been the young woman in question, and not Ethel at all. The second young man had been the booking-clerk. He had been dismissed, and now he had found that his girl, also the chambermaid, had loved not wisely but too well. ''Ell' the booking-clerk had reiterated, 'I gif you 'ell.'

The story as told by Mrs. Duncan in the dining-saloon

was not quite the same. She omitted the chambermaid, and she preferred to think of Ethel as the young woman who had caused the 'ell which the ex-booking-clerk had most successfully made of the dance-room.

Fergus listening, read through it. He knew Italians of old, he understood Neapolitans. Fair hair be damned for a tale. It would want something more than fair hair to turn their heads. Would the cruise never end? he asked himself. All these dreadful people! Until you started cruising you did not know that such dreadful people existed. Only the previous night he had watched an old man from the North of England, who had solemnly partaken of both sorts of soup! He was, he had explained to the steward, 'a rare one for broth'!

There were the romantic people who suffered their romances outside Fergus's cabin night after night, when he was aching for sleep. There was that little fool the A. P. who had picked up a peroxide blonde, with an over red mouth, and he was making an arrant ass of himself. 'One of these days,' thought Fergus, 'he'll get the purser after him,' and the wish was father to the thought.

But the purser wasn't that sort. He was a much older man, and he had seen young officers get into messes before, and out of them again, and do the same thing next trip and never suffer too much for it.

He knew life, did the purser, he knew it very well, and was quite content to live and to let live.

But Fergus was in that mood when he hated all the world and all the people in the world, save perhaps Ann. She reminded him of a butterfly (trite, that, perhaps), something gradually developing, an exquisite and unsuspected beauty emanating from an unpromising shell. And once he had thought of her as an old trout! Inconceivable. At Tilbury she had been so ordinary, one of a hundred other unmarried women over thirty, who see the romantic adventure left behind them, and take on the drab and monotonous outlook which stamps them.

To-night she wore soft blue chiffon. She was a new creature, he thought, and mentally she had changed too. She was thinking now. She had not been thinking when she had come on board. Perhaps a touch of romance had come into his life. Perhaps he also was suffering his sentimental twinge.

Life at sea is so strange.

IV

It was late, much later.

From B deck where they were dancing there came the irresistible melody of 'Auf Wiedersehen', haunting, reproachful, like a memory.

Ann was standing there in the golden path that the moonlight made across the water. Very faintly the ship sighed, though there was nothing in the gentle lapping of the water to cause her anguish. The sea was like a pool, a sweetly pale pool of delicate turquoise, and here or there it seemed as though a needle of gold thread had been run through it by a fairy hand. It was the exquisite artistry of the moonlight.

Ann stood there, her elbows resting on the taffrail. Her hands cupped her chin, and the fairy thread ran through her hair in little filaments of gold where the moon itself touched her. There is something in this, she told herself, that the people ashore must inevitably miss, that golden stream which comes so near, but never near enough to receive them into its beauty.

That was how Oliver found her.

'Well,' he said, 'what are you thinking of?'

'I was thinking if only this could go on for ever, this gay adventure, this romance, the joy. Only it can't. I've got to go back to South Kensington.'

South Kensington with the big strong plane trees in

Queen's Gate, green and fresh in spring with the wide rounded road rising in between their avenue; old and sooty in autumn, stark in winter. South Kensington with the paper-sellers grouped together in the arcade, with the vividly coloured fruit shop at the corner, and the faint hot rubber scent of the Tube, and the hustle of the 'Met', and sometimes the intangible perfume of joss-sticks from the Chinese shop at the end. South Kensington, all very simple, rather unflurried and dignified, what you might have called a very 'nice quarter to live in'. All respectability and quiet gentility, and very little else.

She hated the idea of going back to it.

It is so difficult when you have tasted something much sweeter, essence of lilies blowing under the cedars of the Alameda, gold of the Virgin who guards the sailors passing in and out of the harbour, unruffled loveliness of the dead city under the hill, lulled into long sleeping by the treacherous arm of that devil Vesuvius.

The return would be ghastly, and now she knew it.

'But why go back?' he asked.

'Because it is my job. I haven't the money to continue like this, and London is my home.'

'No, London is where you have happened to live! It isn't your home. You don't love South Kensington or Balham?'

'I don't love them, but they are home.'

'You're a little mole blinding yourself. Well, I'm going to make you see. I'm going to make you see for your own good. Why go back to South Kensington when you can go on touring the world?'

'But I can't.'

Magic of the moonlight, craziness of the fairy who had threaded the pale blue water with gold. She felt herself quiver. She wanted to go from one beautiful place to another. From Vesuvius dark and glowering, with the faint phantasmal tulle of smoke about its crater, and the red passionate glow of fire every little while. From Vesuvius to Stromboli, just as dark, just as glowering, with the eternal cloud lying above it, as though it were too tired to drift away. She wanted to go on for ever. 'Only it can't be,' she said.

'Yes, it can. I am a nomad, a wanderer. I never stay long anywhere. I go on and on, why not come with me?'

'But you don't have to work for your living. I do.'

He laughed. 'I'm a free man now. I'm no longer married. Don't you understand?'

She stood there dazed for a moment, dazed by the suddenness of it all, and the turn that her life had taken. She had never had the chance of marriage before. She was thirty-five, and she had never known love or the opportunities of love, she had never seen the passionate attachment of it all. Now, suddenly in the golden filament of that almost too lovely moon, chance swung wide its doors upon her life. She saw the might-have-beens and the will-be's all dazzling together. She said, 'But you cannot possibly love me?'

'Perhaps not yet, but I am keenly interested in you. I believe that it would be a success.'

'But people only marry for love?'

'Nonsense! Affection is a more stable basis, it lasts longer.'

She felt his hand slipped into her arm, and stood there conscious that it was the first time she had felt the curious rapture of being touched in that way. She felt the passionate desire for something the years had not given her. Then she remembered Lilia. It was just as though the ghost of Lilia, cold and clammy, walked down the golden path of the moonlight, bitterly aloof.

'But Lilia died only yesterday,' she said.

'She died to me a great many yesterdays ago.'

'That doesn't matter. How dreadful we are! How dare we stand here talking like this when she is hardly cold?'

She was shaking a little, ashamed of herself, ashamed of him too. He caught her wrists in his hands, holding them firmly. 'You're a little goose, Ann, it isn't dreadful at all. I've been a widower all these years really.'

'But not really,' she told him. 'I oughtn't to have let you say that to me.'

'Oh yes, you ought. You have blinded yourself to life, and to everything that lay outside your narrow little rut, and for the first time you are seeing things in their right perspective. Their attraction has got you. You won't be able to give them up again. You only think you will, but you won't when it comes to it.'

She knew that he was speaking the truth, and she was afraid of it.

'If you don't marry me now, Ann, you will later. When you sent me that caviare to my cabin, I knew that you would come to me.'

'I oughtn't to have sent that. I oughtn't to have done it. I knew that the moment I saw the steward's face.'

'But you did it; all the same you did it. That showed *me* what I wanted to know.'

From the distance there came the faint frolic of the band – 'A life on the ocean wave'. Then they were indulging in a Paul Jones. They could hear the faint slurring of feet as old gentlemen galloped and young gentlemen chassé-ed. They could hear it above the gentle crushing of the water as the giant bows of the ship ploughed through the turquoise paleness.

She asked, 'Where is it going to end?'

He made a little gesture as though to draw her closer. 'Here, on my heart!'

She broke away, running down the three decks to her cabin in a panic. She was afraid to look at him, afraid to stay. She flung herself on the bed, and found that she was crying, He must not talk to her like this; with Lilia only just dead, it was disgraceful. She must stop it, but how? How?

She wasn't sure that the tears were not of joy.

V

Oliver did not attempt to follow Ann. He brought out a gold cigarette-case and lit a cigarette automatically. He stared into the round wise eye of the moon all the time. He was forty.

He also had thought that life lay behind him, though never in quite the same way as it lies behind a woman. Nature does not curtail a man's love years in the same manner; it gives him the opportunity to love and to be loved even though the sands of time are running out for him. He had been a difficult child, orphaned young, and brought up by a series of relations, none of whom had wanted him, but who had wanted very much the allowance that went with him.

His early life was allotted and partitioned into niches, influenced by the relatives under whose care he had happened to find himself at that particular time. The Banks side of the family had been common. The Montgomerie side grand. Helen Montgomerie, his mother, had stooped to love a man much beneath her in position. At first the Bankses had taken in the child, who had carried with him Helen Montgomerie's fortune.

There had been Uncle Alfred, large and fat with a very definite attachment to check trousers and to strange headgear. Uncle Alfred in private life kept a little 'public' on the Portsmouth Road. In his spare time, he was a student of form, both on the turf and on the stage. He had a very eloquent understanding of a lady's legs and of a filly's capacity. When his nephew stayed at the Britannia, his life was spent in the intimate acquaintance of a beer engine, and of those friends of Uncle Alfred's designated as 'sports'. They were chiefly gentlemen with husky voices and loud ties and a pretty taste in fancy boots.

As a child Oliver had rather liked being with Uncle Alfred, who was noisy, but cheerful, and generous in the extreme; certainly Oliver had liked it better than being with the other Banks relations, dear Grandma and Auntie Miggs.

Dear Grandma and Auntie Miggs lived in a villa at Finsbury Park, and everything was most select. Auntie Miggs was the only one of the family who had never married, and she stayed on to keep house for 'poor Ma'. As a point of fact poor Ma was a great deal poorer for having Auntie Miggs with her; the old lady was frightened to death of her unmarried daughter, who insisted on having everything her own way, and protested that it was always for 'poor Ma's good'.

Everything in Laurel Lodge was polished and cleaned to such a degree that it made life a dangerously disagreeable adventure. It was full of 'mustn'ts' for little boys, very different from the hail-fellow-well-met atmosphere of the Britannia public on the Portsmouth Road.

At Laurel Lodge everything went by rule of thumb and according to Auntie Miggs, who ordered what was and what was not. Everybody was afraid of her. Oliver was afraid of her too, little and insignificant as she might be; in his heart he always despised Grandma for having let Auntie Miggs get out of hand, Auntie who so obviously wanted slapping.

The Montgomerie relations had taken some notice of Oliver when he was twelve, and from these two strange homes of his early youth he had been suddenly taken to his maternal aunt's in a dull square in London. Aunt Daisy was an unapproachable person, prim and strait-laced, who had married late in life, a rich banker. They had had no children of their own, and Aunt Daisy, having nothing to do, from sheer boredom had taken on the role of a chronic invalid.

She needed an interest in life, and she believed that ill-health might provide that interest; it was unfortunate that the Deity, with a strange lack of discernment, should give her such robust health, but Aunt Daisy triumphed over that affliction with surprising fortitude. She talked of her florid colouring as a 'consumptive flush'. Her tendency to put on weight and to do well on her food, she covered by vague allusions to dropsical tendencies. She went to great pains to get ill, and much greater pains to remain ill. She was considerably tried by the fact that she had never developed anything worse than a cold in her head, which, being a very strong woman, she always got over with a remarkable power of recuperation.

Aunt Daisy's house was entirely different from the *ménage* of dear Grandma and Auntie Miggs, and that in its turn had been as the poles apart from the public on the Portsmouth Road, kept by the engaging Uncle Alfred.

Aunt Daisy employed a tutor for young Oliver, until she developed secret passions for the young man, which were immediately discovered by her large and comfortable husband. The husband changed the tutor, and Aunt Daisy as promptly changed the object of her affections. She found tutors to be far more interesting than imaginary illnesses, and probably that was the reason why Oliver found himself somewhat hurriedly sent to school. He was in no way qualified to pass any exam, which would admit him to a public school – his education had been more than a little sketchy – so he was shipped into one of those obliging establishments which are, so the prospectuses state, actually equal to the better-known public schools, though not of the same long standing.

It was in fact a secondary college which gave an

excellent education, though the boys who came there to be educated were a little mixed. Here in term-time Oliver learnt much knowledge (he was a clever boy), and got into the habitual scrapes which every schoolboy of that type gets into.

The holidays were trying, for as he grew older he saw through the subterfuges of Aunt Daisy more and more, and, what was almost worse, her large husband was continually confiding his woes in the boy. He needed someone; he had felt the acute desire for the confessional for many years, and now he poured out his soul to his nephew by marriage. Feeling a traitor, Oliver could not help realizing that his aunt was entirely in the wrong, and his uncle, who was not a real uncle at all, entirely in the right. It was a most uncomfortable position to be in.

Oliver left school at eighteen, having failed in his matric. The reason for this was not lack of brains. During the last two terms Oliver in company with three senior young gentlemen had been getting out at night. They had taken a short cut via a convenient tree that grew alongside the dormitory window, and they had found village girls who had welcomed their advances.

The village girls had been willing to teach them of love. They themselves had been quite willing to learn. These nocturnal overtures had unfortunately sadly messed up the educational advantages offered by day. They had yawned and drowsed over their desks, doing just enough work to keep them out of trouble, and no more.

When the big exams came along, they had failed.

The family had deplored the fact that Oliver's education had been wasted, but he himself was in no way dismayed. He was even at that age a philosopher, he had had his fun, you could not get it both ways, and he wasn't going to grumble about it. It was Aunt Daisy who kicked up the fuss. He had not cared about school too much, though he had certainly cared less for the holidays. Life had been until now a hotch-potch affair, and he could not see how they could expect him to settle down. He had always had a wild longing to see America, and to America he had gone.

America had proved to be a strange jumble of events, an even more hotch-potch affair than anything before. In America he fell in love and out of love. Beautiful women far exceeding anything that he had ever seen in England, strange drinks, perfect ice creams, all blended together into a blur. The statue of Liberty, with the lights blinking in the houses of New York at dusk behind her. Broadway, bustle, stir, commercial confusion, riot.

In America he learnt that Grandma Banks had died, and that he was a little richer. Later it was Aunt Daisy, and he was very much richer. Then he met Lilia.

Bermuda is an island of romance. An island of palms like great feathers, stirring in the wind; of lilies lifting cool white cups, the world suffused with their perfect scent. It had the atmosphere of love, and Lilia herself was love. She was young too, perfectly polished, with that youth of America which is so burnished. She was vivid; her face was almost blanched, for her hair, Titian in hue, had drained every tint from her skin. She painted her mouth. She was the first woman he had seen with a painted mouth, and he found it attractive. So deeply red, why, she did not need any colour in her cheeks with that dark crimson mouth of hers. She wore frocks that tempted him too; backless frocks when everyone else was covered. Directoires disclosing more than was good for a man to see. After the oafish village loves at school she was a startling contrast. She went to his head. She was bitter and cruel, and yet intoxicating. That was how she had affected him.

They were married on the wave of a purely physical

passion, and it could not last. A honeymoon that was the nearest approach to heaven that he would ever reach in this life, and then the awakening.

There had come the knowledge that it had been a mistake, a dreadful, cruel mistake, the dregs of that bitter wine when he thought he had drained the glass. They had parted within the year. It had not meant as much to him as it might have done to some men, for he was not one of the type that takes root. He was essentially nomad. He had never settled in a home or a corner, bricks and mortar conveyed little to him, they were just a temporary abode, no more. People had not held him either. Uncle Alfred, dear Grandma and Auntie Miggs, Aunt Daisy … they were just people who came and went, they were not definite loves or hates. They did not hold him. And, although he had loved Lilia at first with the fierce passionate ardour of a physical emotion, that had gone too. There was no wrench in leaving her, she had never really been part of his life.

Nothing had ever held him for long, he believed that nothing ever would. It was a jar to his pride to let her go, but far better than trying to hold on to her.

He went off travelling to the East. He had a sudden longing to see Fuji-san, and to Fuji-san he went. It gave him ashes and grit, blown about on the wind of chance. Perhaps he had been in the mood for ashes and grit, for figuratively speaking that had represented his life. Then he had gone on. The years had gone on. The hotch-potch scheme that was his life had gone on.

Until now.

He had supposed it would last for ever, and whichever way it was it had not troubled him too much. Then he had met Ann pensively looking at the daffodils in Kensington Gardens.

'They look very pretty,' he had said, but really he had meant that Ann looked pretty.

He had seen the imprisoned soul of Ann, shut in like a bird in a cage, and he had longed to set it free. On such a wheel of chance does our destiny run, it had just happened.

Until to-night he had not known that he had wanted to marry her, and it had been true when he had said that he was not in love with her. Only he was beginning to be in love. That was the difference. He was not in love but he wanted her desperately, and certainly not in the same way as he had wanted Lilia. This was something bigger and greater, something that he felt would grow with the years.

The cigarette burned to near its end. He took it out and flung it far into the sea. The ship trembled a little, trembled and stirred and steamed South.

He had expected Ann to be astonished, even a little shocked. She was like that. At heart he told himself she was unconventional, for all that she had been so involved with the conventions. But, given time to find her true self, she would escape. Oh yes, she would cast aside the shackles of her youth, she would get free.

For Ann would never return to South Kensington. She would never go back to the plane trees in Queen's Gate, and to Mrs. Puddock's moods and tantrums in Onslow Gardens.

Ann had started forth on the great adventure.

CHAPTER 6

I

The *Allando* dropped her anchor with a jerk in the Grand Harbour cut deeply in sapphire blue between the gleaming whiteness of Senglea and Valletta. Ann watched it curiously.

Malta after Naples, which lies like a lovely jewel clasped to the breast of Italy. Naples with its green hills, the wistaria, the bougainvillea flowing like spilled claret over archways and balustrades, the fullness of it, a city of verdure and of beauty, and now an island bald and white with a starkness that hurt.

She had not seen Oliver since last night when he had asked her to marry him. She had been quite bewildered as she had tried to think it over in her cabin. She would, she told herself, never be able to meet him again, it was too dreadful; how could they go on seeing each other? Their first meeting, that would be ghastly; she felt sure that she could never appear natural. Then she had decided that it had been a joke, one of those jokes of extreme bad taste, and she had been silly to take him seriously at all.

All the morning she had written postcards which she had bought in Pompeii, and was getting them into the box on B deck, which announced that it would be closed after eleven o'clock. Postcards for Miss Thomas and little Gelding, and Mr. Robert. She sent some to Gloria too, for surely Cuthbert could not grumble at these, because Pompeii was educational. Then she remembered some of the rumours that had gone round, frescoes, street signs, strange yet fascinating interiors. She had listened to the stories with horror, and it was queer that the old ladies were the ones who imparted them with such a relish. The pure old ladies who seemed to cleave with indefatigable appetite to something impure.

Then she had turned from it in disgust. She had been thinking so much about Oliver, about his proposal (supposing that he had really meant it, but of course he hadn't), and she did not realize how close they were getting to the Grand Harbour. Then she heard the anchor go down; she saw the harbour itself bespattered with little *dghaisas*, the men bending over their oars, their queerly elongated reflections in the water below. She thought involuntarily, 'Venice will be something like this,' which is the one idea that strikes most visitors to the 'island of sunshine and romance'. But Venice is nothing like it; nothing at all.

Ann was anxious to go ashore at once. And here was Miss Bright, with that dreadful panama hat, and all the gew-gaws dangling on her bosom.

'Shall we venture?' asked little Miss Bright. 'It looks most Eastern, I declare I feel quite afraid.'

But Ann said that she had a headache. She did not think she would go ashore this morning, perhaps later, when it was cooler. And, she told herself, not with Miss Bright anyway. Miss Bright turned from her disappointedly.

Really, she thought, people had no enthusiasms, they took so little interest. She could not understand it, and she *had* thought that Ann was different. Well, it just showed that you couldn't tell.

The moment that Miss Bright had disappeared down the companion, deploring the indifference of modern people to the opportunities life offered them, and in search of other prey, Fergus appeared. He was in plain clothes about to go ashore, and he surveyed Ann in the white silk dress with the madonna-blue cape.

'Come ashore with me?' he asked.

'I'd love it.'

She did not know why he asked her, but these days men were taking some notice of her. They were asking her to go with them. It was part of the strange, the sudden overwhelming change of the wonder cruise.

In the deep golden light of the hour before midday, Malta was dazzling like a white flower. She felt a little uneasy as she took her seat beside Fergus in the *dghaisa*. It was such a frail, flimsy little bit of a boat, and the man bent over his oar in such an unusual manner. It was but a little way to the Custom House steps, blazing in the sunshine. You could feel the heat beating down upon you as you stood there. Fergus hurried her through into the roadway beyond, cool and damp and smelling of fetidness.

'Taxi!' he called.

There were two large taxis opposite, but neither of the dark-skinned drivers took any notice. Fergus approached one.

'Didn't you hear me? I want a taxi,' he said.

The chauffeur gazed at him indifferently. '*Festa*,' he said.

Fergus went to the second man; he also was not interested. He shrugged his shoulders and said quite imperturbably, '*Festa*.'

'Hell,' said Fergus.

There were *carozzis* on the opposite side, but gayer, more debonair *carozzis* than those Ann had seen at Gibraltar. The horses wore tassels on either side of their ears like Dundreary whiskers, and a ridiculous single feather stuck in the centre of their heads, like Rosalind.

A driver leant forward. 'I take you, Signor. I take you where you wish ...'

'Oh, all right then,' said Fergus. They climbed in side by side. Climbing in was all very well, but staying in was another matter. Malta was unlike Gibraltar, it was hilly. The driver whipped up his steed, tassels were flung in the breeze, and Fergus and Ann found themselves clinging to the brass rails and the flapping curtains of the *carozzi*. It reminded her of nothing so much as a game of hide and seek she had once played when very young, in a four-post bed with magenta curtains. There is something surprisingly bed-like about a *carozzi*.

'And what is a *festa* anyway?' she asked as they recovered from the anguish of passing the fish market at high noon.

'It is one of their religious festivals, they are always having them ...'

'But what do they do?'

At that very instant a maroon went off at uncomfortably close quarters. The horse shied, and they were again flung into each other's arms.

'That's the *festa*,' said Fergus grimly.

Ann was much embarrassed. 'I'm sorry about this,' she said, 'but I cannot help it. This cab simply throws you about.'

'I know. They always do.'

They spun round a corner on two wheels, and as they did so they became aware of a strange procession proceeding from the opposite direction, and bearing straight down upon them. A policeman waved them back. It was all very well, but they could not go back. The street was singularly narrow, and there was a long string of other wheeled vehicles behind them. Large cars, a taxi, three or four more *carozzis* with tassels tossing in the wind.

There was a jabber between the driver and the policeman, and all the while the procession coming closer and closer, and all Malta in a wild and excitable state of *festa* accompanying it.

'Blast!' said Fergus at last, 'this is what always happens.'

'But I think it is fun.'

'Well, we've got stalls for it, I suppose. That is if the tide of people doesn't sweep us completely away; it may, you know.'

The procession was led by a large quantity of little boys in cassocks and bearing candles, which scattered grease to right and to left of them. This did not seem to disturb the populace, who pressed closer and closer. Women in faldettas, men in rags, all eager for the *festa*. There was then a gentleman wearing a big dark wig and purple robes and carrying a strange gold umbrella raised aloft with pomp.

'What do you suppose he is?' asked Ann.

'Oh, he is representing one of their saints or something. They get up to all manner of tricks half of which they don't understand themselves.'

More little boys, this time with flowers; a tribe of monks; a statue in pink plaster with flowers garlanded round it, and carried by six perspiring penitents who breathed heavily.

'Have you thought,' said Fergus, 'this may be a mile long?'

'I think it is remarkable, and I'm enjoying it.'

All the unwashed of Malta surging round them. A crossbearer leading the multitude and engaging in little pleasantries with the people on either side of him. Good joke, this. Why be long-faced about it, was it not a *festa*?

She could not help thinking of Cuthbert, Cuthbert and his popery inhibition. This was worse than popery, it was almost pagan. At last the crowd had surged on, and the wobbly candles had tottered round the corner, and the gentleman with his umbrella had proceeded with the dignity of a monarch, whilst the perspiring people under the statue had staggered along in compulsory attitudes of humiliation. At last the *carozzi* was freed and able to journey forth up Strada Reale.

Ann had a vague impression of the main street of Valletta. It was hot with sunshine, and it smelt of sand and garlic and sweaty Maltese in one. Reale, with its queer little cabinets of flowers for sale, and with the Porta Reale at one end, and the thin blue line of sea at the other. With Muscat's sports shop standing bravely half way, and the photographers who, judging by their windows, took no pictures save of sports groups from various ships, and Maltese brides in drooping modesty. The car exchange, and the wine shops, and, flourishing at the corner round which they turned, the Wembley Stores, which is the grocery establishment.

'You'll want some lunch?' said Fergus.

'I am rather hungry,' she confessed.

The *carozzi* stopped with a jingle of harness outside the hotel, and she saw a cool porch – really it was very hot indeed, much hotter than Marseilles or Naples; she was quite glad of the uncarpeted floor, and of the fans going.

'Lime and lemon?' said Fergus. 'It's cooling.'

'Please.' She did not argue. She did not expostulate that she wanted to pay; she was so thirsty that really she did not care who paid. Why should she?

Fergus sat there surveying her. She looked very young, he thought, and yet she had once looked so old.

Or had he thought about her differently then? He was not sure. He said, 'I wish I had been free after lunch and could have taken you out to San Antonio gardens. It is lovely there, and you ought to go, only I have to be back at work.'

'I suppose I couldn't go alone?'

'Oh yes, you could. Malta is a safe little island, it is not like Naples in that way. Here you can go about quite well.'

'Then I'll get a cab of some sort and drive out to it.'

'I'll fix that up for you.' He eyed her across the rim of his glass. 'You're liking it?'

'I'm loving it.'

She finished the lime and lemon, and glanced across at him. To him this must all be ordinary and usual, to her it was a fairy tale come true.

'Funny,' she said, 'but I am most terribly hungry, just like a kid …'

'Right. Then come in and have some lunch.'

They went into the dining-room together.

II

Most of the ship seemed to have collected into that dining-room. The waiters were flying about at express speed, they were extremely willing and extremely capable. Ann approved their white drill suits and their canvas shoes.

Ethel and Mrs. Duncan arrived with a young man in tow, who looked as if he had developed jaundice and was not too happy about it. Ann recognized him as having been seen most of the cruise so far through the windows of the ship's cocktail bar.

He had an Hon. attached to his name, she had learnt from the passenger list, and apparently Mrs. Duncan had learnt that too. An Hon. was her idea of bliss.

There was the blazer and beret brigade, and some who had already bought the dark spectacles on sale in the streets; there were the three girls who had worn flannel trousers ever since they had left Marseilles, and their bathing-dress tops, and had actually come ashore in them. 'All very well for the swimming-bath and sun-bathing,' said Fergus, 'and even then it's dangerous with figures like that.'

The unexpected throng caused no little disturbance in the hotel; even the chef – though he had, according to the certificates hung on the wall, first and second class diplomas – had got flustered. There was, so Fergus told Ann, keen competition between this hotel, which was the only one in the island under English management, and the other one further down the same street where a certain Serene Highness had at one time laid his weary body for a night's repose. Ann could not help thinking that Mrs. Duncan had not heard of the Serene Highness, else why was she here? Nobody, Fergus said, had ever decided whether it was better to go for the English management and so lessen more than considerably the fear of food poisoning which was so prevalent in the island of sunshine and romance, or to bask in the aristocratic privilege of having slept under the same roof as a certain Serene Highness.

Fergus put his money on the food.

'The island is full of disease and poison,' he said, 'and here I do know the food is properly cooked.'

'It seems very good.'

How different from the usual lunches, the Miss Thomas lunches when they 'treated' each other. The usual steak and 'kid.' and one veg. Or, on hard-up days, the poached egg and the glass of milk. How would she ever go back to all that? She refused to think of it. She pulled herself up with a jerk.

The worst elements of the cruise continued to pour in

through the dining-room door. The Spinkses large and perspiring. The Frenchman noisy and insistent – he had obviously come for the first and second class diplomas – he demanded to see the menu before he sat down, and then, having misjudged the time, found there was nowhere to sit. ('And serve him right,' said Fergus.) Strange costumes, the sort of costume that the Englishman abroad believes to be cool but which is not. Ann felt that it would be but a short step to handkerchiefs over the head, securely knotted at the corners.

'Let's go,' she said.

'I'll put you into a car for the San Antonio gardens,' he said.

There was some difficulty in getting a car. The *festa* was the excuse. Drivers surveyed Fergus with a complete lack of interest. When he hailed them either they continued to stare, or they shrugged their shoulders with complete indifference, and murmured the single word which appeared to be their be-all and end-all – '*Festa.*'

Then, just as they were wondering what to do, a large car came down Strada Mezzodi, and drew up at the door of the hotel. Inside was Oliver Banks. Ann had thought that when she saw him again she would be covered with confusion, but now, in the heat and flurry of the moment, and the irritation caused by the infernal *festa*, she was almost relieved.

'She was just going to San Antonio gardens,' Fergus explained, 'only there is a dreadful bobbery about getting a taxi to-day. They've got some beano on.'

Oliver grinned. '*Festa*,' he said.

'That's it.'

'I'll take you.' He held open the car door. 'You pop in here beside me. You'll never get a car if you wave your arms about the streets for hours. They are simply taking no notice.'

The Mediterranean was queer in that way. Odd things happened there. You could not go through the day without it changing on the sudden. Here she was, mutely, for she could think of no excuse, getting into the car and sitting down by Oliver's side. Fergus was walking away from the hotel. There was no waving of good-byes, the thing just happened. Could anything be more awkward? she asked herself. And all because of a *festa,* with little boys dripping candle grease down Strada Reale, and a pious-looking gentleman bearing an omnipotent umbrella strutting behind, and the penitents struggling with a pink plaster effigy in the rear.

Fate had taken a hand.

They drove out through the Porta Reale, with the island lying before them, and the Citta Veccian hills beyond. She saw a crimson bougainvillea growing beside a purple one, mingling their wild wine of blossom together on a stone wall.

'You shouldn't have done this,' she said.

'Why not? We're friends, aren't we?'

She wanted to say 'Yes, but after last night ...' only she couldn't. How could anyone? She was annoyed that he was not embarrassed and she was. Yet it did perhaps make it easier to know that he could be natural about it. 'Of course we're friends,' she agreed, and the loveliness of the island suddenly came over her, and the warm beauty of the afternoon. Anyway let them be friendly for the moment, and blow the conventions.

The pastoral, agricultural part of the island lay before them, with the red clover growing wild and rampant and in full blossom dyeing the fields with its Tyrian purple. Here or there was the dim blue of cypresses, or the straggling yellow-green of fig trees already growing dusty. On the right, whenever you looked, there was always the dim thin line of sea on the horizon, clasping close the island which lay like a ruby in a claw setting.

'Glad you came?' he asked.

'It's marvellous.'

A lizard zig-zagged up a crumbling wall, a vivid streak of green against the grey of the stone.

'You'll love San Antonio.'

'I believe I'm in the mood to love anything,' she said, and she resigned herself to her fate. (What were conventions, anyway?) After all, she had never known Lilia. If Oliver remained unembarrassed, why shouldn't she? She told herself that she would make the most of the precious moment, whatever happened. They drove on, along a road thick with dust, which flew behind the car. They passed through villages, fly-blown and indescribably filthy, with the figs growing close to the houses, and the old, old women looking out from under green-black faldettas. There were children everywhere. They played in the gutters; they were herded along in those strange carts belonging to the more affluent Maltese, which have mattresses laid on the bare floor, where the occupants sprawl at full length.

They arrived at the Melita hotel, which stands by the Governor's summer palace in a grateful greenness that is all its own. And after the glare of the road, and the burning whiteness of the island – save where it was red with clovers – Ann was glad. Again the cold tessellated hall, and beyond the glimpse of a little garden through an archway. The garden was unlike the rest of Malta that she had seen, the island stripped stark, for this was verdant and green. Blue plumbago in blossom twined about a marble pool where golden carp swam. An orange tree, white with blossom and gold with fruit, gave them shelter. There was the scent of hot orange flowers, of red roses and nicotiana, all at one and the same moment, and over it all the resinous essence of a tall cedar.

'It is a joy to eat marmalade home-made from their oranges,' said Oliver.

'You've been here before?'

'Yes, twice. Everybody who comes to the island comes here, it is one of the spots.'

'I wish I could never leave it again.'

'Yes, you always feel it when you first come here. But really it is dull, you'd get sick of it.' He poured out the tea with elaborate care. On the wall of the house where a vine trailed its tendrils, a caged bird began to sing. 'It is funny,' he said, 'but they have no birds in Malta save in a cage or a pie. That is the Maltese idea of the place for them.'

'Poor thing! I wonder that it has the heart left to sing,' and though the silence was only broken in the far distance by the jingle of *carozzi* bells, above it came the song of the caged bird.

'Yet,' said Oliver, 'lots of men and women, also caged, still sing. I am sometimes astonished at the bravery of people, the courage with which they fight the most ghastly odds.'

She glanced at him with interest. 'You've had a difficult life?'

'Oh no, better than I deserved, I daresay. It has been odd, nothing really difficult about it.'

He thought for a moment of telling her about Uncle Alfred, and dear Grandma and Auntie Miggs. He thought of laughing with her about the consumptive tendencies of Aunt Daisy. Then it all seemed to be too much of a joke; too much of a hotchpotch; Ann was not used to the different phases of human nature, she might not understand. She had run in a rut. The workmen in the village at home, the ploughboy complex, and the perhaps a little snobbish, certainly a little narrow, influences of her father and Cuthbert. How could she understand that colourful tangle which had been Oliver's life? People as the poles apart, minds vividly contrasting. She couldn't. He did not dwell on his roving, nomadic childhood.

'Your mother was nice?' she asked.

'I never knew her.'

'Your father?'

'I never knew him either. Relations brought me up, I was shuttlecock to their battledores.'

She sympathized, for to Ann the stable certainty of home had meant a lot. Yet although she did not know it, it had extracted a great toll from her, she was only just beginning to escape its greedy demands on her.

Perhaps they were on the brink of confidences, perhaps they were standing on the edge of secrets, when they saw a car load of people disembarking outside the hotel. The lady who had so unfortunately lost her teeth at the very onset of the trip and who had lived on slops ever since. A young man in a blazer of such stripes that no respectable school would have flaunted, his arm round the waist of a young woman in flannel trousers. The Jewess lady with a new 'boy friend', old and solid in appearance, but unmistakably with cash. The Jewess always saw to that, else what was the good of the barber's shop? And oh my, how that man charged! Well, he ought to be ashamed of himself, really he ought, only there wasn't anywhere else to go. And if you didn't make these boys cough up when the going was good, they didn't cough up at all. They just hopped it, always a quarrel or something. It was downright aggravating. Really it was.

'If you have finished we might as well walk round the gardens in the palace,' he said.

'Oh, can we get inside?'

'Certainly we can, and it is rather beautiful. Different from the rest of the island.'

They went out together and in at a wide gateway. Her heart beat faster as they entered the gardens themselves, with their long walks, and their abundance of flowers. A peacock crossed their path, trailing a bronze tail after him, making ripples in the dust. The sun tipped the bronze into gold in places, and all the little feathers on his head shone and glistened. He crossed the path itself, and disappeared into some bushes, where great yellow globes of breadfruit hung.

'Oh look!' she exclaimed excitedly.

'Breadfruit.'

'Does it taste good?'

'No. It is really very dull.' He turned and smiled down at her. 'You're very childlike, aren't you? You've got all a kid's enthusiasms, at heart you are nothing but a kid really.' She laughed. It was nice to be thought like a child. For so long now she had been responsible, definitely responsible, reliable Mr. Robert would have called it, that it was a relief to find somebody thinking of her as just a child. She realized the attraction of Oliver, something that drew her to him. The whimsical mouth which smiled so much, the grey eyes full of dreams, the hair with the darts of silver in it, like the darts of gold that the sun had found in the peacock's tail and breast.

Spontaneously she cried, 'I'm glad that we met, and that we can go on being friends. It is rather lovely, isn't it?'

'It's grand. The best thing that ever happened to me.' Quite naturally he lifted her hand and placed it on his arm, and so guided her through the garden. There were white lilies like those which had blown in the Alameda; there were yellow flags standing stiffly in the stone fountain, against whose swordlike greenery and yellow weight of blossom the water dripped mechanically. There were avenues of trees, and under the grateful shadows they walked happily enough.

'But it is terribly hot,' she admitted. She had meant to buy a bathing dress in Naples, and then somehow she had forgotten. She had been carried away with Pompeii, and with the white city rising in tiers up the hill. She had

had that touch of the sun too, and that had made the difference.

He said, 'We ought to have brought bathing gear with us.'

'Yes, I'd have loved a bathe.'

And instantly she thought of Worthing, where she had bathed from the little huts that smelt of salt, and heat, and rubber caps. She had dried herself on brown and prickly towels, as lent by the Corporation (price twopence) and stamped all over W.U.D.C. just in case you might be tempted to keep them. All her bathing had been spoiled by her extreme modesty, and Cuthbert's very frank opinions about young women who bathed in dresses which disclosed that they were young women. She had had to be so dreadfully decent about everything, that her thoughts had become entirely indecent. She had been quite frightened that something might show – she did not quite know what – or that Cuthbert might have been shocked.

'Where do you bathe here?' she asked.

'Well, Tigné is where the smart people bathe. There are sunbrown competitions and that sort of thing, but really there are possibilities anywhere around the island. A steward told me that Cala Mistra was the place, and I went there last time. We can get a car and go there to-morrow.'

'But I haven't a bathing-dress.'

'I've got a couple. One is a bit open-work, but then there isn't anybody to see, so it won't matter.'

His 'free and easiness' attracted her. It made her feel at home; it made her feel that nothing mattered. She wished that life could go on like this. It was so smooth-running. Oliver accepted the whole bathing party as being settled, and at the moment she was incapable of argument. It was lovely and lazy in the heat, with the shadows falling between the oleanders, and the warm smell of lilies rising in waves. The very impossibility of bathing from any beach alone with a man, debarred it. She just took it as a piece of foolishness. She would not think of it. She preferred to walk, her arm linked pleasantly in his, listening to the conversation which was so completely natural that it enchanted her. To think that she had never dared to be natural before! To think that she had always had to pretend, and that what she really thought about things had had to be hidden behind what the world would like her to think about things! She did not ask more of life at the moment, and the morrow was not disturbing.

At last he said, 'We ought to be getting back,' and she turned quite reluctantly. The sunlight and the shadow of the sweet garden seemed to enfold them still. As she stepped into the car which was to bear her away she felt quite sad about it.

'It was so beautiful.'

'You have much more beauty lying ahead, though you may not know it. What about Venice?'

'Yes, I know. Venice must be heavenly.' And she lapsed again into silence in contemplative appreciation of Venice. They drove back through the Porte des Bombes. They had to slow down for a *carozzi*, ambling along in the middle of the road and refusing to make way for them. At last, with oaths and yells, the chauffeur managed to press them to their proper side. When they had passed, both Oliver and Ann turned to look at the sallow-faced Maltese who was driving; and as they did so, they saw the two strange occupants of the *carozzi* itself. Miss Bright was sitting there, very alert and upright, her enormous gold watch lightly drumming on her virginal breast. And by her side sat a monk in a brown habit.

***

III

It seemed impossible that a monk had 'picked up' Miss Bright, and had taken her for a drive. It seemed equally impossible for Miss Bright to have selected a monk, though the island teemed with them.

'You never know,' said Oliver, 'these old woman are like that. They never realize what they are getting at, and then yell for help when they find things are getting embarrassing.'

'But a *monk*?' persisted Ann.

'Monks are more willing than most, I imagine. We will rag her about it later.'

When the car drew level with the Custom House steps, Ann felt happily tired. *Carozzis* were tearing to and fro, for the *festa* was over. The penitents had performed their penance and were safely absolved, with the result that they could go to the devil again for a whole year quite happily and satisfactorily. The little boys who had dripped tallow up all Reale, had thereby insured a position in the heavenly spheres when their time should come. It was all extremely convenient. Bells were clashing, in the regardless, haphazard way of Maltese bells. A last firework spun up to the sky, and startled the *carozzi* horses grouped together around the Custom House steps.

Ann felt quite sleepy as the little *dghaisa* slipped across the water to the *Allando* lying at anchor. Ann climbed up the gangway.

'I think I'll lie down for a little while before dinner.'

'*Au revoir*, then, don't forget the bathe to-morrow.'

Yet she did not think of the bathe as she lay down on the slim bed in her cabin. She slept late. The heat had had a drugging effect; it steeped her, and when she awoke she was grateful for the first coolness of night coming through the open port. The little lights of

Senglea were peeping out one by one, and on the other side the nearer, greater lights of Valletta. There were ships in the harbour, and she saw their gangways lit by electric lights reflected below in the blueness of the water. It was like a fairy harbour, lit by magic. She dressed and went down to dine, but somehow her heart was not in the conversation of the table.

She could only answer Fergus's enquiries in monosyllables; she had no interest in the Spinkes' indignation at the food and the charges in the island, or the Duncans' complaints that they had thought there would be a lot of young Naval boys, which would have been so charming for dear Ethel. Only Monsieur Vallé was silent, and he had his very own reasons for being quiet, though at that moment he could not divulge them.

For Ann her own adventure had outgrown everything else in her life. Perhaps she was growing selfish (as Cuthbert had said), but she had no interest in outside matters. She had refused Oliver. She could not marry him; it would be positively indecent with Lilia so recently dead. Talk about undue haste! … She got quite hot when she thought about it. Yet she liked him. Yes, she quite liked him …

Something has happened to her, thought Fergus, and what? She is buying experience out of life's shop and getting it at bargain prices. Queer, that, for old merchantman Life generally does everybody down.

Ann made an excuse to go up into the lounge early.

She heard the band playing on B deck, but to-night she could not dance. She was too happy. She saw the A. P. with a girl she had noticed before, blonde, with a mouth red as a wound in the whiteness of her liberally powdered face. The A. P. was making the most of his opportunities. He was not one of the gentlemen who missed chances; he had had his eye on the large and flamboyant Jewess who was for ever being trotted down to the barber's shop to choose herself some little souvenir of an illicit passion. The A. P. had confided to a friend that he 'liked them large'. He had no patience with all this slimming. But he had decided that the lady in question was too expensive; she wanted presents, she wanted to be taken ashore; she liked big cars, and big diamonds, and was not solely satisfied with a manly passion.

'No bon,' said the A. P. reflectively.

You can't rise to that when you have a governor who won't shell out, and a godmother who, having sent welcome cheques during your schooldays on various birthdays, had suddenly gone dotty on retrenching, and only sent silk pocket handkerchiefs these hard times. And as to your pay … The A. P. had something to say about his pay. He called it a damned disgrace.

So he had selected the girl with the mouth like a red wound; she had told him that her name was Kinky, and he thought that was good enough! A girl called Kinky should be plain sailing, he promised himself.

As Ann went aft to where she could see Valletta closer, with its faintly pungent smell of fish market and hot Maltese, she passed several of the beret and blazer brigade just off to dance. But she wanted to be alone. She wanted to stand here and to listen to the tinkle of *carozzi* bells, and the far-away jangling of Maltese in argument. The rather harsh notes of church bells all clanging together, seeming paradoxically like some pagan paean to their deity. A new world, and a new self in that new world. She wanted to be alone with this strange self, in the new strange frock, in the new strange world.

'This is me,' she was saying, 'this is me, and I find that I am quite different from what I thought I was. I don't know myself a bit. I'll never be able to go back again. I shall never be like what I once was.' And it was true. It was dreadful truth, because she could not face the future.

Not the future that was London.

IV

At breakfast – everybody sat where they would at breakfast – Miss Bright, already dressed for the day and crowned by a serviceable little hat that she had brought to withstand the sun, assailed Ann. She had got to explain, she said. The monk had been no ordinary monk at all. Ann must not let herself run away with ideas. Miss Bright had gone ashore and had set herself to see the sights. She had gone to the Cathedral first and had been most delighted with the crypt. It appeared that she had a passion for the morbid. She doted on crypts. She had a complex about vaults. Her whistle well whetted, she had gone on to see the Chapel of Bones, which she found was closed. Some midshipman had made too merry therein, and had thrown skulls about, with the result that the agitated Maltese had in desperation been driven to close it. You could not have young men playing cricket with a dead monk's tibia, and the skull of some departed devout!

Miss Bright had been coming away most half-heartedly when she had met the monk. Getting into conversation – and how that was achieved she treated with a delightful vagueness – he had suggested that as she had unfortunately been unable to see the pleasant sight of the Chapel of Bones, she had better go to the convent where there were skeletons of monks, stood in the crypt, wearing the habits that they had worn in life. The gruesomeness of this had appealed to Miss Bright, and the monk who was a most useful person had offered to escort her. He had expressed the hope that a contribution to the Brotherhood would not come amiss, and reluctantly Miss Bright had been persuaded to part with half a crown.

They had driven out to Floriana in great style, the monk and the *carozzi* driver being on particularly amiable terms, it ultimately transpiring that they were brothers. This had surprised Miss Bright a great deal, for she had no idea how anyone so admittedly respectable as a monk could be related to anyone so villainous as a *carozzi* driver. But be that as it may, they eventually arrived at the convent, which was disappointingly plain in appearance.

Ann was wearying of the rigmarole. She wanted to get on with her breakfast, but Miss Bright would not let it go. She would be heard.

Further parley had been entered into and an English-looking verger had for further remuneration escorted them into the crypt. Miss Bright had been thrilled to the marrow, for not only had she seen the darkest, most gruesome and odorous crypt that she had ever dreamed of, but she had been shown one miserable skeleton of a monk, still draped in the tattered rags of his faded habit. Her appetite for the morbid had been fed to the full. She had actually parted with a still further remittance for the good of the cause, and this in spite of the fact that her people were all Plymouth Brethren and would have been horrified at good money going to the maintenance of popery. But she could not help that. Her lust for the morbid had been sopped. She had arrived back on board only deploring the ridiculous fiat that set the seal of celibacy on the priesthood. And when they had so much in common too! It would have been marvellous to go about with a man like that, seeing things, really interesting things, mummified remains, chapels of bones, sarcophagi, tombs and vaults.

To-day the monk had offered to show her other exciting incidents in Maltese religious life, and she was galloping down her breakfast in a hurry to be off. She had quite forgotten that she had wanted to go ashore with Ann, and that Ann had refused and had gone with Fergus.

'So you must excuse me if I run,' she said.

Ann finished her own meal, and then went up to the lounge, intending to write some letters. It was a glorious day, fine and warm. She saw where the deep trembling purple of the Judas trees ashore burned against the dazzling white of the city itself. She saw the sky rising from haze to deep impenetrable blue, looking as though it went up and up for miles. Space! She wondered vaguely what she, a mere atom in the universe of things, could mean in all this space. Or was she matterless? And if so what was anything but the moment? And did not the moment appear the most vital thing of all?

'Something I want and cannot have,' she thought. Then, looking up from the desk where the letter she had started lay, she saw Oliver.

'Come along for that bathe?'

'Oh, but I don't bathe.'

'Well, then, come and watch me bathe? There's a dress for you if you want it; you may change your mind,' and his grey eyes twinkled.

'I meant to write to Cuthbert.'

'He can wait. You'll have Cuthbert all your life, and Malta for only two days.'

What can you say to such an argument? And anyway she did not want to write to Cuthbert, not really. He was boring. He was dull. Prosy. Exasperating.

'All right,' she said.

V

Cala Mistra is a little bay that is so entirely away from the rest of Malta and so unlike it, that it might in itself be an unknown island lying ready for the exploration. It has fine gold sand, and there are convenient rocks set round it, with little nooks and crannies which can be used in lieu of bathing huts.

The car turned down a road, hot and dusty, across which a green fig tree sprawled indolently. Through the boughs they could see a blindfolded donkey turning a water-wheel.

Round and round it went, too foolish, too blind to stop. Ann could not help thinking, 'I was like that donkey, going round and round, and then something happened to me and I broke free. Now I have this, all this, and I am going to make the most of it.'

The moment. The precious influence of the moment. That was of vital importance now.

The car came to a standstill, and they were in the little bay itself. Oliver got out, and he lifted up a bundle of towels; she saw beneath it a basket. 'What's that?' she asked.

'I got the steward to cut me some sandwiches and things. I thought that we might have a picnic?'

'What fun!'

He gave her the towels and carried the basket, linking his arm in hers again. Somehow that way had become natural to them. She would not have had it different for the world.

The day had come up very hot indeed, and she was glad to reach the shadow of the rocks. What would her tweeds have been like now? she asked herself. And she was quite amused at the silly arguments she had used in London to do with being able to stand the heat, and it only being for a short while.

The sea was clear; it seemed to be a new sea expressive of the new self, for she could peer down to where along the fine sand lay trails of dark weed and starfish and shells.

'It is wonderful,' she said.

He spread the car rug along a rocky surface. 'Sit on this, you'll be comfier. Later you will find you will want to bathe. You'll want to be cool.'

In her heart she thought he was probably right, though Cala Mistra was quite different from Worthing. There were no huts; no pungent smells of rubber bathing caps, and of hot sand mingling with too hot humanity. The sun beat down, and the shadows were violet and claret colour from the rocks across the surface. In shape they were like felled cypresses, lying in long even lines. She hugged her knees and looked down at the small white shoes that Fifinelle had insisted on. The whole dress was juvenile and attractive, white, with the gay scarf she had bought in England fluttering lightly out. She had taken off her hat, and in the heat could feel her hair curling against her neck; it had curled like that when she was a child in the apple orchard at home, she remembered. The heat had always made it twine itself into little ringlets, and only the weight of it growing so long and abundant had changed that in the later years.

'These things are too hot. I'm getting into my bathing dress,' he said, 'you'll be all right here, won't you? There is some fruit in the basket if you feel thirsty.'

She sat there leaning back against the rock, with the bay stretched before her. It seemed that this had always been, and that the old life of South Kensington and of Henrietta Street had existed only in her imagination. It was so far away. She opened her bag to powder her nose, for Fifinelle had given her a small compact – *pour souvenir* – and now she touched her cheeks lightly with the rouge, and ran a red lipstick across her lips. The old life was dead. It did not matter any more. It never had mattered really.

She saw Oliver coming round the bend in his dark blue bathing-dress. He seemed tall and brown, and she noted the big muscles standing up on his arms in knots. He was quite unembarrassed by her presence and sat down beside her. 'Whew! That's better. Men do wear such fearfully unsuitable clothes.'

'They must be very hot.'

'They're deathly. I can't tell you the relief it is to get into this.' He lit a cigarette and then flung across a small blue bundle to her. 'Here is a spare dress for you if you want to bathe.'

'Oh, I couldn't.'

'Why not?'

'There isn't anywhere to undress,' she began in confusion.

'Heaps of rocks, and you need not worry about being disturbed, for nobody ever comes here.'

'It – it isn't that ...'

He looked up at her. 'What is it then? You say it is so hot, and the sea is delightful. Is it convention? Prudism? What is it?'

She tried to explain. 'We used to stay at Worthing ...'

'I understand. That alone says a lot. This isn't like Worthing! What is more it never will be like Worthing. Why not risk a bathe here?'

'You tell me if the water is cold.'

He slid down into the sea and in the clearness she could see his body elongated, and become strangely fish-like with sprawling legs and arms.

'Glorious,' he called to her.

She felt a fierce longing for the cleanness of that sea, and as the sun growing strong beat down upon the hot earth she felt the desire growing keener. Her body's need for coolness was fighting her own prudism. Oliver had swum out to an islet which the tide had left, and he was sitting there with the gulls screaming about him. She knew she could not stem the temptation to join him. She called, 'All right, I'm coming,' and disappeared with the blue bathing-dress behind the rocks.

Ann had never undressed in the open before. She had never felt the air touching her body as she lay her clothes down one by one; she had never felt the fierce joyous intimacy of it, the freedom, the precious heritage of that freedom. She slipped into the bathing-dress. She felt it cover her, far less of her than the dress that Cuthbert had insisted on at Worthing, but somehow here that did not matter. One could be natural, and it was wonderful to be natural. She was entirely primitive woman as she went across the rocks, and lowered herself into the water. Oliver still sat on the little island, slashing his feet in the sea.

She let herself slide down, feeling only the merest chill as the sea touched her body. It was far warmer than Worthing, she told herself. There, bathing on the crowded beaches, in the close intimacy of huts and tents and among the innumerable people, she had been so body-conscious. Here bathing was just what it should always have been, natural and beautiful.

It was, she felt, as though she had no body left. Her arms cut through the water, and as she swam she looked down and saw the weed again, and little rocks, and large shells. The bottom looked so close that she was quite surprised when she lowered her feet and found that she could not touch it. She swam out to the islet and laughed as she climbed up beside him. She was a child again. She was no longer Ann Clements, but the young unsophisticated girl Ann, who had never lived until now. They sat there with hunched knees, and feet dabbling in the water. They talked, and afterwards she could not remember what they had talked about.

Then they swam ashore side by side, and climbed up to the old niche in between the rocks for the picnic. And never once was Ann body-conscious. She was only aware of sitting there with a friend, a dear friend. They ate salmon sandwiches, and meringues, and apples.

'Glad you came?' he asked.

'Enormously glad.'

'I guessed you would be. Not like Worthing, eh?'

'Don't be annoying. Of course it is not like Worthing.'

'What is it like then?'

'The most wonderful day that has ever been,' she said, and she meant it.

After the meal he smoked a cigarette and then they bathed again. It had been hot in the shelter of the rocks, and the sea stung their bodies and received them with a stimulating chill.

'Time we were getting back,' he said as they swam ashore for the last time.

She dressed lazily, for the heat and the general tiredness of bathing had crept over her. She drew on her clothes over a skin sticky with salt. Finally there came out the little compact which she had got from Fifinelle. And as she powdered her nose, she thought with a certain horror that she had been here for hours entirely alone with a man, and almost naked. The complex of clothes had got her again. As she put them on she had donned with them much of her old self. The dreadful dogma of decency as drummed into her by her father and Cuthbert.

In the car returning she was very quiet. He thought it was the first bathe, which always makes you sleepy.

'Have a good lie down,' he advised her, and his hand closed possessively over hers.

If only they could have gone on and on, out there on the little island left by the tide in the centre of Cala Mistra. There she felt that they had been simple and natural people, like children, and now returning to civilization she felt that it had been all wrong, and was overcome with the horror of that extreme decency which had been her undoing all through her life.

'I have enjoyed myself so much,' she said as the *dghaisa* reached the gangway of the *Allando*.

'Something to remember?' he suggested.

'Of course,' but her heart said, 'It should be something that I ought to forget ...'

CHAPTER 7

I

The ship was under way again.

Ann was left with an impression vivid and lasting of the sun slipping behind the Citta Veccian hills; of clover fields ripely red, and small square houses, chimneyless and almost windowless; of the cedars in the gardens at San Antonio, leaning over the breadfruit and the oranges. But keenest of all was the impression of a new world and a new self, as she had slid down into that crystal clear water, as though into baptism.

It had been altogether wrong, she knew, but she had loved every moment of it. Afterwards she had been desperately ashamed. But now, with the island lying behind them, and Gozo a thin shadow along the horizon, she felt different about it.

Either everything in her life had been wrong, and this was the attitude she should have adopted all along; or everything in her life had been right, and she had now gone completely mad, and would have to pay for her folly. She was on the borderline hesitating between the two ideas.

She felt herself to be a traitor to Cuthbert, and to her father and to all the ethics of her childhood. She wanted to get a grasp of her real feelings. Only to get a real grasp on a pleasure cruise is difficult; there is too much diversion, too much dissipation, too much amusement.

As she went down to dine she met Miss Bright. 'You are the very person I wanted to see,' said Miss Bright.

Ann groaned inwardly. Really in so large a ship it was remarkable how you continually ran up against the people you wanted to avoid. And stranger still that in so short a trip there were already so many people whom you were wanting to avoid!

'I went to the central part of the island,' said Miss Bright, 'and it was all so strange, though I must confess a little disappointing.'

'I'm sorry.' Mentally Ann told herself, 'No crypts, and no skeletons! That must have spoilt it!'

'We saw people who live in caves, wild, savage sort of people, but unfortunately no open coffins. They must be a very healthy race, I think,' she sighed regretfully.

Ann had little patience with a woman who could scour an island looking for funerals, and less with the monk who had offered his escort.

'He did his best,' said Miss Bright, 'and in the end he asked me for a small donation for his convent. It is funny but I always thought that they had nuns in convents. I do hope that there was nothing promiscuous about him.'

'I don't suppose so.'

'Well, I gave him a little contribution and I trust it has been put to a good use. You never can be too sure, and we certainly never saw the things he said we were going to see.'

The companion-ways were full of people going down to dine. And now she would have to listen to the boastings of the Spinkses, and the complaints of the Duncans that Ethel had not had so good a time as they had anticipated, or that she had not been the centre of attraction in the island. It was odd how the table boasted, the Spinkses on financial matters, the Duncans on matters matrimonial. If the Frenchman had ever volunteered any conversation at all, Ann felt that his bragging would have been on matters digestible!

Each had seen the island from a different point of view. The Spinkses had gone from one hotel to another, and they had seen the silver gates in St. John's Cathedral and thought that one day they would have better silver gates to their own house. The Duncans had gone from lounge to lounge, and had finally met a woman who had taken them into the club in Strada Reale, where they had met some delightful men. 'Such dear Naval boys,' purred Mrs. Duncan soothingly. The Frenchman had discovered the confectioner's in Strada Lucia, and had come back with huge boxes of chocolates made in Turin, wrapped in silver foil, with curious mottoes in Italian included. The Frenchman, fortunately for him, understood Italian, and had a peculiar mind to which the mottoes appealed. He had spent a busy evening in his cabin, unwrapping a whole two pounds of chocolates in the hope that he would find something even more curious than the last.

Fergus had met a friend from the Leper hospital, and he had gone up there and they had discussed a new sort of leprosy which had recently occurred in Greece. Ann had seen the red fields of clover and the darkness of trees, and the lovely butterfly of the new self skimming between the two! She had baptised the new self in a clear sea, and now she wanted to be alone.

She wanted to think.

***

II

Ann curled into a *chaise-longue* in a corner of the deck. She could hear the band playing. She could watch from the distance, and somehow to-night she did not want to be part of the picture. She just wanted to look on. Through it all there pounded the great heart-beats of the ship's dynamos. She had discovered that when you sat there, almost in the centre, and the ship was moving at a certain speed, you could hear her pulse beating like that, almost like a human heart.

She could hear the slither of feet on the deck, and the tune that the band played, plaintive and yearning, and the ship pulsing. She watched the people passing. Most of them she knew by sight now, and some of them to speak to. They all interested her. The A. P. passed with his peroxide blonde, and to-night she wore blue, an unsophisticated blue, and very little underneath it. Even Ann could see that. The A. P. had eyed it hopefully. So far the lady had been stingy, he had confided to his friends, but he had high hopes. He thought things looked distinctly promising, and she really had very little on.

The beret and blazer brigade had changed into reach-me-down dinner suits, which had been highly recommended by a large London drapery establishment which makes a speciality of that sort of thing. Unfortunately the young gentlemen had not obtained that excellent cut and finish which the drapery establishment had boasted about; and be it said for the drapery establishment, it was entirely the fault of the young gentlemen. They were funny figures, and they wore funny underclothing, which did not fit too well. Each was fostering some romance. Even Ann recognized that in the quickened steps and the heightened colour. The Jewess of the barber's shop was leaning on the taffrail with an entirely new swain. She was an old habitué of cruising. She knew that by the end of the voyage she would have worked all the workable part of the ship. Her cruise would end at Tilbury. For many girls who were unsophisticated and inexperienced, the cruise would not end at Tilbury.

Fragments of the conversation drifted across to Ann. 'I never accept presents,' she was saying and he was protesting.

'But from me? It's different from me?'

'Well, perhaps from you …'

On and on steamed the ship with her great heart throbbing and the sea deeply blue lying calm on either side. Malta had drifted into a hyacinth haze of nothingness. Little scraps of conversation kept being blown to Ann.

Two old ladies. 'Yes, I love these foreign places but they play my corn up so.'

'I've got a wonderful cure for corns. It was recommended to me years ago, and I always travel with it. I wouldn't be without it for the world. You just paint the place!'

'Well, to be sure now!'

'If you care to come down to my cabin, I …' They went on along the deck, their voices died away. Malta in its dim blueness, the star-spangled night … and corns! She smiled a little to herself.

Two girls. 'Oh, but do you think he means it? He sent me a chit across. I'd love to think he was in earnest, it would be too marvellous to go back engaged, but you know what they say about sailors …'

'Oh, but that's just their fun. I expect he means marriage.'

'Oh, he said such things. He said it was simply hell that I'd got Betty in my cabin. *Do* you think that looks like marriage?'

Modern young things! Gay young people, bright

young people. Kaleidoscopic snatches from other lives. Two deck hands passing by, and standing to talk for a moment under the awning.

'It was that there choppy bit off Portugal got her. Told me she was a good sailor, she did, and then brings it all up on me nice clean deck. Just as we'd a-finished scrubbing down too … a fair mess …'

'Well, her 'usband has tried to borrow me number ones for the fancy dress.'

'Don't you lend 'em to 'im. I had enough of that last cruise. Borrowed me best whites and never brings 'em back, until I goes after 'em, and then I finds 'em a-smothered in green paint 'cos he'd got orf and was dancing with a young woman dressed as a Christmas tree. I didn't 'arf swear.'

They passed on and for a moment there was silence, and Ann heard someone coming across the deck, and felt a hand on her shoulder. 'Come and have a drink in the café?' It was Fergus.

'I don't drink.'

'Well, a soft one. Coffee or lemon squash?'

'Very well.'

III

The café was in light mood; it had gay chairs of vermilion-painted wicker-work. People were grouped about in twos and threes, but the majority were dancing. In the corners there was a good deal of coquetry. Fergus took a seat well in the open, his white mess-jacket gleaming against the red of the chair.

'Well?' he said. 'I suppose you did all the proper Maltese things? St. John's? Mnaidra? Tarxien Temples and St. Paul's Cave?'

She shook her head. 'None of them.'

'You didn't go touring then?'

'No.'

She had seen the car-loads as conscientiously arranged by Mr. Thomas Cook, who had a most flourishing office on board, doing a great trade. For the moderate sum of one pound ten and sixpence, so the schedule said, Mr. Thomas Cook was willing to show you pagan temples, the voice of the oracle, skeletons of primitive people, catacombs, village maidens as goatherds, 'geep' in their natural surroundings, and the actual islet where St. Paul was purported to have got himself wrecked some nineteen hundred years ago. Truly a mixed bag! It was a well-worded schedule, for while pagan temples and St. Paul appealed to old ladies, 'geep' and goats certainly appealed to old gentlemen with zoological turns of mind, and the village maidens as goatherds set all the young men's pulses throbbing with desire. Thus nobody should have been disappointed.

'I didn't go on any trips,' she said.

'I went to the Leper hospital.'

'But surely they don't have leprosy in Malta?'

'My dear, in all these places it has a certain sway. You saw the fair side of the treacherous little island, Judas trees and purple clover, palms in the Barracca.'

'I bathed.'

He nodded. 'You never saw the real Malta, fighting its dirt and disease, with its hopeless, helpless ignorance. Its conflict with a priesthood that holds it with a rule of iron, It always gives me a strange feeling to go from Malta to Venice; one is the antithesis of the other; Venice so cool, so dustless, so polished.'

'I expect I shall love it.'

But he was still thinking in a bitter mood of the island he had left. 'Malta is barren, it is full of death. In Venice there is no death.'

'You mean people don't die?'

'No, I mean death is quite separate. It has no part of

the Venetian outlook. I have never seen a trained nurse in the Square. I have never seen a funeral. There are no corpses in Venice, for they are carried away to a separate island. We never see those tombstones expressing their glorious lies for all the world to read.'

'You're very bitter.'

'The truth is always bitter. There are more lies written on tombstones than anywhere else in the world. "In affectionate memory of", "In loving memory of", "Gone but not forgotten", over some grave where the weeds are rank.'

'I never thought of it that way,' and suddenly he was disturbed by the pain in her eyes.

'I'm a pig to talk like this. I get fits, moods of it. You see, cruising has a penalty of its own. I get to look on life just as a patchwork quilt. I meet people, hundreds of people, different temperaments, all little matterless pieces of patchwork flung over me. That's all.'

A man in a paper cap chassé-ed into the café, his hands dug deeply into his trouser pockets. Three women, obviously lady friends of his, clad in a good deal of cheap lace, burst into loud and uncultured laughter. Ann wondered what had induced her to buy that lace dinner frock at Barker's. She had thought that it would be so useful, and now, since she had visited Fifinelle's, she knew that it could only be damning. And by the bye, lace frocks reminded her that she had told Fifinelle to refund the deposit money care of Bunt's, the agents in Venice. Not that she expected to see a farthing of it again, but she was still nursing a faint hope for the best.

'There's a bad piece of patchwork,' said Fergus, and he indicated the hilarious ladies and the dancing gentleman in the paper hat. 'Sometimes I wonder where these people get the money for cruising. One feels that they ought not to have it. It is all wrong that they should be allowed to behave as they do. To-day I saw an amazing sight. I saw a lady passenger kissing her cabin steward.'

'Heavens!'

'Sea-fever they call it. He wasn't enthusiastic. I don't think he could help it, poor chap, but she was all for it. It puts everybody in a most uncomfortable position.'

'Very,' Ann agreed.

The band had changed its tune to 'A life on the ocean wave' again. The dancing gentleman drew his dinner jacket together with a jerk, and produced from his pocket a marvellous pair of slightly soiled white kid gloves; 'Now then,' said he, and seizing one of the ladies violently about the waist chassé-ed out of the café.

'It's eleven.' Fergus's eye wandered to the clock set high up over the door. 'There's a buffet supper in the lounge, not that we stand an earthly chance of getting anywhere near it, but we can try if you are feeling that way disposed, and it might be amusing to watch …'

IV

The stewards had experienced no small difficulty in keeping the passengers off the buffet supper before eleven. It had been displayed with all the pride and glowing content of an ingenious chef, who had worked miracles in marzipan roses. Some of the less nervous passengers, having first enquired if it were free, had pressed close to the tables with their trails of smilax and marzipan roses, only to be wafted back by the stewards.

But now, the moment that six bells sounded – they had been long enough at sea to understand the intricacies of bells, though hardly as yet of twenty-four hour time, which was most confusing – they lurched like a tidal wave of humanity towards the exquisite display. It seemed for a moment that the tables would be rushed, and would be broken under the urge of all these pressing people, then they seemed to ease the strain.

Ultimately they drew back from the sorry spectacle of crushed smilax, greening the white cloths; of crumbs and soiled plates and glasses, of jelly smears and froth of cream, and nothing else! Just nothing at all.

'They've snaffled the whole show,' said Fergus. 'I thought as much.'

Ann laughed.

'I should think the chef is heartbroken having his marzipan roses treated like that,' she said.

'They say that we kill a chef every cruise. Half his heart is buried at sea, and half is taken back to his home town,' said Fergus.

And now suddenly Ann beheld Oliver dancing in a Paul Jones with a dreadful-looking young woman who had a Spanish complex and wore a poppy-red gown, and a shawl she had bought in Gibraltar. Oliver was laughing. He was light-hearted, and nothing worried him too much. He had had such an upbringing that none of these people came amiss. Why should they? Dear Grandma and Auntie Miggs and good old Uncle Alfred had all been much like this; only they had called complexes notions, and temperaments tempers! That was the subtle difference of the years.

He was frolicking with the girl who thought she looked Spanish, and laughing about her shawl. Everything was going splendidly. Fergus saw Ann's glance.

'Rather a nice sort of chap,' he said; 'somebody said his wife died the other day, but that can't be true or he wouldn't be dancing.'

She lowered her eyes.

Then she was not the only one to think such conduct peculiar. 'I am afraid it *is* true,' she said.

Fergus quickly recovered himself. 'Oh well, he probably knows what he is doing. I never believe in interfering with other people's affairs. Do you?'

All the same when she went down to her cabin it rankled.

All the while the great heart of the ship beat on, as they steamed northwards for the city of romance.

V

Some time at sea …

Ann did not know how long, for when at sea the hours seemed to gain a strange matterless magic of their own. They were not the same as when you were on shore; they did not have the same meaning as when the clock chimed the time. It all went in the mystery of bells. Beef tea; the excitement of the tote; siesta; deck quoits and tennis; sunbathing and swimming.

For some the day at sea entailed cocktails in cabins, and rather noisy parties, but Ann had yet to taste her first cocktail. It is true that one of the blazer brigade who slept on her deck had greeted her with the twanging of a banjo, which they had bought cheaply in Mercanti in Valletta, and coming through the pale gold and white door curtain, had called, 'Say, honey, what about a little sing-song?' Then seeing her face he had changed the twanging to 'Ain't it grand to be blooming well dead?' Otherwise nothing had happened. She lolled on deck and she watched people, and sometimes Oliver came and talked to her, and sometimes Fergus.

'Have you seen the man who is wedded to his bowler?' asked Oliver. 'A bowler is a positive disease with some people; he wears it on deck, and if anything ever looked out of place in this world it is to be in the Mediterranean wearing a little city suit and a little bowler 'at.'

'I haven't seen him.'

'It is amazing what the North is responsible for. When

I come on a trip like this, I feel a devout gratitude to the Almighty that I was not born in Manchester.'

He noticed her quietness. 'Why don't you talk? Have I offended you? We were such good friends at Cala Mistra?'

'It's Lilia.'

'But we talked all that out, and we decided that my attitude was the proper one.'

'Only –'

'Only like all women you use the female prerogative of changing your mind. Do you know that I could talk you round again if I wanted to? I could make you see sense, and agree with me again, only I don't see why I should do it.'

'You are being horrid,' she flared.

'I'm being human. Either I'm nice to know or I am not nice to know. That is the point for you to decide.'

'I wish you wouldn't put it like that.'

'It's brutal but it's true. Truth can hurt more than anything else in the world, I suppose; that is why so many of us shy at it. You like me, you know, Ann …'

'I never said you might call me that.'

'Didn't you? Well, I'm taking it for granted. Upbringing has a lot to answer for, hasn't it? Supposing you tell me why I am *tabu*? Supposing you tell me about your early life? For that is what is standing between us.'

'There is nothing to tell.'

'Isn't there? What was your dog's name?'

She turned to him with shining eyes, and somehow she forgot the sea, lying pale blue and shining, and the heart-throb of the ship. She was seeing again the isolated outlook from the rectory at Wadfield, across the fields, red loam, and pastureland of green. She was seeing old Rogan frisking on the half circle of gravel before the front door. She was hearing his bark of welcome. Funny that a dog's name can recall so much. She found herself telling Oliver about it, that and a great deal more. The futility and stagnation of life there among the cottages. Agriculture all around her; wide fields, red and bare in the winter, the long red furrows turned up by the plough; gold and waist-high with corn in harvest-time. A lovely land, and yet not altogether lovely because it had cheated her of her friends and of opportunity, and of her very youth.

She was not fully aware of all that she told him, sitting here beside him on deck; with the enchantment that distance lends, it all became fairer; but he, who was essentially a man of the world, read in between the phrases. He saw the seal of loneliness set upon the place. He understood.

'Tell me about your life too,' she suggested, but his was so different, such a jumble, such a chaotic confusion, that he did not think he could tell her; anyway not yet.

'Some day,' he said, 'I will tell you everything.'

That was his last promise before their arrival at Venice.

VI

It was early morning when they steamed into St. Mark's basin, and dropped anchor in the venerable shadow of the Doge's palace. Ann stood on deck as they approached it. It seemed that Venice swam out to her, like a dream city that had miraculously come true. It was so much lovelier than she had believed possible. It was blue and grey against blue and grey canals. She saw the tall Campanile reaching to the sky, the gold and glittering confusion which was St. Mark's, the white round breast of Santa Maria della Salute.

Nearer and nearer it came, and already, as they slowly steamed to their anchorage, gondolas moved to and fro.

She had expected them to be colourful, she had not thought that they would be all black, and that there would be something almost funereal about them. She was disappointed in that, but she liked the movement of the gondoliers as they bent over their oars. She liked the white gleaming of the city rapidly coming closer.

Venice is a magnet that has attracted many. She had always longed to see it since the days when she sat and stared at the rather gaudily coloured picture of one of the canals which had hung in the rectory schoolroom.

'Let me come ashore with you,' said Oliver.

She shook her head. 'Would you mind? I don't want to seem awfully ungrateful, but I do want to go alone. It is going to be such a marvellous experience. Try to understand.'

And being Oliver, he did understand, though he would have liked to watch her reaction to the loveliness of the 'Queen of the Adriatic'.

Ann felt the heat of the day, for, although she had heard that Venice was cool, it struck her as being hotter than anywhere she had been yet. She changed into a cool pink linen frock which she had thought much too young for her before. Now she did not care how young it was, as long as it was cool. It had no sleeves and ended at the neck with little soft frills. She looked very childlike as she glanced into the mirror above the save-all. She wondered, could anybody having missed youth ever find it again? Could they go back and recapture the lost tenderness? It almost seemed that she had done this.

She went on deck, and the pink linen fluttered a little in the light wind. She tied the slim sash – the colour of delphiniums – about her waist.

'How do I get ashore?' she asked the officer of the watch.

'You take a gondola. We aren't running boats here.'

As she went down the gangway (she would never get

used to that rope banister) she thought like a child, 'I'm going in a gondola, I'm going in a gondola', and she saw one lying there low in the water, waiting for her.

It was one of those precious moments, one of those thrills, just like the time when she had bought her first bicycle, saved from the birthday monies of years, and had wobbled so perilously up the green lane at home. Only this was a greater thrill; it would be the greatest thrill of all, she felt.

She said timorously to the gondolier, 'You speak English?' and the master-at-arms helping her into the boat said encouragingly:

'Oh, they all speak English, miss; you'll be all right.'

She felt that it was hardly Cuthbert's idea of being all right. She lay among the black velvet cushions, in a very comfortable abandonment. She looked at the little heap of notes and silver that the purser had given her in exchange for her good English money. She wished Venice had been like Gib. or Malta in that, for the exchange did complicate matters. It was far easier when you had not got to be continually counting up the lire or the francs.

The gondola came alongside the steps of the Riva degli Schiavoni; it had all been too quick, and she had wanted to prolong it; she had not wanted to be done with it, but the precious moment had passed. She paid what the man asked, and now she saw the Square ahead.

The sun was not fully high as yet, and she was standing between the glittering radiance of St. Mark's, and the Campanile very plain and prudish in contrast. Somehow she had never thought of the Cathedral as being in colour. She had not supposed that before it the great horses would prance. She stood quite still staring at it in wonderment. It seemed that her spirit was drenched in that loveliness which is eternal, age-old Venice. Opposite her the great clock beat out an hour. She watched the huge male figure swing round to wield the hammer, and then when she had drunk in her fill, she walked through the arcade which covers three sides of the square.

It was very hot.

In the shops – and she had never seen such shops before – only the most perfect treasures were displayed. Glass from Murano, in delicate shades of green and heliotrope, and an unbelievable blue. Small bronze statues. Leather-work embossed in colours, much like the precious mosaics of St. Mark's itself.

From Florian's came the tinkle of music, and somewhere in the distance a boy was singing. It was the song of Venice which goes on for ever.

A tombola was evidently in progress, for part of the square was marked off and numbered, and here, in the very middle, the pigeons flew and clustered together, with no fear of the people who walked among them.

Ann wandered with no definite idea of where she was going. She went round and round the square, aimlessly, because for the moment the sheer beauty of the place was making her drunk. She could not settle down to see any individual object while she was so bewildered by them all. She did not want to see any one item, but only to soak herself in the confusion of everything. Round and round she went.

VII

Ann drank some iced coffee, sitting at a small table outside Florian's. After that she became better able to take a grasp of things. She told herself that she would go over St. Mark's first, and then up the Campanile, after that she would visit the clock. Yes, that was the best order in which to arrange them.

She paid for the coffee.

It was all remarkably easy seeing that they spoke English fluently, and were so polite. She began to walk in leisurely fashion towards the Cathedral itself. She went round the cloisters first, inspecting them carefully. The ceiling was all in the same shimmering mosaic that even the passage of time had not tarnished. Into the gold were inlaid biblical pictures of a style that would probably have confirmed Cuthbert's qualms about popery. Ann felt her neck stiffening as she walked along, her head flung back to see it all. It was almost as bad as that time at home when she had tried to whitewash the spare-room ceiling.

She noticed the be-plumed and very much armed gentleman who paraded up and down. Italy obviously believed in swords and pistols for the men; she thought of them in contrast to our sextons and churchwardens, and they were equipped as for the battlefield rather than for the precincts of such a peaceful cathedral.

Probably there was something to pay. Ann approached a large Fascist who stood by the notice-board and she indicated a well-thumbed purse. The Fascist glanced at her with contempt, and in his turn indicated the notice on the board which was translated into different languages. Ann, finding her mother tongue three paragraphs down, read and grew hot with shame. It seemed that His Holiness the Pope had noticed the immodest dress of women in holy church. He deplored this laxity of morals, and to teach that it could not be, he had issued a solemn proclamation that no woman with uncovered arms or neck should be admitted to the churches.

The Fascist watched her, and pointed to her arms nicely browning, as they protruded in their offending nakedness from the pink linen frock! She turned away scarlet.

After all there was a good deal in what Cuthbert had

said, although she had been silly, and had believed him to be wrong. Popery was wicked. The Pope was a silly old man who put himself in the place of God, which was extremely shocking.

She blundered into the vivid sunshine of the square, and even that hurt. To think that she – Ann Clements – should be accused of immodesty! To think …

She did not know that she wanted to see the clock or the Campanile now.

As she stood there, both bewildered and distressed, she saw the office of Mr. Alfred Bunt. It brought her mind back to more mundane matters. The money from Fifinelle should have arrived. It would be exceedingly gratifying to feel that comfortable thousand francs safely in her pocket. That would be at least some small consolation for the humiliation of the morning. She went across and entered the office.

There were a good many people in it, and whilst she awaited her turn she amused herself with looking at the posters hung about. It seemed extraordinary that even in one of the most beautiful cities of the world Tourist Agents should remain undefeated. They had yet more beautiful places to offer – the Dolomites, 'rosy crags piercing a blue sky'; ruined Luxor; the road to Nikko, ablaze with azaleas. She read the wording mechanically – Wagons-Lits – Service – Courtesy – Travel by Land, Sea or Air.

Finally her turn came. Haltingly she made her enquiry. The clerk shook his head. There was no letter for her. She left the office unconsoled.

It was the last straw.

CHAPTER 8

I

Ann went back to the ship.

There was something very C. of E. about the ship, and she felt that she needed it. Never had she been so insulted. Never had she felt so bitterly humiliated, so hurt. For the first time she was really glad to seek the sanctuary of the lounge. It seemed delightfully English, very much like home.

In her cabin, she sat down to debate upon it. Venice, surely the loveliest city of them all, and she would never forget the first wild thrill of it, never, never. Then this to happen! Just as though she had touched the apex of a high hill and then had been dropped with a thud into the valley below. It was dreadful.

It was some time before she could bring herself to venture forth again, more modestly attired in a white frock with a scarf. She was divided between a wild desire to spite the Pope and not to go inside St. Mark's at all, and an innate longing to see everything. She decided that it was hardly worth while spiting the Pope, who would never know of it, since in doing so she would spite herself so very much more. So she marched inside.

The Fascist took no notice of her.

He was engaged in a passionate conversation with an Italian harlot, of whom Ann was quite convinced that the Pope would not have approved. It was absurd making ridiculous laws about frocks in such a hot climate, and then allowing your very beadles to carry on liaisons on the steps of holy church! She felt that if only she had been able to write Italian, she would have sent an expostulatory letter to His Holiness. But Ann did not know Italian, and she very soon forgot her effrontery in the exquisite beauty of St. Mark's interior.

In the dimness of those soft shadows which prevailed, she saw ahead the glittering retable of the high altar, with all its mass of blazing jewels. A guide, who had obviously been taught English – which is rather a different matter from speaking it – detailed a long category of information. She listened, but her attention wandered. His knowledge seemed to be purely numerical. The number of arches, the twenty-five hundred jewels, dates in a string. And who wants numerology in St. Mark's? Who wants dates?

She went above into the galleries, stumbling amongst the beams and the loose flooring, and seeing St. Mark's itself below, strangely out of perspective, grown curiously unreal seen from the height. The galleries are in a state of dirt and dust and unfinishedness. The surging crowds of trippers and excursionists stumble and blaspheme, and laugh and make love, and below in the haze there is the supernatural vision of the church like something of another world.

She went out on to the balcony, where the great horses lift their great bronze feet, and she was almost blinded by the hot sunshine. And here again in contrast she was looking down into the square of St. Mark's, most queerly alive after the jewels gleaming in the darkness within, which were so strangely dead.

The clock hammered out the hours above the commercial confusion of the street beneath it, and it reminded her that life goes on. Life, a very real, a very clamorous life.

She climbed down again and went out into the square, and after the humid darkness of the Cathedral the hot sun was over-radiant. She walked on to the Luna where people were lunching in the street, with the canal lying beyond in the green gloom of shadowy water. She took a gondola.

'Take me where you will,' she said to the man, for now she did not care. All must be beautiful.

'*Si, signorina.*'

They went down the Grand Canal, and she saw the Ca d'or, with its pillars of gold, and the Rialto with its wooden superstructure jutting across the canal itself. They came to the little alleyways which turn off into those lesser canals, all the more beautiful for their quietude and their superb leisure.

The greens and blues and purples that suddenly formed in the water fascinated her. The silent houses for ever keeping guard over their secrets; the dark lace of old wrought-iron gates, and here or there the sudden vivid glimpse of geraniums burning like a fire, or of azaleas rose-red and honey-gold, clustering along some old stone wall. Drifts of song came to her, snatches of it, the eternal song which is the heart of Venice.

'*Ponte di sospiri,*' said the gondolier at last, and he indicated it ahead.

She had expected that it would be the culminating joy, but there was something quite modern about it, disappointingly plain. The Bridge of Sighs holds no hint of tragedy; it keeps no savage secrets locked in its cold stone bosom. In name only does it retain its hold. The gondola slipped under it and Ann hardly knew when she had passed it. On one side the carved and lovely grandeur of the Doge's palace, and on the other the barred and brutal windows of the Doge's dungeons. Such a step from the splendour and the panoply of kingship, from basking in the favour of a court, to the darkness of that prison where so many suffered. Only the Bridge of Sighs between!

They came back to the ship.

'To-night?' said the gondolier enquiringly. 'The Serenata?'

She hardly knew what he meant. 'I shall not be going ashore to-night,' she said.

He lifted his dark face, with eyes that reminded her of the young men who discourse sweet music in Lyons' restaurants, where on affluent days she had sometimes had lunch.

'To-morrow I take you to glassworks?' he faltered. 'Murano?'

'We sail at five,' she said.

He clung to the gangway. 'I come at three? Murano very interest. Very rare. Special of Venice.'

She thought of the iridescent bubbles of blown glass which she had seen in the shops, of the vases rising, tapering and perfect.

'Yes, I'd like to see it,' she said.

He bowed. 'I come for you, *signorina*,' he told her.

II

Ann was sorry afterwards that she had not said that she would go to the Serenata, but she had not had any idea what it was at the time. It was Oliver who told her.

She had grown tired of walking about Venice, for the passengers from the cruise were pouring through the place. The Spinkses were buying expensive souvenirs. The blazer and beret community were taking snapshots in the square. The Duncans had dropped into the Danielli, in the hope of finding an Italian count or two. Everywhere you went you ran into fellow passengers, generally in fierce argument, or hilarious, rather common laughter. It made things very difficult.

Ann had loved gliding along the canals in the gondola; that had been so peaceful, something entirely alienated from life as she had experienced it before. She watched the day dying, the soft amber and rose of the sky behind della Salute, and the little ripples of St. Mark's basin each tinged with amber and rose too.

She watched the gondolas becoming soft shadows upon the water, and heavier boats, with lanterns swinging above them, towed out to the centre of the lagoon. She watched them curiously, wondering what they could be. They were the Serenata.

Later, when the west had been dyed to a tender primrose, and had merged with the ultimate grape-bloom hue of the night, the first strains of music came across the water to her. All the shadowy forms of gondolas turned their curving prows towards the centre of the song. She saw the great round balls of lanterns, citron and orange, flame red and ice blue, reflected dimly in the water beneath. She heard the songs that they sang, Pagliacci, Carmen, Bohème …

She turned from the ship's side, and saw Oliver just come up from dinner, and about to go down the gangway.

'You will come to the Serenata with me?'

She had meant to say no. In her own heart she had decided that although Cala Mistra had been lovely, it had been a little indecent. It could not happen again. Decorum, the death of Lilia, and the fact that Oliver was Oliver and Ann was Ann, forbade it. Nice people did not do that sort of thing. And now here she was, in spite of all her good resolutions, actually running down to her cabin for her coat, and all in a hurry to go out with him to the Serenata. She did not even stop to think twice.

They were in a gondola together.

She had thought the canals perfect by day, and had not realized how much more perfect they were by night. Cuthbert would have been horrified at the intimacy of the gondola in which you lay side by side, yet here nobody seemed to mind. Just at first Ann tried to keep to her own side, but Oliver's hand closed over hers, and after a while nothing mattered. There was the mystery of the music.

They drew nearer to the boats in which the performers were seated, with the gay balloons of light and the water lapping a little against their sides. It was more like a scene on the stage than real life, with the Grand Canal straggling behind in blue and grey and purple, and the wavy outline of the hotels from Danielli to Regina, and the firm round breast of della Salute opposite.

The gondolier moved his boat alongside the others and sat down in an attitude of patient attention. He adored the music. He committed none of the English outrages; he did not whistle or beat time, but sat there in a huddle, and every little while Ann could see the glint of his eyes on the singers, and hear his admiring intake of breath, and his '*Ah, si, si, brava*'.

She felt that she had never heard music, real music, before. She would never hear it again. And now she let her body lie closer to Oliver's. She was glad that he held her hand. For Venice demands love. Venice is love. Once she thought that he turned and kissed her hair, for she felt his lips quivering close. She felt his breath on her cheek, but she could not be sure. He teased her a little.

'What if I touched your lips?'

And quickly she replied, 'Oh, please don't.' The old terrified Ann!

'My sweet, I would not harm you.' And the atmosphere of the place confused her so that she almost believed that his kisses would be lovely, and she wished that he would overcome the recurring modesty of the old Ann.

Enchantment of the moment! She did not know how many times the bronze man hammered out the hour in the square. She did not know how often the weather-beaten sailor clanged his bell on board the *Allando*. What was more she did not care now. She was half asleep, when quietly they slipped away into the light mist which lay above the water of the lagoon. In the dim confusion of sleepiness and mist and music and enchantment, she felt Oliver's lips upon her forehead.

III

Ann awoke in a panic next day. What had happened? She must be entirely crazy. She must be mad. She had made up her mind not to go out with Oliver again, and on the instant she had gone. First of all she had allowed him to pick her up in the park (crude, but entirely true); then they had visited Pompeii; they had gone ashore in Malta and had bathed together. Now this! She took herself very sharply. She must be extremely firm about it, because after all, although on a cruise anything might seem to be possible, it was not quite so possible when you returned to everyday life.

She had got to maintain her self-respect. And now, as she dressed in the little cabin, with the open port disclosing a blue and glittering lagoon without, she felt all hot and cold at the memory of the previous night. She reiterated that she must have been quite mad. She decided that there was something curious about foreign places, which affected you in that way. For instance, you could not do that sort of thing in a level-headed country, in such district as Golders Green or Clapham or Chingford. There people behaved nicely and properly and did not find atmosphere taking hold of them and making them behave oddly. There was no Serenata in Kensington, for instance; if you wanted music you went to the Albert Hall, and the Albert Hall did not supply you with a cushioned gondola, in nature peculiarly like a bed, and your escort did not kiss you.

Worthing supplied you with the most excellent bathing (as the prospectus obtainable on application to the Town Clerk informed you), but it was not quite the same bathing as at Cala Mistra. Abroad, so Ann's father had once told her, things happen. She thought, 'They most certainly do happen.'

Yet that morning everything was serene. There was an excursion from the Riva degli Schiavoni, organized by the painstaking Mr. Thomas Cook; it was an excursion through the picture galleries and the less famous but by no means less interesting churches (this according to the book of the words). Ann loved pictures, but she did not feel that she could possibly go round the galleries in a herd. Miss Bright was going of course. The Spinkses had employed what other people called a guide, but what they were pleased to term a 'courier'. The Duncans had given up the last shred of pretence. They were now frankly man-hunting. The count whom they had met at the tea-dance at the Danielli but yesterday had escorted Ethel to the Serenata, and there had proved himself to be no gentleman! They were trying the Luna to-day, lunch in the street, and they felt that anything might happen.

'Remember that we sail at five,' said Fergus warningly to Ann; 'it would be ghastly if you got left behind.'

Ann watched the gondolas as they passed to and fro,

and she went by steamer to the Lido. It was one of those places that she felt she ought to see, if only because it would shock Cuthbert so immoderately, and now she had grown reckless. She wanted to shock Cuthbert. He did not believe that any woman returned *intacta* from the Lido, and there possibly he was more or less correct. All the same Ann found it dull. It was modern, as against the age of the city of romance. But the magnolias were in flower, and the essence of verbena came to her in every little breath. There were trees too, and after the days at sea, and Venice itself, trees looked strange and almost out of place. She thought, 'How quickly you change your outlook! Fancy being surprised at the sheer beauty of a tree!' She thought of the song, and marvelled at the truth of it – 'But only God can make a tree.'

Even at the Lido she could not be entirely free of the ship. There were a few daring souls who had not fallen in with Mr. Cook's efforts to fatigue them for ten-and-sixpence a head, but who had come to the Lido to flirt. She heard them laughing before she got to them. 'Well, anyway,' she told herself, 'they won't get as far as Murano.' That was some consolation.

IV

The gondolier arrived to time.

Ann lay back on the black velvet cushions. By now gondolas meant no more to her than mere taxicabs; they were more comfortable, they ran more smoothly, that was all. She drowsed as the gondola went forward across the rippleless blue. The rhythmic dipping of the oar, the lapping of the water against the prow, and the lazy heat all soothed her. She closed her eyes. She had recovered from her shocking recollection of last night now, and she was feeling that she had only got to be firm with herself. That was the main thing. Oliver must be brought to understand that matters had gone quite far enough; they could not possibly go any further. She was glad that so far she had not suffered the embarrassment of meeting him to-day. It would be easier when the ship was on its way to Ragusa, and all this atmosphere of romance was left behind.

She blamed the atmosphere a great deal, and herself a great deal more. Her father had always told her that no man overstepped the limits of friendship without some encouragement, however small. Therefore she honestly believed that she was to blame. She was going to be strong-minded about it, she told herself.

She must have slept for some little while, for she awoke with a jerk to find that the gondola had ceased its steady progress forward, and was just floating along in the lagoon. She was not at all sure of its direction. The gondolier was sitting in the stern mopping a somewhat heated brow.

'It 'ot,' he told her frankly.

'It's very hot. Are we near Murano?'

He shrugged his shoulders indifferently. 'Murano very long way,' he said, making no effort to get on with his work.

Ann, becoming less sleepy, sat up and took notice. 'The ship is sailing at five,' she said. The gondolier received this piece of information with a complete lack of interest. 'But you don't seem to understand. We've got to get to Murano and back.'

He said 'I understand,' and then, arriving at the urgent matter nearest to his heart, ''ow much you pay?'

'How much is it?' she asked.

The gondolier named a sum that even Ann knew to be preposterous. 'Oh, but that's absurd,' she said. 'I certainly should not pay all that.'

He shrugged his shoulders again, as though it were a matter of no consequence. It was a very helpless feeling, for here they were drifting about the lagoon, miles from anywhere; she had no idea where they were, there seemed to be islands all about them, and far away, in the direction where she would least have expected it, the faint, almost indiscernible Campanile.

'Very well then,' said Ann, 'we won't go to Murano. We will go back to the ship.'

The gondolier looked his indifference. 'Ship-a long way,' he commented.

All interest in blown glass bubbles had left Ann. She glanced at her wrist-watch, only to find that in the disturbance of last night she had forgotten to wind it up. She felt a rather cruel fear gnawing at her heart. 'We *must* get back,' she said.

Again the unruffled demand, ''Ow much you pay?'

She began to capitulate. 'What is the fare?'

The gondolier once more made one of his staggering announcements.

'But I should never think of paying anything of the sort,' she said. This disturbed her a great deal more than the gondolier, who only settled himself the more comfortably as though prepared to stay the night. She was now getting thoroughly nervous. Anything was better than missing the *Allando*, anything in this world, and anyway she could argue when she got back and refuse to pay, and the purser and the officer of the watch would come to her assistance.

'We will go back at once, please,' she said. The gondolier stared blankly into Space. '*At once*,' said Ann.

Slowly the dark eyes of the young man turned lazily towards her. He had experienced that sort of thing before, and he knew that once alongside she would solicit the aid of officials. 'Pay now,' he demanded.

'But this is infamous,' exclaimed Ann, 'you know it is abominable. You know you have no right to ask it. I won't pay.'

Again he stared absorbedly into space. Ann had a horrid suspicion that she might have been asleep longer than she had originally supposed. The shadows were growing long under the islands; the sun did not seem to be very high in the heavens. Real terror came to her. 'What is the time?' she asked.

Slowly, with an elaborate languor, the gondolier drew out of his sash a large brass watch. He consulted it carefully and then made an announcement in Italian.

'I don't understand,' she cried wretchedly.

He made no attempt to help her. His English had now deserted him, but what did that matter? He was used to dealing with people from cruises, was Antonio. The great secret was never to hurry. He tucked the watch back into his sash. Suddenly Ann, driven to the point of desperation, called to him:

'I'll pay. I'll have to pay. I've just *got* to get back to the ship.'

She brought the bundle of notes out of the small bead bag and began to count them. She was on the verge of tears as she pushed them across towards him. He began to count them with unflurried care; he was not to be disturbed.

'Oh, hurry, hurry!' she begged.

But the gondolier was not going to be hastened. When he had finished counting them, he tucked them into his sash, securing them safely. Then he rose and began to ply his oar. The distance did not seem to diminish. Ann thought that she would never manage to get back in time at this rate. Every little while Antonio would pause to mop his brow, and to complain that it was very 'ot. All her sympathies had gone from her. She now did not care whether he was hot, or whether he was cold. Anyway he was a Venetian and he ought to be accustomed to the climate. The sun was falling behind the islands. She said, 'You can go quicker than this, and you *must*,' and she beat an impatient tattoo with her fingers on the side of the gondola.

'You not pay much,' he complained.

'You can't demand more?' He rested to mop his forehead again; it appeared perfectly certain that he could demand more. 'It must be getting late, very late, and we shall miss the boat,' she panicked.

He echoed her worst fears. '*Si*. We missa the boat. Not much time now.'

It was terror that gripped Ann's throat. Her fingers shook as she drew out a slender stock of lire and held them out to him. 'Take them, only hurry. For goodness' sake be quick. I've got to catch the boat at any cost.'

He tucked the notes away and turned to his oar. Now she knew that he had been doing this on purpose, for the gondola skimmed along. They twisted in and out of the little islands, and she saw the dome and spires of Venice coming nearer. They entered the lagoon itself past St. George's island, and as they did so she saw a great ship moving out to sea. She screamed. The gondolier with true Italian helplessness threw up his hands to heaven in an unavailing gesture of despair.

It was no use.

The ship had sailed.

PART THREE

CHAPTER 1

I

Ann found herself landed on the steps of St. Mark's with night falling and no luggage, no home, no friends. She felt the choky feeling at her throat that she had not felt since she was a child. She believed that if anyone sympathized with her, she would cry. Her first idea was to go to the emporium of Mr. Alfred Bunt, in the hope – an extremely forlorn one – that after all Fifinelle had played the game and had sent the deposit money. She wondered how soon it would be before they discovered on board that she was missing, whether she could possibly go on by train and rejoin them at Ragusa. She was very vague about her geography, and she had no money.

She went into Bunt's, her heart throbbing right up into her very throat itself. Yes, there was a letter for her. The pimply clerk pushed it towards her through the bars which fenced him in behind the counter.

241

She opened it, and the franc notes which were enclosed fell out into her lap. Madame could not think how the mistake had occurred. It had made her most *malheureuse*, and she humbly craved forgiveness. It was all most distressing and she did hope that Mademoiselle had not been put to any inconvenience. Mademoiselle, stranded in Venice, was now looking upon the mistake as entirely heaven-sent. She folded the letter up.

She approached the pimply clerk again, who was quite indifferent to her quandary and enquiries, but said that he would fetch Mr. Harding. Now Mr. Harding was more senior, and he was used to predicaments, more particularly women in predicaments. He had been with Bunt's in Rome and in Naples and now in Venice, and he was very well accustomed to ladies who got themselves left behind, ladies who had missed their trains, ladies who had lost their luggage, and ladies who were in need of financial assistance.

Ragusa, he said, was out of the question, and it would be a most unpleasant journey for a lady to make alone if there had been the time, and there wasn't. The ship would have sailed again before she got there. She could of course cable to Mr. Robert for some more of her money to see her home by train, or she could apply at the British Consulate for aid.

She said that she would go to the Consulate. Mr. Harding thereupon pulled out an enormous watch with a fob attached to it, and said that he thought there would not be much time. Why not let him make arrangements for her for the night at a perfectly respectable and moderately priced hotel, and go to the Consulate in the morning? By then, he went on to say, there might be some message from the ship, as her disappearance would most certainly have been noticed.

This did seem to be the better arrangement, and eventually Ann found herself walking across the square with Mr. Harding, who had become most exceedingly conversational. He thought Ann was a nice-looking young woman. 'Young woman' was the actual term that he used. He did not know why he should hurry, whereas Ann for her part was both distressed and embarrassed.

It was providential that Fifinelle had returned the money, otherwise she would have been stranded with a small matter of eighty lire between her and starvation. It was an additional mercy that she had her passport in her bag, and that Mr. Robert had been so particular about that passport, although the line had said that it was unnecessary for cruising. Now she felt how utterly right Mr. Robert had been. There is a deal of comfort in a straightforward British passport tucked into your bag.

Matters were better than they might have been, though that was a small comfort. Mr. Harding was telling her about his own life, all of which seemed to be a little confusing. Much had happened in his twenty-eight years. Oh, the things he had seen and done too, well, you wouldn't believe it! He twiddled a small ginger moustache, and rolled pale blue eyes to heaven.

Ann interrupted. 'I'll have to go home overland, I suppose?'

'That you will.'

'Shall I be able to start at once?' Her voice quavered a little. What an end to a cruise! What ignominy! What humiliation! 'I suppose there isn't a chance of the *Allando* coming back for me?'

'None whatever,' he snapped.

He had been going to tell her about life in Golders Green, where he had been born. He was proud of Golders Green, it was the sort of suburb you could talk about, nothing inferior like Clapham or Camden Town or that sort of place. Not that he was a snob. He wasn't. But he liked talking, and since he had come to Venice he had not found anyone willing to listen. They were not interested in Golders Green. They were full of Venice, which wasn't much of a place really; old, he admitted, oh yes, old enough, crumbling in fact. And now after all it did not seem that Ann was really sympathetic. Funny how occupied people were with themselves. Very selfish, he thought, most inconsiderate.

As they crossed the square, she said, 'I haven't much money and it mustn't be anywhere expensive.'

'I wasn't taking you anywhere too grand. This place is moderate. It is the sort of place a lady can stay at. You see, this isn't like home, you can't go just anywhere.'

'I suppose not.'

She had an uneasy longing for the cabin on board, which had become home to her. She had a homesick cleaving to her steward; she would have given a lot to see Miss Brown coming towards her now, or even those dreadful Duncans, or the Spinkses, in fact anybody who was even remotely connected with the ship.

Mr. Harding was escorting her through the strangest little back alleys. 'Having no streets makes it seem a funny sort of place,' he said. 'I've never thought much of it myself, a jumble of old buildings, nothing up to date, and I don't believe the canals are sanitary, they smell dreadful in the summer.'

'Oh, but the atmosphere,' said Ann.

'That doesn't impress me much. A good place for a honeymoon, I suppose?' He gave her a quick glance.

Mr. Harding had been living a strictly chaste life ever since he arrived in Venice, and for a moment he was wondering whether the misadventure of the *Allando* might not have provided him with the opportunity for which he had been longing. She was pretty enough, in a shy sort of way, a bit prim perhaps, and all alone too. Ann did not take the hint for the simple reason that she never saw it.

She said, 'It must be a marvellous place for a

honeymoon, and the Serenata too.'

Secretly Mr. Harding did not think too much of the Serenata. A bit gloomy, he thought. He liked the Victoria Palace, you could get a good laugh out of the Victoria Palace, especially when somebody really good like Nellie Wallace was there, and you'd come away feeling all the better for it. The Serenata had never affected him in that way. Still, he thought that if this was her line, he had better play up to it.

'What about going to the Serenata to-night?' he enquired. 'I've got nothing on after the office closes. There is precious little for me to do in Venice. It isn't like Golders Green, you know.'

'No, of course it isn't.'

They turned down a thin alley with high houses shutting it in on either side. She began to feel a little frightened.

'Are you sure this is right?' she asked nervously.

'Yes, of course,' and he pointed ahead to the hotel entrance, where the Grand Canal lay gleaming in the twilight, with the hotel door on the left of it, lit by a blaze of electric light. It seemed so funny that none of these places had got proper front doors. Why, even the Luna had to be approached in a tiny passageway, nothing like as wide as those which she sometimes used as a short cut from St. Martin's Lane through to Leicester Square. She saw the hotel.

'Oh yes,' she agreed, and felt rather embarrassed at having doubted his intentions. A little while ago she would never even have thought of such a thing; it was the cruise. Cuthbert had been quite right. People who went cruising got affected by cruising, they were never quite the same again. Not quite.

They went in at the door, and she saw the enquiry office, and a lounge full of people which opened on to the canal itself. Mr. Harding approached the office, and entered into a long and entirely incomprehensible conversation with a gentleman in blue uniform with many brass buttons displayed on his large chest. The upshot of the conversation, which was accompanied by gestures which at one time Ann had thought were threatening, appeared to be entirely satisfactory.

'I've fixed it up,' said Mr. Harding, 'a small room, but you said that you wanted it done cheap; I'll call for you at nine, and we will have a spot of music and make the arrangements for going to see the Consul in the morning.'

Ann felt very grateful and she wanted to express her gratitude, but here words failed her.

'Oh well, so long for the present,' said Mr. Harding airily, and he went away.

Solemnly Ann was escorted to her room by the lift boy.

II

Ann did not like Mr. Harding. In fact she knew that she quite actively disliked him, but because he was the only person whom she knew in Venice, she clung to him desperately. Without him she would be lost. He had been very kind and he had fixed her up for the night. It was perhaps unkind not to like him.

She had no luggage; she had not even got a nightdress, and to Ann there was something almost disgusting in not having a nightdress. She tidied her hair as best she could, washed her hands – really, she would have to buy some soap, and a sponge and a toothbrush – yet she could not bring herself to go inside these queer foreign shops. What should she do?

It seemed so dreadful to be robbed of everything one possessed, save just the jumbled contents of one small handbag. If only she could have guessed at the freakish whim of fate this morning, and have sent some of her things ashore! If …! The immediate need was very urgent.

She opened her room door and tried to find her way downstairs. She went cautiously, for Ann was extremely suspicious of foreign hotels. She could believe anything of them.

On the second floor she ran into a middle-aged woman who was coming out of her bedroom.

'*Oh*, I'm so sorry,' said the middle-aged woman brightly. Instantly they recognized each other as being English. They started to talk. They went down together.

In the light, Ann could see that her new friend was tall and *svelte*, that she was amazingly well preserved. Although her hair was a lightish grey, she had the supple figure of a girl, and the tender apple-blossom complexion. Her eyes, brown and appealing, were not surrounded by wrinkles. It was a young face.

'You are staying here alone?' she asked Ann. 'Or have you got your husband with you?'

'Oh no. I'm not married. I'm part of a cruise that has gone on without me.'

'You don't mean they have left you behind?'

'I do mean that,' said Ann simply; 'it's dreadful, but it is true. I haven't even got as much as a toothbrush, and I want to go out and buy one, only I daren't.'

'Nonsense. I'll come with you. There is a chemist at the top of the alley. Come along, he may be shut after dinner.'

'It's awfully good of you …'

'Heavens no, you'd do the same for me.'

As they went to the shop they chatted. The new friend was an artist and she gave the name of Eva Temple. She had been staying in Venice to paint it, and she was going on to stay at a little inn she knew of in the Dolomites the next evening. Ann in return gave her the briefest description of herself. A typist. A very ordinary typist who had never been abroad before, and now this had happened to her.

'I always think everything happens for the best,' said Mrs. Temple. 'I even said that when my husband ran away from me with a little chit of nineteen …'

'But how can this be for the best? What about my luggage?'

'Oh, they'll be sure to send that home for you.'

Ann could have wept. 'You don't understand; it isn't that sort of luggage. None of them could be any possible use to me at home. They are the things that I bought in Marseilles. Things that are not really me.' Then she choked back the words. After all, why should she start telling a stranger about all this? The thing was done; nobody else would understand.

The shopping was far easier than she had expected, for the chemist spoke the most excellent English, far more perfectly than Ann did herself, and was most willing to oblige. A sponge, toothbrush and paste, soap, and a small wooden-backed hairbrush were bought. It meant parting with more of the precious lire, but she could not help it. These things were necessary. Eva Temple suggested a nightdress, and they crossed to quite a humble little *lingerie* shop. It was not of the kind that flourish in Venice, but something far simpler; for all that it seemed to Ann that the plain nightdress cost more than it would have done in England. The little wad of notes was depleting too rapidly to be assuring. She must not spend a penny more than was actually necessary, she reminded herself, and she returned in a most subdued frame of mind.

'But it was good of you to take me,' she told Mrs. Temple. 'We might perhaps dine together? I am sure that the waiter will put you at my table if I ask him.'

'Yes, let's.'

Ann ran upstairs to put her purchases away, and then returned to the dining-room. She felt nervous. The waiters were obsequious; on the small tables were golden baskets of fruit, the small black Italian grapes, oranges, mandarinos, the wizened-up apples that are so prevalent abroad. In the centre of the room hung an enormous chandelier, glittering with lights. It was an alien setting, and again Ann felt a yearning for the ship. She was glad for the friendship of Eva Temple, for the shelter of her presence and for being able to sit at her table. She noticed her new friend more closely. Perhaps Eva's eyes read more deeply into hearts than most people's. Her nostrils were finely cut. Her mouth was sensitive and whimsical. Gradually, bit by bit, Eva won Ann's story from her. She had decided on that from the first, for Eva made it her business to learn from other people. They interested her, until she had pecked the flesh from their bones, figuratively speaking; then, when they represented nothing more than an empty husk to her, she lost her attention.

Ann told her of the early days. South Kensington, Balham, Balham, South Kensington, with occasional interspersings of Henrietta Street. In return Eva told her a little of her own life, a life so strangely different that it read like a book. Eva had been born with the nomadic soul; she could not rest long in one place; she was a wanderer, she for ever pitched her tent from place to place. She picked the world bare, as she picked people's minds bare, and then she left it. Somewhere in Cheyne Walk she had a little studio, that was if it hadn't been already pulled down, for the place had been condemned for years. It was a little studio overlooking the river, pearl in summer, pale blue in spring, blue and grey and unutterably lovely in autumn and winter. She had had pictures in the Academy, and in the Salon. She had had what the world may call success, but it had not satisfied her. For the heart of Eva Temple was the heart of all creative genius; it does not want what the world can give it. Her manna was of heaven.

She had married, and they had not got on. He had not understood her; he was a rich stockbroker, she said, and he had the Stock Exchange mind. That conveyed nothing to Ann. Then he had gone off with a mere chit of a child, and perhaps the proud soul of Eva had been hurt, bruised a little. She had not wanted him herself, but she certainly had not wanted somebody else to have him. And a child too. Well, she had told herself at the time, they would never get on. Herbert wasn't that sort. Herbert liked comfort. He liked home well kept, and a lovely wife. He had got neither.

'It didn't worry me,' she lied to Ann. 'I don't suppose I ever gave him a second thought. The divorce went through and that was that. I don't know even if he has married her.'

But that was a lie too. She had taken good care to know. She had been staying outside Rome at the time, when the spring was turning the hills to pink with almond blossom. The Apennines were hazy with blue veils drawn about them. The news had come to her in an English paper, nearly a week old, brought up to her bedroom by a frowsty-looking chamber-man. There had been a picture of Herbert leaving the registry office, and a ridiculous caption; the girl had looked very young, and very childish, and Herbert had looked smug. She had noted with an evil appreciation that his coat was beginning to fit tightly at the waist – too tightly – he'd have to watch that!

There had been a few bad days, when she had not cared what she did. In the hotel they had shrugged their shoulders, for nothing suited the Signora. Then she had buried her love. She did not care. She told everybody she did not care, and now she was almost beginning to believe the lie herself.

Ann listened to it all. She felt herself growing more and more the new self. She was actually talking to a woman who had employed divorce to free herself of an irksome husband. That in itself was polluting. But somehow now she could not think of it polluting quite so much.

After dinner they went on to the veranda, and sat there on the very edge of the canal drinking their coffee. The lights from the Serenata were reflected in mid-stream on the water, rippled in places. It was all very quiet, very enchanting. It seemed as though time stood still for them, the future did not matter so much.

'In the morning,' said Eva, 'I will come with you to see the Consul. He is a personal friend of mine, and I am sure he will do something to help you.'

'You're very good.' Then her voice faltered.

'Why, what's the matter?'

'Don't you see I don't *want* to go home? I don't *want* to go back to South Kensington and the toil of Henrietta Street. I don't want to be my old self again.'

Eva eyed her. She was interesting. On the spur of the moment she said, 'Then why on earth don't you come on with me to the Dolomites for a while?'

'Because I'm stranded. I've got practically nothing in the world save a brand new toothbrush and a sponge. I've got a few lire, just the few that beast of a gondolier left me, and the money that Fifinelle returned. That's all.'

'But the *Allando* won't keep your things. They can't. We will cable on to them in the morning to return them. They'll send them to my inn. It's cheap there, and you could stay months for practically nothing. Has the purser got your money?'

'Some of it. I left a deposit with him.'

'Was it much?'

'It seemed a terrible lot to me. I don't suppose you'd call it much. There must be at least thirty pounds there.''

'They shall cable it from Ragusa.'

The spirit of adventure suddenly seized Ann in deadly earnest and she turned to Mrs. Temple. 'But where are you going, and could I really come? I'd wire home for the rest of my money to be sent out to me. I put a hundred and twenty-five aside to be invested for my old age ...'

Eva laughed. 'You *would*! My dear, old age never comes. Who was it wrote "Yesterday is dead, forget it! To-morrow is not here, forgo it! Now is the time that matters"?'

Just what the old woman in the Alameda had said, only differently. Ann felt that she would do anything to postpone going back to the ineffable boredom and monotony of life. One hundred and twenty-five pounds invested would bring in a very modest six pounds a year if she were lucky, and she wasn't usually lucky over things. She could claim six pounds a year's worth of fun from it, and cram it all into the next few months. She was not due home for another fortnight. Perhaps Mr. Robert would understand, and take her back in the autumn, any time ahead, only not now ... she could not go back now ...

She saw Venice rising out of the night, a lovely frail cluster of flowers, her domes and colonnades like lilies, white and shadowy against the haze of the canal. From the boats anchored in the middle of the lagoon there came the first quiver of the music. It was Pagliacci.

A much-buttoned pageboy brought her a card on a brass tray.

'Mr. Harding is waiting in a gondola, signorina,' he said.

***

III

They were rowed across the canal.

Now the spirit of all mysterious adventure took shape. It might be very different from last night, when Oliver had been with her, less tender, less provocative, and she had to admit that deep down in her heart she had certain qualms about Mr. Harding with his little ginger moustache and pale blue eyes, and his best Golders Green style. There was something about him that was not entirely inducive of being at your ease. For all this it was adventure, and as such Ann loved it.

'I always think the music is a bit slow,' said Mr. Harding. 'I'm keen on jazz myself. Something that has a little pep in it.'

Ann, trying to enter into the spirit of the thing to oblige, suggested 'Auf Wiedersehen'. It was a melody linked up with the memories of the ship; the dancing on B deck. Taffrail conversations. Drifting in a haze. Sea-fever.

'No, I think that is a bit too slow. Too dreamy. I like a tune with some go in it. There isn't any go in what they are singing now.'

It was the love song of the passionate Neapolitan at his lady's window. 'But it's delicious,' she said.

The gondolier attached their boat to the long trail of gondolas beside the one which contained the Serenata. She could not help comparing the difference between this and the London theatres. Here late-comers made no hustle, no confusion, no noise. Gondolas glided into position, with only the ceaseless ripple on the water, so slight, so evasive that it might have been but the gentle breathing of the lagoon itself. But then Venice will not be hustled. Even an invasion of Americans had failed to bustle the city of romance. It was still a ghost town, reflected in the blueness of its waters; it was still a phantom that time did not touch.

While one of the men was singing, Ann was aware that Mr. Harding was watching her very carefully. She turned abruptly to him, vaguely uncomfortable.

'Well,' she said, 'what is it?'

'I was thinking how good it was to be out with an English girl again after all these dago misses.'

Girl! He thought her a girl! Prudish though she might be, it brought a pleasant thrill to her heart, a new warmth to her lips and cheeks. 'It's nice of you, Mr. Harding,' she said.

'Rot! It's nice of you to come out with me, and please don't call me Mr. Harding; my name is Cyril.'

She could think of nothing to say, save, 'Is it?'

'Yes, what's yours?'

She did not want to tell him, yet she could not think of a reasonable excuse for refusing. She said as coldly as she could, 'It's Ann, but very few people call me that,' and she added the last as a sop to her reserve, for it was quite untrue that she had been called anything but Ann.

'Well, what do they call you? A nickname, eh?'

She said, 'I'm not prepared to tell you that,' which he immediately accepted as being encouraging.

'Oh, go along! Very well then, I'll guess it.'

He settled himself more comfortably in the gondola, prepared for a thoroughly jolly little flirtation. And she had not looked to be that sort either! But then you never could tell. Girls were so deceptive, and some of them so deep.

'Well, what letter does it begin with? A, B, C, D?'

It was too late for Ann to extricate herself from the tangle. Somewhat horrified at her deception, she still dare not be honest and say, 'I haven't a nickname at all. I only said that to prevent you calling me by my real one.' So there was nothing for it but to persist, 'I shan't tell you.'

'Oh, come along, yes you will. I'll make you. You see if I don't.'

A lady in the next gondola who was fond of music turned her head at the loudness of his voice, and muttered a warning 'Hsh.' Then everybody else said 'Hsh.'

'We're getting unpopular … what a crowd!' said he, and he gave directions to the disappointed gondolier. The gondola slid out into the canal itself. 'Where we can talk without all this shushing,' he explained.

IV

Blue. Blue like love-in-a-mist and delicate hyacinths. Blue like river fog and water. It enfolded her. It drew them both to its heart. She felt his hand closing over hers, as Oliver's had done last night, though not in quite the same manner. Oliver's hand had been tender and sympathetic, something she sought not to escape, but rather to encourage. Cyril Harding's was crudely amorous.

'Come on, be a sport. Tell me?'

She was playing up to the rules of the game of flirtation; she was in her ignorance playing the game as it should be played. The little secret that he must discover; intimate, revealing, yet modest.

'Please,' said Ann with what dignity she could summon, 'let go of my hand. I shall not tell you. I certainly shall not tell you. Besides, what possible interest could it be to you what my people call me?'

But he could not believe that she was snubbing him. It was all part of it, trying to put him off. Well, he wasn't going to be put off as easily as all that. 'Of course it is of interest to me,' he averred, 'you must know that. You can't get away with it like that, you know you can't.'

Ann hadn't known that she couldn't, but she knew

now. His arm crept round her, and it was the first time that any man's had done that, in flirtation. It was a grim irony of fate that it should be Cyril Harding's arm!

'It's no good being stingy,' said he; 'we are two English people alone here together and you must know how I feel about you.'

His lips touched her cheek. Cold horror mixed with a strange and thrilling fascination tore Ann two ways. The horror won.

'You hateful little bounder,' she said.

She turned to the gondolier, who was lazily plying his oar and singing softly to himself in that tender crooning voice all gondoliers seem to possess. She knew that he had seen the kiss, and had heard her rebuff. Both were the same to him. He took life philosophically. He took love philosophically, for was this not the city of love?

'Back to the hotel!' she ordered.

'*Si, signorina.*'

Cyril Harding looked at her indignantly. 'Well, I do call that a bit hard. You encourage me. You do all you know how to lead me on, and then you let fly like that. Back to the hotel, indeed! What did you come out with me for?'

'Not for that.'

'Well, what the devil did you expect? You knew that I fell for you.'

'I didn't,' she declared, a little wildly. She thought that he must have been drinking. How dreadful to be out here in beautiful Venice, in the middle of the lagoon, with an amorous young man who had been drinking.

'A pretty girl like yourself,' said he hotly, 'why you ought to be ashamed.'

The words fell as seeds on fertile soil. She had started the cruise as a woman, a woman nearing middle age, who had had nothing out of life, and less out of love, and who expected nothing. She had been awakened vividly in the Alameda by an old hag who had warned her to take what she could. She had taken what she could. And now she had become a pretty girl who tempted strange young men to kiss her. Whatever you might say, the change was a gratifying one to your vanity. She was going on to the Dolomites. She would never go back. Never. Never. She would take every penny she had got, plunge it all, invest it in the capital of happy memories, and what was more she didn't care. Why should she care? She had become a pretty girl.

'I am going back to my hotel at once,' she said.

'I say, don't be silly. Come and have some supper at the Luna and don't make a fuss.'

'I certainly shall make a fuss, and anyway I've had my supper.'

He picked her up for that. 'You've had dinner, not supper. Supper is yet to come. This is going to be awkward to-morrow, isn't it?'

'Not at all. I've decided that I don't want the Consul to see me home. I'm not going home.'

'Well, I'm damned.' He thought instantly, 'She's picked up with some bloke at the hotel, and found a game worth two of that, the little devil!' But aloud he repeated, 'Well, I *am* damned.'

'You said that before, ' Ann reminded him.

'Yes, and I'll say it again. You're a deep one, you are,' and he chuckled. 'Only what about the hotel? They only took you in because I saw to it. Who's going to foot that bill?'

'I'm cabling to the *Allando*, and the purser will send me my money. Also I'm cabling home.'

'That's what I told you to do, and you turned up your nose at the idea.' She loathed him for reminding her of it. The gondolier was not hurrying, why should he? The night was yet young, he had had some experience of lovers, they would probably make it up in a moment or two, and then keep him out until dawn. As they passed the Serenata, Cyril Harding said, 'I wonder who the lucky fellow is?'

'Lucky fellow?'

'Well, somebody has made you change your mind.'

She went hot and cold that he should think that of her. She said with some dignity, 'Nothing of the sort. I met a woman friend,' and was hurt when he laughed.

Once again he put out a hand and took hers. Ann felt that perhaps she had been rude, and she did not withdraw it, whereupon the ardent Cyril immediately interpreted her acquiescence as encouragement. His lips came closer.

'A bit stingy with your favours, eh?' he said, 'and me a lone Englishman trying to do my best to entertain a lone English girl.'

Girl again! She was entranced at the idea, but aloud she said, 'I'm sorry if I seem to be unkind, Mr. Harding, but I don't think I'm your sort. I'm not used to this style of thing. I'm very old-fashioned,' and she left him with that on the steps of the hotel.

He ordered the gondola to take him home, and he looked apprehensively at the gondolier, who must have heard every word. But the gondolier was quite philosophical about it, quite used to the ways of women, and of love, and of rebuffs. That was that, he told himself. Cyril Harding lit a cigarette and cocked a weather eye towards the supple figure bending over the oar as they turned from the Grand Canal's blue and grey into the green gloom of the canals which run to the heart of the city. 'Women,' he said, 'are rum creatures.'

The gondolier looked down at him passively. '*Le donne*,' he philosophized, '*sono sempre diavole*.'

'You're right, old cock!' said Cyril in English.

CHAPTER 2

I

Ann slept amazingly well, and she had a confused jumble of dreams in which two men kissed her, Oliver Banks and Cyril Harding, and she liked it. She was quite ashamed when she awoke.

She went down to breakfast and found this proceeding quite wrong, because first of all nobody fed first thing save in their bedrooms, and secondly there was not any breakfast. The dining-room was in a state of chaos; chairs were set in preposterous positions on the table-tops, their legs raised in protest to the ceiling. Shell flowers and artificial carnations were being dusted with feather brushes, flicked indolently by waiters who were in the process of much animated conversation. They gazed at her in dismay. No, she could not possibly breakfast here. They indicated the veranda, perhaps in a state of a little less undress, though displaying a large number of inverted wicker chairs and legs. What did the *signorina* desire? Some coffee? The *signorina* was desiring a good deal more than coffee. Bacon and egg, or fish. Something solid, for she was intensely hungry. The waiter protested to heaven! Only the continental breakfast, or perhaps they could procure a boiled egg. There had been some boiled eggs once, some time ago, he would see! Ann hastily disposed of the idea of the egg. She would have coffee and whatever went with coffee, and she would eat it in a corner of the veranda without being a nuisance to anybody. After a long delay a tray arrived. The pungency of the hot coffee made her feel hungrier than ever, and she tried a crisp roll. But the crisp roll was most deceptive. The crispness flaked away, and revealed a dismally hollow inside. Just when Ann was feeling very hollow inside too! She could have wept. Having regard to the outraged virtue on the waiter's face, she did not like to ask for a second roll, therefore she ate all she could and left a large accumulation of crumbs. Eventually Eva Temple arrived.

'Oh, but you poor dear,' said Eva; 'the thing is to get them to send it up to you, and then clash the bell for more. I always do.'

'You needn't worry, I'm not so hungry as all that. I want to get the money fixed up.'

'First of all,' said Eva, 'you must wireless to the ship. They had better send your luggage and the money to the inn.'

'And where is this inn?' asked Ann.

For the first time her interest had become keen. An inn in the Dolomites. She thought of the fascination she had felt that evening when she and Miss Thomas had gone to *White Horse Inn*, and now she was going to something very much like it. Ecstasy.

'It isn't very far from Merano, in a fir forest. It is adorable. Are you sure that you want to come?'

'Quite, quite sure.'

'I shall be painting; you'll be left entirely to yourself. There'll be hardly anybody else there.'

'I don't care.'

Eva helped her to word the Marconi to the ship. She also helped send the message to Mr. Robert that he was to wire the money immediately. It took a very short time; Ann had had no idea that it would be so simple.

'And now,' said Eva, with the whole day before them, 'we will go and see the Consul, just in case there is any delay over the money: we have got to catch that train.'

Last night Ann had felt confident and assured, but now she felt a little afraid of the Consul. She thought he would probably be a superior sort of policeman. To-day she saw that her linen frock was creased. She felt both dishevelled and untidy and she had nothing into which she could change.

'What shall I do?' she asked Eva.

'They'll press the frock for you at the hotel, you'll find. The moment the money comes I'd buy a neat travelling suit to last until the luggage arrives. Give your present frock to the chambermaid and tell her to be quick.'

So that when she arrived at the Consulate she was at least tidy, and that gave her an additional confidence. The moment she was inside she knew that she need have had no fears. Eva Temple and the Consul knew each other very well; they had been brought up in adjacent villages in the epoch when neighbours were really neighbourly. They had remained friends, meeting at odd intervals in strange parts of the world. Seeing the Consul resulted in a lunch at the Luna, a pleasant and quite happy affair, with the sunshine splashing goldly on to the square. The Consul himself was a mild old man, quiet and reserved, and most enraged at the infamy of the gondolier who had been responsible for Ann's being left here stranded. He felt that Ann should have taken his number, but she had never thought of gondolas as being taxicabs, which in truth they were, whereas in London (if she had ever taken a taxi, which was most unlikely) she would have had no compunction in reporting such perfidy to the police. Here in Venice she had not even thought of such a thing. And now she wasn't sure that it mattered. Life had taken on a new twist. She was amazed at the adventure of it; it was alluring.

They spent the afternoon in the picture galleries, which Eva was determined that Ann should see. They were almost too beautiful; you could not absorb so much loveliness all at once, and she came away confused.

That evening Mr. Robert sent the money. Ann had not realized how relieved she would be, until she felt the crinkle of the notes in her hand. She thought that she would cry.

'We'll catch the eleven o'clock in the morning for Verona,' said Eva Temple.

'I feel as though we might meet the Two Gentlemen!'

'Possibly! One each!'

Ann went round to Bunt's just before it closed, for she felt that she must explain to Cyril Harding that everything had been arranged satisfactorily, and that he need not worry any more on her behalf. Little did she know that he was not worrying. The pimply clerk consulted an inner office, where Cyril, upon hearing who it was, said, 'Good God! Get rid of her,' and grabbed at a seedy-looking panama. The clerk came back with the news that Cyril was engaged in a most important business consultation, and perhaps she could leave a message or could call again. He suggested the calling again as an after-thought, and without much enthusiasm, for in truth he did not want her to call again, and then have all the bother of getting rid of her for a second time.

Ann left a message. She was impressed by the fact

that Cyril was in an important business consultation, and she left word that she had fixed things up satisfactorily and that she would be leaving for Verona in the morning. The pimply clerk eyed her with a grin. He had half an idea that she might be leaving for Verona with Cyril, who also was taking a holiday to-morrow. Ann regarded him coldly; she had of course got no idea as to what he was thinking. If she had had she would have collapsed.

She walked out into the square again. There remained only the purchase of the suit.

II

Ann bought herself a light flannel suit at a little shop that Eva had recommended. In spite of its severe lines, there was something schoolgirlish about it, something that fitted closely to the hips, which were still as slender as when she had been in her teens, and which gave her the hallmark of youth. She carried it home herself. Well, she supposed that the *Allando* would be sending on her luggage from Ragusa, but at the moment she possessed only two garments in the world, the tailor-made and the linen frock, and while they washed the underclothes she would have to stay in bed. A stale old joke, she thought with a wry face, but in her case it was coming true, and she failed to appreciate the humour of it.

They were ready to start for the Dolomites in the morning; to start on the new adventure which should always be the best adventure of all.

'But,' she told Eva, 'I'll be sorry to leave Venice.'

Eva nodded. 'You'll come back, for people always return to Venice, it has that curious quality about it. I've been back again and again, and have always discovered something new about it, something I have failed to see before. Venice is like a woman in a new frock; she changes every time.'

'I wonder if I'll come back?' She wrapped her few small belongings in a sheet of rather brittle brown paper which the hotel had scornfully provided. 'It looks very feeble,' she explained, 'but it will save a lot of trouble with the Customs if we want to cross frontiers.'

Again there was that odd thrill within her. Customs. Frontiers. Going across Europe overland. In the boat it had all been lazy and quiet; it demanded no effort to live. Now suddenly life was demanding quite a big effort, a very real but very thrilling one.

'I'm ready,' she said.

They went to the station in the gondola, cutting through the little canals, and coming out by the Rialto. Ann felt sorry in case this really was farewell, in case the old spell did not hold good and she did not return to this city of enchantment. Cupolas and spires faded into the blue mist which held them for ever; it seemed to her as though a giant forest of michaelmas daisies rose between her and the city, and blotted it out. They were the blue and heliotrope daisies of fantasy. It seemed that the new and unreal Ann was setting out on a voyage. Opposite her, Eva, whom she had only known a few hours, and yet knew so much better than people she had known for years. Yet journeys are like that; they make the impossible suddenly possible. They make fiction become fact. They make dreams come true.

Behind them a blue island, which had started the whole adventure, and now the actual adventure itself, and anything possible.

She looked out eagerly on either side, and somehow she wished that Oliver was with her, for he would have enjoyed it so much. The vines straggling along the hedges, their leaves yellowing in places already, the first little bunches of hard green fruit forming and lying against the earth. The rice fields. The ground lying in long furrows, and the line of hills beyond. It was most disappointingly English. Ann had hoped that Italy spread out before her would be something different, something as remote from England and the English scenery that she knew and loved, as she herself now was. But it was much as England; much more so than Malta had been with its rectangular houses and its ripe clover fields. She had unfortunately come to that part of Italy with the sombre fields that lie in the north-east, dull, and devoid of the brighter colourings, in some ways reminiscent of the Shires.

It changed at Verona.

They ate their lunch in the station, a typical lunch of tough chicken, and wide rolls between which were sandwiched large unappetizing slabs of meat. They drank Chianti in its straw-plaited bottles, and all the while the dismal disturbance of station life went on around them. A hot porter conversed in a noisy offensive with an even hotter *confrère*. Two peasants were having a pleasant little conversation which might equally well have been the fiercest argument. The heat beat down.

'Thank God we are not going on to Milan,' said Eva, as after an unconscionable delay the *rapide* – which was not *rapide* at all – snorted out of the station. 'Milan is the hottest place I know. It is exactly like sitting in a frying-pan at the station and every train waits there for an hour.'

'Isn't it hot in the Dolomites?'

Somehow at sea it had never been too hot, because they had made their own draught, but here for the first time she found the air fetid; she found her fellow travellers large and ponderous, with a tendency to demand closed windows.

'In the Dolomites,' said Eva, 'it is delicious.'

***

III

Morning at the inn.

Ann had forgotten the journey, the heat bearing down in the humid night, the exploration of Verona, and the subsequent missing of the correct train and coming on here by the next, a poor affair of inadequate accommodation and stuffy carriages.

Here was a new country, something she had never dreamt about. They had stayed a few hours at Bolzano with its deep arcades, and the ancient fountains which played like musical instruments harmoniously tuned in. They had sat down and had an alfresco meal in the cool beer gardens lying under plane trees, green and freshly inviting. Ann had a vivid memory of it, plane trees, red striped umbrellas, and grinning porters in green baize aprons.

Then they had climbed higher, and had eventually come to this isolated inn in the forest of fir trees. The inn had been a miraculous discovery of Eva's one holiday two years ago when the economical situation had threatened to become embarrassing. She had hired a tin car in the village and had come to the inn quite by accident, with the idea of painting the blue mountain which rose opposite to it. Far beneath a little village curled into the shadow of the mountain. She had fallen in love with the spot. Ann fell in love with it too. The firs grew right to the very door and whispered the secrets of their green hearts each to the other. In early spring a cherry tree scattered its snow of blossom about the threshold. Already the first little hard green fruit was showing, hanging in clusters among the thin leaves. The house was built almost entirely of wood; it was rather like a Swiss chalet, sweet-smelling as though the timbers still carried some half-forgotten memory of their happier days when they were living trees and lifted delicately flowering branches fragrantly each to the other. The one great *salon* opened on to a veranda where red and white lilies were in flower. Inside there was a steam-heating stove which seemed to occupy rather clumsily most of the space. One corner was dedicated obviously to the necessities of '*essen und trinken*' and it was filled by trestle tables and a weird pattern of chairs, which had never any possible relationship one to the other. A winding wooden stair curled fanwise up to the top floor.

On the walls were antlers and horns, a jumble of trophies, and here and there a stuffed deer's head, staring down with timidly reproachful glass eyes, as though in death he were regretful that he was forced to continue the farce of pretending to live. But everywhere there was the keen clear air, hot and sweet, yet with the hint of snow in its breath from the cold bosom of the Marmolada Glacier.

Everywhere was the pungent tang of fir forest and of fragrant boughs clustering round the kind old house which gave them guest-room. The charges were absurdly small. 'At this rate,' thought Ann, 'I can stay for months.' Then she wondered what Mr. Robert would have to say about it. After all, some explanation was due to Mr. Robert. He could not give her indefinite leave of absence. Almost at once she met the other people who were installed in the inn, and they put the bothersome anxiety of Mr. Robert out of her head.

Mein Herr and the *Frau*. *Mein Herr* was large and fattish; he would not see forty again; the *Frau* was large and comfortable too. She had not a mind beyond *Suppe* and *Brötchen*. She occupied herself entirely with the creature comforts. The *Frau* in her full skirt, and her fitted bodice which revealed the ample curves of her voluminous bust, was a worthy woman. She did not believe in physical attractions, and she devoted herself to making as little of that body that God had given her as was possible. She wore heavy boots, and chaste stuff frocks. She braided back her fair hair, bleached by the sun, which had once been so lustrous.

Mein Herr was less pure. He had his little peccadilloes with the serving-maids. Just now it was Sophie (it had been Irmingarde before, but the *Frau* had expostulated, and Irmingarde had gone off post-haste). Sophie was not likely to go so suddenly. Irmingarde had gone, sent off to one of the pleasant inns at Pordoijoch as more suitable to her particular capabilities. *Mein Herr* had cursed all women, and had got very drunk on beer, and had had a bad headache and a worse stomach-ache after. Then Sophie had come along and he had found her agreeable. Kind too, not stingy. She was young and slender as yet, and he appreciated *die Backfische*. It was an ill wind, thought *mein Herr*, when he had got over the effects of the beer orgy.

In the hostelry was Pablo.

Pablo had been a student; he had come from Budapesth University, where his health had broken down as a result of over-study and wild living.

'It ees sad,' said *mein Herr*, 'to see so fine a man so seeck.'

But Pablo was not seeck now. He was twenty-three, he was tall and dark with the figure of a young god, and the eyes of an old devil. His hair, grown long, curled lightly as a boy's about his head and slender neck. His mouth was whimsical.

Ann, coming to the hostelry, saw Pablo standing on the veranda cutting himself a new stick and shaping it with a clasp-knife, and singing to himself one of those intriguing Teuton songs which seem to go echoing through your heart long after the singer has become silent.

'O Tannenbaum, O Tannenbaum,
Wie grün sind deine Blätter!

Du grünst nicht nur sur Sommerszeit,
Nein, auch im Winter, wenn es schneit.
O Tannenbaum, O Tannenbaum,
Wie grün sind deine Blätter!'

Ann stopped dead. All around was the scent of the *Tannenbaum*, faintly resinous; the green arms, almost blue in places, a delicate dark lace of fronds which were like ferns, and opposite to them the mountain with the village at its foot.

Pablo turned. 'You the new come?' he asked, and he smiled. 'English? *Nein?*' There was the flash of teeth between his lips; she took it as a welcome.

'I've just arrived from Venice.'

'Venice. A city what you call dream. Much love. Much linger,' and he laughed.

Somehow here she was not shy or afraid or even conventional any more. She was not herself. It was as though the hostelry were swung between two worlds; nothing outside it mattered.

They were entities, not people.

He straddled the low rail which ran round the veranda, and glanced at her. Perhaps in his dark eyes she saw something keenly alive and alluring. Perhaps he saw something vivid in her fairness and Saxon colouring, and the linen frock which she had put on after the journey, disclosing slight outline and firm white skin.

'What were you singing? Please go on?' she said.

'I was singing of … what you call 'eem? … the fir tree.'

She dropped into a chair, and listened. Pablo did not demur. It was enough that anyone wanted him to sing. He went on in that untrained, natural voice that was so pleasing.

'Du grünst nicht nur sur Sommerszeit,
Nein, auch im Winter, wenn es schneit.'

It seemed to Ann that a spell was cast upon her. The spell of the fir forest, of the lonely hostel, and of Pablo sitting there singing.

After, in her own room, she was ashamed. She sat down on the single iron bed and gave herself a talking to. 'I'm impressionable, and I must be fast. I never knew it before, but since I left England, just look what has happened to me!'

Youth had come, chance and opportunity, and they might never occur again. She must grasp them on the instant and hold them fast.

She went to the window, high and narrow, opening it with difficulty, for *mein Herr* and the *Frau* were in truth terrified of fresh air, although they urged it as so beneficial for medicinal purposes. Outside there was a little wooden balcony which did not look as though it would bear her. And down beneath her, stretching in waves like a great green sea, the fir forest. Right down into the valley it ran, in among the clustering roofs of some small town, with here or there the darting silver of a river. It was like some lovely painting, and it stirred her in the same way. It stirred her so that she told herself, 'This is my chance and I am taking it. What does it matter what comes afterwards? One is old such a long long time,' and she stood there drinking it in until it half intoxicated her.

IV

At dinner-time they all met.

There was another woman artist staying at the inn with her husband. She was a large, rather strident woman, and he was a small man – French – who wore extraordinary clothes, and wore them in a very extraordinary way. Although Madame Heriot and Eva Temple seemed eager to compare work, it struck Ann that before long there might be jealousy. Madame Heriot was of the impressionist school, while Eva disliked modern art.

But over the strange meal in the one big sitting-room, with the stuffed animals hung around them, they discussed their art as though they had a fellow-feeling about it.

Ann thought it was one of the strangest meals she had ever eaten. Veal cut in a new way, cooked in butter, with long thin slices of beans on either side of it. Cheese made from goat's milk by the *Frau*, green figs clustering together in a hand-made basket. There was Pilsener in long, slender, horn-shaped glasses, and beer frothing out of tankards. Ann asked for water and was told that it was not procurable. 'Eet is *nicht gut*,' said *mein Herr*.

So she drank Pilsener, which tasted bitter, and which she did not like but conformed to, as being better than typhoid. Cuthbert would of course have considered a serious illness to be far preferable to such sin as strong drink, but still ... and after all, she wondered, was Pilsener quite strong drink? Everybody seemed to take it.

Mein Herr waited on them all, running to and fro with quick, short steps, and carrying on an agitated and guttural conversation with the *Frau* through the kitchen door. And every time the door opened there came the hot savage odour of veal mingling with the resinous fir forest, the green tender essence of Pablo's *Tannenbaum*.

Afterwards they drank coffee, thick *café-au-lait*, set before them in wide bowls with double handles. Ann, still remembering the nursery tuition that it was rude to use both hands when drinking, stooped over hers a little nervously. Then she saw Pablo across the table, his hands set on either side the bowl, his lips to the crude thick china, his eyes challenging hers across the rim. (What was it the old hag in the Alameda had said?

'Make much of life while you are still young. Look at me.')

Only now she was not looking at the old wizened face, but at the young attractive face of Pablo. The eyes that were lit by flame, the high cheek-bones, the laughing audacious mouth.

'Afterwards let me show you the forest, *ya*?' he asked.

'Please,' she said.

That night she went to bed and she could not sleep, for such thoughts pursued her. 'I'm old enough to be his mother,' she kept telling herself, but in her heart she knew that she was not. Mothers of twelve are not abundant. Last thing of all, she heard the sound of the trees whispering together, and a little laugh from the kitchen where *mein Herr*, the toils of the day over and the *Frau* safely asleep, was occupying himself with Sophie. And she heard Pablo singing tenderly. These sounds were her lullaby.

V

The next afternoon they walked out into the heat. All around them it was fiercely hot, yet under the trees it was cool. Pablo had said that it would be like that. He showed her the path which led down to the valley, with the dwarf rhododendrons in rosy profusion, and through the moss and tattered grasses of the undergrowth orchids and columbines and large gentians spearing up into the light.

'There are much flowers here,' he said, and then quickly, 'you like flower?' and he stooped and gathered some of the columbines, pale mauve and pink and amber, and bringing them to her tied them into the little scarf on her frock. She felt his fingers lightly against her skin, something impish about it, faunish, something that fascinated.

'It is seldom someone young come here,' he said, 'all are so old, and so ugly.'

'But I'm not young.'

'So?' and he laughed, adding gallantly, 'in Venice all are old or young. You are of my age.'

She had not the heart to tell him that she was not his age. It was a pleasant dream, a sweet delusion, let it last while it would.

'I shall be glad when my luggage comes,' she said, 'you see I was on a cruise, and the ship went on without me. My luggage has to come here all the way from Ragusa.'

'What?' he demanded, 'the Customs? The frontiers? That will take beeg time.'

'Don't say that, these are all I have got.'

'Then,' he said, 'we go to the village and buy clothes. Beeg clothes.' He laughed and made a gesture of flowing skirts from the hips, of full bust, of great sleeves and a snug waist.

'You mean national dress?'

'But it is very become,' he said. 'We will go to the village, but it not like this. I love not commerce. I love not buy and sell. I love the forest, the *Tannenbaum*, the quiet.'

As he spoke she found herself glancing at him; his slender hips, and wide shoulders, his long slim line of thigh and leg. She felt different about him. Something she had never felt before about any man, and because of it she was afraid of herself. She wished for a moment that Oliver were here. If he were here with her she would not be so afraid, for whatsoever his faults may have been, he had understood. He was very understanding of emotions and it had helped. Never before had Ann been attracted by the physical loveliness of a man, but Pablo was very beautiful. He was, she felt, irresistible.

They were two people standing alone and staring

down into the world, where in the valley below the village lay. It was a kaleidoscope beneath them, unimportant and matterless, for it was the other people's world, and this green forest was their very own.

'You've been here long?' she asked.

'Some time. I come here from Budapesth. Over-study, the doctor say. I come here to be quiet. No study. No wine. No women. No music.'

'And you like the hostel?'

He shrugged his shoulders. 'Peoples come, and peoples go. Now you come.'

It seemed to her that she had been here for an age. The ship was already a mere phantom. Venice was disappearing into its own blue mist. The station at Verona with its unappetizing food, and now only this forest of the moment, and this young man. He turned abruptly. 'We will go back now.'

She felt as though she had failed him at a critical moment. As though she had suddenly and unforgivably disappointed him, and she herself was at a loss, for she had no idea what he had expected of her.

They came out of the forest to where the hotel stood vivid in the light. *Mein Herr* was singing as he chopped wood at the corner of the house. At this time of day the *Frau* slept, and often Sophie (who did not sleep) came creeping out for a word. He sang to her so that she should know that he was alone, and ready for a little of that *flirten* over which the *Frau* was so frugal. He sang for very gladness of heart, for if the affair with Irmingarde had been discovered and torn up, there was Sophie to take her place; and if Sophie went, there would perhaps be somebody else; some Minna or Gretchen or Luisa. There was the pleasant ringing sound of his axe against the logs, and his voice, deeply bass, singing one of the *Volkslied* and echoing far.

'Bald gras ich am Neckar

Bald gras ich am Rhein.'

Ann sank down into the chair on the veranda. 'Oh, I am so hungry. I want my tea so much.'

Pablo stood looking at her. 'You English pine much for the tea. We drink it not. But wait …' He went into the house and he came out again carrying two bowls of coffee. '*Mahlzeit*,' he said graciously.

She had no idea what it meant.

It was a meal remotely different from the office tea. She thought of that by contrast. Whose turn would it be to buy the biscuits? Whose turn to wash up? The tea that would slop into the saucer when she took it in to Mr. Robert! The little *festa* which was Bourbon biscuits, the everyday affairs of Osbornes!

'I wish life could stay still here and now,' she said suddenly.

'Well, and why not? There is only the moment. Now is the only time. Why not make much of it?'

She watched him as he sat there. A young man with his shirt open at the throat, rolled up above the elbows; the old pair of flannel trousers was girded about his slight hips by a faded leather thong. He was looking at her with dark eyes which reminded her of something vividly alive. She did not know when she had ever seen anyone so much alive before.

'Time must go on,' she said.

'But not for us.' He leaned closer. 'Shall I tell you what will happen to you? Shall I …?'

But Eva Temple came out of the house.

VI

Ann did not know if the hours stood still, or if they went on. She saw nothing of Eva, for she had entered into a competition with Madame Heriot. On the face of it, it was quite friendly, but underneath lay a streak of enmity.

Eva secretly thought that Madame Heriot's work was 'quite dreadful', Madame Heriot thought that Eva's was too dull for words.

Ann was alone – yet beautifully accompanied by Pablo – only she felt that she wanted her clothes. Surely they should have come by now? Surely something might have been arranged? Never before had she realized the extreme difficulty of having only what you stood up in.

The *Frau* was obliging, and she was very courteous over the linen frock, and the first evening all the underclothing was laundered and brought up with the *Frühstück* the next morning. For only the first day in Venice had Ann sinned in coming downstairs for *Frühstück*. She had become quite accustomed to some beaming male (it was never a woman) coming into her room, bearing the tray, and depositing it upon the bed. There was a luxurious joy about drinking the coffee and eating the roll, which was invariably hollow. She was fascinated by the laziness of it, the lack of hurry, and the un-English atmosphere.

Mein Herr brought up the meal, set the tray down, and handed Ann the newly-laundered lingerie, with a rather embarrassing attention to detail. 'I put them how you wear him,' he explained, and laid them out along the ottoman sofa.

Ann found herself reddening, though she ought to have become accustomed, really she ought. To these foreign people underclothes and bedrooms and general intimacy were not things of which you were ashamed. You accepted them. *Mein Herr* arranged the garments with admirable knowledge of their sequence and, smiling encouragingly, he departed again. He never gave it a second thought.

But you could not go on with this distressing shortness of attire. On the third day Ann toiled all the way down to the village to send a cable to the purser at

Ragusa entreating him to hurry up and to send her her luggage. She toiled down the mountain side, through the forest, taking care not to slip, and it was very difficult. When she arrived at the little cottage, which was also labelled *'Polizist'* and in an outer shed of which the fire-engine was housed, she remembered that the ship would have left Ragusa for England. All this walk and for nothing, only herself to blame which made it a little more maddening. The toil back to the hostel was not easy. It was a good deal steeper going up than it had been coming down. The late afternoon seemed to grow disobligingly hotter instead of cooler. It seemed to her that the distance came no nearer, walk as she would. Instead of it being cool under the fragrant boughs of the *Tannenbaum* she found it far hotter. In the steepest parts she was reduced to going upwards clinging to the dry tufts of grass above her. She was very late indeed, and very cross. When she eventually got back to the inn she found a letter from Cuthbert. Cuthbert was outraged. He could not understand what had come over his sister; he could only think – and he stated this quite baldly – that she must have gone a little queer in her head. To behave like this! Such a reflection on his life, and on Eleanor's life, and on poor dear Gloria's life too! Blighted in the bud, so to speak.

Ann could not follow his line of argument at all. His letter had the effect of egging her on to do worse. It incensed her. On the veranda she saw Pablo straddling the balustrade and singing softly to himself.

He said, 'Good news, I trust?'

'No news from my home is good,' and then wearily, 'I went to the village to cable for clothes, and then remembered the ship had sailed. What am I to do?'

'But you look most nice. You are pretty. I like you like that. I not mind if you haf no clothes,' and he went on singing.

He did not seem to understand that he had said something quite dreadful. Or did he? She had a vague suspicion that perhaps he did. She turned, feeling her colour coming, and she went into the house.

CHAPTER 3

I

Sex is a strange factor in life.

It was just as though it had taken Ann and Pablo and had shut all the rest of the world away; they had to act out their own romance, come what would. She felt it coming, and she was afraid of the new Ann who lived inside the old Ann, and who acted so bewilderingly. She did not understand how far the new Ann might go.

Pablo's outrageous remarks; his calm acceptance of life in the more intimate phases. For instance that morning when the old priest came to the inn. The old man was doing a walking tour clad in a time-greened cassock and propped by a stout 'stock'. He came in for a rest and was irritable and demanding, sending *mein Herr* running this way and that, and complaining to the *Frau* about the badness of the beer and the poorness of the *kleine Kuchen*. Nothing suited him.

'A thoroughly cross old man,' said Ann when they watched him depart.

'He what you call celibate,' Pablo explained, 'it make man angry. Man not meant to live without woman. It good for him and make him more pleasant to his fellows.'

She should have been shocked, but queerly enough she was only surprised at the frankness of his admittance of the male need. 'People do not talk like that in England,' she told him.

'Oh *nein*. In England,' and he laughed, 'there are no men and no women in England. No love, no making love, just all pretend.'

'You shouldn't say things like that.'

'Why not? They are true.'

He refused to argue. She felt that she ought to pull him up, but unfortunately it was not so easy as that. Besides, he fascinated her; he fascinated her by his strange contrast to the world that had been hers. She told herself that Eva should not have left her so much alone with Pablo. Eva Temple was one of those women who love new friends. She loved making new acquaintances, enquiring into their lives, learning all about them, and then, when she had sucked their store of information dry, passing on to pastures new. Perhaps she had learnt all that she wanted to learn of Ann. Anyway the first few days at the inn she was not seeing much of her.

The absence of Eva flung Ann into the friendship with Pablo. It grew on the instant. It was big and blooming before she could cut it down inside herself. The moment she had realized its bigness, it was too late. She could not stay it.

He had sex attraction. He had the physical beauty of youth that she had never met before. The friends of her father and Cuthbert had not been beautiful, they had been hideously clothed. They had not been developed. In the office there had only been Londoners, muffled in smart overcoats, nothing to attract, nothing that she had found noticeable, just people. But Pablo was a personality. To her he was a god.

'I shock you, you tell me,' he said, 'but then you are so virgin. So shy.'

'You say things you should not say.'

'About love? Ah well,' and he laughed. 'Tell me, do you not sometimes theenk of love?'

'Never,' she said, and thanked heaven that it was – or rather until recently it had bccn – true.

He took her arm in his hand, and he shook it a little. 'What if I make you theenk … what if I make you …?'

Providence mercifully aided her.

They heard the rumble of wheels on that rough road which twined through the last part of the forest to the hostelry. It had been made one winter, *mein Herr* said, and he was proud of it. It was rough in the extreme, it had no surface at all. Horses slipped on it, cars refused it, yet every now and then some vehicle more intrepid than the others would come up from the village bringing new guests to the inn. Instantly Pablo was all thrilled. He peered forward with a childlike interest.

'*Mein Herr* said new peoples come to-day.'

He pointed through the break in the trees to where a dilapidated old car had come to an unoiled standstill. An Englishman, wearing the peculiar clothes Englishmen on holiday do wear, had alighted. He was expostulating with the driver. Standing in the car, collecting smart patent-leather luggage together, was a young girl.

'But she is *schönste*,' said Pablo admiringly.

Ann stared. Fuzzy gold hair, not guiltless of peroxide; a too red mouth, plaintive blue eyes. She decided that she did not like her.

'No brain,' said Pablo, 'nuzzing but the body.'

'What do you mean?'

'How I say? She knows love. She understand love and what love would ask, thees Mrs. Temple.'

'Mrs. Temple? But that's Eva?'

'*Nein*, thees is also Mrs. Temple. It not matter.'

A horrid thought darted through Ann's brain. The world is small; surely this could not be Herbert Temple and his chit?

She looked chittish enough in all conscience, and had not Pablo himself admitted that she was all body?

'You don't think …?' she began.

'*Ya?*'

'You don't think that it could be Eva's husband and his second wife? It … it's rather dreadful, but she divorced him.'

Pablo nodded. He did not think it was dreadful at all, it was just the usual thing, and he could understand any man sickening of Eva. Much too prim. A prude. Far too proper, 'Oh *ya*,' he said, 'divorce, I see.'

But the world is bigger than that, Ann told herself. It must be. She watched them as they entered the inn. They would be safe enough at the moment for Eva was out painting, and would not be back until the shadows grew long. Ann waited until she thought that the register would be signed, and the form of identification and all the rest of the paraphernalia which was insisted on, then she tip-toed into the salon. *Mein Herr* and the *Frau* had escorted the new arrivals upstairs, where there seemed to be some little discussion about the bedrooms in progress. Seeing that they were a married couple, *mein Herr*, who had all the good Teuton belief in a comfortable double bed, and no nonsense about it, had put one room aside for them. It appeared that they wanted two. The chit – if of course it were the chit – did not wish to sleep with Herbert – if it were Herbert. She was explaining quite frankly that he snored too much for that, and she couldn't stand it. She must have another room and she would prefer a choice. So *mein Herr*, the *Frau*, and the chit were peeping into all the unoccupied rooms, while

282

the despised Herbert, left entirely to himself, rather ruefully proceeded to unstrap his luggage. He had apparently no interest in the room the chit chose, seeing that he would not be allowed inside it.

It gave Ann a noble opportunity, and she went to the corner of the *salon*, which was screened off by a dilapidated screen labelled *Bureau* in large inked letters on a cardboard box-lid. There on the little desk lay the register open and still wet. Mr. Herbert Temple. No occupation. Nationality, British. Aged forty-nine. From Budapesth. Mrs. Gwynneth Dolores Temple. No occupation. Nationality, British. Aged twenty-three. Also from Budapesth.

It did not help very much, for, as Ann told herself, there must be lots of Herbert Temples in the world. Yet she was still suspicious. It would be so awkward and just the sort of thing that the fates delight in. She felt that she ought to protect her friend just in case. Eva and Madame Heriot had taken sandwiches and were out to lunch in the forest, therefore *Mittagsessen* was a very friendly affair. Mr. and Mrs. Temple, Ann and Monsieur Heriot, and Pablo. Everyone was very amiable with each other except perhaps Mr. Temple and his wife. He had been distinctly galled by the affair of the bedroom. So humiliating, that, and as if it could matter how much anyone snored just for a couple of nights!

Gwen had taken to Pablo, just as Pablo had taken to Gwen. They talked animatedly and quickly together, and their voices were not raised loud enough to permit of the rest of the table hearing, for Monsieur Heriot, who was a distinctly French eater – almost as bad as the young Frenchman on the cruise – rather drowned any but the loudest noises.

Mein Herr ran to and fro as fast as his fat legs would go. Finally when the meal had arrived at the fruit and coffee, he heaved a sigh of relief. When there were so

283

many it made it more difficult, but more money, and the money went a long way.

'We shall be rich,' the *Frau* assured him, 'our inn is getting known more and more, soon the whole world will know of heem.'

And she liked to imagine the whole world pouring in to be housed there, and *mein Herr* running about on his funny little fat legs trying to get them served.

Afterwards, while Pablo showed young Mrs. Temple the first threshold of the forest with the red and white lilies, and the great gentians and the columbines, Ann talked to Herbert Temple. She tried to pump him, but he told her little. No, they had not been married long, and he had always been interested in travelling. He had found it very pleasant wandering about Europe with someone gay and young and enthusiastic like Gwen. They had been everywhere together. Iceland, and Norway, Holland and Germany, Italy, Hungary, and now here. Gwen had always wanted to come to the Dolomites, but he had not been anxious.

'But why not? It is such a beautiful part of the world?' Ann urged.

He said, a little apologetically, 'You see, I've been married before – not very happily – and my first honeymoon was spent in the Tyrol.'

Then Ann knew that he was *the* Herbert Temple!

II

Ann went out among the trees. 'I will stay here,' she promised herself, 'and when I see Eva coming, I'll call her aside, and tell her. It would be dreadful for her to come bursting in on this scene unexpectedly.' Whilst she was sitting there on a fallen log waiting, Pablo and the chit went by. They did not see her. They were entirely occupied with themselves. That hurt Ann, to see them like that. She had not believed that man could be so fickle, for so recently Pablo had appeared to be attracted by her. She had woven her own dreams about him. She had hoped … Silly, of course, but you cannot help your dreams. They are a cobweb illusion thrown about your brain.

Now he was looking at the chit in the same languorous way as he had looked at Ann. And he had admitted the chit had no brain, only a body. It sent cold shivers down her back, it hurt her a little more than that. She had a sudden longing for the security and peace of that rut and routine of Henrietta Street and South Kensington, where this sort of thing did not happen.

It was providential that she did not speak German, for while she was sitting here awaiting the return of Eva, more than a little disturbed as to how her friend would take the news, *mein Herr* and Sophie were in the wood shed, which was alongside. They were conversing freely, for the *Frau* would be resting, and they believed that the land lay clear. The *Frau* was large and ample, and she found it convenient to rest a little during the late afternoon before occupying herself with the evening meal, therefore there was no need for caution on their part. *Mein Herr* and Sophie carried on their liaison mainly in the wood shed, and though not very comfortable they found it acceptably shadowy. It was really quite convenient. Their voices were raised a little. '*Liebchen, Liebchen, aber du bist meine …*'

And from Sophie, '*Nein, nein, kommst du …*'

All of which conveyed nothing at all to Ann who was sitting there awaiting Eva Temple. Finally she came. She carried her easel heavily, as though she were very tired, and she did not look too well pleased to see Ann there in an attitude of patient resignation.

'What are *you* doing here?' she asked.

'I was hoping to see you first. I want to have a word

with you. Things have been happening in the inn.'

'Things?'

'Yes. There are two newcomers, I'm afraid.'

'Afraid of what?'

'Their name is Temple, too.'

Eva gave a start. 'You don't think it could be Herbert? I mean Temple is quite a common name, but –'

Ann gulped, 'His name is Herbert, because I looked in the register. He put it down as Herbert Temple, and he is forty-nine.'

'My God,' said Eva, 'it *is* Herbert!'

'And her name –'

'You don't mean that she is here too? That chit?'

'Yes, she is.'

'Oh, but this is monstrous!' Eva flung the easel down and stood there armed only with a camp-stool, and staring a little wildly. 'What a horrible thing for them to do! How on earth did they come to hear of this place? It isn't the sort of place where you'd expect to have your divorced husband turning up, is it?'

'Well, no, of course not.'

All Ann's early training said, 'Only why have a divorced husband at all? Why not have tried to make the best of your marriage, instead of letting it come to this?' But of course she could not say it aloud. She could do nothing but sit there, very still, and rather quiet, and try to help as best she could. It was a dreadful situation for Eva.

'What's she like?' asked Eva after a moment, womanly curiosity stifling her natural reluctance to speak of the chit.

'She's rather common-looking. Yellow hair ...'

'Dyed, of course.'

'I rather thought so.'

'I know the type. Blue baby eyes, and cheap rouge and all that. Where is she now?'

'She's been out walking with Pablo.'

'She *would* be. That nasty physical young man who looks like a cheap musical comedy thrill would be her sort. Poor Herbert! Still, it serves him right for having brought her here. They must go. They must go right away. I never heard of such a thing.'

But she still showed a diffidence in approaching the inn. And as she stood there, maudlin sentiments mouthed in German suddenly pierced her comprehension from the wood shed.

'Oh, *mein Becchützelein.*'

And then tenderly, '*Möcht ich mit dir …*'

'I suppose the chit isn't in there?' demanded Eva hotly, pointing to the wood shed with the business-end of the camp-stool.

'No, I think it is *mein Herr.*'

'Then he ought to be ashamed of himself. I suppose it is that fat kitchen-maid again; still, that's no concern of ours. Let's get into the house without being seen, then I had better make sure that it is Herbert. Not that there is any doubt, and then, well, perhaps a note.'

'I could take him a note,' said Ann helpfully; 'it is most awkward for you, and having her here too.'

'Except that at the moment she isn't here, and if I know anything of that type of young woman, she won't be here until after dark. Not seeing who she is with.'

Ann was hurt that Eva should think like that of Pablo. She had been particularly injured by the allusion to him as a 'nasty physical young man who looked like a cheap musical comedy thrill', but she adopted an air of Christian forgiveness. After all, Eva was in such a position that quite possibly she did not know what she was saying. She needed friendship. Together they approached the hostelry.

It happened that Herbert Temple, who felt the heat and had gone to lie down during the hottest period of the afternoon, had just decided that his chit's absence was a little prolonged. He had gone to her room, and had found it in that superb state of chaos in which she habitually left it. Intimate underwear lying about, a lot of blue bows and *écru* lace scattered everywhere. There was the pervading essence of Patchouli scent, which she frequently used and in far too large quantities, and which he disliked intensely. The chit herself was missing. Marriage had taught Herbert that she was very seldom missing alone, and so he had come downstairs with the idea of seeing who was to blame this time.

He had arrived in the sitting-room, when he collided with Eva coming in at the open door. Eva was prepared, Herbert was totally unprepared. He said, 'My God!' and clasped his head with both hands as though he had suddenly seen a ghost.

'Don't be silly, Herbert,' said Eva, which was easy for her seeing that Ann had forewarned her.

Ann made good her escape. There are some scenes at which you cannot be present, and Eva and Herbert Temple were still man and wife in the eyes of God, however much they might choose to think otherwise. And, as she slipped into her own room, she only hoped that they might arrive at some definite conclusion.

III

As Eva explained with rather much emphasis, so Herbert thought, the inn had been her discovery two summers ago, and he had only come across it by accident. She declared that she had a moral right to it, and he had none, seeing that he would never have known of it if that stupid porter in Merano had not told him. She had been here repeatedly – she dwelt on that – and again she brought in the words about it being hers by moral right.

Herbert didn't care whose moral right it was; he

hadn't wanted to come at all, which was singularly hard lines. It had been Gwen's idea. The porter at Merano had said that young students sometimes stayed here, and that it was all very 'of the country'. That had been enough for Gwen. Personally he had already had quite enough of it. He had had enough of the Dolomites, and the Tyrol, and all the rest of the beastly places on that first honeymoon ages ago, but he could not very well tell Eva that. It was all very fine her kicking up a fuss and insisting that he should go at once. He wanted to go. He hadn't ever wanted to come, only how could you go when the place was miles from a station, and hadn't even got a 'bus service? You chartered an old tin car from the village, at a prohibitive cost, and took the funicular down to a town where if you were lucky – and apparently you were not, more often than otherwise – you caught a train. You couldn't get away from it, and at this time of day it was more than was reasonable to expect there would be any trains. There probably wouldn't be any funicular. The shades of night were falling fast.

'If you are going to start quoting poetry at me I shall scream,' said Eva.

But Herbert hadn't had any idea that he was quoting poetry. He was just muddled. Gwen had gone out and she hadn't come back, and he could not go until she did get back, and anyway he couldn't go to-night.

'She's out with that young student,' said Eva coldly; 'my friend lost her head over him too. He is a dangerous and owl-eyed young man, but he understands women.'

Herbert had gathered that much. After a few hours in the forest with an owl-eyed young man who understood women, he wasn't at all sure that she would be willing to go. He did not suppose that he would be able to persuade her. It was all very well for Eva to stand there laying down the law, there was Gwen to be dealt with as well as Eva, and when a man had two wives to consider it made it very much more than twice as hard. Really it did.

Gwen had never been too pleased about the alimony that went to Eva, and she would probably be very rude – she could be quite insulting – she would be only too glad to say a few things to the point when it came to it. It was extremely unlikely that she would want to curtail her visit. Moral rights and common decency would not worry Gwen. She'd go when she thought she would, and not a moment before. It would be far easier if Eva did the going, though he was not courageous enough to suggest it to her.

'It is almost indecent our all being under the same roof,' said Eva witheringly. Herbert felt that it wasn't quite that. They all had separate rooms, hadn't there been trouble enough about that earlier in the day?

'What's the first time you can get away in the morning?' asked Eva.

Herbert didn't know. He had only just come, and he knew nothing about arrangements. *Mein Herr* was called into the argument, for Eva believed in getting things cut and dried. *Mein Herr*, fresh from the affair in the wood shed, and hopelessly at sea with time-tables, could not understand why there should be such enquiries. You could go to Modzerene and catch the funicular there which would take you to the town where you could get a train to Merano. Where did they want to go from Merano? Herbert didn't know. He just wanted to get away, he explained; he did not care much where he went. *Mein Herr* came to the conclusion that they must be quite mad. It was rather an insult to the hostel that they should want to go, and having only just arrived too.

'When you haf *Abendessen*, you change minds, *nein*?' he suggested.

Herbert didn't see very well how *Abendessen* could

make any difference seeing things were as they were. So Eva, believing that she had gained some ground, and had at least got Herbert to consider an early move elsewhere, dragged her easel and camp-stool upstairs, and she explained to Ann that she had done her best and had so far avoided meeting the chit face to face. Only there was the rather desperate predicament of supper all together in charming intimacy. She and the chit! What a position!

'Have your meal up here, and pretend that you have a headache,' Ann suggested.

'And let her think that I am frightened? Not me!' snapped Eva. It was very complicated.

As she was changing into her solitary pink linen frock, Ann heard Pablo and the chit come in from the forest. She leant over the little balcony and watched them. How young the chit looked! How aggressively young! She came inside her room again and told herself that she had been a fool to look. The chit made her feel old, desperately old, and she knew that Pablo could never really have cared for her. She should not have looked out upon their return, hand in hand, like forest lovers, both full of youth and the dreams of youth, and the brittle, inconsequent magic of youth!

Somebody else had also been watching the return. It was Herbert. He knew all the signs. He knew the pinkness of cheeks and the sparkle of eyes, and the 'Reely nows,' and the 'Oh, I says.' The chit wasn't going to be easy.

He tackled her the moment he could, going into her room where she was changing. She was clad in cami-knicks, and powdering her back with a huge pink puff, fixed on the end of a ribbon-swathed stick.

'Oh, it's you,' said Gwen disappointedly, as though she had expected somebody else.

He stated his case. He thought if they could catch the funicular as *mein Herr* had suggested, and went back to

Merano, they could go on to Garda from there and see the lake, the largest and grandest of all the Italian lakes, he had read in one of Mr. Thomas Cook's informative little books. Purposely he left Eva out of the question; it would be much better for all concerned if Gwen never knew of the presence of the first wife. If Gwen met her without knowing who she was, she would not be so hostile to the project. Herbert cherished no secret conceits as to his prowess at intrigue, but he thought he could handle this affair with discretion. Eva would hold her tongue because she was a lady. Gwen, he was afraid, could not be trusted on the same score. Frankly, she wasn't.

'But I don't want to leave this place, we have only just come here, and I like it,' said Gwen.

'Yes, I know, but …'

'Oh, that's all nonsense. It's so green and naice. I want to stay here for weeks. It's luverly.'

'I don't think the drains are good,' began Herbert. It was the only excuse he could think of.

'Rubbish. You're always worrying about drains; it is that blasted inside of yours.'

'Well, I don't like the place, and if you stay here you stay on alone,' which he knew at heart was impossible.

'That'll suit me down to the ground,' announced Gwen, and she went on powdering herself liberally.

It did not seem to be a propitious moment for argument. Matters were not panning out at all properly according to Herbert. He decided that he would leave it for the moment; after supper there might be a change. A change that he hoped would be for the better. Nothing was to be gained by pressing matters at the moment.

IV

Supper was divided into two camps, the one composed of people who were not talking very much, and the other of those who were talking a great deal too much.

Eva and Ann came down late, to find that the meal had started very gaily in their absence by the chit putting the salt down Pablo's neck, and by Pablo smacking her gaily, in the way people of such short acquaintance do not usually smack.

Now he was sitting beside her talking amorously, and on the other side of her was Herbert talking not at all. The Heriots were trying to lead him into conversation and were thinking what a dull man he was, and Madame Heriot what an awful girl the chit was. Monsieur had his own ideas. Once he had been a devil himself! Once he would have fallen for just such a little *méchante*. A pity he was not younger. Rheumatism baulked you in so much.

Mein Herr was running to and fro.

He had high hopes of the success of this supper, and then the English lady and gentleman might perhaps change their minds and not go back to Bolzano to-morrow. There was *Kalbfleisch*, exquisitely grilled, with *gelben Rüben* arranged about it. Such sweet little *gelben Rüben*, young and tender, surely they could not fail to be entranced by such cookery. *Mein Herr* felt that a great deal depended upon this meal, yet had he only known the truth, nothing depended upon it whatsoever. Nothing would make any difference to the strained relationship around the table.

So far, the chit had no idea who Eva was, or what was really the matter with Herbert. She thought perhaps he was jealous of Pablo, and with good reason. The chit had had a very happy afternoon with him in the forest, and his kisses had been sublime. There would probably be more later. She filled up her glass with red wine, knowing perfectly well that she could not drink red wine. It always went to her head, but she was prepared to make a night of it.

The chit was heartily sick of Herbert, whose first clumsy ardour had waned, and who was now only a trying old man she considered, who snored, and had false teeth, and was fussy. The chit liked flirtations; she liked a little more than flirtation if the truth may be known; that was why she enjoyed travel.

You met with such successes and in such unexpected places. Now who would have thought in this out-of-the-way hotel …? Well, it wasn't even a proper hotel when you came to see it, stuck in the backwoods of the beyond. It had been different in the Weimar at Rotterdam, where a certain commercial traveller had been so generous, and had come sneaking to her room, carrying his boots in his hand. 'But why bring your boots?' the chit had demanded, 'you won't want them?' Or in Standvers Hotel in the cold purity of Norheimsund. You wouldn't suppose anything like that could happen in Norway, would you? Yet at the very Steindalsfoss she had met that blond young man, a Viking lover, she had sentimentally told herself, and while Herbert had gone back to the Standvers, there had been what the chit could only describe as 'Oh, such goings-on!' That had been a wonderful week, for Herbert's unfortunate stomach had played tricks with him, and he had had to remain in the vicinity of the Standvers, while the chit had taken good care to remain out of the vicinity, with her Viking lover.

In Italy of course there had been romance everywhere, and she had grown heartily sick of Herbert. It was just that his money was so useful, but really she couldn't stand the sight of him. So prosy. So old-fashioned. So prim.

But there had never been so beautiful a lover as Pablo. His dark eyes. His way of saying things. The touch of his hands. The chit was full of delicious plans for the hours to come, and consequently she was more than usually blind to the circumstances which were making the evening such an embarrassing one.

She just glanced up as Eva and Ann came in, and when Monsieur Heriot, as the father of the family, said, 'This is anuzzaire Mrs. Temple,' the chit murmuring, 'Pleased to meet you,' went on with her food.

Eva didn't reply. She wasn't pleased to meet the chit. She wasn't going to make even a pretence of being polite about it. She sat there grimly.

Ann tried to cover awkward moments by making pleasant conversation in which nobody joined. All the time her eyes were wandering back to Pablo. His attention to the chit was most distressing. If only he wouldn't! She felt quite humiliated by his ardour, and to think that only a few hours previously she had thought that he was attracted by herself. She must have been mad.

'It's pleasant weather,' Herbert observed.

'Isn't it?' said Eva, and darted him a look as much as to say, 'and such a pleasant evening too!' Herbert in a dilemma had never been able to rise above the weather. It was his be-all and end-all.

'You come from Bolzano?' asked Monsieur Heriot.

'And we are going back there,' said Herbert.

'I'm damned if I am,' murmured the chit carelessly. Mercifully only Ann seemed to hear.

'Delightful there,' said Monsieur Heriot; 'did you not admire the fountains? So many of them, and all so old.'

'Do you like old things?' enquired Eva coldly, knowing perfectly well that Herbert did not know old from new.

'Oh yes, what did you say? No, I don't understand anything about them,' said Herbert, who was trying to catch what the chit was saying to Pablo; more than a little difficult, for the chit was past mistress in the art of the *sotto voce*.

'Are you slightly deaf?' asked Eva with ice in her voice.

'Not to my knowledge,' said the miserable Herbert.

Mein Herr congratulated himself. Everything was going splendidly, everybody so *glücklicher*, no need to worry at all, and the Herr Temple had had two helpings of the little *gelben Rüben*, really the *Frau* had excelled herself in the cooking. It was superb. Everything fried in butter, and so rich.

After this, *mein Herr* assured himself, they would never be able to leave. They would say, 'If this is the type of meal, let us see what else the *Gasthaus* can produce.' He beamed in high good humour, and with the delicious essence of fried carrots and veal, he did not notice the flagging conversation. He did not see the venomous glances that Eva darted every little while at the chit, nor the miserable looks of Herbert placed in such an unfortunate position. Nor did he observe the unhappiness of Ann, obliged to watch Pablo and his new love.

Afterwards they foregathered for coffee. Pablo's ardour had increased. The rising of the moon was significant of the rising of his desire. He watched Gwen across the rim of a cup. His eyes said what his lips could not; at first she pretended not to notice, then suddenly her lids drooped. He knew that she was willing. It sent triumph through him, success, as though he were riding on the clouds.

'Come into the forest, it is most perfect at night,' he said.

'There is a dew,' commented Herbert, 'I don't want her to go –'

Gwen rose. 'Don't take no notice of him. He wants putting back into the oven for a bit. He's half-baked. It's liver, that's what it is.' And she laughed.

She went out on to the veranda. Ann, watching her, saw her as she turned and motioned to Pablo. She saw Pablo's quick response, as he followed her out to the forest itself. Eva was staring after them, and there was a look on her face that the company were not likely to forget in a hurry.

But in Ann's heart there was a certain sickness. It was like a pain. She saw youth, the butterfly, flitting by. It would not come back again, she told herself.

Suddenly she was terribly unhappy.

V

That was a wretched evening.

The Heriots going to bed left Ann as the third in a triangle in which she had no wish to intrude. She made an excuse, and went up to her room, pretending that there was some sewing to be done.

Downstairs Herbert and Eva jangled. Eva felt that he must have done this despicable thing on purpose. It was inconceivable that any man could have picked on this one inn in the whole of Europe, and she told him so. Herbert protested in vain. He wished he had never seen the beastly place. It had been no wish of his, it was Gwen. Eva shot him a look! Gwen indeed! What a girl to have married! What a chit! And here she was going off spooning in the woods with the fast young man she hadn't known five minutes, and Herbert sitting there like a fool and never saying anything about it, or doing anything to stop it. She hadn't any patience with him, really she hadn't. Herbert was feeling too weak to argue. During the year of his marriage with the chit he had at times remembered Eva kindly, and with some regret. He had thought when there had been the trouble with the commercial traveller at the Weimar, and the bother at the Standvers, that perhaps he would have done well if he had clung to the tattered remains of his marriage to Eva, rather than attempt this farcical marriage with the flirtatious Gwen. Now he wasn't so sure. He recalled the old nagging. Goodness, how she had nagged! Women were all the same. Only this was not a good moment, for he wanted to think. He wanted to invent some suitable excuse for getting Gwen away in the morning. And knowing Gwen, he could think of nothing that would do. She had a little habit of taking root where she thought she would, and there were evident signs of her having taken a fancy to this place.

'And to think that you preferred that girl to me,' said Eva, and she sniffed.

Herbert could offer no reply. 'Let's say no more about it,' he pleaded.

But Eva had a great deal more that she wanted to say. She would have sat up half the night saying it too, save that *mein Herr* came in, and showed symptoms of wishing to sing to them (he occasionally had musical moments), and that was more than she could bear. This scene and *mein Herr* sitting at the old yellow-keyed piano and mouthing out *Lorelei* or *Roselein* would be more than she could stand. She went up to bed.

Ann was sitting miserably enough in her own room, and wondering whether she had not made rather a mess of things, and if the arrival of Herbert and his chit at the inn had not been in a way propitious; it had at least shown her that she could not go on as she was doing. She sat down on the simple bed and brushed her hair. Across the forest, on the opposite mountain, a church bell tinkled. It reminded her dismally of Wadfield, as though with reproach. She was depressed almost beyond endurance, and yet she knew that it served her right. She wasn't young really. She had just been playing at youth. She felt that the glory of her St. Martin's summer had waned – it is always short-lived – and that now it was over, and she must give up the idea of anything that was really lovely.

It seemed to her that there was no future save to return

to the office, where she would probably be laughed at for ever. To return to work for the rest of her life, while Miss Thomas bragged about saving her money, and the miserable little odd fifteen pounds a year it brought in – or whatever it was. Ann would be constantly reminded by Cuthbert of how she had frittered away her fortune. She was quite sure that he would consider it a fortune by that time.

She heard all the familiar sounds of the hostel; Eva creaking up the wooden stairs to bed; later, Herbert. Below in the kitchens the lights went out, and there was the sound of stout shoes and of stuff skirts swinging as the *Frau* adjourned to rest. There was light chatter in the lofts where the maids lodged. The blind of the room over the wood shed was drawn, and against its pale yellow, lit by the flickering candle flame from within, there came the shadow of Sophie undressing. Curves, large curves and dents, and outlines! Sophie who evidently wore corsets and unhinged them carefully, and then spread enormously with relief.

And bye and bye *mein Herr* creeping furtively out of the house like a cat, and keeping always in the shadow as he edged towards the wood shed. Really, thought Ann, it was all rather dreadful.

Mein Herr was supposed to sleep in the little back bedroom allotted to him by the *Frau*. When the little Minna had been born years ago, the doctor had said that there must be no more children. They had had no ideas of contraception, but had decided that they must sleep apart, and therefore the *Frau* had allotted the back bedroom to *mein Herr* – one could never let it to a guest anyway, for it had only a skylight, and was not considered healthy – and he had remained there ever since.

Ann heard it all from her balcony. Last of all she saw Pablo and the chit, coming like lovers, hand in hand, out of the forest. The dark and lovely green of the *Tannenbaum* at night lent them a glamour. They came closer, carelessly, thinking that the whole world slept, and they alone were awake.

Under the balcony they stopped.

'Oh no, he doesn't sleep with me,' the chit was saying, 'come right up.'

'None will hear?' whispered Pablo.

'Well, and who cares if they do?'

She was brave, this chit! She had the high courage of youth. She dare laugh in the very face of fate. Ann felt a tremendous responsibility on her shoulders. A certain smugness seemed to possess her. She thought of the woman taken in adultery, and it seemed to her that the chit was that woman. She heard the two of them coming up the stairs. They were not trying to be quiet about it; love had made them very bold. It is horrible, Ann told herself, and they must not be allowed to do it. For Eva's sake. For Herbert's sake. For her own sake too.

She opened her door.

They were just going into the room that the chit had chosen, she with her arm round Pablo, he looking down into her eyes. There was something about his languorous attitude which incensed Ann, and she grew quite brave.

'Look here,' she said, 'you can't do this. I heard.'

The chit released her hold of Pablo, and eyed Ann quite coldly. 'Well, upon my word, you've got a nerve! What business is it of yours?'

'I shall call your husband,' said Ann, knowing quite well that she would never dare to do so, 'it's positively disgusting. Here in the hostel, with the first Mrs. Temple not two doors away.'

'What did you say?'

It was the first inkling that the chit had got of the truth. Her eyes went glassy, her mouth grew hard. 'You aren't going to tell me …?' she began hotly.

'Oh, my God!' exclaimed Pablo. 'What the 'ell for did you tell her that?'

'Herbert's first wife is here – in the hotel? She isn't that sour-looking old trout at dinner?' demanded Gwen. There was something about her face that frightened Ann. She stepped back, put out a hand to protect herself, and touched Pablo. But he had scant sympathy.

'It would haf been most all right,' he said grudgingly, 'the ozzer wife keep the 'usband busy, and now you go tell her. Oh women, what fools! Oh God!'

'How can you be so disgusting?' flashed Ann, stung to retort. 'They were divorced. And now to have this happen.'

The chit came closer. Her eyes were round and hard, her mouth was set. 'You mean your friend was the first wife?'

'Yes, of course.'

'Then that's why Herbert came here. He wanted to see her again. The dirty little beast! It's because of her that I can't have the three-carat diamond I wanted in Vienna. It's because of that stinking alimony that we have to pay her, blast it! It's because of her, and all the time he had a sneaking love for her, and comes back here, brings me, he …'

Ann and Pablo bundled the chit into the bedroom between them. They tried to calm her. She was making a dreadful noise, the sort of noise that Ann remembered, too late, a very common girl does make when she is angry or miserable. She refused to be quiet.

'It ees all your fault for telling her,' complained Pablo, 'a darn fool thing to do. No wonder she ees angry. You make the beeg meestake.'

Calming the chit was not easy! She fought like a mad thing. She wanted to go and see Eva and to tell her what she thought of her, and 'that stinking alimony'. She'd been longing to meet Eva for some time, she explained, and she wasn't going to miss this chance, not for anybody, she wasn't. She seemed to have forgotten Pablo, and the night which had promised so well in the lists of love. Ann wished that she had never interfered, for anyway, though she might have been behaving as the woman taken in adultery, it would have kept her quiet, and that was something.

'Oh, do please go to bed, and we'll talk it over in the morning,' begged Ann.

What a hope!

'Think I'm going to be talked to by a bit like you?' retorted the chit. 'I'm going to do what I think best and I won't be bullied by anybody. It's my business, and not yours.' Which was of course true.

Into this scene Herbert walked. Herbert was not looking his best. He was one of those unfortunate men who are not blessed with a waist, and therefore he could not wear a belt, but had to rely on braces to support his more necessary articles of apparel. Pyjamas refusing to remain tied about his ample middle, he had long ago given up the attempt, and therefore he wore a neat little nightshirt. Why a man should look so ridiculous in a nightshirt nobody yet has been able to explain, but he does. Herbert, his dressing-gown only hastily hung about him, looked merely absurd as he came into the chit's room. He had heard the noise. He had tried to ignore it, but there had come a moment when he could do so no longer. She was making too much noise for that. He had been obliged – oh, most reluctantly – to come and see what the trouble was.

'Whath all thith?' he demanded. His speech was slightly difficult, for some of his teeth were reposing on the wash-hand-stand in a glass of water. It was the absence of these teeth which made him lisp. At the moment it seemed difficult to understand how such a girl as the chit could ever have accepted such a poor spectacle for a husband as Herbert. It was also quite easy to understand how Eva had given him up.

'Whath all thith?'' he demanded.

The chit stared at him. 'I've found out why you brought me here. I know now what you're playing at, you snake in the grass, you! Do you take me for a perfect fool, you old devil with your two wives?'

Herbert could think of nothing more tactful to say than, 'Who told you?'

'I did,' said Ann.

'But why? Why?' asked the miserable Herbert.

Ann had no idea why. She now had no idea whatsoever.

It was obviously the wrong thing to have done, and she could not see what was the thing to do to put it straight. The chit was furious. She was dangerously furious. Her eyes were hard and savage, her colour was coming and going in patches. There was no gainsaying her. Pablo was angry too. With all this fuss and flurry he did not see how he was going to get what he wanted out of the night, and he blamed Ann for the whole thing. Jealousy, thought Pablo, *sempre la donna*!

Herbert was furious that Ann could not have kept quiet just when the most difficult meal had been safely negotiated, and he had thought that he was round the worst corner! He had been asleep when the noise had started, and he had had a most beautiful dream that a convenient 'bus ran before breakfast to Bolzano, and he and Gwen were in it with no further ado. Then he had awakened to the savage sounds of argument, to a noise like a hell-fiend let loose, and old associations had warned him that it was Gwen. No other woman would make a noise like that.

'How dare you bring me here, you dirty little devil?' she challenged him, 'with that wife of yours under the same roof. I won't stand for it. Now I'll damned well tell her off about that filthy alimony trick. Why should we starve while she grows fat? Money's no good to an old trout like she is.'

Very unfortunately Eva heard the noise. At first she had thought that perhaps the *Frau* had discovered the infidelities of *mein Herr*, and she had therefore ignored it; but then certain familiar sounds had dawned on her intelligence, and her curiosity had overcome her. She had pulled on a dressing-gown, intending only to peep out into the passage, then she had come as far as the doorway. She must have heard every word. She was for a moment transfixed with horror. Herbert saw her first. He swallowed hard and he waved frantic fat hands in deprecation, but owing to the regrettable tooth trouble the words would not come. Ann went across to Eva.

'Oh, go away,' she implored, 'do go away. You don't know what a dreadful girl she is.'

'Yes, that's it. You call me names,' said the chit, 'you're a lady, I must say. Both of you, I don't think.'

Pablo leaned across the bed to her. He laid a restraining hand upon Gwen's arm. 'We send all to bed?' he suggested. The idea obviously presented its possibilities to the chit. She hesitated. Then it was that Eva drove home her shaft. She wasn't going to be bested by a girl like this.

'Herbert. Do you realize what that young man is suggesting to your wife? How can you stand there and listen to it? It's disgusting enough that you married a girl like that, but more disgusting that you allow her to carry on like this under your very nose.'

'Pleath,' besought Herbert, still frantically waving his fat hands. 'Do go to bed. Everybothy. Do go to bed.'

Eva pulled herself up. She looked at the chit. There was something compelling about her; the only thought that struck Ann was how on earth could she ever have married Herbert?

Eva was Junoesque, there was no gainsaying her, even the words died on the lips of the agitated chit. She had met her match. Herbert was sadly handicapped by the nightshirt, and the lack of the teeth, and the fact that he ran so much to fat, but even at his best he could not have been an Adonis. Beside him Pablo looked like a god. The ripple of muscles under the live skin of his throat; the long slender lines of thigh and body, the dark eyes, flashing amusedly from Eva to Gwen, from Gwen to Eva, glancing a little coldly now and then at Ann. For hadn't she caused it all? Hadn't she come sneaking in out of sheer jealousy, to see what was to be seen? And when she had seen it she hadn't liked it, and serve her right too! He had no patience with her.

'I won't be talked to like that,' shrieked the chit; 'if you don't take that woman out of my room, I'll slap her, I will. I tell you I will. I don't care. She's an old trout, and she's jealous of my being young and pretty and having fun …'

Her voice suddenly became dulled, for Herbert, very red in the face, had bustled them out and had shut the door between. They were in the passage, Ann and Eva and Herbert. An ill-assorted trio. The mild eyes of a stuffed elk looked down on them regretfully, a creature of the wild and of the forest, which, had it been able to speak, would have said with Puck, 'Lord, what fools these mortals be!'

'Really, Herbert,' said Eva, 'you must remove that impertinent little chit. She's to go first thing. How you ever dared to have come here at all is more than I can understand.'

'I didn't mean …' began Herbert.

Eva lost all patience.

'And don't stand there lisping at me. Go and get your teeth if you *must* talk, but I'd much rather you went to bed.'

'I wanth to go to bed,' lisped Herbert.

He went.

But Ann did not sleep. She lay there in between the cool sheets, and she listened to the noises of the forest like a sea around her. The sighing of trees heart to heart, the stirring communion of the branches. She listened also for those very noises that she did not want to hear. Everybody seemed to have forgotten that the chit had been left with Pablo and that he had not come out of her room. What was happening there? She felt herself going hot with shame. Life, how cruel it was! Love, how inconsequent!

And until to-night she had actually allowed herself to fall half in love with Pablo. She felt that must always be the most terrible part of it. He had attracted her. He still attracted her, even in spite of all the wickedness of to-night.

She must get away, run away, escape from all this. She must be the one who caught the train from Merano. She had behaved like a child and it was the most humiliating thing in the world. It was absurd to suppose that you could cheat life of so much as a year. That had been part of the glamour of the cruise, the infection of the sea-fever that had got her. She had imagined that she was young again, and she wasn't. She was thirty-five. She was thirty-five all through, every hour of it.

It was ridiculous.

She could not sleep, because still some fragment of her being clung to Pablo. Still she loved him in that stupid physical way which refused to be silenced. In spirit she was with him.

She was jealous of the chit, she knew that, although she had tried to believe that she was just indignant with her. She coveted the embraces that Gwen would be receiving. It was all very wicked of her, she told herself, but she could not stem the tide within her. She *did* love him.

And things being as they were she must leave as soon

as ever she could and get out of this unreal world, back
to the old world, where typewriters tapped, and the only
diversion the day offered was the debate as to whether
they could have Bourbon biscuits for tea, or not. What
possible excuse could she offer *mein Herr* and Eva? And
anyway, would she not have to stay until her luggage
came, and the rest of the money? Or could she go now,
uproot herself as it were, and get aboard a train for
somewhere – she did not much care where – before
Mittagsessen?

Then mercifully she turned sleepy.

VI

She awoke with the exquisite beauty of the dawn
flooding the room. The air was like wine. In the forest,
hundreds of birds twittered an overture to the morning.
Bells were ringing in the village below, and from the
Kirche on the opposite mountain. The forest green rolled
down and down to the village, where the darkness of
cypresses and cedars and ilex changed to the fuller,
younger green of larches. Gradually the trees gave place
to the meadows, where the cows grazed, their bells
tinkling against their soft throats. Opposite, the clouds
rolled up the mountain sides, and above their grey tulle
wisps the jagged peaks pierced the pink of the sky, and
turned rosy themselves. 'In the Dolomites,' Eva had told
her, 'the very mountains blush.' They were blushing
now.

She got up, for somehow she could not sleep, and she
felt the longing to walk. She wanted to smell the earth,
and the gentians and the columbines, and the clustering
red and white lilies which grew beside the hostel.

Outside her room, on the landing, Sophie was
indolently dusting with a feather brush. She looked
surprised to see Ann, but stifling a yawn she went on

with her work. She was not interested in it; she thought the English lady must be mad to get up when there was no need for her to get up. But then most English ladies were mad. They were a mad race.

On the veranda Ann came face to face with Pablo. He was very creased and crumpled, he had obviously slept – that is to say if he had slept at all – in his clothes. His eyes were ringed with tiredness, his hair rumpled. He stopped her as she would have passed him by.

'I suppose that now you hate me?'

Ann wished that the very fact of his being there did not thrill her. She said, 'What you choose to do is obviously no business of mine,' and tried to pass him.

But Pablo would not be passed so easily.

'I come to the forest also,' he said, 'it is most nice in the early morning, *ya*?'

They walked a few steps side by side. Then Ann stopped, she was indignant, she was furious. This could not be. 'How dare you come with me after last night?' she demanded. 'Everybody else seems to have been blinded to what happened, but I know. You were with that dreadful girl all the time. I suppose you have only just left her now?'

He did not deny it. 'That is truth,' he said cheerfully.

What could you do with such a rogue? He linked his arm in hers, and although she longed to cast him off she could not. The green received them as it had received him with Gwen the night before. The irony of it! The warm tarry smell seemed to engulf them, the earth smell mingling with it, dry and powdery, the faint essence of lilies and gentians.

He said, 'You do not understand the man so well. With men when they desire a woman they do not need to love her.'

'I don't want to discuss this.'

'*Ya*, but you do. I desire you. You refuse me. I see the

girl. I zink she is also woman. Any woman. It does not mattaire. The woman I want, wants me not, therefore anyone. I not care. *Ya*?'

Ann could not see that it was *ya* at all. She replied, 'You are talking disgustingly, and I don't want to hear about it. I don't care what you did. I am going away from here, right away, and at once. I've finished with it all.'

He came to a standstill. 'You go away?'

'You can't expect me to stop.'

'But, Ann, why do you go away? Do you run away from me? Is it that you are afraid?'

It was the truth but she denied it. Suddenly he put his arm around her, and drew her to him. She wanted to resist but she could not, he was so strong. She just cried. Ann had never wept on any man's shoulder before, and it was a beautiful experience. Now she felt that she did not care what he had done, most probably it was the chit's fault anyway, and she would forgive him. Like this she would forgive him anything. Pablo kissed her. He kissed her hair, whispering soft and tender phrases in a consoling German; her eyelids, her cheeks, and at last her mouth. And, as she told herself afterwards, the awful part was that she did not attempt to stop him. She liked it. She would have given anything for more. It was just as though she were putty in his hands, and he could mould her into any shape, and do what he would with her.

'That girl she mean nothing to me,' he persisted, 'she was all experience, all knowledge. But you are simple. You are all virgin.'

She wished that he would not say such things, and in particular that he would not use that word.

'You not go? You stay? Promise me you not go?'

'There is no point in my staying.'

He made a last daring suggestion. 'But what if we marry?'

She could not believe the full significance of the words, but stood there staring at him, with the golden spears of sunshine piercing through the dark trees, with the up-rushing essence of earth scent and *Tannenbaum*, with the day rising above them. Then suddenly, only half understanding, she broke from him and ran out of the forest back to the inn.

If we marry!

And she would marry him; she knew that. She could not stop herself. It was all very well of people preaching, all very well for them to become common sense about it, but she could not help herself. The curious atmosphere of attraction had got her in its control. She felt much like a fish caught in a net, flapping and struggling through the meshes. Such a marriage could only bring disaster, surely last night had shown her that? Yet she knew that she had not sufficient sense left to reason that way.

Eva had been quite right when she had described Pablo as being a nasty physical young man who looked like a cheap musical comedy thrill. Only unfortunately none of these things helped Ann to see sense; she felt that she never would again. 'If I'm not careful, I'm going to make an awful mess of my life,' she told herself, 'and I just can't be careful.'

For here she was in her own room, offering quite good and plausible excuses to herself as to why she should not leave the place. There would be such complications about her luggage, and it would probably end in her losing it altogether, and she did not want to do that. Whereas if she waited a few days it would be bound to come. There would be difficulty over the money the purser was sending. She had no reason for going, and Eva would think her mad, or guess the real reason, which would be even more trying. On the other hand in a few days a letter from home could explain the whole thing. An illness there – preferably appendicitis, which she always felt was such a convenient illness – or domestic business. She told herself that she could not possibly go to-day.

Sophie brought up coffee and rolls. She set the tray down and departed. Outside there was a banging of doors, and a chattering of keys. The keys to all the rooms were large and cumbersome, and hung on a key rack behind the screen marked *Bureau* on an old box-lid. There was the sound of heavy luggage being pulled about, and calls for Andreas. Andreas acted as out-porter and boot-boy and kitchen lad, and quite often understudy to *mein Herr* in more intimate matters than *mein Herr* dreamt of. Andreas, in a green baize apron, was hauling luggage about, and the old tin car from the village was waiting at the door. Andreas and the boy who drove the car entered into a bright conversation. Good business, commented Andreas, guests coming, guests going. Much good business.

Herbert came out first. It had cost him the three-carat diamond from Vienna, and God alone knew where he would be able to raise the money for it, but he had got to do something to get away. Ann went on to the balcony to watch. Herbert was crestfallen and rather subdued, and he was followed by the chit who was far from subdued.

'I hated this beastly place,' she was saying, 'if it hadn't been for you wanting to see that wife of yours …'

Herbert made vague and quite useless gestures of expostulation. They climbed into the car.

And as Ann watched, she heard a new sound. It was a strangely disturbing sound, coming as it did into the stillness of the forest. A second tin motor-car was struggling up the mountain road, pulling badly, and wheezing as she came. She rounded the corner and clattered on to the open space where already the first tin car was loading up.

The idea of two cars where one alone was even a

rarity horrified Andreas so much that he dropped the chit's dressing-case and it rolled down the steps.

'Here, I say,' called the chit pleasantly to Herbert, 'look what that bloody boy's been and gone and done.'

But no one noticed her.

Out of the second car a man descended. He was indicating a trunk which was stuck in the back. Ann's eye became fastened on the trunk; she could not move her gaze. She recognized the trunk as having been bought at Messrs. John Barker's, one of their famous family of nineteen-and-sixpennies, initials extra. And there were Ann's initials added at small cost but carrying with them, so she had felt at the time, the hallmark of distinction.

'My luggage!' she gasped aloud to no one.

There was in fact nobody to hear.

And the man was Oliver Banks.

CHAPTER 4

I

Ann went inside her room and she closed the windows and stood there, her hands still on the latchet, holding fast. She supposed there had never been a moment in her whole life when she had been more glad to see anybody. She was almost afraid because she was so glad. It seemed obvious that Oliver must have left the ship at Ragusa, and taking her luggage had brought it all the way for her. She did not know what to do, nor what to think.

She stood there, quite still, and all the little impressions of the room were grafted into her mind. The slender bed, the simple dressing-table, with its *bouffante* skirts of chintz; the icon hung in the corner, the dreadful garish pictures.

Outside the first tin car chuffed away, and the shrill voice of the chit attacking the unprotected Herbert faded into distance. Presently there was a knock at the door, and Andreas came in bearing Mr. John Barker's nineteen-and-sixpenny trunk on his back. He let it down with a crash which should have broken every bottle inside it, but Ann was so grateful at seeing it that she never even thought of rebuking Andreas.

'*Mein Herr* for you to see,' said Andreas with some difficulty. He was not fluent with English.

'I'll come down. I won't be long, tell him.'

For in Ann was the urgent longing to unpack. She was so dead sick of the pink linen frock, and the grey flannel suit which was so desperately hot. She undid the box and opened it. Miss Brown had obviously been called in to do the packing, and she had done it splendidly. She had employed a great deal of tissue paper and padding, which was a nuisance, as every bit had to be carefully unwrapped in case it concealed some bottle or jar. One by one Ann drew out her things. Another hat. The white frock with the little madonna-blue cape in that heavenly shade. She felt that she must put it on at once, for she was sure that she should be sick if she had to go on wearing the same old things. New shoes. A crisp clean petticoat. In them she felt that she herself was a new woman.

It was Eva who came in to see her.

'Well, that's got rid of Herbert. I never heard such impertinence as his bringing that awful woman here. What could he have been thinking of? Oh, has your luggage come? Very quick, surely?'

'A friend brought it from the ship.'

'A friend?' Eva looked at her queerly. 'That's odd, isn't it? You've lost no time, I see.'

Ann shook her head.

'I am so dead sick of the old things. I think I shall never be able to look a piece of pink linen in the face again.'

And in this frock she felt like a new woman, just as though she had flung away an old self with that crushed dress on the floor. Now she would be able to start the journey home. For she must go back while she still had got the strength left. She must not let herself be swayed by Pablo. He was not a good influence. With him anything was possible, or nothing. Now that Oliver was here, he was older and more stable – although he had once told her that nothing held him and that he was nomad through and through – but if she could only bring herself to tell him about Pablo, he would take her to Bolzano or Innsbruck and he would put her on the train for England and for safety. For the clatter of the typewriters in Henrietta Street, and the cheerless English summer, its hot days marred by thunderstorms, its cold days soaked with dismal rain.

Such fun the English summer after Italy, and the Dolomites, and all the exquisite beauty of dawn rosying the mountains. Such fun, she told herself, and pulled a wry face.

And now as she went on to the landing she was not so sure that it was going to be easy meeting Oliver. She felt self-conscious, and wondered how she should start … 'So good of you to have brought my trunk' (it sounded most insincere). 'Have you had a rotten journey?' (far too trivial; after all, he had done a lot for her coming all this way). She went downstairs resignedly.

Half way she met Pablo.

'Oh, but how divine, like a little sweet madonna,' said Pablo, and his hand was laid arrestingly on hers; 'we go and sit out of doors and drink in poetry, *ya*?'

'I'm afraid I can't. A friend of mine has just come.'

'A friend?'

'Yes, from the ship.'

A cloud drifted across his face; she saw him turning sulky, darkening.

'I do not like much your friends,' he said.

'I did not like much *your* friend,' she agreed, and she

went on, leaving him standing there.

It took courage to do that, but she did it.

In the *salon* Oliver Banks was eating the most enormous breakfast she had ever seen.

II

'Ann!'

'Oh, it was good of you to come all this way and to bring that trunk. It was awfully good of you …'

'Well, you would not have got it for ages. Directly I discovered what had happened I went to the purser. He was awfully decent about it, and he said I could bring it along. Ann, whatever made you lose the ship like that? What happened?'

'It was the gondolier. We were going to Murano, and he just would *not* hurry. He kept on wanting more money.'

'The dirty skunk! You can never trust those old Ities, they are always doing something like that. I suppose he was not bothered when you missed the ship?'

'Not in the least.' Now she could afford to laugh at the gondolier's lack of interest, though at the time it had been a veritable tragedy. 'I went straight to Bunt's, and luckily there was the money there from Fifinelle's. I saw the Consul and I met Eva. She suggested that we should come along here to this inn.'

'It is a very charming spot. A little lonely, out of the way spot. Nobody ever finds it, I imagine. Nothing ever happens here.'

'Oh, doesn't it?' and she laughed.

She met his eyes across the enormous plate of bacon and eggs, and somehow she went off into schoolgirlish sniggers. Nothing ever happened here! Nobody ever came here! Why, things had been happening from the very moment that she had arrived, and they were going on happening. More happened here than in Piccadilly Circus, or perhaps you came closer to it, more face to face, as it were.

'How did you persuade *mein Herr* to give you all that?' she demanded. For *mein Herr* had a rooted preference for the Continental breakfast; it was less trouble. He always said that the English ate too much, rolls and coffee were better, so much healthier, and the idea of anybody having persuaded him to venture on bacon and eggs was almost miraculous.

'I told him I'd got to have it,' said Oliver, 'after that journey I was feeling pretty deathly. And Bolzano, I got there in the dead of the night. What a place!'

'The ancient fountains …' said Ann mischievously, quoting Monsieur Heriot.

'Not much use to a *bona fide* traveller in the dead of night.'

'The arcades.'

'Equally futile. I came on to a little one-eyed place in another train – not a *rapide* – God knows what it was, and then I got a funicular, and after that the most broken-down old car God ever made.'

'I saw it.'

'I'd got to get here somehow, and nowhere had they heard of food. When I left the *rapide* and got into this region of the Dolomites or the Tyrol or whatever it is, the restaurant cars and the sleepers left me. When I tried to get breakfast at one place they offered me *café-au-lait* in a cardboard carton, the same kind you buy jelly in at Harrod's food department.'

'I expect you were ravenously hungry.'

'Ravenously, and I told *mein Herr*. He made no bones about it.'

'It was good of you coming all this way, and for me …'

Oliver swallowed a mouthful of bacon and egg. 'It

was for you that I came. Otherwise wild horses wouldn't have got me here.'

Ann felt that she ought to say something, to be polite, to thank him for the compliment, only she couldn't. 'Now I've got my luggage I am going home,' she told him.

'Money run out?'

'No,' and then she told the truth, and it was bitter and cruel and it hurt, 'sense has run out, I think,' she said.

III

Oliver did not pursue the subject then. There were several interruptions. Eva came down armed with all the painting apparatus, and prepared to march off back to yesterday's scene of operations. She had to be introduced and to make her adieux in one and the same breath. She would not be back until evening, when it grew too dark and the light changed, and she would be taking Madame Heriot with her. Madame Heriot was all smiles too. Her picture was coming out very well. She had even dropped a few hints to Eva as to how to do this or that, and they had been received with surprising coldness. Eva did not want Madame Heriot's hints. She hated modern art and could not see which way up the picture was supposed to hang; that was if any particular way up mattered, for it looked the same either way.

Then Pablo appeared. Oliver gave Pablo one glance and then looked away. Ann had the horrid idea that he also had formed Eva's opinion of Pablo looking like a cheap musical comedy thrill. Well, perhaps he did. They might be right, only in spite of all that he attracted her. He attracted her all the same.

The strained conversation was at its worst when *mein Herr* rushed in exclaiming, '*Der Postbote*,' and indicating that there was money to be paid on a letter obviously from Cuthbert.

Cuthbert took great exception to the imposition of foreign postage. He considered that it was a great deal too expensive, and he for one could not afford to pay it. Ann was rich, and therefore he put on a stamp of the value which he considered was just and reasonable, and she must pay the other end. Ann had been paying all the time, and she was heartily sick of it.

Also the contents of his letters were not worth paying for And this one was dear at any price.

He was as usual scandalized, and he implored Ann to come home. Eleanor was not well. Gloria was thinking of taking on a job. She was attending a course of secretarial work, and she hoped to qualify at the end of six months, but at the moment she found the speed at shorthand most baffling. It was highly necessary for Gloria to earn. Cuthbert emphasized this point, 'highly necessary' was underlined several times. All the sources from which she had had expectations had failed her. By this, Ann gathered, he referred to the insurance money and the three hundred pounds that Ann had won and had spent on herself in riotous living.

Poor girl! It was all very sad.

Ann could not see that it was any sadder for Gloria to have to earn her living than it had been for her. She folded the letter and she put it away into her bag.

To go back to that. To go back to routine, to greyness, and the sure and certain knowledge that nothing could ever break the drabness through again. For luck does not hold to that extent. You don't win two sweepstakes in your life. You don't go cruising about the Mediterranean twice over. And after the Mediterranean what of Worthing? I ask you!

It would almost have been better never to have seen the loveliness, never to have dreamt the dreams, than to have had them for this brief span and then to be forced to return.

It would almost be better to marry Pablo, who was

young, and glorious, and glamorous, to go on living here, where at least there was sunshine and joy and the keen gladness of living, than to return to South Kensington and Henrietta Street.

He would be a most unsatisfactory husband. He would cause her bitter grief and dreadful humiliation, but she would have some moments; she would have moments when she stood on the top of the mountain hand in hand with him, and that would be something.

You cannot have everything in life.

'Something is worrying you,' said Oliver, looking at her across the table.

'Yes.'

'Come out into the garden, if there is a garden …'

'There isn't. It is just forest, but it is all rather beautiful.'

'Well, come into the forest and tell me all about it?'

She said humbly, 'I'd like to.'

And she felt like a penitent going to confession.

IV

The forest struck her as being like a great green cathedral.

Its branches met overhead in arches. The softness of the undergrowth drowned the noise of your footsteps, so that it was held in a sacred hush. The yellow sunshine fell in streams through the branches.

'It is all rather wonderful,' he said.

They stood there, and the *Tannenbaum* stood round them like columns supporting the dark arches of some ancient church.

'Now what has been happening?' he asked. 'It is that young man, isn't it?'

'Well, in a way.'

'Poor Ann! You came out into the world entirely unsophisticated, you knew nothing of life, much less of love. You have come against something far too big for you.'

'Oh, I'm not in love with him,' said Ann.

'Not mentally perhaps, but a little physically.'

She wondered whether she dared confess the truth, and for a moment hesitated, then suddenly it seemed as though she had known Oliver such a very long time. She recalled that bathe together in Cala Mistra; that night at the Serenata. Pompeii.

'I'm so dreadfully afraid I might marry him,' she said.

'Oh Lord, you mustn't do that! Live with him if you like, but don't be a fool and marry him.'

It was hopeless. Oliver would not understand. A man of his age suggesting such a thing, such a wicked and sinful thing; it made her quite sick.

'You have no right to think of anything so awful,' she said.

'My dear, it would be far less sinful to have an affair of that sort than a lifetime's misery for both of you. That's what marriage would mean with him, I can assure you of that.'

'I know,' she admitted.

'And you still want him, I suppose?'

'I'm afraid I do.' And then she started to tell him the truth. She started to tell him of the amazing happenings of the previous night; of the arrival of the chit and Herbert, and the affair of Pablo and the chit. 'And yet even *that* wouldn't make any difference to what I felt for him,' she said despairingly, 'it's awful, isn't it?'

'It's natural.'

It was nice of him to say that, but she knew that he was only trying to be kind.

'You see,' he said, 'you had got to experience some reaction after your cooped-up little life. It had to come. Pablo is the reaction.'

'Look here,' she said, 'you've got to help me. You

have got to make me see sense. I want you to arrange about trains home. I know nothing about such things, but I've got to get away at once. I want to go right away from here, I want to go home. Will you take me to Bolzano or Innsbruck or where-ever it is I go from, and see me aboard the right train and send me home?'

He took her hand and drew her down to the grass. They sat there close to the earth, with the dry powdery smell of it, and the trees stirring about them.

'You've told me what you feel. Now I want to tell you what I feel.'

'Please?'

'I'm afraid you've got to listen. It is no good fighting against it. I've got to tell you and there is a lot to tell. When I first met you, you attracted me. You were a new experience in life. You were so fresh, so untouched, opening like a flower, and it was interesting to watch that opening.' He paused a second, then he went on. 'I did not realize that I was growing fond of you. I knew of course after Pompeii. I knew for certain that day we bathed together at Malta. In Venice I was wild about you. Then, when the ship went off without you, I started thinking seriously. I told myself that it had been a passing phase perhaps, there are so many of those in life. I've always been a nomad. I haven't wanted to settle down. I didn't believe I ever would.'

'You said you wouldn't.'

'I've wanted to go on and on and always on. Perhaps it is never having had a home as a youngster, not a proper home. You couldn't count Uncle Alfred's, and Auntie Miggs', and Aunt Daisy's, they weren't home in the true sense of the word. But after you had left the ship I knew that I couldn't go on without you. I just couldn't, Ann, and that's the truth.'

She did not know what to say.

'I got your luggage and I came back after you. I

guessed something like this might have happened. I guessed you would have turned homesick and frightened and afraid of going on, and that you would want to turn back and go home. But, Ann, the heart of you doesn't want to go back to work and to London. The heart of you wants to go on searching through life, with me.'

She said, 'I don't know what I want,' which was true, but not helpful.

'Supposing you risked it?'

'But Lilia has only been dead for such a short –'

He put his hand over her mouth. 'The old silly argument. It doesn't hold water, my dear. Lilia has been dead to me for years, and you have been alive to me for years though we only met such a little while ago. Do you think you dare trust me with your future? Do you think you could possibly risk it?'

'I'm afraid of my own future,' she told him.

'I know. Risk it with me. You can't go back. After a cruise like this you can't take up a drab existence again. You can't marry your young man. He isn't your age, and he isn't your sort. Ann, I'm understanding, I'm tolerant, and I find I do care for you most tremendously.'

There was something humble in his voice, something reverent in his touch. It was not only the glamour of the cruise, and she knew it. They had met in drab London, they had met before any of the illusion had started. She knew that she would be safe with Oliver. She did not question his understanding her.

Funny to end the cruise here in a wood of *Tannenbaum* sweeping down a mountain side, into a village flanked by green larches. Funny with the tinkle of cow-bells in the distance, and the one bell from the *Kirche*. One of the queer happenings of life that a chain of circumstances will set going.

She lifted up her face to his.

'Take care of me, Oliver,' she said. 'It is absurd, I

know, but I feel dreadfully young and irresponsible.'

His lips touched hers.

'You're both, my dear, and I'll take great care of you. You see, I love you very much.'

V

In Balham Cuthbert read and re-read the letter. He read it with his glasses on and then he took them off and re-read it, having polished them up, as though he hoped he had mis-read the first time.

'Upon my soul,' said Cuthbert.

He looked across at Gloria. Poor little Gloria! Poor little Gloria done out of all that money! And she having such trouble with her shorthand speed, it was a shame of Ann behaving so wildly.

'She is married,' he said, 'they are going on to see the East. Mr. Banks is a widower of independent means, she says that he is rich …'

'She must be mad,' said Eleanor.

'I always thought winning that money turned her brain,' commented Cuthbert, 'now I am sure of it. We ought to close our doors on her, turn her away, but –'

She had said that Oliver was rich. That was the chief point to Cuthbert.

'We must show a Christian forgiveness,' he said.

'But,' sniffed Gloria over her shredded wheat, 'why shouldn't Auntie marry?'

'Of course she shouldn't,' said Cuthbert.

'Don't be silly,' said Eleanor.

It was disgusting of Ann marrying. It was disgraceful. And now what would happen about the insurance which was ultimately to have come to Gloria? How could they make sure that she would keep the instalments paid up, or anything else if it came to that? She might even have children of her own, Eleanor thought, and blushed for the very idea. That same suggestion had presented itself to Cuthbert, but he had repudiated it as being unworthy. Ann had no right to have married, she would have no right to have children. That was unthinkable.

But unfortunately Oliver was rich.

'We … we ought to send them a wedding present?' he commented.

'I suppose we ought,' lamented Eleanor.

Money was tight. The papering of the spare room this spring-cleaning had been a big consideration. She did not want to give Ann a wedding present. She would have liked to smack her hard for being so silly. Only you couldn't very well.

'Haven't we something about the place that she would like? A sentimental value is far greater than a mere mercenary one,' said Cuthbert.

'Yes, dear, of course,' agreed Eleanor.

They put their heads together. They abandoned the idea of the portrait of her father; a dealer had told them that it was valuable, and one day they might need to raise the money on it themselves.

They thought of the biscuit box which had been given to them by grateful parishioners, and then remembered that it had been tactlessly engraved with the good wishes of the same parishioners.

They decided on the Sheffield plate candlesticks at last. Ann had never seen them, and they had been rolled up in tissue paper in the false roof for some time. They would strike a very good note. They were delightful, and they would be so useful. Travelling about in all those dreadful foreign parts she would need a light quite often, and though a little cumbersome, it would be nice to have your very own candlesticks.

Cuthbert packed them himself. He and Eleanor wrote 'With loving wishes, from us both.' Afterwards when they had gone, they suddenly remembered that the message had not included Gloria. That was most remiss. Gloria would have to give something. She would have to fall back on a pin-cushion; she made them rather well, and it seemed to offer the solution.

The candlesticks arrived at Bombay.

'My God,' said Oliver.

Ann, who had grown very rapidly more modern, said, 'My God' too, and 'isn't that just like Cuthbert?'

The parcel was delivered to them as they were getting into rickshaws to go to see the Towers of Silence.

'What do I do with them?' asked Ann.

Oliver leaned out of his rickshaw. He handled them with suspicion. 'What muck!' he said.

A beggar clawed closer, and pushed thin fleshless hands out pleading for alms. For one instant Ann had a vision of a face much like the old hag's in the Alameda. '*Malo* piccaninny,' and then 'Look at me.' Oliver thrust the candlesticks into the clawing hands.

The rickshaw coolies bore them swiftly onwards.

THE END

ABOUT THE AUTHOR

Ursula Bloom was one of the most popular bestselling authors of the twentieth century. She wrote over 560 books, a feat which earned her a place in the Guinness Book of World Records for many years, as the world's most prolific female writer. She also wrote short stories, radio and stage plays, and worked as a Fleet Street journalist.

During her long career, as well as writing books under her own name, Ursula used the pen names Sheila Burns, Rachel Harvey, Lozania Prole, Mary Essex and Deborah Mann.

You can read more great stories by Ursula Bloom, and find out more about her life, by visiting her official website www.ursulabloom.com

Printed in Poland
by Amazon Fulfillment
Poland Sp. z o.o., Wrocław